The
INDICTMENT

The
INDICTMENT

Barry Reed

CROWN PUBLISHERS, INC.
NEW YORK

Published by Crown Publishers, Inc., 201 East 50th Street, New York, New York 10022. Member of the Crown Publishing Group.

Random House, Inc. New York, Toronto, London, Sydney, Auckland

CROWN is a trademark of Crown Publishers, Inc.

Manufactured in the U.S.A.

Library of Congress Cataloging-in-Publication Data
Reed, Barry
 The indictment / Barry Reed.
 I. Title.
 PS3568.E3647515   1994
 813'.54—dc20   94-8346
                                         CIP

ISBN 0-517-59433-1

10 9 8 7 6 5 4 3 2 1

First Edition

To Susan, Barry, Rie, Debbie, and Marie

At his best,
man is the noblest
of all animals;
separated from
law and justice,
he is the worst.

—*Aristotle*

The
INDICTMENT

PROLOGUE

DAN SHERIDAN studied Senate bill 486, then passed it to Tom Buckley.

"Interesting," he said, "proposed legislation to abolish investigative grand juries and indictments."

"Long overdue." Buckley spread the document on the walnut-veneer conference table, scanning it as he lit a Camel. He sent several puffs billowing toward the fiberboard ceiling. "But got about as much chance of surviving the Joint Judiciary Committee as a can of gasoline in a forest fire."

"Timing is lousy." Sheridan fanned the air with a yellow scratch pad. "Sixteen indictments in the last four months. Pols on the take, school bus contractors, bankers . . ."

"Not to mention four lawyers, two of whom we represented," Buckley added.

Sheridan shook his head. "This bill is doomed. No legislator in his right mind would support it—not even the Beacon Hill liberals."

Buckley took another drag on his cigarette, this time letting the smoke seep slowly from his lips. "The sponsor must have a cushy inheritance. Can't be from around here. The DA and law-and-order guys will send him packing."

"Name's Farnsworth, from Northampton," said Sheridan.

"Sure. Farnsworth of the Northampton 'got more money than God' knitting mills Farnsworths." Buckley ran his hand through his thinning reddish hair. "His grandfather sold blankets to the Union army at two hundred dollars apiece—and those were 1860 dollars."

"But I think we ought to write a letter to the editor—the *Boston Globe* and maybe the *Herald*, backing up Moneybags Farnsworth."

"Are you crazy?" Buckley ground his cigarette into a Cinzano ashtray. "We're already in Dutch with Mothers Against Drunk Driving, the DA hates our guts, and the Boston Police—they're getting very unfriendly."

"Hey." Sheridan laughed. "We need controversy. You got to be in the thick of it. Did you ever think what would happen to us lawyers if people were reasonable? Settled things with a handshake?"

Buckley grinned, nodding his head. "I'd be a forty-year-old lifeguard in a tight-fitting orange bathing suit at Nantasket Beach, tanned, tagging a lot of nineteen-year-olds.

"And you'd still be playing baseball. A middle-aged catcher, struggling in the Piedmont League."

"Seriously." Sheridan reflected inwardly for a moment. He sighed and his eyes seemed fixed on some thoughtful distance. Buckley knew he was in for one of Sheridan's lengthy dissertations. It was well after six. The office staff had long since departed. He needed a good scotch. But Sheridan was his boss. He reached for his pack of Camels.

"You know," Sheridan began slowly, as if he was lecturing a first-year law class, "grand juries are archaic anomalies. They've been abolished in thirteen states, even in England, where grand juries were first invented."

"Runnymede field, 1215." Buckley nodded as he lit a second cigarette. "The barons forced King John to sign the Magna Carta. No one could be charged with a crime against the Crown except on information or indictment by twenty-three of his peers."

Sheridan always was impressed by Buckley's sense of legal history. He could quote Bellarmine, Jefferson, Cardoza, even St. Luke, with instant recall. And they had been together for fifteen years—Sheridan & Buckley. They defended every faker, fraud, embezzler, scalawag, drunk driver, narcotics dealer, bookie, and hooker who congested the streets of Boston—even a child molester. They thought, maybe like the barons at Runnymede, that everyone was entitled to a defense, was innocent until proven guilty, and that the Crown had to prove charges beyond a reasonable doubt.

Sheridan again waved his scratch pad.

"You know, Tom, DA Harrington and I never got along. We're both Irish, came from the same neighborhood. But he's Ivy League Irish, Harvard, Yale Law. I'm Salem State, an ex-cop, night law school. He tried to get me indicted once, but that's another story.

The point is that the DA's office abuses the grand jury process and no one gives a damn."

"Except you and me."

"Well, what the hell is a grand jury?"

Buckley knew he was in for a bit of legal philosophy. The question wasn't meant to be answered. He shrugged, as if he was conceding a three-foot putt.

"Twenty years ago, the old DA, Maurice Delaney—that was Harrington's predecessor, before your time—convened a grand jury to investigate corruption in state government. Delaney ran the show. The jurors were simply sheepherded at his direction. But things got out of hand. It was a runaway grand jury—lasted three months, a real fishing expedition. Four judges, the lieutenant governor, and the chairman of the school committee were indicted. They were absolutely destroyed. Made no difference that all were later acquitted. And the media was touting Delaney for higher office. That's when Harrington came along. . . ."

"Would you like a drink, Dan? It's after six. Sun is way over the yardarm."

"Sure."

Buckley ground out his second cigarette in the ashtray. He reached under the conference table and pulled up a half-empty bottle of scotch.

"Well, what have we here!" Two inverted paper cups dangled around the neck. He set them upright on the conference table and poured.

"We're out of ice, but it's good stuff—eighteen years old."

"*Slainte,* as we say in Irish," Buckley toasted.

"*Slainte mhaith,* as my grandmother would say." Sheridan raised his cup.

"You know, Tom," Sheridan began after a deep swallow, "the whole concept of investigative grand juries has gotten out of hand. Sure, when John Hancock and the Adams boys were around drafting it into the Constitution, it was a noble idea. No one could be charged with a felony except by grand jury indictment. It was a protection. Citizens had to answer to citizens. But those were different times. And even then grand juries refused to follow the law. Sedition cases against the Crown were dismissed. In the 1850s, here in Boston, jurors refused to indict abolitionists."

"Hey, I'm supposed to be the legal historian," Buckley said, then drained his scotch.

"Today, in 1994, an indictment can leave a hard-won reputation in shambles. Makes no difference the defendant couldn't tell his side of the story. The rules of evidence go out the window. All sorts of hearsay come in. Counsel can't object. Can't elicit testimony in his client's behalf. There's no cross-examination of adverse witnesses. The jury hears only the prosecutor's case. The DA makes sure exculpatory evidence is deep-sixed. There's no requirement that the person under investigation even has the right to be present. It's a one-way street. Christ, even the presiding judge tells the jurors they're an accusatory body and should be guided by counsel of the prosecutor; charges them that if the evidence is unexplained or unrefuted, the jury must return an indictment. What a crock!

"In federal court, the defendant's attorney isn't allowed in the grand jury room. And in state court, we can't participate or make any statement in behalf of a client. We can only whisper advice, and to jurors, that looks like hell. In their minds, the defendant is guilty as sin or he wouldn't be there, wouldn't even need an attorney."

Buckley poured himself another scotch.

"This district attorney of ours, Harrington, is the one who determines who'll be accused and who'll be passed over. Got more power than the governor, even the attorney general. And the jurors are overawed by those good old law-and-order boys in the blue pinstripes. They could indict Mother Teresa. Really. All they need is twelve out of the twenty-three jurors to raise their hands—a bare majority.

"And let's say the defendant asserts his Fifth Amendment right against self-incrimination."

"Gonzo!" Buckley killed his second scotch. "Accusations of the grand jury are sacrosanct."

"You know what really bothers me?" Sheridan still had his hand curled around his cup. "The way the press takes over—Madame Defarges with typewriters. Especially if the defendant is from a privileged background or a lawyer. They'll make sure his head will roll. The DA feeds them like the pigeons on the Common. We start to counter with a press release or two—bang! The judge hits us with a gag order.''

"Want one for the road, Dan?" Buckley held up the bottle, giving it a slight jiggle.

Sheridan checked his watch.

"No, I think I'll put in a couple more hours in the library, then call it a night. This isn't an issue we can settle anytime soon.''

1

MCCAFFERTY lit a cigarette from the stub of another. Karen Steadman watched the slight quiver of his hand. She glanced at the clock on the far wall: 5:10 A.M. It was that hour before dawn when the hospital was silent; even the pain seemed asleep. They would be coming in soon, the nurses, the hospital staff, the kitchen help banging pots and slinging dishes onto breakfast trays: the morning ritual, the abrupt awakening.

McCafferty took a long drag, savored the smoke piercing his chest, exhaled slowly, and tried to relax.

"Sorry to roust you at this ungodly hour, Dr. Steadman," he said apologetically. "This is a priority case. Unusual. I got a call an hour ago from the commissioner's office telling me to get my ass over here right away. I haven't even seen the police report."

He tapped his cigarette ashes onto the floor. Standard rules of sanitation did not seem to apply in the morgue.

"All I know is the body was found sometime around midnight in the bushes off I-Ninety-five. A motorist got out to take a leak and tripped over it. Must have scared the bejesus out of him."

Karen Steadman nodded but could think of nothing to say. She was beginning to feel queasy.

"I don't even know if it's a man or a woman—not that it matters," he continued. "But you can be sure of one thing: It'll be some lowlife—a hopeless druggie or a punk who crossed the mob. It won't be one of the Beacon Hill crowd. And it won't be pretty."

Death, whatever its form, was always hideous. McCafferty faced it often, and just as often he flinched from it. He studied Karen Steadman. Her fresh Nordic complexion was turning the color of the cement floor.

"Initial autopsies always make you feel squeamish," he offered with a trace of a Scottish burr. "Like when you sliced into your first frog in Bio One. But you'll get used to it."

"Oh, I'm all right, Doctor. I sectioned a few cadavers back in med school." She tucked her silken blond hair into her blue rubber cap.

They waited. At the far end of the corridor, they would soon hear it: the metal doors clanging open, the squeak of spoked rubber wheels against linoleum as the orderlies pushed the gurney down the hall. They would be in no hurry. The patient had all the time in the world.

Karen Steadman, P-G1 in Pathology, snapped on her latex gloves and sucked in her stomach, trying to keep it from churning. She wondered why in the world she had ever wanted to become a pathologist, or even a doctor. She returned McCafferty's gaze. Dr. Bernard McCafferty, five years ago one of Boston's leading surgeons. Now, after too many OR fatalities, too many malpractice suits, too many gin-filled nights and weekends with crazy nurses, he was at the end of the surgical road, carving up inanimate objects. Now a mistake couldn't threaten a life.

In his late forties, he had sad eyes underlined with drooping pouches like a Labrador retriever. His Gaelic face was florid and puffy. Little beads of sweat mingled with freckles on his balding head, disappearing into a thin tuft of rust-colored hair. His lower lip began to quiver and he bit into it to halt the tremor. Karen Steadman recognized a boozer when she saw one.

There was a banging at the far end of the hall—a muffled, ominous sound. Karen's stomach lurched. They heard the creaking of the approaching gurney along the corridor.

Then the doors clanked open and death came wheeling in. McCafferty saw that Karen Steadman was not yet ready to face it. Somehow he had to calm her down.

"You have excellent credentials, Doctor," he said brightly. "Today it'll come together. All the textbook learning in the world can't replace the three-dimensional dissection. McKettrick said you'd make a great pathologist."

A great pathologist, she repeated in her mind. So much bullshit. Here she was, at twenty-five, a medical zero. No clout, not even the marks for a decent residency, and about to spend a year with a drunken hack in the bowels of a run-down brick ark called the Boston Memorial, more aptly tagged the BM.

The orderlies wheeled the gurney to the stone table and cranked it to a level a few inches above the slab. They eased the draped body onto it as though it were a fragile antique. Exchanging nods with McCafferty, they departed quickly.

Karen looked past the shrouded form. The morgue was cavernous and eerie, with soapstone tubs, a few battered white metal cabinets, bottles and vials everywhere, even stacked on the floor. It had a strange smell—formaldehyde, sulfur, sweet odor killers—not the scrubbed antiseptic smell of a hospital. She thought of her home in Kansas. How she had hated growing up there, the prairie, the flat sameness of the land. But the air was clear and the wind had a harsh purity, stirring the wheat as far as the eye could see. And everyone spoke their mind, like Harry Truman. You knew where you stood.

McCafferty sensed her discomfort, also her hostility. "Stomach doing a little turn?" He would try an academic tack.

"More like a one-eighty." She forced a small smile.

He adjusted the kettledrum lights over his head and clicked them on. The stone table with its troughs to collect bodily wastes was suddenly bathed in white light. Karen shuddered. It was grotesque, like some grisly Aztec altar, and soon high priest McCafferty would be cutting into a human form and plucking out a human heart.

"Well, look at it this way," he said. "Pathology is the queen of the medical sciences. Without it, we couldn't check on disease, treatment, surgical techniques."

Karen had heard the rhetoric before at University Med, McKettrick's second lecture: ". . . Vesalius in the sixteenth century pillaging scaffolds for bodies . . . the Austrian physician Rokitansky with his thirty thousand autopsies. Modern medicine dates from the first postmortem. . . ." She tied the strings of her faded blue tunic around her waist and pretended to listen.

"And sometimes we just don't know." McCafferty heaved a little sigh. "A person dies suddenly, unexpectedly, at home, in surgery, or in recovery. No reason. Everything's going fine. Then zap, it's curtains. You a Catholic, Dr. Steadman?"

"At times." There was a subtle defiance in her tone, a laying of ground rules for the future, formalizing the large gulf between them.

"From Boston?"

"Kansas." She was going to add *Wichita*, but McCafferty had already plowed back into his dissertation.

"Well, most families around here are Catholic. When someone dies, they feel the person has suffered enough, that the body is the sepulchre of the Holy Spirit and can't be desecrated further. So, no autopsy. Cause of death? An educated guess.

"Some young filly marries old moneybags. He's got every disease known to man, but hell, she's afraid he'll live forever. She goes up one night to give him his medication, adjusts a pillow *over,* not *under,* his head. Bang. He's gone!" McCafferty snapped his fingers. "She calls his doctor. 'No need to view the body,' he says. 'Sounds like the old ticker finally gave out.' No post; the old wastebasket diagnosis—acute coronary thrombosis, cardiac arrest; natural causes. A few suppressed tears. She takes it like an heiress.

"The point, Doctor, is that ninety percent of all deaths never go to autopsy. Cardiac and respiratory arrest, even coronary thrombosis, are pretty good guesses. But that's the terminal event, the way we all go. Fall off a building, get hit crossing the street, the heart stops and we cease breathing. But that doesn't delineate the exact cause, or the manner or time of death."

McCafferty dropped his cigarette onto the floor and mashed it with his foot. "There is a certain dignity to the procedure we do here. We treat the victim with utmost respect. We'll keep the body partly draped throughout." He pointed to a pile of clean linens on the stone table, near what she assumed was the victim's head. "This is a medicolegal autopsy. Our job is to find the manner and cause of death.

"But sometimes even after sectioning all vital organs, tissue analysis, histologic and microscopic studies, we're baffled."

Karen Steadman was only half-listening.

"Remember Juliette Krisler, the TV personality on Channel Five, two years ago?" McCafferty didn't wait for an answer. "Well, I did her post right on this slab." He patted the table as he spoke. "She was thirty-two. A beauty. Found dead in her apartment. Had everything going for her; just signed a new contract, five hundred thousand dollars a year. We did everything—blood studies, H and E stains, tissues. Her coronary arteries were like the inside of soda straws—not a platelet or smidgen of arteriosclerosis. Pancreas, brain, liver as beautiful as she was. No marks, bruises. No sign of foul play. Absolutely nothing to cause her death. But I signed the death certificate—ventricular fibrillation. You know what that is, Karen?" He had dropped the *Doctor.*

"When the heart's ventricles contract and dilate so fast, they fail to expel oxygenated blood into the aorta." The undertone of resentment was still there, but weakening.

"Yes. Well, again the educated guess. Ventricular fibrillation, cardiac and respiratory arrest. I listed all three as the terminal diagnosis. No one could quibble with the last two. The ventricular fibrillation? Maybe. Maybe not. Why should a young woman's heart, with absolutely nothing wrong with it, suddenly start squirming like a snake pit?"

"It does happen." Karen Steadman leaned back against the stone table, folding her arms defensively. "My dad used to get spasms of tachycardia. For no apparent reason, his heart would start racing, then it would abate just as fast as it had commenced. It's anatomically rare, but it does account for a lot of unexplained sudden deaths."

McCafferty liked the distraction of medical banter.

"When I finally knew what I was looking for, I pieced it together. Krisler consumed three vodka martinis that evening. The blood alcohol was moderate. The girlfriend who found her said she used to take two chlordiazepoxides before retiring each night. Know what those are?"

"Trankies." Karen almost smiled.

"Mood elevators. Krisler was high-strung. Pressure cooker business. Two little greenies on top of three vodka martinis. No big deal, but the combination at a given time, when the physiology is out of sync, can kill a weight lifter."

"Synergistic reaction." Karen supplied the medical metaphors. "Anaphylactic shock."

"That's right. Deadly as Russian roulette. Two comparatively harmless ingredients, mix them together and they kill like the South American dart poison."

"D-Tubocurarine," Karen added.

"Right, Tento, curare, dart poison, whatever."

Karen nodded deferentially.

"I revised the autopsy: 'Accidental death, toxic reaction, cardiac and respiratory arrest.'

"It made no difference to Juliette Krisler, but her relatives came out of the woodwork. Double indemnity for accidental death.

"And you know what?" Like the old fraud from Oz, behind the curtain of an impish grin, McCafferty worked his rhetorical dials and levers.

Again she nodded her head.

"Krisler had it all—celebrity, wealth, boyfriends. But you wouldn't believe this. . . ."

"She was a virgin." Karen beat McCafferty to the forensic punch.

McCafferty had let her. "Yup. *Virga intacta.*"

Their eyes locked. The laughter started there—in the eyes—and rumbled across their faces. Karen fought for control, putting her hand to her mouth. It was too late. The uncertainty, the tension, dissolved in the moment.

"You know, Karen," he said, snapping a blade from his X-acto holder, examining it closely, "you're making the right choice becoming a pathologist."

"Perhaps." She nodded. A feeling of nausea was creeping back into the pit of her stomach.

"No perhaps about it." McCafferty ran his thumb along the sharp edge. "You'll see a variety of things no GP or surgeon will ever see—the ravages of cancer, multiple sclerosis eroding the spinal cord like rust in a storm pipe."

McCafferty held the blade up to the light. The knife passed scrutiny. It was sharp enough. He pulled on his latex gloves. His face suddenly tensed. "Okay, here we go. As I said, don't expect a Cabot or a Lodge."

He whipped back the upper drape with the flourish of a magician, exposing the head. McCafferty and Karen gasped at what was revealed. The face was stunning—calm and serene. Her long black lashes were closed as in sleep. Her skin was smooth as weathered marble, creamy, the color of café au lait. Although she was evidently part African-American, her high cheekbones gave her a slight Asian cast, with a small delicate nose and thin but perfectly shaped lips. Her luxuriant raven hair cascaded onto the slate gray slab.

She was the most beautiful woman, living or dead, McCafferty had ever seen.

2

PHIL RILEY received the call from Katie MacLennan, the police dispatcher at Precinct 4.

"Christ, are you sure, Katie?" Riley knew she was, but he had to let her know he wasn't enthralled with the message.

"No Celtics game tonight, hondo. Captain Furlong wants you to pick him up in front of Boston Garden at five-thirty. A possible homicide. He'll fill you in."

"Jesus, Katie, Furlong knew I had these boxes for the Bulls game months ago." Riley spit it back. "That son of a bitch . . . Shit—we'll be screwing around all night."

"Careful . . ." Katie was steeled to the profanities. It came with the territory. She genuinely liked Riley. But she also liked her job, and she needed it a lot more than she liked Riley. And she knew the dispatches were wired.

"Know how you feel, Riley, but the captain has to work, too. You'll catch the last five minutes. That's when the game's won or lost, anyway. . . . Good hunting."

"Yeah, kiss my ass," he growled into the dead mike.

Riley sat there, fuming, mumbling expletives, running down a slope of frustrated anger. Detective Lieutenant, Boston Police. It had been fun at first, even the middle years. The camaraderie with fellow officers, the breaking rumors, the special details—all had a quality of adventure. The feeling that something was going to happen and being there when it did. A quarter of a century on the force. Now just a job. Stymied, underpaid. Forty to fifty hours a week, scrounging a few overtime bucks, surviving until retirement—and that was four years away. And then what?

He listened to the idling motor, the rhythmic swish of the windshield wipers, and mulled over his dreary existence. He watched the unseasonable April snow fall in big silent flakes, melting upon impact on the slick dark pavement. He wondered about his boss, Charles "Buddy" Furlong, who always managed to spend Februarys in Boca Raton, never fretted over college tuitions, owned a three-decker in Jamaica Plain, and had a place on the Cape. Some said the captain was in line for police commissioner—if Mayor Jimmy Kane decided to seek reelection.

Furlong was waiting on the sidewalk in front of the Garden when Riley pulled up at 5:27.

"We're going to check out the victim's apartment," Furlong said as he fastened his seat belt. "I'll fill you in on the way."

Riley eased the car into the early-evening traffic.

Hawthorne-on-the-Charles fronted the river, halfway between MIT and Harvard. It was a moderate high-rise, skins of glass stretched over fifteen stories, the newest, most chic location of address-conscious Bostonians. Angela Williams lived in the penthouse; that is, she had until sometime last night, before she was found quite dead a few minutes before midnight. Detective Riley was always uneasy, intimidated by posh surroundings or by important people. But it was an environment that Captain Furlong seemed to relish. Perhaps it was *his* chance to intimidate, to exert authority.

Mr. Schofield, the manager, impeccably attired in a double-breasted navy blazer with bright gold commodore buttons, let them in. His gray flannel trousers, carefully coiffed pearl gray hair, and a wisp of a white mustache blended easily with his crisp British accent.

"Gentlemen," he said, "Miss Williams was a lovely lady. She had exquisite taste, as you can readily see." His arm swept in a graceful arc toward the elegant interior.

Riley, who had migrated from Ireland by way of England (it seemed like centuries ago) and who had spent a hitch working the Liverpool docks, detected a trace of a Cockney accent. The way he said *loidee* gave Schofield away.

"Nothing's been touched?" Furlong addressed Schofield, taking charge. It was more a statement than a question.

"Nothing, gentlemen. It's as if Miss Williams never left. . . . We are deeply troubled by what happened. . . . If I can be of assistance, I will be in my office."

"Thank you, Mr. Schofield. We'll be in touch." By a quick nod of his head, Furlong motioned to Riley to start the inspection.

"Never seen such a place." Riley surveyed the glass walls—ceiling to floor—encompassing a sweeping panorama of the city of Boston.

There were Oriental rugs, furniture of delicate teak and sandal-
wood, and on the few panels between the glass hung etchings of
Chinese masters, terra-cotta statuary of Ming emperors, and gold-
leaf Buddhas. Riley whistled to himself as he walked gingerly on
the rich Chinese rugs woven in subtle hues of ivories, soft blues,
and mint greens that covered the parquet floor. In the center of
the living room, surrounded by white cushions, was a Japanese garden spreckled with jagged rocks, pebbles, exotic plants, and bamboo shoots. Goldfish quivered and darted among the lilies and
water flowers that shimmered on the surface of the sunken pool.
It was not ornate, almost understated. Soft lighting, muted tranquillity. Angela Williams had an eye for class, Riley surmised.

"Don't know a helluva lot about the broad. Autopsy was started
this morning. We'll have the preliminary report tomorrow." Buddy
Furlong looked at his notebook. "Born Loretta Chichari 11–22–64.
Dominica, British West Indies. No criminal record, as far as we
know. The FBI is checking her prints. All routine. No family around
here. Maybe a brother in New York. We're trying to locate him."

Riley was sure of one thing. Angela Williams was in love with
Angela Williams. Her pictures were everywhere. There were shots
of Angela on horseback, on a yacht, with movie stars—Tom Selleck
types—celebrities, and sports figures, on the walls, propped up in
the bedroom. She had squeezed a lot of life into twenty-nine years.

Furlong noted the inscriptions, recognizing the photos, scribbling in his notebook. He wrote on top of the white baby grand
piano. "Ever see a white Steinway?" It was Furlong's way of talking
down to Riley. "Must go fifty G's."

Riley noted the score positioned on the music rack, Mozart's Piano Concerto in C. He played a few notes—the theme from *Elvira
Madigan.*

"Jesus!" Furlong clenched his eyes shut and brought Riley's playing to a quick end. "You fuckin' jerk, Riley," he exploded. "What
in Christ's name are you doing putting your paws all over the keys?
You may have blown this whole thing. You do any more bonehead
things like that and you'll be back at the corner of Beacon and
Tremont flagging traffic for the duration."

Riley reddened but said nothing. He knew he had goofed. And
he should never have let Furlong know he could play. One more

tally in Furlong's ledger. If Furlong did count—and Riley knew he did—being bumped back to patrolman was more than a remote possibility.

The search continued by rote: wardrobe, shoe boxes, mattresses, nooks, corners, shelves, dressers, the coffee canister—nothing overlooked. Everything was carefully cataloged, described. Riley made mental notes.

Furlong checked the library shelves. "Hmm," he said, "Shakespeare, Proust, Dickens, Thoreau." He moved off without further comment.

What an ignorant asshole, thought Riley as he continued to canvass the library. He opened a volume of Cervantes, skimmed the pages, and put it back. Either she was well read or someone had advised her what to buy. There were expensive-looking paintings on the walls, a French countryside by Corot, a seascape by Winslow Homer. Riley ran his fingers over the raised brush strokes on the canvas. Probably duplicates. Originals would run into the millions. But then, he thought, seems like the real McCoy.

Nothing looked out of place. Nothing unusual for a twenty-nine-year-old girl from the Caribbean who could afford a $25,000-a-month apartment with a million-dollar interior—nothing except two packs of cocaine—in a bureau drawer—pure Colombian prime, worth at least as much as the furnishings—along with a few receipt books. Not much more; the girl was obviously well connected—hard drugs, probably handling well over $10 million a year.

Then Riley opened the top drawer of a black lacquered table, revealing a thick packet of letters bound with a slim blue satin ribbon. As he reached to pick it up, the entire room began to move, almost imperceptibly. And there was music—classical—maybe Handel. Riley wasn't sure. It was a little heavy.

"What's going on!" yelled Furlong, bounding out of the bedroom.

"The room's rotating, Captain," offered Riley.

"I can see that!" sputtered Furlong. "You activated this thing?"

They stood there. The room turned slowly. The lights of Boston quietly disappeared as the view swung upriver toward the Harvard Bridge and the Tudor rectangles of the university. "What a sunset," remarked Riley. The men watched the city twinkle to life. The Hancock and Prudential towers came into view, bathed in an orange glow.

"All right," Furlong rasped, snapping the moment. "Let's get this goddamned thing stopped. You must have triggered something."

Riley returned to the table, fingered the rich ebony finish, opened the drawer—then closed it. The room and the music stopped. He opened the drawer slightly. Again the room began to move. Again the music. "Hey, I got it," he exclaimed. He shut the drawer, but not before taking out the packet of letters.

"Well, let's not get carried away. Turn the thing off," demanded Furlong, "and let's finish up here." The view had not quite come full circle. The bedrooms now faced the city. The living room caught the grungy warehouses and freight terminals of North Cambridge.

Riley read one letter quickly and scanned a few others. Romantic stuff. To Angela Williams from one Christopher Dillard. Dillard wrote well. No question that he was deeply in love with the Williams woman. He said so in each opening and closing. They bore postmarks from distant points—Granada, Spain; London; Dublin, Ireland; Algiers; Caracas, Venezuela; Mexico City; San Francisco. Why did Dillard travel so much? Riley wondered. He handed the packet to Furlong.

The police photographer arrived and went to work. The ID boys would be over from the lab to check for prints on the crystal, teak furniture, whatever, if Riley hadn't screwed them up. The new electronic scan would test for human hair, other footprints on the costly Orientals; for fiber traces that could pinpoint Angela's recent guests, friends—maybe her killer. Furlong also called for the boys from Vice. They would take over the drugs.

They had just about finished. Riley glanced at his watch: 8:25. Boston Garden would be packed with screaming fans by now. The Celts and Bulls would be banging heads down the stretch. Maybe he'd catch the finale on the radio. Christ, how he detested Furlong. They should have wrapped it up an hour ago.

Then he saw it. Riley thought it was strange that Furlong hadn't noticed. Lodged between the lineup of expensive shoes—perhaps twenty pairs—was a small green book covered with reptilian skin and fastened with a gold clasp, together with a tape cassette wrapped with a rubber band. Furlong was giving the sumptuous marble bathroom a final look.

Riley skimmed the pages and whistled to himself. There were some incredible names in the book: U.S. Senator Irving Crimmins; the letter writer, now listed as Dr. Christopher Dillard; CIA head Vance Cranston; television and media personalities; Mayor Jimmy Kane; others. Riley slipped the book and tape into his pocket. Perhaps he held the key to Mayor Jimmy Kane's return to private life and to Furlong's future. Maybe his own. He had a hunch about the tape. He'd play it at home. He could turn it over to the captain later.

"Not much to go on," said Furlong, coming back into the living room. "She sure knew how to live, perhaps too well. Someone wanted her scratched. . . . I think we'll pay a call on this Christopher Dillard. Right?"

"Right!" Riley answered too quickly, like a novice responding to a drill sergeant. He could have kicked himself.

3

THEY FACED each other, McCafferty and Karen Steadman, two figures in blue, separated by the body on the table. McCafferty carefully removed the remaining linen, then exhaled audibly. Most
bodies were ugly, scarred with folds of hideous cellulite. This one
had an exquisite symmetry: perfectly rounded shoulders, long, slender arms, delicate neck, beautifully formed breasts, with chocolate-
tipped nipples protruding sensuously, a navel that was flat—not a
scar—black pubic hair, carefully cropped, perfectly developed
thighs and legs, and childlike feet, the toenails varnished with choc-
olate-colored polish.

McCafferty paused a moment; for the first time this morning, he
had nothing to say. Finally, he spoke. "Cause of death should be
relatively easy when we consider the pathological facts with the
crime scene description. Read me the ID report."

Karen picked up the chart attached to the gurney and rattled it
off. "Fully clothed black female found in a rest area by motorist off
Interstate Ninety-five, Burlington, Mass., ten miles north of Boston,
at eleven-fifty-eight P.M. Officers Turco and Stephenson dispatched.
Arrived eleven-fifty-eight. Body identified from clothing tag—Angela Williams, d.o.b. 11–22–64, Hawthorne-on-the-Charles, Standish
Drive, Boston. Body located facedown in dense, swampy underbrush. Body warm. No pulse. No respirations. Dispatched to Boston
Memorial via Burlington Police ambulance. Officer Turco investigating."

"And the ER report." McCafferty's voice was packed with authority.

"Boston Memorial, twelve-thirty-six A.M., 4–3–94. Body warm, lips
cyanotic, no sign of rigor mortis, no bodily bruises or other markings. No sign of trauma. . . . Pupils round and regular, dilated bilaterally, nonreactive to light. No vital signs. DOA. To pathology
one-oh-four A.M. Signed, D. Supples, M.D."

"Fine, Karen," McCafferty said. "What's your guess?"

"Probably midline subdural hemorrhage, rupture of a cerebral artery in the brain stem. Most likely the circle of Willis." Karen touched the back of her head.

"Why midline?"

"Since *both* pupils are dilated. If it was a unilateral hemorrhage, the pupil *opposite* the site of the lesion would show more dilation. The blood would encroach upon the ophthalmic division of the fifth cranial nerve controlling the ciliary response. The cranial nerves cross in the optic chiasm, the left nerve controlling the right ciliary reflex and vice versa. Also, there's no indication of unilateral injury, tongue protruding to one side, mouth sagging, nerve palsy—things we pick up in first-year med and promptly forget."

McCafferty was impressed. "I'll say you haven't forgotten your neuroanatomy. But this woman is dead. Her pupils dilate bilaterally, remember? Okay, jot things down as we go along."

Karen scribbled as McCafferty recited the gross examination of the head and scalp.

"Zero. Zero. Zero. Negative. Negative."

McCafferty palpated the carotid arteries in the neck.

"Negative."

Anticipating him almost automatically, Karen handed him an ophthalmoscope.

McCafferty grunted approval.

With a finger and a thumb, he opened the victim's eye. A glazed black depth stared back at him. He focused a beam of light and peered into its recesses. The retina was normal. He examined the only blood vessels capable of exterior view in the human—the retinal artery and vein. He followed their course as they disappeared within the optic nerve.

"Hmmm, might not be a brain hemorrhage after all," McCafferty said. "No signs of papilledema—that's swelling of the optic nerve due to pressure from the brain, a cardinal sign of cerebral injury."

Karen knew this. She even knew how to spell it. She nodded agreement.

"Optic nerve, macula normal. Retina and retinal vessels exhibit the box cars of death." Then the other eye. "Take a peek," said McCafferty. Karen followed McCafferty's routine. Everything was normal.

The lips were blue and the body was now taking on a sepia-blue tinge. Cyanosis. But now, there was full rigor mortis.

The gross examination took about twenty minutes. McCafferty feeling, probing, peering, pinching, right down to the toes. No burns, no scars, not a wrinkle.

They turned the body over gingerly. Beautiful shoulders, straight back, hips, buttocks, legs, calves—perfect.

"See these splotches," McCafferty said. There was purplish mottling underneath the skin on the back of the shoulders, the buttocks, and the posterior thighs. "This is livor mortis. The blood is pooled after cessation of circulation and settles in dependent areas. . . . The body was found in a prone position. The mottling should have been anterior, not posterior. This is our first big clue. The victim died elsewhere and was transported."

"Or the police could have turned the body—or the ambulance attendants, or the orderlies," Karen offered.

"Yeah," said McCafferty. "Check that out, Karen."

They returned the body to the supine position.

McCafferty's pelvic and genital examination was deliberate and time-consuming. Every dead female was a potential rape case. He inserted a speculum into the vagina and peered and peered. "Hmmm. No Juliet Krisler. . . . She's been around. But no evidence of rape, no seminal fluid."

"Well, Karen, the gross examination is absolutely normal." He shook his head. "It's as though she were sleeping.

"Let's open her up and have a look. Sometimes a guy gets hit by a Mack truck. Not much damage outside, but inside . . . hamburger.

"Three power on the lights," McCafferty barked, as if he was back in surgery. Karen reached up and clicked the control knob, intensifying the light that bathed the delicate figure. For a moment, it was macabre, a scene from a class B horror movie, the mad scientist trying to find the secret to life, abetted by the beautiful young assistant.

McCafferty changed his specs. He now had on thick lenses that made his magnified eyes bulge and swim. Karen repressed a nervous giggle. He looked comical, the way a mad doctor should look.

His mouth tightened.

"Number twenty-two Brad-Parker scalpel." His voice bristled.

Karen handed him the blade. He held it aloft like a baton. Karen placed a white linen sheet over the body as McCafferty moved toward the victim's head. He cut deliberately from ear to ear, over the top of the head, and then reflected the hair and scalp back over the face, the way an Indian would scalp his victim. The skull glistened white in the bright light. They inspected it carefully.

Karen gave him the Stryker vibrating skull saw. It hummed and whirred as McCafferty cut and removed the skull cover, revealing a pulpy mass of cerebral tissue. He sliced deep within the skull, cutting delicate attachments at the base, shaking, cutting again, severing cranial nerve roots, then removing the brain with the stem attached, like lifting a rooted plant from a flowerpot.

"There it is," McCafferty said, raising it gently. "Can't tell Hitler's from Mother Teresa's. Same sylvian fissure, same ventricles, same gray matter, same frontal lobes. Murderer, poet, Einstein, all the same. But something, Karen, way within holds the secret."

Again, Karen felt as if she might get sick, but she handed McCafferty a white tray and he placed the delicate mass upon it.

"Hmmm, no signs of contusion or hematoma. We'll do coronal sections later."

Karen handed McCafferty a fresh scalpel.

"Now this will be a little easier than removing the brain."

Karen draped the head with white linen. McCafferty started at the shoulders, crossing to the midsternal notch, and cut downward, avoiding the umbilicus, cutting down to the pubis. She handed McCafferty the spreaders and they looked inside.

"Heart, pancreas . . . okay. Spleen, liver, intestines." He examined the interior anatomy. "No lacerations. No internal hemorrhaging. Everything is in place."

He saved the tissues for later staining and study, then took samples of the mucus in the stomach, the urine in the bladder. The blood was collected for analysis. The toxicology tests would come back negative, but McCafferty wouldn't know that for a day or two.

Finally, McCafferty yanked off his cap, stripped off his gloves, and untied his tunic. He reached for a cigarette.

It was over. Somehow Karen had survived. It was 1:10 P.M., eight grueling hours. McCafferty bent over his desk and scribbled some notes.

"Time of death?" Karen inquired.

"Eight-thirty to nine P.M., give or take a few minutes," McCafferty replied.

Karen frowned slightly. "Cause of death?"

"I haven't the foggiest idea. There's not a goddamned thing wrong."

4

IT SEEMED that Riley spent most of his time waiting—waiting for Sunday Mass to begin at St. Brendan's in Dorchester, or for his next assignment at Station 4, or for Buddy Furlong's retirement or advancement. The world was passing him by and he was painfully aware of it. He fidgeted with some loose change in his pocket.

"Dr. Dillard will be with you gentlemen in a short while," the nurse said. "He just left the OR. Why don't you go down for coffee." It sounded like an order.

"We'll wait, thank you." Furlong spoke for them both, hardly glancing up from his black notebook. He ceremoniously flipped a page. The nurse was quick to notice.

Furlong turned to Riley, his big hand shielding his mouth, and spoke in a husky whisper.

"Imagine the boyfriend being a doctor. And from the looks of this place, his patients aren't Southies."

Riley took in his surroundings. He had been to doctors' offices before: fiberboard walls painted pink or light blue, a brass clothes rack, black Naugahyde sofa, white acrylic chairs, a magazine rack with *Popular Mechanics*, medical throwaways, and outdated copies of *National Geographic.* There was always a sliding glass panel separating the nurse's alcove from the patients. Someone dressed in white served as receptionist, typist, medical assistant, and bill collector. The inner office was not much of an improvement: an untidy desk, a collection of paperweights, family photos, and other memorabilia. On the walls, usually painted green, was the requisite display of degrees—Brandeis or Northeastern, occasionally Brown, and very occasionally, Harvard Med. The decor never seemed to instill confidence. But you knew the price wouldn't exceed Blue Cross.

Riley now felt uncomfortable. Dr. Dillard's intimidating office at St. Luke's Hospital was not what he had expected. The teak paneling reminded him of the hoary foyer of a London inn. The red-patterned Sarouk had to be at least ten by twenty. (Along with the footage, Riley tried to assess the cost—around forty thousand dollars, equal to his annual pay.) The truth was that the nine-by-nine Kirman, just to the left of the Sarouk, cost as much as did the shorter Takiz. The burgundy leather chairs had the scent of quality, old English, of richness and style. Suspended shelves of polished oak held the latest issues of magazines—*Vogue, Architectural Digest, Business Week,* and the morning edition of the *Wall Street Journal.* Riley surveyed other artifacts, pre-Columbian statues of ancient Aztec gods, slender vases, and tableaux frozen in Steuben glass. Silk-screen etchings—birds, flowers, bamboo—in soft blues and teal greens gave the decor a blend of elegance and tranquillity. There was soft music, semiclassical, and Riley felt less awkward. The room bustled with activity, nurses coming and going, attractive, young, carrying X-ray films or records. Several patients waited.

It was all planned. Furlong would handle the interrogation, keep it all "friendly." He would zero in on Dillard's alibi and subtly work into his relationship with Miss Williams. There was no question but that Dillard was the target. His initial responses to Furlong's inquiries would lock Dillard in. Riley was along as witness.

The nurse with Orphan Annie curls and a Mary Poppins smile ushered them into the doctor's office. If the reception area was out of character with what Riley had read about the great Dr. Dillard, there was no mistaking his interior office. It was the Oriental motif that struck Riley immediately as he saw reclining Buddhas, terra-cotta Ming dynasty figurines, Tang horses, bronzed-patina temple bells, Chinese porcelain, and antique pottery. Yet it was an atrium of light, with exotic plants—ficus, bamboo palms, and various cacti dappled by shafts of sunlight from the skylit roof. A large window looked over the city as seen from Mission Hill.

Dillard was ensconced behind a burnished rosewood desk upon which an onyx-base pen set, a jade-handled cigarette lighter with matching letter opener, and a small silver-framed photo of a youthful-looking wife and four beaming children were neatly arrayed. That was it: not a medical book or a degree anywhere in sight.

He greeted them warmly. "Gentlemen, come in. Please sit down." He motioned to two dark blue suede-covered chairs in front of his desk. The nurse with the auburn curls stood at the door for a moment, smiled, then departed, closing the door with a discreet click.

If Dillard was nervous or upset, he didn't betray it. Furlong didn't have much to go on. Dr. Dillard was a highly respected cardiovascular surgeon who had earned a reputation on a par with Cooley, De Bakey, and the Stanford Medical group. He did over two hundred coronary bypass operations annually, plus heart transplants, artery grafts, and was now experimenting with laser surgery, unclogging vital arteries of the brain. Graduating with honors from Harvard College and Yale Medical, he had been gifted since his formative years at the Choate School. In college, he had been an outstanding athlete in football, basketball, and track. There were those who said he could have made it in the NFL. He was a naval officer in Korea, much decorated, still hold-ing the rank of commander in the Naval Reserve. His six-two, 190-pound frame, handsome square-jawed face, and smoked silver hair belied his sixty-one years. He was well connected politically, academically, and socially. Also, he was a millionaire several times over.

Riley was more intuitive than Captain Furlong, and the whole situation seemed incongruous. He recognized instantly the striking similarity between the Williams woman's apartment and the interior of Dillard's office. Then there were the love letters (blackmail?) and the cocaine. Hospital labs, the pharmacy—he had the perfect setup for supplying drugs. But Riley thought it went deeper. With twenty years of gumshoe experience, he knew something that even the police commissioner didn't know: Christopher Dillard, the Brahmin surgeon, eastern Establishment, homes in Marblehead and Oyster Harbor, yachtsman, confidant of governors, politicians, college presidents, heads of television and the news media—this was a bigger incongruity—Dillard, who had old Boston roots, old English ties, was the biggest benefactor of the Irish Republican Army, the IRA. No one seemed to know why. Perhaps the answer would be entombed with Angela Williams.

"What can I do for you gentlemen?" It was not an effusive greet-ing, which would have been suspect, but crisp, that of a busy pro-fessional.

"Just a few questions, if we may," said Furlong. "We're from the Boston Police. This is Detective Riley. I'm Captain Furlong. Mind if I smoke?" Furlong had already wrestled open a pack of filter kings and offered one to Dillard, who declined. He took deliberate time to light, puffing on it, then with great ceremony replaced his lighter in his back pocket with some difficulty.

"Did you happen to catch the Celtics–Bulls game two nights ago, Dr. Dillard? I understand you're quite a fan."

"Sure am!" replied Dillard. "I have box seats. In fact, we run an athletic clinic here at St. Luke's and we've operated on a few of the players. You might say I'm a basketball filbert. Played varsity ball back at Harvard."

Riley felt they should apprise Dillard of his rights—the right to remain silent, to obtain counsel. If he felt any hint of surprise or concern, Dillard's face and demeanor did not disclose it. He should have asked why, or what the inquiry was all about. Maybe his coolness gave him away? Of course, there had been nothing about the homicide in the press. There'd be no release until after they received the autopsy report.

"Actually, it was the first game I've missed this season. I stayed in town at my apartment on Beacon Hill. Caught the last fifteen minutes on television before I turned in. Great comeback. I think they'll win the play-offs."

Furlong could now fill in the pieces. His mind quickly calculated that, according to Dillard, he had been in his apartment from 10:15 on.

"Were you with anyone? I mean, watching the Celtics game?"

"No, I had dinner with a young lady. I was operating the next morning, and when I do, I usually stay in town."

"May I ask whom you were with, Dr. Dillard?"

"Certainly," Dillard replied too quickly, as though he had been asked a question by one of his medical students. "I was with a Miss Williams at her apartment in Back Bay. She's an old friend."

"How old?"

There was a masked arrogance in Furlong's inquiry. Riley knew that Dillard at that moment was being destroyed—his career, his prestigious insulated life, his family. And he, Riley, was part of it. In a few moments, they would nail Dr. Dillard, one of the most respected citizens in Boston.

"I've known her for a long time. I sponsored her American citizenship. She's originally from Dominica, an island in the Caribbean."

"What time did you leave her apartment that night?" Furlong was surprised at his success.

"Time?" Dillard unconsciously glanced at his gold-braceleted Piaget. "I'd say about ten o'clock."

Riley thought it strange that Dillard didn't ask whether anything was wrong. He remained unruffled. His voice had a spontaneity about it, a ring of sincerity.

"May I ask what time you arrived at Miss Williams's apartment? What you did during the evening?"

If fissures were to appear in Dillard, this should have been the time. Also, he should have called a halt to the inquiry. Riley felt that the doctor was unaware of Angela Williams's fate.

"We had a candlelight dinner. Soft music, that sort of stuff. Miss Williams loved to cook. She was part Carib Indian. Great island recipes. We had the works—duck à l'orange, gratinéed potatoes, crêpes Bayaldi, a bottle of Chardonnay, and a few after-dinner brandies. She had just bought a restaurant on Newbury Street. We were sort of celebrating."

Furlong was unimpressed. He sensed Dillard was lying. Perhaps it was his use of the past tense when describing Miss Williams. "Loved to cook," he had said.

"Something's wrong, isn't it?" Dillard said, rising. His voice started to crack.

Furlong reached over to rub his cigarette into the small silver tray on Dillard's desk. "Yes," Furlong said. "Angela Williams has been found dead. . . ."

Dillard staggered slightly and slumped back into his chair as his composure deserted him. Then his face crumpled. He buried his head in his hands and began to weep, racking sobs that shook his large frame.

At this juncture, Riley chose sides.

5

DR. BERNIE MCCAFFERTY sat in the outer office of District Attorney Neil Harrington. He had a sense of well-being, of belonging. As county medical examiner, he was part of the system. The room was elegantly decorated with pecan-wood paneling, celery green broadloom carpeting, muted marine prints on the walls, and the great bronze seal of the Commonwealth of Massachusetts sculpted above the foyer that led to the inner office. Above McCafferty, a portrait of Cardinal Richelieu, attired in scarlet ecclesiastical robes, glared down. The doctor couldn't avoid his imperious gaze. It was intimidating. Perhaps it was meant to be.

After one unsuccessful attempt, he struck a second match and lit a cigarette. He hoped the attractive young receptionist hadn't noticed.

"The district attorney will be with you shortly," she said, smiling tolerantly. McCafferty had handed her his business card. She had glanced at it without comment. Between puffs on his cigarette, he chewed some mints. He had had a few scotch bracers earlier that morning and felt reasonably well. Never a stylish dresser, even in his good days, his white button-down shirt was rumpled and stained and his tweed suit was too small. He unconsciously adjusted his tie.

The receptionist seemed uninterested in striking up a conversation, although the doctor had commented on the portrait of the cardinal, even peering at the artist's signature. She smiled, halfway between a smirk and a smile—nothing inviting—and returned to transferring incoming and outgoing calls and typing memos.

He had been cooling his heels for forty-five minutes. He glanced at his watch and sighed. The girl looked his way and arched her eyebrow slightly, indicating that her boss was really busy.

Kristina Collins, the young receptionist, had the book on the county medical examiner: two divorces, alcoholic, involved in a paternity suit. In fact, there was little that Kristina Collins did not know about the Boston political and social scene. She knew that four years ago Harrington had saved McCafferty's ass. And right now her boss was not pleased with the postmortem report on Angela Williams.

"Mr. Harrington will see you now, Doctor," the receptionist said. She turned the burnished brass handles on the double oak doors and ushered McCafferty in.

"Bernie." Neil Harrington came to him, shook his hand warmly, and clapped him on the back. "Good to see you, old friend."

Another figure caught McCafferty's eye, a striking young woman in her late twenties or early thirties. She wore a gray business suit with a white ruffled shirt and was leaning back in a wine leather sofa, her perfectly shaped legs crossed at the ankles.

"This is Mayan d'Ortega, first assistant district attorney in the Criminal Division, Bernie. She'll be handling the case."

"What case?" inquired McCafferty diffidently.

Harrington looked at McCafferty for a moment. His smile hardened a bit. "The Angela Williams case . . . the folder under your arm . . . this is why we're here."

"Oh yes." McCafferty felt the unhappiness in Harrington's smile. He suddenly became pensive.

"Good to see you, Miss d'Ortega. I've heard a lot about you. High marks, believe me."

"I believe you," she said softly, accepting the compliment but not returning it. She smiled faintly, an enigmatic, far-off smile. Her dark brown eyes were large and round and her jet black hair, shaped carefully, framed her olive Hispanic face.

She's a beauty, McCafferty thought to himself. A Mexican beauty, known admiringly as "the spic with the big chocolate eyes," who hadn't lost a criminal case in four years, including five first-degree murder convictions. And her father was also the richest man in El Paso, Texas.

In the old days, say ten or twelve years ago, when Neil Harrington was cutting his legal teeth, getting bounced around by judges, court clerks, and the criminal bar, he would have come right to the point. But he had learned the art of being elliptical, of listening, cultivating, manipulating. Now he was a master of the technique.

Harrington seldom sat at his imposing desk, even during press conferences. He reasoned that it was a place to work, not to serve as a barrier. Motioning McCafferty to join Mayan d'Ortega on the sofa, he sat in a chair opposite them, various folders and documents spread out on a nearby glass-topped table rimmed in bronze. This was the first time McCafferty had been invited into Harrington's inner sanctum. The muted earth tones of the interior, he thought, blended perfectly with the olive-skinned beauty who sat to his right. She said nothing, which made McCafferty nervous. He felt her wide inquisitive eyes watching him closely—like an Indian—which was partially accurate, since her name came from the Yucatán, her mother being part Mayan. McCafferty reached for a cigarette, offered one to Mayan d'Ortega, who declined, and Harrington lit it with a silver cigarette lighter that was conveniently within reach.

"I can't understand your postmortem, Bernie," Harrington began. "We have a heinous murder on our hands, involving some big people, big connections, and your autopsy protocol is completely meaningless."

McCafferty sensed the niceties were over. "Well, Neil, it was an eight-hour post. The most..." He looked at Mayan d'Ortega. She nodded. "Mind if I call you Neil? We go back a long way...."

Harrington's mouth tightened but then relaxed.

"A long way.... Yes, Bernie, call me Neil."

"As I was saying, Neil, it was an eight-hour post. The most exhaustive and thorough study I've ever done. We overlooked nothing. Sectioned everything. Lungs, trying to spot an embolism. Arteries, veins, capillaries—everything. Pathologically, there wasn't a goddamned thing wrong with that woman." He again looked at Miss d'Ortega. She nodded her okay.

Harrington was used to talking to city and state workers, even to expert witnesses—doctors, psychiatrists, economists. He had spent a decade with them on both sides of the law. The experts, he felt, were whores. Once at a bar seminar, he defined an expert as being a guy who's fifty miles from home with slides. And experts had to be culled, cajoled, romanced, honed, then led predictably to the end that best suited his needs, be it legal or political. And in his scheme of things, McCafferty was no exception.

"Please, Bernie," he said, "this woman had high connections. She was found dead off a major turnpike ten miles north of Boston. She didn't walk there. Right?"

"Right."

"Your report indicates posterior livor mortis, and yet she was found facedown. So she was murdered elsewhere—my guess is in her Back Bay apartment—transported to Burlington, and deposited where she was found."

"But why?" inquired McCafferty. "Why go to all that trouble? If someone wanted her out of the way, leave her in her apartment. There'd be no suspicion of foul play. No marks, no bruises on the body. Probably never would have been an autopsy. . . . Or wrap her in a cement overcoat and dump her off Minot Light. Why was she found so quickly? . . . And by whom? Neil, it looks too easy. I . . ."

Harrington had let McCafferty ramble. Now he cut him off, displeasure creeping into his voice. "Bernie, the ifs, buts, and whys are for me and my office. We have a prime suspect, and we're going to nail him. . . . You just do your job and I'll do mine. . . . You must have overlooked something—potassium cyanide, curare poisoning. We've had many of these homicides in Boston. Inject a little potassium and it's curtains. Kills without a trace."

McCafferty lit another cigarette. His hands shook noticeably. All along, he was conscious of the large brown eyes of Mayan d'Ortega watching him.

"Now, two reporters will be arriving shortly, Fletcher Porter from the *Globe* and Pat Nolan from the *Herald*. I can't stall them forever." The irritation crept back into Harrington's voice. "They're good people. My press agent, Susan Iannella, will parry them as best she can. But listen, Bernie. I don't intend to bullshit these guys. . . . They can do a number on you. I want something concrete by the weekend . . . and that means the *exact* cause of death."

"Well, I can recheck, do another post. The vital organs are all refrigerated. So's the body. I'll look for a mystery toxin. My assistant and I will—"

"Your what?"

"My assistant, Karen Steadman. She worked with me."

Harrington looked at the signature on the autopsy report, then at McCafferty. "There's no mention in this report"—he shook the documents—"of an assistant."

"Well," McCafferty stammered, "she was doing a little moonlighting. . . . She's an intern in pathology. It was her first post. . . ."

"Okay," Harrington replied, again interrupting, his voice calm but still pinched with displeasure. "Bernie, quite frankly, I think you were hungover and did a slipshod job. . . . Dr. Myron Gellis is flying in from New York today and will conduct a new postmortem."

"Myron Gellis?" McCafferty looked stunned. Gellis was the dean of American pathologists, who was former chief medical examiner of New York City, was author of numerous books, lecturer with international credentials, president emeritus of the American Board of Pathology. It was Gellis who gave pathology a good name, tried to elevate it from the pit of the medical disciplines.

And McCafferty knew there was another side of Gellis. He wasn't exactly Albert Schweitzer. He testified professionally in civil and criminal cases worldwide. His credentials were of the highest quality—and so were his fees. McCafferty could only begin to wonder how much this was going to cost the taxpayers.

Harrington could read McCafferty's mental calculations.

"Yes, you'll be his assistant. Give him your utmost courtesy and cooperation."

McCafferty doused his half-lit cigarette with a spiraling motion, grinding it out into an onyx ashtray. Harrington knew McCafferty would breathe a deep sigh. McCafferty did. It was a sign of acquiescence, servitude, defeat.

Harrington smiled. It was a genuine Irish smile, full of wit and charm, devoid of rancor and pettiness. They understood each other. McCafferty gathered up his papers and started filing them into his valise.

"Okay, Neil. Okay. I'll give Professor Gellis all the support he needs."

"Fine," Harrington said, rising. "Nice to see you again, Bernie. Mayan, why don't we escort Dr. McCafferty to the lobby. Go out by my private elevator. I'll deal with the *Globe* and the *Herald* in a few minutes."

McCafferty smiled weakly and stood to leave.

The elevator was a mere outline in the walnut paneling. They stood there for a moment, Harrington, McCafferty, and Mayan d'Ortega. The district attorney made eye contact with McCafferty and held it. Their entire relationship was locked in that gaze: McCafferty saved from the junk heap by Harrington; Harrington now calling in the chips.

6

NEIL HARRINGTON had never been an insider. He had attended Harvard on a football scholarship and was a starting linebacker in his senior year. In the final game against Yale, he staved off defeat by intercepting a pass. For a while after that, he was toasted, and he dated young women from Radcliffe and Smith who had surnames like Mellon and van Sturdevant. He even got invited to summers in the Hamptons and yachting weekends out on Nantucket and the Vineyard.

But he was always the tough Irish kid from the inner city, born on a side street from respectability in the brick-bottom section of Boston's South End. One of six children, he had ordinary parents and ordinary brothers and sisters. His father held menial municipal jobs—City Water Department, Public Works, Redevelopment Authority, from rate clerk to field supervisor, depending upon who was dispensing patronage at city hall. In a way, his family was an embarrassment, and this fueled young Harrington. He owed the world a success.

Despite his rugged good looks, a six-foot frame, and the adulation and connections made in college, he quickly realized the enormous gulf between himself and his classmates. In his senior year, the corporate teams were conducting interviews for candidates, and the parrying and jostling started for grad school. Then awareness struck home.

At gatherings at Oyster Harbor or in the Hamptons, Harrington recognized the interlocking of power. Eastern Establishment families moved among themselves, intermarried, wielded further influence. Money, he realized, not title, was power; athletic fame, even a superior academic record, was not a passport to status.

Perhaps he had always known it—even before he'd been on the beach in the Hamptons just a few weeks before graduation. He was with his best girl, a senior from Radcliffe whom he had dated for two years. He was in love. So was she. They were at her family's beachfront sprawl on Long Island. They had picnicked on a sand dune, sipped white wine and eaten French bread. As they sat watching white puffy clouds scudding over the Atlantic, he asked her to marry him. He was entering law school. They'd have children, lovely children, a future.

She held his face in her hands and began to weep. She alone understood the hopelessness. She shook her head. It was impossible. She asked him to drive her home. He caught a glimpse of her tanned aristocratic features, her flaxen hair catching the wind as she stood in the doorway, her back to the ocean. Neither waved good-bye.

It wasn't a rejection, just simple recognition. The young girl with the hair of spun gold had known. It took Harrington a little time before it finally sank in. It was a long way from the South Shore of Long Island to the redbrick playgrounds of the South End of Boston. Harrington never looked back. He'd been in overdrive ever since.

Harrington sat at his desk now, reflecting. He had set impossible goals for himself, a series of overachievements. After Georgetown Law came three years of naval service in Vietnam, where he was wounded in the last stage of the war at Cam Ranh Bay. He was discharged as a lieutenant commander. At the urging of friends, he ran against Maurice Delaney, Boston's aging, near-senile district attorney, who vowed to die in office. It was Neil Harrington's initial encounter with the political process and he was a resounding success, thoroughly trouncing the incumbent. In a show of graciousness, he retained the defeated Delaney as first assistant. True to his word, the old DA died four months later.

The second time he asked a wellborn golden girl to marry him, she did not refuse.

Neil Harrington spent the next decade building his fiefdom. He gained a reputation for fighting crime when and where it counted—street crime, prostitution, pornography, bookmaking, drugs. "Make the streets of Boston safe" was his motto, and if it confined blacks and Hispanics to narrower corridors in the ghetto, it was not without the approbation of his lower-middle-class white constituency, be they Polish, Italian, Jewish, or Irish, not to mention the upper-crust residents of Back Bay and Beacon Hill. He became a gifted after-dinner speaker—at bar associations, the cardinal's annual charity ball, college commencements, and various politically oriented functions up and down the Eastern Seaboard. He kept himself in superb physical condition, was a respected squash player, and jogged five miles daily. At age fifty-four, he ran the Boston Marathon in under three hours.

There was no question that Harrington wielded more power than any political figure in Massachusetts, and that included the mayor, the governor, and Irving Crimmins, the only black to sit in the U.S. Senate, a seat Harrington was zeroing in on. Harrington decided who was to be indicted and who wasn't, for what offense and for what reason. More importantly, he knew where all the skeletons were hidden and in whose closets. His PR staff was carefully tailored to promote close ties to the press, particularly the *Boston Globe*, and the rest of the media. He employed the daughters and sons of movers and shakers. That was the key to gaining the respect of their parents. He became a social intimate of television stars and sports celebrities. His Irish good looks and the blondish hair with a tinge of white at the temples made him a prime candidate for the talk-show circuit, for which he often served as a moderator or host. His attractive, unassuming patrician wife had produced three handsome children—a son at Georgetown Law and two daughters at Mt. Holyoke. If there was a blemish on Neil Harrington's profile, it was that he worked too hard. He was an indefatigable exemplar of the American work ethic; he thrived on eighteen-hour days, never stopping to savor his accomplishments.

His next stop was the U.S. Senate, and nothing or no one would keep him from getting there.

Dr. Myron Gellis chatted easily with Harrington as he leafed through his papers, sorting them in the index of his mind. He wore a dark blue suit with a light blue tie and a white-on-white shirt. In his late sixties, he had a great shaggy mane of gray hair, lively brown eyes, a scholarly face, and a high forehead encasing a magnificent brain. Einstein and Oppenheimer immediately came to mind. He spoke in German-accented analytical tones, lacing his esoterica with earthy analogies. His credentials fitted the man. He was an expert's expert.

Gellis removed his glasses, polishing them carefully. "Essentially, what Dr. McCafferty found was correct," he said, holding the spectacles up to the light. "His postmortem followed the Rokitansky technique, with organ-by-organ dissection. It was a little slipshod, but by and large, he touched all the pathological bases. Of course, after forty-eight hours, certain poisons and toxins leave no trace at all—curare, potassium." Gellis detailed them carefully.

Mayan d'Ortega sat next to Dr. Gellis, following every word, making mental notes of her own.

"I did find a minute fracture of the cricoid cartilage in the anterior neck. Measured one point one centimeter in length by point one in width. McCafferty apparently missed it."

"Could the fracture of the cricoid cartilage have been traumatically induced by, say, strangulation?" Harrington came right to the point.

Gellis looked thoughtful, placing his thumb to his cheek, forefinger on his right temple. Police departments, district attorneys, and private litigators paid him to supply the answers. This was why he was here.

"It's quite possible," he said carefully. "I would like to have done the original post and viewed the anterior neck musculature first-hand—the longus capitus, the sternocleidmastoid, the scalenus."

"Essentially, what we have is a broken neck, isn't that right, Doctor?" Harrington was catching Gellis's signals.

"You might call it that. The anterior neck is very flexible, yet highly insulated from injury; all sorts of soft tissues give it protective cover. But such a fracture is consistent with being induced by exterior force."

Harrington let it go at that. Each man understood the other. At that moment, a pact was formed. The testimony would take a little honing, a little probative polish, but even now it was enough for an indictment. By the time of the trial, Dr. Gellis's expert opinion would be persuasive beyond a reasonable doubt.

Gellis supplied other details. The victim was indeed a great beauty. McCafferty was right in many respects; there was not a mark on her. "If she was trafficking in heavy drugs . . ." He looked at Mayan d'Ortega, then at Harrington, who nodded that full disclosure was okay, that he fully trusted his assistant prosecutor. "Well, if she was a heavy trafficker, she wasn't a user. No needle marks or punctures, no inflamed nasal passages; blood serum and enzyme studies—all negative."

"We found ledgers and receipts indicating she did over ten million a year," said Harrington. "Obviously, she wasn't a loner. She had to have connections. I don't think she was tied to the mob. We're checking it." He glanced at Mayan d'Ortega. "The feds are interested."

"You say you have a prime suspect?"

"We do. Probably the last person who saw her alive. They ate dinner at her place, full gourmet meal, wine, the works. He says he left her about ten P.M." Harrington threw it out matter-of-factly.

"He's lying." Gellis took a pipe out of his jacket pocket, packed it carefully from a tobacco pouch. "Mind if I smoke?"

"By all means, Doctor."

Gellis lit his pipe with great ceremony, puffed it vigorously to ignition, then sat back on the couch, crossing his legs in a contented posture. "Except for natural acid and stomach mucus, the stomach was *empty.* There is absolutely no evidence that she had eaten anything that evening."

That was the clincher.

"Dr. Gellis," Harrington inquired deferentially, "from your postmortem, based upon your clinical experience, what would be your estimate of the time of death?"

"Probably eight-thirty that evening; nine P.M. at the latest. I would agree with Dr. McCafferty's assessment. This can be pinpointed with reasonable medical certainty."

Harrington changed the pace. "We're fortunate the Commonwealth can rely upon a medical expert of your caliber and renown, Dr. Gellis. At the national district attorneys' conference in Houston last January, Barry Cormack, the DA of Chicago's Cook County, told me how you blew E. Lyle Coopersmith out of the water on a rape/incest/murder case."

There was a faint smile on the Einstein physiognomy.

"Yes. We exhumed the body. From the food content, I was able to demonstrate that the defendant, who was the father of the little girl, testified falsely as to when the child last ate and when he had put her to bed for the night."

"And this is the reverse of what we have here, Doctor."

"Is the Commonwealth willing to underwrite . . ." It was an unnecessary question, but from experience, Gellis wanted the money up front before committal.

"Doctor, please. No question about it. The Commonwealth is

solvent.'' Harrington trusted Mayan d'Ortega in most confidences. But she was still young, and at times her eyes had an ancient glow of fires burning somewhere far away that was disturbing even to Harrington. He'd rather leave the financial assurances for a private meeting.

Harrington knew Gellis's testimony would not be inexpensive. Barry Cormack had told him that Gellis's fee was in the range of a twenty-thousand-dollar retainer, plus expenses—costs for associates, research, hotels, incidentals—which often added up to more than fifty thousand dollars. Harrington knew that and Gellis knew that Harrington knew. It involved a certain amount of risk. Gellis's reputation was on the line, and so was his future. This had to be factored into the cost, which could reach six figures. There was a mutual accord between the men; and only peripheral discussion was needed.

"Now, Dr. Gellis, in your professional judgment, what was the competent producing cause of death in this case?"

Gellis took a languid drag on his pipe, allowing the smoke to curl slowly toward the ceiling.

"Death by strangulation—sufficient to fracture the cricoid cartilage, a most resilient piece of gristle, I might add. I feel fairly comfortable that I can support that pathologic diagnosis.''

Harrington had his expert—and his case.

7

DR. DILLARD slid into the last row in Courtroom 806. An elderly man to his left nodded a welcome and shifted his cane and raincoat to make more room. Dillard gave him a half smile, placed his top-coat on the vacant seat, and put on his dark glasses. He sat motionless for several seconds, trying to adjust to the strange tableau in front of him. The spectators' benches were partially filled and in the front row, sitting rigid and upright, he could see a man and woman wearing Thomas neck collars.

To Dillard, the scene lacked reality—somewhat like a stage production—a senior-class play. The black-robed judge with white shaggy hair peered down from his perch with the proper degree of judicial disdain. The bailiff, portly and ruddy-faced, told the jurors to be seated. They did so with a series of muffled clacks. The attorneys fidgeted at their tables, awaiting the opening click of business.

"You just missed the prosecutor's statement," the elderly man whispered as he leaned toward Dillard. "That Matson fella—good TV sportscaster, but he'll be wearing the denims by tomorrow night. Third charge of drunk driving."

"*Commonwealth* vs. *Charles T. Matson*," the bailiff boomed. "The jury is all present, Your Honor."

"Fine." The judge leaned forward. "Mr. Sheridan, do you wish to make an opening for the defense?"

Dillard was snapped back into reality as he watched Daniel Sheridan slowly rise from his seat at the defense table. For all that Dillard had heard about him, his reputation of being Boston's premier trial lawyer, Sheridan looked unimposing. In his plain blue suit and button-down shirt, he looked a little chunky. Dillard guessed he stood just shy of six feet and was perhaps on the better side of forty. He had reddish brown hair flecked with gray. When Sheridan nodded toward the prosecuting attorney, Dillard noticed his nose was slightly pug—perhaps from physical encounters, athletic or otherwise. To Dillard, it was a good sign—the face of a fighter.

"I'd prefer to make my opening after the prosecution puts in its case," Sheridan said, addressing the bench but nodding slightly toward the jury.

"That's your prerogative." The judge gave a fatherly look to the jurors. "Ladies and gentlemen," he said, "you have just heard the Commonwealth's attorney, Mr. Wayne Elkins, outline what he intends to prove as the elements of his case against the defendant, Charles T. Matson—namely, that the defendant operated a motor vehicle on a public way in the town of Barnstable while under the influence of an intoxicating beverage and operated recklessly, so as to cause his vehicle to collide with the rear of a vehicle stopped on said public way. Now let me caution you—keep an open mind. Don't discuss this case with *anyone* until all the evidence is in, one way or the other. The prosecution has the burden of proving beyond a reasonable doubt all elements of its case, and on the other side of the ledger, the defendant has the benefit of the presumption of innocence. Mr. Elkins, call your first witness."

The jurors hunched forward. From his loft in front of the judge's bench, the clerk shuffled some papers. The stenographer's fingers hovered over her recording machine, poised for the opening salvo.

Wayne Elkins, the young assistant district attorney, turned toward the spectators. A shock of blond hair tumbled down almost to his eyebrows; his horn-rimmed glasses added a studious touch to his boyish face.

"Sgt. Martin F. Hanlon," he called out audibly.

"Martin F. Hanlon," the bailiff cried. "Come forward and be administered the oath."

Sergeant Hanlon, attired in his state trooper's uniform—electric blue jacket with gold chevrons, a row of citations embroidered into his lapel—was an impressive figure as he stepped from the spectators' section. He carried a notebook in one hand and his Smokey the Bear hat in the other. His jodhpurs with the gold stripe along the seam were tucked into glistening black boots. He paused midway in front of the jury and raised his right hand. Sheridan eyed him carefully.

"Do you promise to tell the truth and nothing but the truth so help you God?" the bailiff intoned.

"I do." Sergeant Hanlon's voice was authoritative and crisp.

Hanlon stood in the witness box, placed his hat on the seat, and opened his notebook on the lectern in front of him.

The preliminary questioning went quickly. Hanlon was on patrol out of the Cape Cod barracks and noticed a car speeding near the center line, heading north on Old County Road. From his check-point, he estimated the car's speed at seventy to seventy-five mph in a fifty-five-mile zone. He started to give chase but was delayed by several cars passing in each direction. When he finally got under way, he came upon an accident scene where the suspect vehicle had collided with a car stopped for a red light. He questioned both drivers. The occupants in the stopped vehicle claimed neck injuries. He called the barracks for assistance, then walked back to the other car. The driver who had caused the collision was standing outside his vehicle, leaning against the passenger door.

Prosecutor Elkins waited several seconds, then removed his horn-rimmed glasses and pointed them toward the witness. "Sergeant Hanlon, did you form an opinion at that time as to the driver's sobriety?"

"I did." Sergeant Hanlon looked at the jury. "He was drunk!"

Elkins, yellow scratch pad in one hand, glasses in the other, walked toward the witness, stopping just beside the foreman of the jury. "What was the basis of your opinion?" he asked.

Hanlon proceeded to run with the question. "I observed that he was glassy-eyed and had the strong odor of alcohol on his breath. He claimed to have had only two beers, but his speech was slurred. I asked him to focus on my pen." Hanlon produced a ballpoint pen from his lapel and held it next to the right side of his eyes. Jurors in the last row stood to view Hanlon's demonstration. "His eyes couldn't focus. They jiggled from side to side. We call this phenomenon nystagmus—a cardinal sign of intoxication."

The sergeant went on to describe other field sobriety tests, finger to nose, walking the center line heel-to-toe. "All of which," he said emphatically, "the subject flunked! I then had him accompany me back to the barracks in the cruiser."

"What happened next?"

"I asked him to take a Breathalyzer test voluntarily. He refused."

"He refused?" Elkins pursed his lips halfway between surprise and disapproval.

"That's correct."

"Did you then place the subject under arrest?" The prosecuting attorney stole a glance at the jury. They sat in rapt attention.

"I first read him his Miranda rights, the right to remain silent, the right to counsel, and also told him he could make a phone call. He said he knew his rights and didn't need to make a call. I then placed him under arrest. He was booked and sent to a cell."

Elkins surveyed the jury. They were grim and receptive. The testimony had been concise, graphic, and persuasive. "Thank you, Sergeant Hanlon. Please remain where you are for the defense lawyer's cross-examination."

"Okay." The elderly man again leaned toward Dillard cupping his hand to his mouth. "Watch the defense attorney. He's a tiger. I've seen him before."

"Mr. Sheridan?" The judge peered down from the bench.

"No questions, Your Honor."

Charles Matson, sitting next to Sheridan, slumped in disbelief. There was a noticeable stirring among the spectators.

Sergeant Hanlon nodded and began collecting his notes and hat.

"No cross-examination, Mr. Sheridan?" The judge stared down, his eyebrows arched.

"That's right, Your Honor," Sheridan said quietly.

Several patch-quilt witnesses fleshed out the remaining evidence—the driver and passenger of the stopped vehicle. A local photographer, who happened on the scene, explained blowup photos of the accident, highlighting skid marks left by the vehicle that did the rear-ending.

Sheridan again had no questions.

"Do you wish to make your opening?" the judge inquired.

"Does the prosecution rest its case?" Sheridan looked over at Elkins.

"The prosecution rests," Elkins said with finality.

Several seconds went by.

"Mr. Sheridan?" The judge looked impatient.

"Your Honor, I move at this time for a directed verdict for the defendant."

"On what grounds, Counselor?" The judge's look of impatience suddenly changed to irritation.

"The prosecution has failed to identify the defendant personally as the driver of the car in question and has failed to put in proof that Old County Road is a public way," said Sheridan.

"Your Honor!" Elkins bolted from his seat. "That was an oversight; if I may be permitted . . ."

The judge knew that Sheridan was right. Elements, however minor, were lacking in the Commonwealth's case. "I'll see all counsel in chambers!" he barked.

No one spoke for several seconds. The judge took off his black robe and handed it to the clerk. Sheridan sat tight-lipped. Elkins was turning the color of the judge's beige rug. He knew he had booted it.

"What do you want me to do?" The judge looked at Elkins.

"Reopen the case, Your Honor. Allow Sergeant Hanlon to point out Matson as the man he arrested. He's been sitting with Mr. Sheridan all day.

"And Old County Road is Route Six A, a state road, Your Honor. Everyone knows that."

"Where did you go to law school, Mr. Elkins?" The judge tried to engage in some conciliatory banter.

"Duke University, Your Honor, class of '92."

"First job—with the district attorney's office?"

"This is my first case, Judge. . . ."

The judge turned toward Sheridan. "You have any objection to allowing Mr. Elkins to reopen his case just for identification purposes? Sergeant Hanlon can also testify that Old County Road is a public way. Take thirty seconds. You can cross-examine on all points. Recall all witnesses."

"Judge, you know I want to be fair. But my client doesn't have to prove or disprove a damn thing here. The presumption of innocence continues throughout the entire trial. And I owe a duty to my client. If I waive the rules of the game just because the DA's office made a mistake, hell, I'd be sued for malpractice, perhaps reported to the bar overseers. And Judge, those so-called neck injuries? This was a fender bender—maybe fifty dollars' damage tops." Sheridan rolled his eyes toward the ceiling. "Certainly I object to reopening the case."

The judge heaved a long, deliberate sigh. "Well, Mr. Elkins, perhaps I can put in a word with your boss, Neil Harrington. You tried a beautiful case except for a tiny oversight. It's not the end of the world. There'll be other cases, and you'll never forget the lesson you've learned in this one."

The judge didn't look happy. "Defendant's motion is granted. Bill"—he turned to his clerk—"discharge the jury. Tell the defendant he's free to go."

Elkins slumped dejectedly in his chair, shaking his head. Sheridan didn't feel all that great, either.

Dillard stood by the bank of elevators in the corridor next to the courtroom. It was a mangy place, with dirty tiles and cigarette butts spilling from dusty bins; even the unpolished brass on the elevators had a greenish tinge of decay.

He watched the jurors as they waited for elevators or took the stairs. They were ordinary lower middle class, some prattling about their new experience, others impatient that their lives had been interrupted, but all expressing dismay at the trial's outcome. "You can get away with murder in this town," some muttered. "All it takes is a slick lawyer."

Dillard wondered.

"Mr. Sheridan." Dillard hurried to catch up with the lawyer as he headed down a side corridor. "I'm Dr. Christopher Dillard. Your office said I could catch you here." Dillard extended his hand.

Sheridan shifted his raincoat onto his briefcase to shake hands.

"I watched you perform." Dillard smiled slightly. "I can't say I understood what went on, but I overheard some of the jurors say you won on a legal technicality."

"That happens sometimes," Sheridan said diffidently. "The law is full of fine lines."

"I thought you were going to get steamrolled," Dillard offered, "but whatever you did paid off for your client."

"How can I help you?" Sheridan wanted to dismiss the Matson case.

"Mind if I walk with you?" Dillard said. "I think I'm going to need a counselor of your caliber. You come highly recommended."

"Okay, Doctor. Let's go down the corridor and take the rear

elevator. I'd prefer not to run into the jurors. I could tell they were not too pleased. They probably thought we made a backroom deal."

The thought had occurred to Dillard, too.

"What sort of problem do you have, Doctor?" Sheridan opened. They dodged traffic across Beacon Street.

"Wouldn't it be better to go to your office?" Dillard asked.

"Sure. But let's see if your problem falls in my area of expertise. Might save us both a lot of time."

Dillard surveyed the pedestrians in his immediate vicinity.

"Well," he began guardedly, "I think I'm going to be charged with a crime I had nothing to do with, and I understand you're the best criminal lawyer in Boston."

Sheridan didn't bite at the accolade. "I win some and lose some," he said. "What do you think you're going to be charged with—malpractice?"

"Murder."

"I see." Sheridan didn't register surprise. They continued walking.

"I dined with a young lady one evening a week ago. Left her apartment about ten. That same night, she wound up dead."

"You married, Doctor?" Sheridan noticed a gold band on Dillard's ring finger.

"Yes. That's why I'm in a jam. Nothing's been in the papers yet, but I've already been questioned by the police—and a reporter from one of the national tabloids called and left his name. Everything's going to hit the fan. I need help."

Sheridan stopped at the corner of Tremont and Beacon and studied Dillard. "You're the cardiovascular surgeon who owns a boat or two. Live in Gloucester, I believe."

"Marblehead."

"Okay." Sheridan checked his watch. "Where will you be tonight, say about seven?"

"I'm available anytime. You just say it, time and place, I'll be there."

"There's a little hole-in-the-wall on Beacon Hill, Lazzarie's. We can have a drink, then go for a walk."

"Fine." Dillard, who had been looking grim and tense, suddenly breathed a sigh of relief. "Seven at Lazzarie's. I'll be there."

"What was the young lady's name?" Sheridan lowered his voice.

"Williams. Angela Williams."

Sheridan called Claire Doherty, the DA's indictment clerk. She called back from a pay station. They went back many years. Sheridan got her son off when he and a group of Boston College sophomores, dressed as Indians, stole the *Mayflower II* from her mooring in Plymouth Harbor and ran her aground off Manoscet Light. The judge, an old Yale grad, excoriated them in the courtroom but gave them suspended sentences, not even assessing costs for damage to the vessel. He later told his clerk that he thought it was a pretty good prank. As a youngster, he had once given a fresh coat of paint, Eli blue, to the statue of John Harvard the night before the football game.

Claire Doherty checked on the name. "Yes, they're investigating the murder of Angela Williams." She'd get a copy of McCafferty's autopsy. She understood a Dr. Gellis came in from New York and did an additional post.

"Dr. Dillard was the prime suspect; made some incriminating admissions. They've got love letters." She'd try to get details, but they seemed to be zeroing in on Dillard's statement that he had had dinner and then left about 10:00 P.M. The estimated time of death was an hour earlier and no food was found in the victim's stomach or other organs. Cause of death? She'd get back.

Claire had one final word of advice. "I heard how you knocked over Little Lord Fauntleroy this morning. Harrington is ape. You were never one of his favorite people, Dan. I'd stay out of this one if I were you. Farm it out to Jakey Weisman or Larry Cantone. Looks like a married goodbody was fooling around. The girlfriend leaned on him. You know the rest of the score. Mayan d'Ortega will be handling it. She's the first assistant, never lost a homicide case."

" 'The spic with the big chocolate tits'?"

"Eyes, Dan. Eyes. You know, you trial jockeys are all alike. But don't mix with her, Dan; she's a barracuda."

"There's only one thing I like getting better than baked barracuda." Sheridan added some whimsy to his voice.

"What's that?" Claire was getting irritated.

"Scrod."

"Scrod? You mean young cod?"

"No, Claire, I mean the past participle." Sheridan heard an audible click, then silence.

They sat in a corner and poked at crabmeat cocktails, Dillard working on his second martini while Sheridan nursed a bourbon. For a hole-in-the-wall, Lazzarie's had a quiet rendezvous ambience. A man in a black velvet jacket played the piano, a medley from Richard Rodgers. It helped to keep conversations private.

They talked about mutual acquaintances, sports, things in common—a psychological confidence builder for both of them.

"Allow me." Dillard reached for the check the waiter had discreetly placed at the center of the table. Sheridan didn't argue. He caught several media types mixing with local celebrities, then glanced out at the Public Garden and the Common. It had started to rain. Not the greatest night to discuss business.

The tuxedoed maître d' brought their coats and again Dillard was quick to respond. "Keep it," he said, tucking a twenty-dollar bill in the man's hand.

They walked into the cold night, along the bosky strand of Commonwealth Avenue, then turned onto Charles Street. Sheridan should have hailed a cab, but he thought it best to walk back toward Dillard's hospital. Charles Street still contained the memory of Colonial days, a rustic mix of Georgian brick and cobblestone. The simulated gas lights flickered as young people in jeans and L. L. Bean parkas shuffled past.

"My father had his medical office on the second story of that building." Sheridan pointed to a renovated brick structure that now housed an antique shop on one side and a flower boutique on the other.

"He was a doctor?" inquired Dillard.

"A general practitioner. Delivered half the babies from here to Kenmore Square. Used to get paid in turkeys, hams, eels, salami. It was the fifties. We never got rich, but we didn't starve."

Sheridan thought back on his father, Dr. Frank Sheridan, who died of cirrhosis and drug addiction, leaving a grieving widow, unpaid bills, and unkept promises.

"My father succumbed of a broken heart, as the Irish say. Too much booze, late hours, emotional problems. He was thirty-three when he died. He used to hit the Old Howard burlesque when Ann Corio was in town. That's where they found him—in an alley off Scollay Square."

Dillard appreciated the candor but wondered about it. He knew that Sheridan was an ex-cop. There had been some sort of internal-affairs investigation. But what emerged was that Sheridan was a fighter, ruthless when it came to defending a client. It bordered on obsession. Just the kind of man Dillard desperately needed.

"I received a subpoena today to appear before a magistrate Thursday morning." Dillard pulled it out of his raincoat pocket. They stopped at the corner of Chestnut Street and Sheridan studied it under the gaslit post.

"Well"—Sheridan's voice took on a serious tone—"looks like you're the target for a homicide charge. The DA is convening the grand jury and you've been 'invited' to testify."

They moved on, walking slowly. The rain had abated into a soft drizzle. "Tell me about it," said Sheridan.

"It's like a nightmare." Dillard gave the essentials, the same story he had given the police. "I haven't seen the body. I'm not even sure it's her."

"It's her, all right. Count on it. Let me explain where we stand. You were the last person to see her alive. You have no alibi."

"How do you know that . . . ?" Dillard stammered.

"Oh, I have my sources." He studied Dillard. "I want you to level with me. Did you kill her or have her killed?"

"Are you kidding?" Dillard halted.

Sheridan stopped, too. "I've got to know. If you killed her, there are pleas we can make—temporary insanity, self-defense. What you tell me now is held in absolute confidence. Like the seal of the confessional, it can't be broken. . . ."

"The whole thing's preposterous. I loved her."

"Okay. Fine. You loved her. Everyone kills the one he loves . . . eventually."

"Sheridan, I'm being framed."

Sheridan didn't have enough information yet to form an opinion. In addition to Claire Doherty, he had his investigator, Manny Raimondi, getting a quick read on Angela Williams—what the street was saying before anything broke in the papers. It all looked too easy. Incriminating letters. The body found quickly. By whom? And why? This was being checked.

Dillard was vulnerable. Even if acquitted, he'd be destroyed. The indictment would see to that. They walked toward the Storrow Drive overpass. Neither spoke for almost a minute.

"Can we get this thing taken care of, Mr. Sheridan?"

"Call me Dan."

"All right, and call me Chris."

"Sure," Sheridan said with cynical buoyancy. "You can fix anything in Boston—parking tickets, homicide. Takes a little scratch. But unless you've got more money than God, you can't fix Harrington. And if that's why you retained me, shit"—Sheridan's voice had a steely edge—"we'd better part company right here." They both stopped. "I can't help you there, pal. I can only defend you within the system." Sheridan resumed walking.

"What are my options?"

"Right now, you're between a rock and a hard place. You'll be indicted. I can't do a goddamned thing about that."

"Why not?"

"The system. It's the system. You'll be asked to testify before the grand jury. Asked? I should say required. It's a one-sided show. Counsel can only advise. He can't speak or make objections even to hearsay. The prosecutor runs the show. I understand that Harrington's first assistant will be putting in the evidence. She's a piranha. Particularly stupid was trusting the Boston Police. They were out to skin you alive. They'll relate your conversation. There'll be no rebuttal evidence on your side, nothing. Right now, I don't know what else they have." Sheridan held back a few things; the estimated time of death didn't jibe with Dillard's story.

"This will destroy me professionally and personally." Dillard stopped and looked at Sheridan.

"No question about it. The way I look at it, we play dead. We can't avoid an indictment. Battling the prosecutor at this point is like fighting submarines with a flamethrower."

These were things Dillard didn't want to hear. But Sheridan had learned long ago never to gloss a case, particularly with a client. Give him the worst. No assurances. Then if the chips fall your way, you're a prince.

"Isn't there anything you can do?"

"I'll work on it. Right now, I want you to hole up in Marblehead. No calls, no press . . . nothing. Don't want you going to work."

"But I'm booked solid in surgery for the next month."

"Doctor," Sheridan said patiently, "I don't think you're listening to me. Take a temporary leave. One slip of the knife, one patient fatality, and any chance of pulling this out goes pffft!" Sheridan flicked his fingers outward. "The press, the TV crews, every ghoul in Boston, will camp outside your office. It's not every day that Boston's leading surgeon is charged with killing a high-priced hooker." Sheridan meant to sting.

"Hooker! What are you talking about?" Dillard's jaw tightened.

Sheridan didn't answer. Then he said, "Look, there've gotta be other surgeons at St. Luke's who are just dying to use the knife. Maybe take over your practice. Right now, you retire from the world. No press, no statements, no comment from you or your family. Understand?"

"I understand." Dillard buried his hands in his pockets.

"I've got a few ideas," offered Sheridan. "It's a long shot. You were never apprised of your constitutional rights to remain silent. You were a target for the Boston Police when they came to your office. The very fact they were police was its own badge of intimidation. If I can convince the DA's office that the conversation will be thrown out, then they might be disinclined to convene a grand jury. Lot of ifs."

"You get me out of this hole, Dan, and you can name your price."

The rain subsided. Sheridan hailed a cab. "I think I'll walk back to my office," he said. "You take the cab back to the hospital. I'll call you tomorrow. Keep out of sight for a few days until I get a read on things." As a cab swerved out of the night traffic, Sheridan gripped Dillard's arm. "Tell me, Doc. I've got to know. Did you kill her?"

The cab, a few feet ahead, waited.

"Of course not." Dillard's response was emphatic. It had the ring of credibility. Sheridan looked deep into the doctor's eyes.

"Forget about me, Doctor. But why should a jury buy that?"

"Because," Dillard began slowly, his voice cracking, "I'm telling the truth." Sheridan noticed tears welling in the doctor's eyes. He almost believed him.

"Will you take a lie detector test?" Sheridan studied him carefully.

"Absolutely!" Dillard didn't hesitate. Then he stepped into the waiting cab.

Sheridan walked along the waterfront. He watched the black hulk of a tanker slide silently out into the stream, the green starboard lights glowing eerily in the billowing dark mist.

"A rich man with a problem." Sheridan smiled inwardly. "A defense lawyer's dream."

A chill wind blew off the Mystic River and he turned up his coat collar. Yet he felt something else, something from far off, a whiff of danger.

8

SEPIA BEAUTY SLAIN. Sheridan saw the lurid headline on the front page of the *Boston Herald*. Somehow, the reporter had secured a photograph of Angela. He bought the *Globe* and the *Herald* at the lobby newsstand and scanned the story as he rode the elevator to his eleventh-floor office. No mention of Dillard. It would give them breathing room, maybe a day or two.

"Good morning, Judy." Sheridan flashed a smile to his longtime secretary, who served as typist, receptionist, and faith healer and who had been with him since he'd first hung out his shingle fifteen years ago. Judy Corwin accepted the welcome, gave him a sheaf of messages, then nodded imperceptibly toward a carefully groomed man, late fifties, face tanned, seated in the small waiting room reading the *Wall Street Journal*. The man looked up from his paper and nodded, smiling slightly.

"This is Mr. Bradford Kyle," Judy Corwin said, introducing the visitor. "Mr. Kyle has an appointment."

Kyle folded his *Wall Street Journal* and seemed to bound out of the chair.

"Pleased to meet you." Sheridan extended his hand. "I'll see you in a moment."

"The pleasure is all mine . . . and you can call me Brad." He gripped Sheridan's hand, his crisp voice aristocratic, almost Etonian.

Judy Corwin tweaked the blinds in Sheridan's office partially open, then attached several pieces of correspondence to files on his desk. Sheridan hung his coat on the rack next to a portable bookcase, looked in the mirror behind the door, and straightened his tie and smoothed his hair. "Who's that?" He mouthed the words to Judy Corwin. She closed the door discreetly.

"Vice president of Commonwealth National Bank and looks the part. Has a legal problem with a girlfriend, and as the song goes, 'he's as rich as Rockefeller.' "

"Sounds like a client we can help." Sheridan enjoyed the early-morning banter. "Send him in."

*   *   *

Sheridan sipped his coffee from a white plastic cup and listened to banker Kyle's tale of legal woe.

"I have the canceled checks right here," the visitor said, producing photocopies from his valise. "They total three hundred thousand dollars. I paid for her condo outright. The understanding was that we were to be joint owners, but in view of the sensitivity of the situation, the deed was put in her name."

"You married, Mr. Kyle? Er, Brad?"

"Yes. We've had our ups and downs, but my wife's a dear person. We live in Wellesley Hills."

"Children?"

"A daughter at Brown, a boy at Princeton. Wants to become a lawyer." Kyle gave a patronizing smile.

"Who recommended me?" Sheridan drained his cup.

"Well, I've read about you in the papers, Mr. Sheridan, and George Whitemore, formerly with our foreign finance department, told me you knew how to handle these difficult situations."

Sheridan thought back. Sure, Whitemore. He had gotten him a suspended sentence for bank fraud.

"Oh yes," Sheridan said. "Where's Whitemore now?"

Kyle adjusted his glasses as if he was disapproving a bank loan. "Well, he's doing quite well, as a matter of fact. Teaches applied economics at B.U. Straightened himself out."

For a few moments, Sheridan studied the canceled checks and a photocopy of the condominium deed. Without asking, he could surmise what had happened. With the girlfriend finally ensconced in her own pad in her own name, the relationship had suddenly cooled.

"What do you want me to do?" Sheridan studied banker Kyle.

"Well, the way I see it, I paid for the property with the express understanding that we were joint owners. Get me back my three hundred thousand and you can pocket a hundred-thousand-dollar fee, plus expenses. That's the usual contingency, isn't it?"

"How old is your girlfriend?"

"What has that got to do with it?" Kyle was becoming annoyed. "I'm sure you can bring legal action to enforce a constructive trust. She can keep the property."

Sheridan started to dislike his new client. Kyle had been snook-
ered, no question about it, but no jury in the world would empa-
thize with him.

"Well, the way I see it," Sheridan said, "your friend will claim
it was a gift or payment for services rendered, a quid pro
quo."

"But isn't the law supposed to remedy this sort of stuff? This girl
is stealing. . . . Listen, I'll give you a ten-thousand-dollar retainer.
Let me write you a check." Kyle reached for his wallet.

"Save your money, Brad. Cut your losses and go back to Wellesley
Hills." Sheridan pushed the documents across his desk toward
banker Kyle.

"You're not taking the case?"

"That's right. It's a no-win situation. I'm giving you the best advice possible and it isn't costing you a dime. Go forward with a
lawsuit and you'll spend another twenty-five grand, have your name
plastered all over the tabloids, and wind up with zero."

"Well, I guess I made a mistake with that fucking whore!" Suddenly Kyle's patrician veneer deserted him. "I'll see Porter Wainwright over at Wainwright and Gray. I'm not done with that bitch
yet!" Kyle departed quickly, not bothering to shake Sheridan's
hand and forgetting his *Wall Street Journal.* He grabbed his coat
from the rack in the reception room and stomped out of the
office.

"What was that all about?" Judy Corwin inquired.

"An expensive piece of ass, Judy." Sheridan grinned. "I hope it
was worth it."

Judy shook her head in mild disapproval. "Speaking about love,"
she said, "am I to start a file on Dr. Dillard?"

"I haven't committed to taking the case, but make up a folder.
I want to see how he handles the polygraph we've scheduled for
Tuesday night with Rochford Steinmetz over at MIT."

"If you gave all your clients a lie detector test, you wouldn't have
any left. To think of the cock-and-bull stories they feed us, and you
still bail them out. What's so special about Dillard?"

"Well, he's got no alibi—that's for openers. He made a lot of
damaging admissions to the police. And he last saw the victim at

ten P.M. So *he* says. The estimated time of death was an hour earlier.

"He's a cool customer. Somehow, I think he'll fold Tuesday night. Then I'll try to cut a deal.

"And Judy, tell Manny Raimondi I want to see him. Have him check into the victim's background. I want to know what the scuttlebutt is out on the street.

"And tell young Buckley to get me the latest cases on motions to suppress under the Fourth and Fifth amendments. There was no arrest or custodial interrogation of Dillard, but it came damn close. I think they tricked him. He wasn't advised of his right to counsel or his right to remain silent. There's got to be a case or two out there covering this sort of stuff."

Judy Corwin scratched herself a memo. Young Buckley was Sheridan's assistant, had been for fifteen years. At age forty, he wasn't so young anymore. But despite his thinning rusty hair, Tom Buckley had a round baby face and the perpetual enthusiasm of a teenager. He would always be young Buckley to Sheridan and Judy. And Manny Raimondi was their investigator—an ex-cop like Sheridan, he had an uncanny knack of infiltrating the street, finding missing evidence, reluctant witnesses, and lost heirs. Short, compact, Manny was growing slightly plump from the pasta he loved to eat. Judy had heard more than one doting woman say he looked like a teddy bear. A teddy bear with a mind like a fox, she thought.

"Oh, by the way, Dan"—Corwin peered out over her glasses—"our account with First National is forty thousand down."

"Only forty thousand?"

"That's the good news. The bad news is that Caitlin O'Malley is five months along."

"Five months? Is she going to marry the guy?"

Corwin shrugged. "Who gets married these days? I think it's high time we started lining up a new secretary."

"Okay. Do the necessary." Sheridan sighed. Forty thousand down, he thought to himself. It was expensive running a law office. And the cash flow was tight. Maybe he'd been a little too abrupt with banker Kyle. No. That was a loser from day one. Dillard? Maybe.

*   *   *

Tommy Buckley picked up Sheridan at his waterfront condo and they drove along the Charles River embankment, headed toward the gray columned porticoes of MIT.

"Dr. Steinmetz is the number-one guy in the country on the polygraph," Buckley said as he edged into the outer lane of the early-evening traffic. "I spent three hours with him going over the test. It's foolproof. He rigged me up and asked some control questions. I was relaxed, not a care in the world. I picked a red card from a deck of playing cards. Said it was black. 'Do you like apple pie?' Could have asked if I liked good-looking broads. 'No,' I said. The needle almost hit the ceiling. Everything else followed. There's no way anyone can beat that machine." Buckley glanced over at Sheridan. "And he's discreet. Bad results never surface."

"Dillard exhibits a lot of bravado." Sheridan checked his watch. "We're to meet him at Steinmetz's office in about twenty minutes. I think he'll choke at the last minute. Say something like he's read up on the test and it's inadmissible in the courtroom, so why take it."

"Well, there are some jurisdictions that allow the results in evidence," said Buckley.

"Yeah, but Massachusetts isn't one of them. What I want right now is Dillard's reaction. If he goes through with the test and flunks, we've got real problems."

"Assume the best scenario," young Buckley said as he maneuvered around the Storrow Drive overpass, then proceeded to make a right turn onto the Longfellow Bridge. "Let's say Dillard passes, that he had nothing to do with the Williams woman's demise. We write a letter to Harrington's office asking if Dillard is a target, then make a courtroom motion for an impartial polygraph, with a stipulation that the test results be admitted before any tribunal, grand jury, or trial court. We leak it to Pat Nolan at the *Herald.* Now Harrington and the Mex are in a box. Maybe the DA will back off. Harrington's going to run against Crimmins for the Senate. He's not going to risk lousy press coverage. He agrees to our request; Dillard passes the impartial and walks. If Harrington doesn't agree, the media will have a field day."

"Well, we have to watch extrajudicial statements. Might get us in a raft of trouble."

"What trouble?" said Buckley. "No one's been arrested; no

charges have been filed against anyone. And wait until Harrington starts feeding his choice morsels to the Fourth Estate. They'll crucify Dillard. Then after the damage is done, the Mex will come in with a gag order directed specifically at us."

"I'm not quite following you," Sheridan said, questioning Buckley's logic.

"Well, there's another way. Say we're hit with a gag order. We say nothing—no press conferences, no leaks. But all the judicial gag orders in the world can't prevent Professor Steinmetz from lecturing on the validity of the polygraph, citing an example or two—and who happens to be in the third row?"

"Pat Nolan of the *Herald* and Fletcher Porter of the *Globe*." Sheridan smiled. After years of association, he was beginning to appreciate young Buckley. "You're forgetting one thing." Sheridan again checked his watch.

"Suppose Dillard flunks." Buckley filled in the answer.

"That's a good possibility. And maybe Dillard won't even show."

As Buckley parked in the faculty lot, Dillard was there to greet them, having just alighted from his silver-blue Porsche.

Sheridan, Dillard, and young Buckley were welcomed by Professor Rochford Steinmetz in his white cinder-block office in the basement of MIT's Brown Hall. Sheridan was a little uneasy upon viewing the small room furnished only with a gray metal desk and two plastic chairs. Documents, books, magazines, and papers were strewn everywhere. From the size of his office, Sheridan felt that either professors of psychology were not paid too well or the polygraph business had come on hard times.

Steinmetz was short, maybe five four, portly, wore thick-lensed glasses and sported a carefully trimmed Vandyke beard and mustache. His quiet, dignified voice complemented his intense appearance. Sheridan, never a firm believer in the polygraph, thought it bordered on the occult and that examiners were only a step above spiritualists and charlatans. He wondered whether he was doing the right thing. He had wanted to leave the assignment to Buckley, who had engaged Steinmetz. But he was curious. Did the lie detector really work? Could it ferret out cheats and liars? *How* did it work? How would Dillard respond?

The three men chatted easily for a few moments and then followed Steinmetz down a concrete hallway, where he ushered them into a padded enclosure. In contrast to the disarray in Steinmetz's office, this room was completely devoid of clutter. The walls were padded with white waffled fiberboard.

Steinmetz clicked on the recessed overhead lights and pulled a thick burlap drape, shutting off exterior light from three small windows. The floor was carpeted with deep-piled gray broadloom. The room was completely soundproof.

"It is necessary to have total quiet during the test," Steinmetz said. "No distractions whatsoever, and I need your absolute attention and cooperation, Dr. Dillard."

Dillard nodded.

"And here, gentlemen"—Steinmetz picked up a black leather case, placed it on the table, and snapped it open—"is the polygraph machine." With its lights and dials, needles and corrugated tubing, the machine, a small black oblong box, looked intimidating.

To Sheridan, it seemed quite sinister. And although Buckley appeared to be impressed with Steinmetz, Sheridan had reservations.

Of the trio, Sheridan, Buckley, and Dillard, Dillard seemed the least nervous. He looked at the machine curiously as Steinmetz unraveled and then plugged in the wires, checked the voltage, and "warmed the machine up," as he put it.

"The polygraph, gentlemen," Steinmetz said as he watched the stylus make squiggles on the graph paper, "is really quite simple. It measures and records basic physiologic functions—respiration, heart rate, blood pressure, and galvanic skin response.

"Dr. Dillard, if you would kindly take off your coat. You may keep your shirt on, but roll up your sleeve for the blood-pressure cuff—just as if you were taking a reading of one of your patients.

"Now, there's no trickery involved here," he lectured. "I'm going to ask you a short series of questions that Mr. Buckley and I have prepared. Two are innocuous, nonsensitive questions and I want you deliberately to misrepresent. Two are control questions just to get your response. There will be a few throwaway questions, but the rest are very important.

"So that you'll know what will be asked, we've written it all out. Answer each question with a simple yes or no."

He handed Dillard and Sheridan the sheet of questions.

"There'll be no surprises. I want you to be perfectly at ease during the examination."

Dr. Dillard studied the questions, displaying no emotion.

Steinmetz felt things so far were favorable for an objective examination. He had established the necessary rapport; and if Dr. Dillard showed any anxiety he managed to disguise it well.

"Now let's hook you up, Doctor, and I'll explain how all this works." Anticipating him, Dillard rolled up his right sleeve. Steinmetz wrapped the blood-pressure cuff around Dillard's bicep. "As you know, Doctor, your cardiovascular activity is measured by this cuff. I'll inflate it halfway between diastolic and systolic. When the heart contracts, the increased blood supply passes through the brachial artery, resulting in expansion of the arm. A reduction of blood flow and reduction of arm size occurs when the heart is more at rest. Changes of these variations in blood flow and arm size are transmitted ultimately to a pen that records an upward swing with increases of blood flow and a downward swing for decreases."

Dillard again exhibited outward calm as Steinmetz inflated the cuff.

"Your respirations will be recorded through the use of these two corrugated tubes." Steinmetz put them around Dillard's chest and abdomen, buckling them into place. "Each inspiration results in an upward swing of the pen; each expiration causes a corresponding drop.

"Not too snug, is it, Dr. Dillard?"

"No, feels just right."

"Now these two little caps with wires leading from them are electrodes. I'll slip them over two fingers of your left hand. These measure your galvanic skin response. An imperceptible amount of current will flow through the fingers. You won't even feel it, Doctor. An increase in perspiration reduces the skin's resistance to electricity, and produces an upward swing of the pen."

"Let me see if I've got this right," Sheridan cut in. "If someone is lying, his blood pressure goes up, he sweats, his breathing increases, and this is all recorded?"

"Well, it's a little more complex than that. I have to interpret the results."

"How many of these tests have you done, Doctor?" Sheridan inquired.

"Over two thousand. Mostly for the federal government—security cases, also the armed forces and industry. People applying for sensitive jobs.

"We usually ask candidates if they ever stole anything in their life. Everyone has stolen something as a kid or fudged in an examination of some sort. They think if they say no, they'll get the job. What employers are looking for is basic honesty. A yes is not a deception; it demonstrates integrity."

Sheridan tried to inject a little humor into a situation that was becoming tense. "I remember Sister Mary Bernadette, my eighth-grade teacher. Kept me after school one day and asked me if I had ever masturbated. Well, I goddamned near choked, and before I could answer, she said with a heavenly grin, 'Danny, my dear boy, remember: There are two types of individuals in this world—masturbators and liars!' "

Dillard was hooked up. He still looked relaxed. "What is the basic principle behind this phenomenon?" he said.

"Conscience, Dr. Dillard," Steinmetz said authoritatively. "Conscience. . . .

"A person being tested brings with him all his beliefs, biases, attitudes, judgments, values—in short, his conscience. Now the more the examinee has to lose if found deceptive, the greater his tension, anxiety, and fear. Deceptive behavior indicates some degree of guilt, causing physiologic change. These can be easily analyzed.

"Now the innocent and guilty respond in a similar manner, but in a reverse fashion to control questions. The guilty subject, despite the fact that he is lying to both the control and relevant questions, will manifest larger responses to the latter and only minimal to the former.

"Okay?"

Dr. Dillard would be alone with Professor Steinmetz for approximately an hour while Sheridan and Buckley went down to the cafeteria to await the outcome.

Steinmetz delivered the neutral questions and watched the cardio tracings and blood-pressure changes on the graph paper. "Is your name Dr. Christopher Dillard?

"Are you a doctor of medicine?"

Dillard answered yes or no to each question.

The only other sound was the scratching of the stylus as it recorded in blips and squiggles Dillard's reactions to each question.

Now came the relevant questions, the hard ones.

"Did you dine with Angela Williams that evening?

"Was Miss Williams alive and well when you left her apartment at ten P.M.?

"Did you have anything to do in any way with the death of Angela Williams?"

Steinmetz watched the heart and respiration rate and skin responses carefully.

Dillard waited, as instructed, for four or five seconds before each response. He answered all questions in a calm voice, devoid of emotion.

Steinmetz knew what he was looking for. It wasn't the answer to the question so much as the subject's reaction to the question—this was the bone and marrow of the polygraph. The subject didn't even have to answer. The nervous system would be kicked into action by every relevant question. Steinmetz watched for suppression or acceleration of breathing, amplitude of heartbeat, slight sweating, and activating galvanic skin response. His trained eye watched for subtle indices, tiny nuances, interpretive of deceptive or nondeceptive patterns.

Steinmetz finished up.

"Have you ever committed a serious undetected crime?

"Have you been perfectly truthful in your answers here this evening?"

Buckley took Dillard for coffee before the cafeteria closed and to get him out of the way. Sheridan sat in Steinmetz's cluttered office as the professor put on even thicker glasses and pored over the tracings. Several minutes elapsed. Steinmetz looked through a magnifying glass and continued to scan. Sheridan was beginning to get a little uneasy. In between the uh-huhs emitted by Steinmetz, he thought he heard the psychologist humming.

"Aha!" Steinmetz broke the silence, then furrowed his forehead and continued reading.

"An interesting subject, your Dr. Dillard." Steinmetz nodded, rocking his head as he put down the magnifying glass and removed his glasses. Little beads of sweat had gathered on his forehead. He wiped his eyes with the sleeve of his white frock coat.

"The polygraph, like the X ray, doesn't lie," he said. "But both depend upon who reads them."

Sheridan had a premonition of what was coming.

"It's not possible to beat the lie detector," said Steinmetz. "It's all involuntary. No one can control his heart rate and galvanic skin response just by thinking about it."

"Well, what's your conclusion?" Sheridan was getting impatient.

Steinmetz looked at Sheridan. "My preliminary investigation indicates your Dr. Dillard has answered without deception."

"One hundred percent?" Sheridan wasn't sure whether he should be elated or alarmed.

"Ten out of ten," said Steinmetz.

Sheridan didn't have to add it up.

9

MAYAN D'ORTEGA sipped coffee from a plastic cup and motioned to Detectives Riley and Furlong to help themselves to ham-and-cheese sandwiches that had just arrived from the Beacon Deli. Riley had heard about the d'Ortega woman—the accolades, the innuendos, the rumors. He knew there was discontent and jealousy among the assistant DAs on Harrington's staff. Mayan d'Ortega had risen from obscurity. A Texas University law graduate, she had started at rock bottom, assistant to the third prosecutor in the misdemeanor division. At first, she was a chauvinistic joke, privately disparaged as a skirt and a Latina. A tall Hispanic beauty with a slight south-of-the-border accent (it was the way she drew out her *eez*es), she took the sniggering and put-downs, never flinching from menial assignments that deluged her in her apprentice year. Now, at age thirty-one, she was the chief prosecutor. She had a string of impressive victories, all felony convictions, and in her five-year tenure had never lost a case. The plea bargaining was handled by others, sometimes by Harrington, but when it came down to a trial, Mayan d'Ortega had no peer, not even Harrington himself.

Mayan d'Ortega was the one real incongruity in Harrington's office, which consisted of 135 young law graduates, mostly male Caucasians—moderately aggressive, predominantly Irish Catholic—a few mellowed veterans, a smattering of minorities—three Jewish, six Italians, a token black. Three daughters of prominent businessmen shuffled enough papers to feel needed, settling an outstanding favor or two and rounding out an annual budget of forty-plus million dollars.

Neil Harrington had carefully forged social, political, and fiscal alliances that would provide the necessary capital, clout, and manpower to topple Irving Crimmins, the black Republican senator from Massachusetts. Enmeshed in financial and domestic problems, Crimmins appeared vulnerable. If he decided to run, Harrington had to carry Boston by 70 percent of the vote to ensure statewide victory. He needed to infiltrate the black and Hispanic communities. This, then, was the reason for Mayan Castalanes Malinichi d'Ortega.

Buddy Furlong felt uneasy having a woman prosecutor lecture him on criminal procedure. He would have preferred one of the veteran prosecutors—Charlie Ready, or Kevin Costello, or even the legendary Neil Harrington. Riley, for the first time during the week-long investigation, seemed comfortable. He liked d'Ortega's approach to what had to be done, her fluid, melodic voice, and, most of all, her no-bullshit intelligence.

As she spoke, at times gesturing with her hands, Riley came under her spell. It was not difficult. He could now see why she had risen from the pack to become chief prosecutor and why Neil Harrington had taken a shine to her.

She was a shade over five seven, had raven black shoulder-length hair and Mexican features, nose slightly pug, more defiant than delicate. She had large brown eyes and amber bronze skin. She was more handsome than beautiful and held her striking figure in a proud aristocratic posture. She spoke perfect English, but at times she lapsed into her native Spanish. As Mayan talked with Riley and Furlong, she occasionally broke into a smile, a tack to win their confidence, since what they were discussing was serious business. When she did so, she displayed even white teeth.

"In our system of justice, an investigative grand jury is unlike anything under the sun," Mayan began, not in a professorial tone— serious yet engaging. Even Furlong, who had testified before many grand juries, hunched forward to listen.

"It can be a harmful vehicle. Our office decides who is a target and who isn't. Just being subpoenaed before the grand jury can be emotionally draining. An indictment can be devastating. No question in my mind," she said, "that our predecessor, Maurice Delaney, used the grand jury to assassinate people. Once the media picks up on it, the defendant is gone—even if he's found not guilty a year down the line. The public feels the target got off due to clever lawyering. But, I wouldn't present evidence unless I'm dead certain we have a case."

"Well, I think we got the goods on Dillard," Furlong interjected, "and there're a few other things." Furlong reached for the mustard, then squeezed it over his sandwich. He lowered his voice. "We're on the verge of uncovering the biggest drug ring on the Eastern Seaboard, and I think Dillard's mixed up in it."

Mayan merely nodded and continued.

"We'll have twenty-three jurors, men and women from Suffolk County. But we need only twelve to return a bill of indictment," she said. "I'll present evidence sufficient for the jurors to return a true bill. Dillard's subpoena has been sent out. Ordinarily, I wouldn't call him as a witness, because conceivably he could carry the day in his own behalf. From what I understand, he makes a good appearance, has tremendous respect in the community, and could exonerate himself by his own testimony. I'm taking that chance," Mayan said. She looked at Riley and then at Furlong.

"I understand Dillard has retained Dan Sheridan," Riley said as he sprinkled salt on the remainder of his sandwich.

"No love lost between Harrington and Sheridan." Furlong threw this out, hoping d'Ortega would take the bait, perhaps give them a few asides that they weren't yet privy to.

She let a few moments pass, saying nothing. She thought Dan Sheridan predictable and unimaginative. She was fairly certain that Sheridan would have Dillard invoke his constitutional prerogative against self-incrimination and take the Fifth. That apparent cop-out, coupled with Furlong's and Riley's testimony, topped by that of Dr. McCafferty and Dr. Gellis, was all the grand jury had to hear. They would indict Dillard for the murder of Angela Williams.

"The bottom line," she said thoughtfully, as if Furlong hadn't spoken, "is that the grand jury is a one-way street. Only evidence against Dillard will be presented. There'll be no presiding judge in the grand jury room, just me interrogating both of you and the pathologists, and a steno taking it all down. There'll be no testimony in behalf of Dillard, no alibi witnesses, nothing in mitigation. His lawyer can't object or cross-examine, merely whisper advice to his client.

"And the lawyer can't make any statement or be present when other witnesses testify.

"I won't put in our entire case. We may come up with an additional witness or two whom we'll use at the proper time."

Riley was quick to pick it up, but he said nothing. Mayan d'Ortega didn't elaborate.

"Why do prosecutors do this?" inquired Furlong almost chattily. "Why not bury the defendant at the outset."

Mayan looked thoughtful. "We just put in the bare bones, enough to warrant an indictment. You see, the minutes of the grand jury are available to defense counsel. If we parade our entire case, inconsistencies might develop. Witnesses might be impeached if later testimony doesn't jibe with what was given earlier. We minimize this chance of conflict."

"Can the jurors start asking questions?" Riley felt he wanted to become more involved.

"They can," replied Mayan. "Often do. Although we run the show, technically it's their investigation and they can come up with some far-out inquiries. They have unlimited subpoena power, and sometimes what starts out as a routine felony case can develop into a bizarre fishing expedition lasting months.

"That's called a runaway grand jury. Happens every once in a while. It's usually brought on by some smart-ass on the panel who realizes how much power he or she has and explains it to the other twenty-two sheep on the jury. Then, no matter how good the shepherd is—and Harrington is good—the whole herd takes off. Last one we had in this county was 1975. The foreman was an unemployed architect—good government type. The jury indicted four judges, three state representatives, and the secretary of health and welfare before their six-month term expired. The DA had to nol-pros them all, and the media had a field day.

"But in my experience, Suffolk County jurors—especially hard-core wage earners—want to get it over with quickly. And you can bet at least twelve of them will believe the target is guilty or he wouldn't be there in the first place. And with Dr. Dillard, his status may actually hurt him. The grand jury started in England, but it really came to fruition in France during the Reign of Terror. Not too many citizens worried about civil rights when aristocrats ascended the scaffold."

Mayan spent the next two hours going over Furlong's and Riley's testimony. "Keep it simple, no gingerbread. Just the facts," she said. "And I would prefer you wear your uniforms with your brevet citations and gold chevrons." She paused to glance over her brief. "Okay. I think we've got it down pretty well.

"No discussion with your family, the press, your friends," Mayan concluded. "You know the protocol. The work of the grand jury is secret. We could blow a solid case quickly with even a minor leak."

Furlong nodded in agreement.

Riley said nothing. He had received word through the network that Dillard was on a par with the legendary Joe Cahill, and that certain elements of the IRA would intervene. Dillard was off limits. He wondered how Dan Sheridan would fare in a one-on-one with Mayan d'Ortega—all things being equal. And all things would not be equal, since Neil Harrington would be in the background, deploying hordes of investigators, court personnel, and a handpicked judge. It was Harrington who had headed the judicial nominating committee responsible for the last ten appointments to the bench. Things could get sticky for everyone. Riley thought it was time to listen to the tape. It might be nothing—but it could bury Dillard even deeper. He should have turned it in, he knew, but now he was stuck with it. And criminal charges—obstructing justice, secreting evidence, and a few more—loomed if it ever surfaced.

Sheridan wasn't quite convinced that Dillard had really passed the polygraph. He delayed advising his client of Steinmetz's initial appraisal. Something must be wrong. He was waiting for young Buckley to come back from checking the Burlington Police, the ambulance drivers who had transported the Williams woman's body to the hospital, and the traveler who had just chanced to go into the woods off the rest stop on I-95 and happened upon the body.

Sheridan sat at his desk, chewing on the end of a pencil. How in the world had Dillard ever gotten by the questions, especially those relating to the dinner and time of death? It flew in the face of the facts. Steinmetz was emphatic on the integrity of his examination. "Chances of error or mistake were remote," he had said, "infinitesimal."

Sheridan still doubted that the test was on the level. He had watched Dillard closely during the preparation and examination. It was his nonchalance, the dead calm, that bothered him. Not a flicker of emotion. Could Steinmetz have been bought off? Unlikely.

Steinmetz said his assistant read the tracings independently and came up with the same opinion. Sheridan reread Steinmetz's report. How in the hell had Dillard passed?

"Tell me, Dr. Steinmetz," said Sheridan, calling from his car phone, "how could Dillard have been telling the truth about eating with the Williams woman, when the pathologist found absolutely no stomach contents?"

"I didn't say Dillard was telling the truth." Steinmetz was getting irritated with Sheridan's persistence, and his fee was going up with each phone call. "All I said was that I found no evidence of deception. The polygraph doesn't weigh credibility or lack of it or measure facts.

"I can't understand your attitude, Mr. Sheridan," Steinmetz added. "You should be doing handstands."

"Professor Steinmetz," Sheridan said, "I only want to make sure I'm not going to be sandbagged. You said the basis of the lie detector was the subject's response to stress and that this was regulated by the autonomic nervous system's control over cardiovascular activity."

"Yes."

"Well, Dillard's a cardiovascular surgeon. You know that, of course."

"Certainly I know that. But it makes him no more or no less a favorable subject than if he was a garbage collector. No one has conscious control over the autonomic nervous system. You can't say, 'Heart, beat faster,' or 'Slow down' and cause it to do so, or 'Blood vessels, constrict,' or 'Please, no sweating.'

"When a person attempts to deceive, the autonomic nervous system is activated, and that comes about through conditioning during all of our lives. Look, Mr. Sheridan, the test is not designed to verify truth; it's designed to verify what the person believes to be true."

"Well, couldn't a person control his breathing, the number of breaths he takes and the depth of his respirations?"

"Sure, but I would detect this."

"Okay, let me see if I get this straight," said Sheridan. "Is it fair to say that the polygraph does not determine guilt or innocence?"

"Yes."

"Would it be fair to state that the polygraph is a method of truth verification?"

"As it pertains to belief, yes."

"Okay, assuming that it's the subject's sincerity of belief that's important, would it be fair to say that if that person was mistaken about his belief, it would not appear on the tracings? I mean, one could be dead wrong about what he believes, but if he believes it, the tracings will fail to show him deceptive."

"That's correct."

"So if two individuals give divergent stories about a situation, diametrically opposed, if both believed in what they were saying, then they would both pass the test? Is that right?"

"That's what I've been trying to tell you." Steinmetz's voice was etched with irritation.

"So if a person rationalized his behavior by some method—even if he had killed someone—he might beat the machine."

"I doubt it," Steinmetz said. "But conceivably it could happen."

"One last thing, Doctor. Do you know about the CIA mole, Aldrich Ames?"

"Yes, I'm well aware of his counterespionage activities for the old KGB."

"Well, how come he was tested several times by CIA polygraphers and passed with flying colors?"

"Again, Mr. Sheridan, it depends on the expertise of the examiner."

Sheridan thought he had some of the answers he needed. Perhaps a call to Mayan d'Ortega to lay some groundwork, measure her receptivity. Maybe a deal could be struck.

10

HE SAID his name was James Callahan and he told Judy Corwin that he would like to speak to Mr. Sheridan for a few moments. No, he had no appointment. It was about the Dillard matter. He looked ungainly in his dark gray flannel suit. His shirt collar was rumpled and his bright red tie was off to one side, the knot drooping slightly. He was a bear of a man, well over six feet, mid-sixties. He eased into a chair and sat with his rumpled fedora resting on top of a battered leather briefcase that he held on his lap. His gray-blue eyes peered out over rimless glasses that perched halfway down his porcine nose. His lips seemed pursed in a slight perpetual smile and his cheeks bunched up, giving his plump face a hint of merriment . . . or mischief.

Sheridan was perturbed that the man had come in unannounced, but he signaled his secretary that he would make an accommodation.

Sheridan knew who he was. Most people in Boston knew Sonny Callahan, although few had actually met him. He was more a name than a person. He rarely attended social functions, sporting events, or other public affairs. His world was his construction firm, Callahan & Sons, and various spin-offs—cement and iron works, lumberyards, home improvement and building supplies, a dozen laundries sprinkled about greater Boston. Summers were confined to his rambling twenty-room compound on the "Irish Riviera" at Green Harbor, south of Boston.

Sonny Callahan was the Machiavellian power behind Boston's political throne, the kingmaker. Without Sonny's approbation, the governor couldn't function with the legislature, Mayor Jimmy Kane would find a disruptive city council, and state senators and representatives would be forced to seek early retirement. He was the catalyst; he made things work. No one bucked Sonny Callahan— no one with good sense, that is—not even on a national scale. U.S. Representative Margaret Devaney and Senator Irving Crimmins knew he had to be reckoned with, tolerated perhaps, but never

insulted, never alienated. Sonny had friends in all places at all levels—judges, school committees, contractors, lawyers, corporate
boards, ward heelers, prat men, runners, stoolies. His recommen-
dations received quick approval and his cadre of municipal workers
ruled the neighborhoods from West Roxbury to East Boston.

But Sonny was beginning to have detractors. Lately, Sheridan had
heard hints of a federal investigation for misappropriation of federal funds for Boston redevelopment and harbor improvements.
But Sonny had weathered these storm warnings before. Since the
day he'd stepped off the boat from County Clare, Ireland, fifty years
ago with seven dollars in his pocket, fortune had seemed to smile
his way. Gifted with enormous physical strength and a penchant for
hard work, he and three ambitious, educated sons had parlayed
their talents into an empire. Sonny's laundries supplied the needs
for all of Boston's hospitals, private as well as municipal and state
owned. Invariably, he was the lowest bidder on contracts for construction and maintenance of state and municipal buildings. Or if
not the lowest, his was deemed to be the most responsible. There
had been investigations before, mostly local. Unseasonable cracks
had developed in the cement foundations of some of Sonny's buildings. Inspectors felt that Sonny scrimped on the footage of gravel
to the yard of concrete, contrary to specification. And there had
been a lot of noise and clamoring when, on a Tuesday morning
five years ago, the Carillon Tower at the state university's Boston
campus suddenly collapsed as if it had been dynamited. No one was
killed or injured. There was the usual perfunctory legislative inquiry; a few committees made noises; one newspaper editorial com-
plained about Sonny's shoddy workmanship. But not much more.
The dust cleared. Things quieted down.

But no one denied that Sonny was a go-through guy. If you
couldn't afford to admit your ailing grandmother to a private nurs-
ing home, call Sonny and, like magic, she'd get into the state's
chronic-care facility—at the taxpayers' expense. Or if a street
needed plowing or a neighborhood wanted extra police patrols
cruising the area, Sonny would see to it. He could make things go
right.

No one really knew how much Sonny was worth—$30 to 40 mil-
lion perhaps, give or take a few million. There was talk that he
owned three midtown hotels, most of the waterfront properties,

numerous condos, and four restaurants. During the last decade, he had acquired run-down warehouses, dilapidated wharves, parking lots, and vacant landfills—some at foreclosures, some from private or municipal sales, some simply deeded as leasebacks or for past favors remembered.

Sheridan had never met the mysterious kingmaker, but he had heard all the stories, the rumors. He stole a glance in the side window; when the early-morning sun was right, it reflected images like a mirror. He tugged at his suit coat, straightened his tie, and swept the correspondence on his desk into the top drawer. He wondered what it meant. Why Sonny Callahan? He had a strange apprehension that the visit did not augur well.

"Send Mr. Callahan in," he addressed the intercom, pushing the volume button so his voice was audible to Callahan. "And Judy," he added, "hold the calls." It signaled a certain deference, not unrecognized by his visitor. Sonny Callahan removed his glasses, chewed thoughtfully on the end of the ear frame, and smiled at Judy Corwin as she led him into Sheridan's office.

Sheridan stood up and greeted Callahan cheerfully. This was no time for the moderate con, like pretending not to know who Callahan was.

"Mr. Callahan." Sheridan welcomed him with just the proper amount of enthusiasm. "It's indeed a rare pleasure." He extended his hand and Sonny shook it with his strong bricklayer's grip.

"Mr. Sheridan," he said, his eyes quickly taking the measure of the man and assessing the surroundings. He bent his head slightly and peered out over his glasses. "Heard lots o' good tings about ya, Mr. Daniel O'Connell Sheridan. 'Tis a shame now we haven't had a few jars t'gether."

"Sit down." Sheridan motioned to a chair in front of his desk. "Like a cup of coffee, a cigar?"

"The cigar t'would be foine," Callahan said.

Sheridan reached into a bottom drawer and pulled out a box of Raphael de Coronas, the finest Cuban cigars available under the counter in the lobby smoke shop.

Callahan unwrapped the silver foil carefully, smelled the cigar along its length, then bit off the end. Sheridan reached forward with his desk lighter.

"May the saints be good to ye," Callahan said. He took a few puffs, then held the cigar lengthwise at eye level and studied it with satisfaction.

Seconds dragged by. Both men waited.

"A foine cigar, Mr. Sheridan"—Callahan reached into the silence—"like foine whiskey. One of the last great enjoyments in life."

Sheridan knew Callahan wasn't there to discuss the relative merits of Cuban cigars and Irish whiskey. Their eyes locked. In that instant, the preliminaries, the niceties, were over. Each was aware that something extraordinary would be demanded of the other. The why was there; the whats and wherefores would take a little ironing out.

"I'm sure you've heard of me, Mr. Sheridan," Callahan opened, a slight smile on his face.

"I have," Sheridan said, curious that Callahan's Barry Fitzgerald veneer had suddenly disappeared.

"Well, most of it's pure malarkey. I'm a businessman, a builder. I've busted my ass to get where I am today."

"So have I," Sheridan parried.

Callahan's smile broadened. Callahan was never known to bullshit. "Tell me I'm devious, a grafter, a manipulator," he often said, "but don't bullshit me." Now, he came right to the point.

"I understand," he said, dropping his voice as though someone might pick up the conversation, "that you're representing Dr. Christopher Dillard in the bit of trouble he now finds himself in."

Sheridan merely nodded. Years of lawyering had taught him not to volunteer. He needed to draw Callahan out, to see where all this would lead.

Callahan took another drag on his cigar, tilted his head back, and exhaled slowly. Wispy gray smoke floated toward the ceiling. He then brushed an imaginary particle from the lapel of his ill-fitting suit. "I know of your legal reputation, Mr. Sheridan. Fine Irish Catholic lawyer. Nothing grander than a fine Irish Catholic lawyer. Chris's getting the best representation possible. But Mr. Sheridan, sir"—Sonny cleared his throat—"I think *we* can be of a wee bit of assistance. If ye follow me."

"I'm not sure I do." Sheridan hesitated, having an inkling of what was coming.

"There's two hundred thousand dollars in cash here." Callahan patted the briefcase on his lap. "From the friends of Christopher Dillard—sort of a defense-fund kitty."

"That's a lot of defense." Sheridan's voice had an amused quality.

Callahan's face hardened. His cheeks flattened and all sense of merriment disappeared from his eyes. He looked directly at Sheridan. "We think Dr. Dillard is being framed."

The thought had crossed Sheridan's mind. The initial evidence against Dillard was devastating; the circumstances too pat—a prosecutor's dream. Sheridan let Callahan talk.

"We feel there's been an illegal entry and search made of Miss Williams's premises, evidence procured illegally, and interrogation made of Dr. Dillard in violation of his constitutional rights."

"Hmm. Hmm," Sheridan hummed. "I'd say legally you're pretty well informed. So why do you need me?" Sheridan realized that Callahan's source of intelligence must be remarkable and that it had been collated with adroit legal counseling. It might not hurt to have Sonny in his corner.

Callahan thought for a few moments, trying to assess the impact of his words on his listener and also to avoid a direct reply. "Let me put it this way." He took another puff on the Corona, slowly exhaled, then put the cigar in an ashtray on Sheridan's desk. "I think even the district attorney's office knows they're way off base." Callahan's voice was crisp, perfect measured English. "Dr. Dillard is a fine surgeon, a fine man. A petition should be presented in Suffolk Superior Court Monday morning before the grand jury convenes. . . ."

Before *what* judge? Sheridan thought to himself. And he wondered again what had become of Callahan's begorras and bejabers.

"To preclude tainted evidence from reaching the jury."

"And just how am I going to do that?" Sheridan waved aside the smoke that was drifting toward him from Callahan's cigar.

"Bring a motion . . ." Callahan began. "Call Johnny Flaherty, the clerk of courts. He'll set it up."

"Look." Sheridan didn't mask his annoyance. "The DA will claim Dillard is not a target or even a suspect, just a citizen questioned as to the whereabouts of a missing person. Pure routine. He was not charged, not under arrest. Not even now. The constitutional safeguards against self-incrimination as well as the right to counsel are inapplicable . . . and even if he was a target, what did he say that was so incriminating?''

Callahan was about to reply, but he suddenly surmised that Sheridan was trying to string him out. A correct assumption.

"Well, why not try it? A motion or petition to suppress, say before Judge Israel Katzmann. Probably'll hear it in his chambers. That should end Dillard's involvement." Callahan was getting edgy, knowing he was drifting off track.

Funny, Sheridan thought, I never used the word *motion* or *petition,* let alone *suppress.* Sonny was getting some good legal signals from somewhere. Maybe the DA's office.

"No, it won't end Dillard's involvement," Sheridan replied. "We have an unexplained death of a young woman." He put a little sting in his voice. "Probably murdered. The grand jury can inquire into the circumstances surrounding that death. There'll be twenty-three citizens in there and they can ask a lot of foolish, possibly embarrassing questions and get some crazy and revealing answers. Everything comes in—hearsay, a lot of irrelevant stuff. There's no judge in there with the jurors. And there's not a damn thing I can do. No cross-examination tests the reliability of the evidence. It's a one-way street to indictment. Do you understand what I'm saying?''

It was Sonny's turn to remain silent.

"When Dillard takes the witness stand, I'll tell him to give just his name, rank, and serial number. Period. Nothing else. Invoke the Fifth Amendment on everything. And stonewalling will sure as hell lead to an indictment. Right now, we're playing with loaded dice. We can't possibly win. So we hedge our bets—get ready for the big roll when the stakes are all or nothing.''

It was a speech. Sheridan hadn't intended to make it. Neither did Callahan intend to receive it.

"Well, then, you've got to make a motion to dismiss with prejudice, a sort of double-jeopardy petition to prevent the DA's office from reconvening the grand jury at a later date." The maneuvering was over. Callahan's stratagems were falling flat.

"Dismiss what! . . . Are you crazy or something!" Sheridan spewed at Callahan. "There's no such animal in the law. I could draw up some ridiculous motion, but no judge in his right mind would allow it, let alone hear it.''

"Why not?" Callahan's face suddenly flushed.

"Precedent. Legal precedent. That's why not. We just can't carve something out of nothing simply to accommodate one client. The law has certain rules of the game, out-of-bounds markers, baselines, so everyone knows where they stand and where they're going. That's true for the prosecution and the defense and for those accused as well as for the accuser. Dillard is not special. Whether we like to believe it or not, there's basic equality in the law."

"Okay." Callahan patted his briefcase. "Suppose Harrington's office goes along with the motion. The police officers were overzealous, the evidence was illegally obtained, and so on."

This was the first time Harrington's name had been mentioned. Sonny's finally getting to the point, Sheridan thought.

"It will be a blow for justice, the safeguarding of human rights, a prosecutor protecting the innocent as well as the guilty," Callahan continued. "No one should be railroaded. Precedent? There's a host of precedent. The Sacco and Vanzetti case. Julius and Ethel Rosenberg. The Salem witches. The Scottsboro Boys. You see *To Kill a Mockingbird,* Mr. Sheridan?"

Sheridan momentarily closed his eyes. He now knew what he was supposed to do, what the $200,000 in the briefcase was meant to pay for. The right judge, Harrington, the police officers, Mayan d'Ortega. Callahan wasn't even subtle or smart.

Sheridan had heard that you could fix anything in Massachusetts, even murder. But it had to be done with style, a certain amount of class: season tickets to the Celtics, stock options, buying property at foreclosures for a tenth of its value. But never with a bucketful of greenbacks. And yet here it was. Sheridan wondered whether there actually was $200,000 in Callahan's satchel. Temptation passed through him like a sigh, then it was gone.

"What you want me to do"—Sheridan eyed Callahan with increasing disdain—"is to bag the case from the outset? Right? But why involve a judge when all you need is the DA?"

"That's not what I said or intimated." Callahan seemed startled.

"Cut the bullshit, Sonny!" Sheridan decided to terminate the meeting. "Win or lose, I'll operate within the law. I don't need any thumbs on the scales of justice. I need no assistance from anyone except my own staff—and that includes you. Particularly you!" He rose from his desk and jabbed a finger at his visitor.

Callahan smiled, an impish, leprechaunish kind of smile. He had underestimated this guy. He had heard that Sheridan was a man with a past—some difficulties as a police officer—and now was ruled by principle. Callahan had met these types before. It would take some doing, but in the long run they were the easiest to deal with.

"Look," said Callahan apologetically. He, too, knew he had nothing to gain by further discussion. "I only wanted to ensure that an innocent man wasn't going to be railroaded."

"Noble," Sheridan said sarcastically. "I'm sure that was your intention." He suddenly disliked Sonny Callahan, more than he had disliked banker Kyle. And he felt he might just as well let Sonny know where they both stood.

"Where were you last year about this time, Sonny, when Isaiah Rawlins, that black boy, was convicted by Harrington's office of raping a whore and sentenced to life at Walpole? And when that skinny spic kid, Santiago Roches, was shot by that Southie boy, Dermie O'Connell, and the Boston Police broomed the whole thing as self-defense?"

"Mr. Sheridan"—the smile drained from Callahan's face and his voice had the tinkle of ice—"I'm now asking you to withdraw from representing Dillard. Joe McNurney will take over his defense. The money in this briefcase"—he lofted it for a moment, then passed it to a position in front of Sheridan's desk—"is yours . . . for your fee and expenses to date."

"I think, Mr. Callahan"—Sheridan's eyes bored deep into those of his visitor—"the request for my withdrawal should come from Dr. Dillard, not from you."

Sheridan walked around his desk to the briefcase, hefted it, and weighed it mentally—it probably did contain $200,000. "One last thing, Mr. Callahan, perhaps the most important."

"Yes?"

"Take this briefcase with the cash and shove it up your ass! I think it'll fit. And now get the hell out of here!"

Callahan broke into uncontrollable laughter. He bolted from the chair, reached out past the briefcase, and grabbed Sheridan in a bear hug, locking him with two strong arms. Again the muscular grip of the bricklayer.

Callahan's eyes danced and his cheeks swelled into tiny bunches. "Ye're me man, bucko! Ye're a foine broth of a lad!" Again the thick brogue. He shook Sheridan, who didn't quite understand what was happening.

"Only testin' ye, Danny me boy! Knew ye were a man of principle! That's what we want. That's what Dillard wants! I told *them!* By God, I told them! We're with ye all the way, boyo!"

Before Sheridan could recover, Callahan took the briefcase and made his way out. He stopped at the door. "Ye really didn't think there was two hundred thousand big ones here, did ye?" Callahan shook the case at eye level. "Just putting you to the iron, lad. Ye'd have a foine time countin' rooled-up newspaper.

"*Slainte,* Mr. Sheridan, as we Irish say." And with that parting salute, Sonny Callahan was gone.

"Yeah, fuck you, Callahan!" Sheridan addressed the vacant doorway. "As we Irish say."

11

DETECTIVE RILEY extracted a can of Budweiser from the kitchen refrigerator and pulled the tab. He took a few swallows and checked the digital clock above the oven: 2:30 A.M. Marge and the kids were asleep and the only sounds were a dripping faucet and the muffled drone of traffic from the nearby expressway.

He went into the living room, still carrying the Budweiser, and looked momentarily at the closed bedroom doors before he unlocked a small cabinet on a bookshelf. Only he had access to this cabinet. He reached past his service revolver and removed a small package sealed with masking tape and a tape recorder. Returning to the kitchen, he closed the door gently, unwrapped a gray cassette, and inserted it into the recorder. He watched the spools start to spin, turned up the volume slightly, and took another sip of beer.

"Coochie darling." The voice was softly mesmerizing, like the stirring of mountain snow. "I really must see you. It's been a whole week."

"Look," a man's voice interrupted, "I think we have to let things ride for a while. Wait until November. Things will be different. We'll have a future."

"I am your future." The softness was still there, but Riley detected a subtle tonal edge. The woman was probably Angela Williams. But the man? It didn't sound like Dillard. But the quality wasn't that good. A taped telephone conversation? "Don't try to run out on me, Cooch." Still the softness. "I'm sure you understand me."

"Okay." The man's voice seemed to harbor frustration. "Look, I've got to go. I'll call you sometime tomorrow." There was an audible click and that was it.

It wasn't much of an exchange. But there was the hint of a threat in the woman's voice. And who was Cooch? Was it Dillard's nickname? He'd check it out.

*   *   *

Sheridan sat at his desk and wondered what it was all about. He steepled his fingers, resting them against his lips, almost as if he was praying. The briefcase. The $200,000. Sonny Callahan. Was he on the level? Or was it his way of using people—corrupting them, forcing them into a corner, then coming up with the crunch? And what about the Irish connection? A Brahmin like Dillard, no less. Things didn't add up.

Sheridan had heard the stories for years but tended to discount them. His father had told him all the Homeric tales of the Sinn Fein, the Easter uprising in 1916, the great liberator Daniel O'Connell, who was on a par with Abraham Lincoln, and for whom Sheridan was named. The Irish patriots all the way from Wolfe Tone to Kevin Barry. The men of Irish Republican brotherhood: Clark, Pearse, Connolly, De Valera. And the women: Countess Markiewicz and Maude Gonne. The ghosts, the legends, and the battered sanctuaries had never been far away in the Sheridan household.

He remembered his grandfather, Eamon, and the deference and respect the Sheridan family and relatives had paid him. Sheridan was a young boy then, eight or nine, and at gatherings, Eamon, dressed in a rumpled black suit, would sit in the sunshine, leaning on a cane and quaffing a pint of Guinness. He had soft blue eyes and gray shaggy hair and a face lined with history. Occasionally, his bony fingers would smooth out a faded green ribbon pinned to a dark bronze decoration on his lapel. It was more than a medal. It was a sacred relic. Gen. Michael Collins had pinned it on him in Cork City two days after a British lorry with all hands sank to the bottom of Ballycotton Bay. Six women and four children went with it.

Young Dan Sheridan knew that his parents and relatives held his grandfather in high esteem, bordering on reverence. Eamon was a Provo; he had fought in the hedgerows with Pearse and Barry and was a member of Collins's "Twelve Apostles," a hit team that systematically weeded out informers and British colonels and assassinated them. His grandfather had longed to return to his native Clare, where the River Shannon flowed and the bluebells and poppies dotted the hillside above Lough Derg in the early spring. But there was no going back. Even then, four decades later, there was a price on the head of Eamon Sheridan.

Dan Sheridan never had been to Ireland and somehow over the years had lost touch with being Irish.

He sat at his desk, mulling over the morning's events. He was confused, but his sensors were all in the red. Sonny was too well informed. . . . Callahan's visit did not augur well. Sheridan had a feeling that by some nimble legal machination, the district attorney's office would close the Angela Williams case. Certain exchanges would take place, subtly, above suspicion. A campaign fund enriched, alliances shifted, liaisons realigned, endorsements proffered. Harrington would announce his run for the Senate against Crimmins. And Sheridan would be the legal formality, the window dressing for an artful subterfuge.

But then again, suppose his client was innocent. He had aced the polygraph. Steinmetz was emphatic that it showed no deception. What difference did it make how Dillard gained his freedom? This was how the system often worked.

But Sheridan's mind spun. Thoughts tumbled like leaves in a wind tunnel. A storm was gathering and he wasn't sure whether to angle into it or give it a wide berth.

First, he had to check with his client. He was still disturbed about Dillard's insistence that the Williams woman had dined with him, even though the autopsy had disclosed no stomach contents. And the time of death—this was a greater incongruity. He also needed to bounce a few ideas off his associates. He was expecting a call from Manny Raimondi, his private investigator.

"Judy." He buzzed his secretary on the intercom. "Get Dr. Dillard on the phone and tell him I want to see him. Tell him it's important and to be in my office at nine tomorrow. And please send down to the florist for a dozen roses to spruce the place up."

"Yes, sir, Mr. Sheridan."

"And Judy?"

"Yes?"

"Clear the diary for the rest of the day. Let young Buckley handle Mrs. Coulter on her estate problem. She's due in at four. I'll be gone for the afternoon."

"May I ask where I can get in touch with you?"

"No, I'll call in."

Judy looked at the intercom quizzically, then shrugged. This was apparently going to be one of Sheridan's mysterious Wednesday afternoons. Not even Buckley or Manny Raimondi knew where he went. Last week, Raimondi had spotted Sheridan's red Le Baron on the Mystic River Bridge, headed toward the North Shore. "Could be a new girlfriend," said Manny. Judy didn't want to think about that.

12

HARRINGTON didn't like it one bit. He had received the call on his private line and then asked his secretary, Kristina Collins, to call his driver. He'd be gone overnight, he said. Kristina knew enough not to ask where when her boss didn't volunteer information. "And tell Mayan to call Dr. Gellis; he's lecturing at Harvard Med, Thursday. We have accommodations. She'll know what to do."

The drive to Logan Airport was a short run, twenty minutes through the East Boston Tunnel. The roads were slick with rain, but the late-morning traffic moved evenly. Harrington's chauffeur, Declan Haggerty, had driven for the best of them, from James Michael Curley to John F. Kennedy. His eyes were still keen despite his seventy-six years and he knew when to keep them open, when to avert them. He was a storehouse of information—of what was going on, what had happened or would happen. If someone said, "Isn't it a beautiful day?" Declan might reply, "Sure'n 'tis that—but who now would be wantin' to know?" He was Harrington's radar, had been for ten years. There wasn't much Harrington didn't know about the Boston scene, and part of his intelligence came from his chauffeur. There were few individuals Harrington really trusted—perhaps a handful. Declan Haggerty was one of them.

They turned off at the United Airlines terminal, Declan driving the unmarked Plymouth past rows of smaller carriers—Allegheny Commuter, Vermont Air, Business Express—past rows of twin-engined Otters waiting or taxiing to pick up ten or twelve passengers. Declan waved at a state trooper and maneuvered out onto the asphalt apron, easing past a row of Cessnas, Pipers, and single-engined planes tied down at the far end of Runway 160.

"There by the copter." Harrington motioned. Declan saw the chopper, electric blue and with white trim, sitting like a giant bug, its overhead propellers whirling slowly. Harrington hadn't said much on the way over—small stuff, inquiries about Declan's son and grandchildren. It was unlike Harrington not to tell his driver where he was going.

Declan opened the door and helped Harrington out onto the slick pavement, then handed him his valise. Declan didn't recognize the pilot, an early thirties air force type, sporting military sunglasses. There were no markings on the copter, just a serial number that Declan quickly memorized. Harrington knew Declan's thoughts, knew he'd check it out. But Harrington would also check Declan out. He trusted the man. Yet lately, Harrington had come to realize that trusts and loyalties had an ephemeral quality and could shift or erode, depending on the vagaries of the moment.

The copter flight to Green Harbor, just north of Plymouth, took an uneventful twenty-five minutes. They swung on a direct line at about seven hundred feet from Logan across Boston Harbor toward Cape Cod Bay.

"I used to fly in one of these in Nam," shouted Harrington above the clatter of the propeller. "We were losing three a day toward the end."

The curly-haired pilot smiled, surveyed the horizon, then looked toward Harrington. "I was too young for Nam," he yelled, "but I served in Desert Storm."

"Navy?"

"Navy. . . . We flew off the *Eisenhower.*"

"Know Rear Admiral Cawley?" Harrington was softening.

"Sure do. He was my CO. Hell of a skipper." There was in that moment instant camaraderie, a sense of friendship, of implied loyalty. Sometimes the chemistry is just right.

They landed gently, touching down like a lunar module. The heliport was just off a putting green on Sonny Callahan's sprawling estate on a bluff overlooking the Atlantic.

The propellers whirred to a gradual stop. Bobby Callahan and his passenger emerged to a warm welcome from Sonny and his wife, Moira, as they smiled and waved a greeting. Bobby took Harrington's bag and they headed toward the glass rotunda facing the sea.

Sonny Callahan never went past the eighth grade. But he didn't amass a fortune or gain his station in life by being stupid. Sonny

was a master of the oblique maneuver, of opportunistic manipula-
tion. He had an innate craftiness that enabled him to judge men
and a sense of cunning that could divine the shifting of moral tides.
And he knew when to strike.

Callahan knew that Harrington, like Mayor Jimmy Kane, had
stayed in office too long. Kane was politically through, but Harrington could still make his move. But if he didn't beat Irving Crimmins for the Senate, he, too, was done, perhaps returning to the
private practice of law. Harrington couldn't imagine a crueler fate.
And Harrington knew that Callahan knew. It would take money to
topple Irv Crimmins—tons of it. And support. And workers. In his
years as district attorney, Harrington hadn't really developed a network. Strangely enough, a U.S. senator was one of the last persons
who could get a street plowed in South Boston—or fill a janitor's
job at the Endicott School in Dorchester. Maybe a federal postal
inspector's position. Callahan could do them all. He also had a
machine; it was geared, oiled, and ready to move at the snap of
Sonny's fingers.

The afternoon was amiable, Callahan showing Harrington the
manicured grounds. The two men walked out to the Point, a craggy
shoal where the surf crashed in thunderous claps against the rocks,
sending salty spray into their faces. "The next parish is Ireland,"
said Callahan. His gray-blue eyes looked wistfully at the ocean.

"It's a beautiful land," he said, turning slightly toward Harrington. "All green and grand like Easter Sunday. And yet so melancholy . . . and the Irish people, how they've suffered.

"It's just over there, Neil." He pointed out to sea. "Ballingarry,
Kilgarren, the Cliffs of Moher. My cottage on Bantry Bay." He
looked at Harrington. Tufts of gray hair fluttered in the cold wind.
His eyes were misty. "Oh God, I love it so."

"My grandmother was a Casey," Harrington interjected, "family
came from County Kerry."

"Cahirciveen," Callahan noted.

"And your father's people came from Tipperary," Callahan
added quickly. "What a place, with its emerald plains, the Rock of
Cashel—and the Harringtons. What fighters! They marched with
Red Hugh O'Donnell, the Earl of Tyrone; beat the English at Con-
naught and Kinsale."

Sonny could spin it—thick, maudlin. You could almost hear the war drums pounding and the bagpipes skirling.

Harrington pulled up the collar of his jacket, trying to signal that he would like to return to the house, or at least get out of the wind. And Callahan's fund of information on Gaelic genealogy, particularly concerning the clan Harrington, was disconcerting. Harrington had never heard that his ancestors were particularly bellicose. As far as he knew, they were peasants, poor peat farmers who stuck to the land.

He turned from the wind to take in the vast compound. There were two heliports, docking facilities, barns with stables, pickup vans. It was ideally situated—remote enough, yet central. He suddenly had an eerie inner sense that Sonny was into something more than bleaching bedsheets and the home-improvement business.

"I wonder what county the Dillards come from?" Harrington turned suddenly and looked at his host.

Callahan didn't even blink. He had half-expected it. But the subject matter was premature. Callahan wanted dinner, a few brandies, cigars, stories. His son would join them, his daughter, Meghan. They would light a fire. Discuss Harrington's run for the Senate. How much money it would take. Ted Kennedy had spent $4 million and ran virtually unopposed. This certainly would be mentioned.

Then perhaps later, after the camaraderie, the brandy, and the stories had glazed the evening—Christopher Dillard. It would seem a natural extension of the conversation.

"What do you know about Dr. Dillard?" Callahan, too, came right to the point.

"Oh, I know he's a distinguished doctor, great humanitarian, trustee at St. Luke's, Harvard Medical School, professor of cardiovascular surgery at Tufts, married, a charming wife, fine children, patron of the arts, excellent yachtsman. There aren't many negatives to apply to the eminent Dr. Dillard. . . ." (Except sometimes he kills people. Harrington kept that notion to himself.)

Sonny gave a short, decisive nod and thrust his hands into the pockets of his overcoat.

"Let's get out of this wind, boyo. It's time to change for dinner."

* * *

The evening with Callahan's family—his son, Bobby, who had flown the chopper; Meghan, who held engineering degrees from Rensselaer and MIT; and Sonny's wife—had been a delight. There was light talk about the local political scene, Ted Kennedy's future, the economy, the intervention in Bosnia, and, finally, sports trivia. Moira served dinner, hearty staples—roast beef, carrots and peas, servings of whipped potatoes heaped with gravy, Irish soda bread. Not fancy, just delicious.

It was late. Mrs. Callahan had cleared the table and Meghan played the piano. Sonny sang "Rose of Tralee" and "Galway Bay." He wasn't half bad. Even Harrington joined in. Meghan brought in snifters of brandy. Bobby Callahan stoked the fireplace, putting on a few more logs, and soon had the hearth crackling. The den, structured with low-beamed ceilings, pecky cypress walls, and a wraparound fieldstone fireplace, was a far cry from Sonny's thatched cottage in Bantry Bay, but it shared its warmth and coziness. There were more stories—poignant, funny, some sad—as the evening drew to a close.

Mrs. Callahan retired and the rest of the family were in the glass rotunda watching the late news. Callahan had lit a cigar and Harrington knew that Sonny would now play his trump card for Dillard. He beat him to the punch.

"Tell me, Sonny," he began as he watched the smoldering fire now dying with the remainder of the evening, "why all the sudden activity in behalf of Dr. Dillard? That's really why I'm here, isn't it?"

Callahan removed the cigar from his mouth, studied the tip for a moment, and watched the blue smoke curl upward. "Partly," he said. "Primarily, I want to discuss your candidacy for the U.S. Senate. Get the campaign rolling. Generate the help that the business community of greater Boston could throw your way. It'll take big bucks.

"But the thing I like about you, Neil—and that's why you'll make a great senator—is that you tell it as it is. You're up front. I like that in a man. And I'm not going to bullshit you. I'm going to give it to you straight from the shoulder."

It was buttery, Harrington thought. Maybe the Callahan con. Maybe not.

"Dillard does a lot of good work for Ireland, Neil. You'd never

know, but many an Irish family owes its very existence to Dr. Christopher Dillard."

(And because of Dillard, a lot of British families are bereft of
breadwinners. Harrington repressed the temptation to vocalize his
thoughts.)

"What is it with Dillard?" Harrington said. "Non-Catholic, Brahmin. What's his angle? What's with the Irish connection and who's
behind him?" Harrington searched Callahan's face.

"He's a freedom fighter, Neil. Might seem strange to you, but
there are guys like that out there. Sure, he's Ivy League, Eastern
Establishment, forebears probably signed the Mayflower Compact
and knocked down all the castles in Ireland.

"Wolfe Tone was an Irish patriot. And a lawyer," Sonny added
with a slight grin. "Lost his head fighting for Ireland against the
Crown. And you know, Neil"—Sonny paused a few seconds—"he
was a Protestant."

Harrington pretended to be impressed. And he knew well
enough not to get embroiled in Irish history. Not at this hour. Not
with Sonny Callahan.

"Okay, let me give it to you straight." Sonny looked directly into
Harrington's eyes. "If Dillard is indicted, everything will get sticky.
There's a lot more involved, believe me, Neil, than even you know
about. Big names."

"Who, for instance?"

"Jimmy Kane, for one." Callahan started at the top. "His name
will come out. He was very friendly with the Williams girl. The
whole Irish movement in Boston will go down the drain. We've
been building it for a generation. They're all good people, Neil.
You and Jimmy go back a long way. *We* go back a long way. It's the
clan, Neil. You're one of us. You can't desert us now."

Harrington stood up and walked toward the fireplace, put his
hand on the fieldstone mantel, and looked thoughtfully into the
embers. "What do you want me to do?" he said.

"Tuesday, Dillard's attorney—you know, Dan Sheridan—will
meet with you. Evidence was obtained illegally. I understand evidence may have been taken from the victim's place without a warrant?" Sonny let the question hang in the air as he drew on his cigar
and gazed thoughtfully at the smoke wafting toward the ceiling.

"Dillard wasn't apprised of his constitutional rights," he continued. "I want you to give Sheridan assurance that his client is not a target."

Harrington continued to stare into the dying fire.

"All we're asking is what any prosecutor interested in protecting a person's civil rights would do. Illegally obtained evidence is tainted. I want the case to go away, Neil."

"In short, Sonny"—Harrington looked over at Callahan—"you're asking me to bag the case."

Callahan sidestepped the accusation.

"See what you can do, Neil. Believe me, you don't know what it will mean to all of us."

"I'll sleep on it," said Harrington.

"Have a good night, Senator. God bless," Sonny said as he took his leave.

Harrington's gaze returned to the dying embers. He adjusted his tie. The tiny microphone was still in place.

13

NEIL HARRINGTON was certain of two things: There was a leak some-where, either in his office or with Boston Police headquarters, and—more importantly—it was time to break with the clan. Sonny Callahan was privy to too much information. How the hell had he found out they had taken Dillard's love letters from the Williams woman's apartment? Riley and Furlong had had no search warrant, but they hadn't needed one. That was the opinion of his staff. The manager had let the detectives in voluntarily. The victim was dead and the letters belonged to her, not to Dillard. Sonny hadn't men-tioned "love letters," explicitly. "Tainted evidence," Harrington recalled, were Sonny's exact words. And Sonny was probably feed-ing information to Sheridan. Well, things would change—damn soon. When Sheridan made his pitch for Dillard, both he and Ma-yan d'Ortega would be wired. But Harrington had a broader plan.

After briefing Mayan d'Ortega of his intentions, Harrington called U.S. Attorney Norman Wright on his private red line to set up a meeting. Wright promptly cleared it with the Justice Depart-ment and Operation Blackstone was about to have its genesis. Named for the famous English jurist, the exercise would be far-reaching, aimed at legal practitioners involved with the criminal element, particularly at those who earned lucrative fees from the mob or from drug dealers. Dan Sheridan was specially targeted.

Mayan d'Ortega and Neil Harrington were ushered into the U.S. attorney's office without delay. His secretary closed the door and U.S. Attorney Wright motioned them to enter a side conference room where two FBI agents waited.

Introductions were cordial. "This is Agent Brian Loughlin," said Wright. "Holy Cross College—comes in from the Memphis office. And Sheila O'Brien—Loyola of Chicago, Northwestern grad school, and Fordham Law, Class of '92. Another good Jesuit product. Just graduated from the FBI school at Quantico. This is her first assignment."

Loughlin was sandy-haired, boyish, with a good-natured grin that could be disarming, although his hazel eyes seemed packed with intensity. He had a linebacker's frame and his nose showed the results of more than a few gridiron encounters.

Sheila O'Brien had creamy tan skin and silky blond hair that fell in a cap of natural waves that just covered her ears. She looked radiant, as if she'd just come off the slopes of Stowe or Aspen. Expressive blue eyes and a girl-next-door smile complemented her wholesome face. Even before she spoke, Neil Harrington knew he liked her.

Wright and Neil Harrington had first met as students at Harvard. Wright, a transported New Yorker with blue-chip roots, had served in various governmental agencies and was now the newly appointed U.S. attorney for the Boston area. Two more attorneys, young assistants from Wright's office, joined the group. Wright motioned all to be seated at the glistening walnut conference table; Operation Blackstone was about to be launched.

"I'm going to play a copy of my taped conversation with Callahan," said Harrington. "The original is in my office safe. I believe extracts from this will be sufficient to secure the necessary electronic surveillance on lawyer Sheridan, Mr. Callahan, and Dr. Dillard from Magistrate Rae."

The group hunched forward as the tape spun out its tale of intrigue. One of the assistant U.S. attorneys cited several U.S. Code violations, including RICO Act conspiracy. No one mentioned that it was a criminal offense to tape-record someone without that person's consent, as Harrington had done.

"Callahan's a cute operator," remarked Wright when the tape ended. "He never actually offered a quid pro quo, Dillard for the U.S. Senate. But I'm sure we can get the magistrate's okay for phone taps, including pay phones if necessary. And our cameras will show who's coming and going.

"We may have lucked out," Wright said as one of his assistants slid a newspaper clipping across the table. "In yesterday's *Globe,* Sheridan's office advertised for a secretary." He nodded toward Agent O'Brien.

"Miss O'Brien has some exceptional skills," Wright continued.

"Sharpshooter with a forty-five automatic at Quantico. But best of all, she can work a word processor, types eighty words per minute, and takes reasonable shorthand. During law school, she went to one of those crash secretarial schools off Broadway. Even has a certificate. We've already set up an interview, designed a suitable résumé, and if she lands the job, we'll be able to get the best inside information since we infiltrated the Santiglia mob in Philadelphia."

Harrington was impressed. And he knew that U.S. Attorney Wright had political aspirations. But he was a latecomer to the political arena. Maybe somewhere down the line, they'd clash. For now, though, Harrington welcomed the feds. They had the power, the resources, the ear of the judiciary. They could intimidate, overwhelm, and eventually crush. And he liked the idea of Sheila O'Brien. She had such a fresh, healthy look about her. And she could type.

Dr. Dillard arrived promptly at 9:00 A.M. and sat on the brown Naugahyde sofa next to a young woman who was also waiting for an appointment. Judy Corwin brought him a cup of coffee and made up a story, telling him that Sheridan was delayed on a court matter but would be in shortly. He nodded a thank-you, removed a medical journal from his valise, and began to read.

Young Buckley walked in.

"Dan will be a little late." Judy Corwin gave him a warm smile. "Would you cover the phones for a while? Caitlin called in sick again and I have to interview someone for her job. We'll be in the library."

"Boy, she's had a rocky time," said Buckley as he checked his messages. "Sure, I'll cover them from my office."

"Miss . . ." Judy Corwin hesitated, searching the notes in front of her.

"O'Brien. Sheila O'Brien."

Pleasant-sounding voice, thought Judy. Pleasant-looking, too. Not beautiful—but then again, they weren't running a modeling agency. And Judy Corwin was protective of Dan Sheridan. Caitlin O'Malley had gone gaga over her boss, fortunately from a distance.

And Sheridan was reaching his midforties, a vulnerable age for a single man like Dan. A dangerous age even for a married man, Judy reflected.

"I've been over your résumé." Judy read aloud from her notes. "Sacred Heart Academy, Evanston, Illinois. Loyola of Chicago— bachelor's in English; postgrad Northwestern—majored in drama and fine arts." She glanced up at Sheila.

"I thought I'd change direction." Sheila O'Brien crinkled her nose and her blue eyes seemed to dance.

"Burdett Secretarial School, New York City. Single, age twenty-seven." Corwin skipped through the résumé. "Eighty words per minute, shorthand, and skilled with all forms of the word processor. Not bad." She nodded, directing a slight benedictory smile toward the applicant.

"What did you do down in New York besides going to secretarial school?"

"I was an actress."

Corwin detected a slight reddening in Sheila O'Brien's cheeks.

"Mostly I waited on tables."

"Ever work in a law office?"

"No. This will be a first for me."

"Well, we pay six hundred dollars a week to start. Two weeks vacation, eight-hour days, sometimes ten when it gets hectic—which is most of the time. When can you start?"

Sheila O'Brien caught her breath. "Uh, uhm," she stammered, but quickly regained her composure. "Right away."

"Fine. Follow me. You'll be working mainly for Tom Buckley, but we switch around a lot. Let me introduce you to Mr. Buckley. And you'll like Dan Sheridan, our boss. Helluva guy. I've worked for him since he first hung out his shingle."

Sheila O'Brien breathed an inward sigh. It had been easy. Those acting classes at Northwestern had paid off, after all. She followed Judy Corwin out into the waiting room. The distinguished Dr. Dillard was still engrossed in the *New England Journal of Medicine,* and he looked curiously calm.

Crowded on the sofa next to him was an Hispanic family. They sat ramrod stiff, wearing cervical collars. Both the man and the woman wore army fatigue jackets. What was almost laughable was the child, perhaps five, also wearing a cervical collar. O'Brien didn't know they made neck braces that small. It was obviously an accident case. The whole eclectic mix looked comical. But seated near Judy Corwin's desk was another dark Hispanic type, nattily dressed. He had black beady eyes, pockmarked cheeks, and a Fu Manchu beard and mustache. His face resembled the target poster on the Quantico rifle range. Nothing distinguished-looking or comical about him.

Dr. Dillard seemed relieved when Sheridan told him the results of the polygraph. "That should do it," he said, as if his life would now be back to normal.

"Far from it." Sheridan scribbled a few notes and looked over at Dillard. "I'll use it as best I can, but it has no evidentiary value in our Massachusetts courts."

"Then why did you make me go through all that rigmarole?" Dillard asked testily.

"I didn't say it has *no* value. For one thing, I wanted to see how you'd react. You didn't hesitate when I asked you to take the test. That gives me a little insight into where we're headed. And I can use it in other ways."

"What other ways? Look, I've been living on tenterhooks for the past few days. Certain parties assured me you could handle this."

Sheridan had been going to inquire about Sonny Callahan but decided to wait. "What time did you say you left the Williams woman's apartment?"

"About ten."

"How did you get into and leave the building? Was there any security check?"

"The guards and doorman know my car. I drove into the underground garage at about seven."

"Did you sign in?"

"I just waved at the guard. His name is Julian."

"How did you gain access to the garage elevator?"

"I have a key."

"And when you left, did you sign out?"

"No. I just waved at the guard."

Sheridan jotted down more notes. "I have information that the autopsy disclosed no food contents in the victim's body. You and Williams had dinner maybe two to three hours before her body was found?"

"Yes." Dillard seemed composed; his expression didn't change. Didn't this guy ever get rattled?

"You're a doctor. How do you explain the autopsy findings?" Sheridan studied Dillard carefully.

Dillard hesitated, then ran his hand over the top of his head. "Angela was bulimic," he said. "I tried to cure her for years, but she said it was the only way she could enjoy her food and keep her figure. Ironic, isn't it, that she managed to have her cake and eat it, too. Now, of course, it couldn't matter less."

Dillard always seemed to have the right answers. Might even be true, Sheridan thought. He is a doctor, after all. Maybe a jury would believe him.

"Okay, we're taking your case on." Sheridan tapped a manila folder on his desk, then leveled his gaze at Dillard. "I don't want any outside interference . . . understand?" Their eyes locked.

"I understand," Dillard said, suppressing a sigh. "Should I tell my wife? She's wondering why I'm just cruising around Marblehead in my boat."

"I can't give you advice on that. That's up to you. Nothing's been in the papers, just that the police are investigating. Let me get a read on what's going on and I'll be in touch. But sooner or later, she's going to hear something. Why don't you take a few days this weekend, go to some resort in the Catskills."

"Might not be a bad idea," said Dillard. "They have a little airport near Lake Champlain. Kim and I can fly up. She doesn't know about Angela. I think I'd better start filling her in."

They shook hands and Dillard left. Dan did not envy him his weekend of explanations and rationales.

Judy Corwin appeared at his office door. "Tom is in with the Hernandez family." She rolled her eyes, smiling slightly.

"Mr. Escarda is here, too. Wants to discuss the fee. And"—Judy motioned for someone to enter—"I want you to meet our new secretary, Sheila Kathleen O'Brien."

Sheila hesitated in the doorway.

"Just what we need, another harp around here. Let's—" Sheridan turned and stopped in midsentence. The perky smile, the sprinkle of freckles across her nose, the large blue eyes with that look of Irish wonderment—all hit him.

Well, well. Sheila O'Brien would be nice to have around.

14

ASSISTANT U.S. ATTORNEY SHELDON FINE, accompanied by Mayan d'Ortega and FBI agent Brian Loughlin, entered U.S. Magistrate Shirley Rae's chambers on the tenth floor of the Federal Building. The room was Spartan: a witness stand, counsel tables, wooden chairs, and the magistrate's bench, flanked by the American flag staffed in a metal stand. Although the judiciary and the U.S. attorney's office were separate federal entities, the relationship was quite close; geographically the magistrate's chambers were right down the hall from Fine's office and politically there was that undefinable comity that at times brought into question the magistrate's role as an impartial dispenser of justice. Attorney Fine sat down at a vacant table and began to review his motion for necessary surveillance and wiretaps. It was airtight. Electronic surveillance and wiretaps involved infringement upon one's Fourth Amendment right of privacy, which guarantees protection against unlawful search and seizure. To get a court order, the government had to document sufficient probable cause to show that criminal activity was being perpetrated or contemplated.

Magistrate Rae carefully read the affidavits and recorded extracts of the Harrington-Callahan tape.

"Have you something more to add, Mr. Fine? It is an unusual motion. I mean, the subjects aren't your everyday traffickers in criminal activity."

"I understand, Your Honor." Fine rose to his feet. "But we have it from reliable sources that the Dillard matter goes beyond the homicide investigation presently being conducted by the Suffolk County District Attorney."

"Isn't that the Williams woman?" the magistrate said, glancing over at Mayan d'Ortega. "I read something about it in last night's *Herald*."

"That's right, Your Honor." Mayan d'Ortega rose and stood beside Attorney Fine. "The homicide probe is fairly complete. An investigative grand jury will be convened shortly. But, as you can see in the accompanying affidavits, we have reason to believe that Williams was a courier in the international drug trade aiding certain terrorist organizations."

"Why should I allow wiretaps of Mr. Sheridan's office, car phone, and residence? You say he's defending Dillard and has a close liaison with Callahan? Isn't any communication between lawyer and client absolutely privileged? You certainly wouldn't bug a confessional."

"If I may, Your Honor," Fine answered for d'Ortega. "The reasons are enumerated in our motion signed jointly by the U.S. attorney and District Attorney Harrington. We have a reliable informant whose identity is confidential, indicating that all three suspects—lawyer Sheridan, Dr. Dillard, and Mr. Callahan—are connected in an illegal enterprise and were involved in conspiracy, bribery, racketeering, and obstruction of justice, as the tape clearly indicates."

Magistrate Rae still looked somewhat quizzical. "Okay," she said finally, emitting a soft sigh, "I'll sign the warrants."

Detective Phil Riley showed his badge to the building manager, who motioned him to have a seat in his small cubicle of an office.

"Were you on duty the night of April 2, Mr. Schofield, when a Dr. Dillard checked in around seven in the evening?"

"No. I'm on duty from nine to six. I left at six P.M."

"Who came on duty after you?"

"The assistant manager—Colson. But that was his night off."

"Well, who was in charge?"

"The security guard, Julian Montoya."

"Only one security guard in an establishment like this?" Riley's arm stretched outward.

"That's right." Schofield didn't elaborate or apologize.

"Did Dr. Dillard come here often?" Riley opened a small notebook and jotted away.

"I really don't check on who's coming or going." Schofield tried to mask his displeasure. "I manage the properties, collect the rents, supervise maintenance, things like that."

"How long had Angela Williams occupied the penthouse floor?"

"Without consulting the books, I'd say about three years."

"Did she sign a lease?"

"Year to year."

"What was the rental?"

"Twenty-five thousand monthly."

"A month?" Riley whistled inwardly.

"That's right. . . . Look, I'm awfully busy."

"Just a few more questions, Mr. Schofield. Do you know anybody, perhaps a tenant, by the name of Cooch or Cuz or something sounding like that?"

Schofield pretended to search his memory. "No, I can't say that I do."

"Ever hear that name before?"

"No. That I'm certain of."

"Who paid Miss Williams's rent?"

"Why, Miss Williams did."

"How did she pay?"

"By check."

"Drawn on what bank?"

"Commonwealth Trust."

Riley scratched a notation in his notebook.

"Did she own a car?"

"No. A cab would usually pick her up, sometimes a limo."

"Did she have many visitors other than Dr. Dillard?"

"Mr. Riley." Schofield didn't hide his impatience. He tweaked the end of his white mustache. "I really wouldn't know."

"Is Julian Montoya on?"

"He'll be here at five."

"Who's on now?"

"Christian Montoya. They're cousins."

"Here." Riley handed Schofield a large envelope addressed "Boston Police: Attention Detective Riley." "I want you to send me a list of the owners and tenants, apartments and telephone numbers."

"That may take some doing . . . and most of the phone numbers are unlisted." Schofield reluctantly accepted the envelope, noting it was unstamped.

"Get it in to me by Friday," Riley grunted. "It'll save you a court appearance."

* * *

Riley waited in his car for the changing of the guard. Sure enough, promptly at 5:00 P.M. an angular dark-skinned man with fuzzy close-cropped hair sauntered up from the underground garage and entered the kiosk. He was wearing dark blue pants and a white shirt with epaulets. He began exchanging greetings with the guard on duty.

Riley alighted, walked to the enclosure, and waited until the salutations seemed to cease. "Mr. Montoya?" he called out in an authoritative tone.

The recent arrival popped his head out. "Yes, mon," he said in a high-pitched Kenyan accent, "what is it?"

Riley flashed his badge and Montoya's eyes widened.

"Phil Riley, detective, Boston Police. Are you Julian or Christian?" The other security guard poked his head out.

"I'm Julian Montoya and this here is my cousin Chris. We have our green cards properly certified," he began.

"Look," Riley said, "you could be third generation for all I care. . . . Either of you on duty the evening of April 2?"

"That would have been me." Julian smiled in relief, revealing a set of big white teeth.

"Do either of you know Dr. Dillard?" The smile slowly evaporated. Security guards knew all the scuttlebutt, more even than the occupants.

"We both do." Julian Montoya's voice was supplicative and obliging. "He was a friend of Miss . . . er"—the guard cleared his throat—"Miss Williams."

"Did he come here often?"

Montoya's eyes slid from side to side. "Quite often," he said. "Right, Chris?"

Christian now emerged from the kiosk carrying a clipboard. "Yes. He used to visit Miss Williams."

"How do you know that he called on Miss Williams?"

"Er . . ." Julian Montoya again cleared his throat. "We know his car—a silver-blue Porsche, low-number license plate with an M.D. on it."

"Did he have a sticker?"

"Not exactly." Again Julian's eyes slid toward his cousin as if he needed buttressing. "Miss Williams told us to let him use her spot in the garage. It comes with the apartment and she had no car. In fact, she had two spots."

"Did you check Dillard in on your clipboard?"

"No. Just the actual occupants."

"Were there any other similar arrangements that Miss Williams had?"

"Not that we knew of."

Riley noticed the front door to Hawthorne-on-the-Charles was a good fifty feet from the kiosk. Several leafy acacias obstructed a direct view.

"When occupants drive into the garage"—Riley signaled in that direction—"how do they gain access to their apartments?"

"They all have keys to the elevator in the garage," said Christian Montoya.

"And I take it," said Riley, "that Dillard had a key."

"We assumed so. He always drove in and out."

"Did you see Dillard drive his car out that evening?"

Julian Montoya seemed a little more relaxed. "Yes. I waved in his direction."

"Was the driver alone?"

"I'd say so."

"Did you actually see Dillard driving?"

The guard looked quickly at his cousin. "Well, I was in the security enclosure. But it was Dillard's car, all right."

"What time was that?"

Julian Montoya conversed with his cousin in Swahili for a few moments. "I'd say about ten to ten-fifteen P.M."

"Anyone else leave after Dillard?" Montoya again looked at his cousin. "And listen"—Riley's eyes narrowed—"speak Anglo-Saxon—no mumbo jumbo."

Montoya exhibited a wide grin, but Riley failed to note the defiance in his eyes. "No, mon. It was pretty quiet after that."

"One final question." Riley looked at both guards. "Ever hear the name of a person called Cooch or Cutch or something that sounds like that?"

The Montoyas looked quizzically at each other. Both shrugged their shoulders. "Name does not sound familiar," Christian Montoya said.

"Okay." Riley nodded. "Let me know if you hear anything."

Manny Raimondi waited in his nondescript Ford Taurus about a half block from Hawthorne-on-the-Charles. He watched Phil Riley drive off and jotted down his license plate number. He assumed he was Boston Police, but he'd check it out.

"I'm Detective Raimondi." He greeted the Montoyas with an affable smile, handing the nearest guard his card.

"We already spoke to a detective." Julian Montoya's voice was etched with caution.

"Hey, listen." Raimondi continued to smile. "I'm not a cop. I'm a private investigator trying to help a client. Can I just have a few words with you gentlemen?"

"If it's about Miss Williams, we have nothing more to say." Julian Montoya's tone was leery. "You'll have to talk with the super—Mr. *Schofield*."

"I just talked with Schofield." Raimondi fed them a white lie, hoping they wouldn't check. "He said it would be okay. I just need a few answers, and believe me, I know it's an imposition on your time." Manny extracted two one-hundred-dollar bills from his wallet.

"Well, if, as Mr. Schofield says, it's all right." Christian Montoya pocketed the bill in a quick motion, as did Julian, not even bothering to check the denomination. The benign green image of Ben Franklin had registered.

Raimondi went over the same territory as Riley. Julian Montoya now didn't recall actually seeing Dillard at the wheel. It was raining, so he had remained in the enclosure, pushing the button that lifted the traffic stake. But he was certain that it had been Dillard's car, even though he hadn't seen the plate number.

"Could you get me a list of the building occupants?"

"No. That would have to come from Mr. Schofield."

"What sort of person was Angela Williams?"

"A nice lady." Julian Montoya answered for both of them. "Always pleasant, tipped real well."

They were unaware of visitors other than Dillard, who called upon her at least once a week.

Raimondi smiled, thanked them for their time, and turned to go. Like Columbo, he hesitated for one last question. "Did she have any enemies, like someone who wanted her out of the way?"

They both shook their heads. Hard to tell if they are leveling, thought Raimondi.

"Do you know what she did? I mean, for a living." Raimondi's arm swept skyward toward the penthouse.

This time, the negative nods were accompanied by blank stares and pursed lips.

"Okay, fellas, many thanks. If you come across anything"—Raimondi gave them a quick Boy Scout salute—"give me a call."

"Sure thing, bwana," Christian Montoya said. Even his eyes smiled.

It was after six and Claire Doherty was tidying up her station by the typing pool. The secretaries had departed and only two assistant DAs were still poking through some books in the law library. Friday afternoons were the same for all municipal divisions. The district attorney's office was no exception, especially with the prospect of good weekend weather. The place was deserted. The criminal justice system could wait until Monday morning. Claire covered her typewriter, tucked a few stamps into her purse, then made her way toward Harrington's office. Mayan d'Ortega had asked her to delay getting subpoenas out on the Dillard matter until further notice. No reason. And Claire was smart enough not to inquire. But she'd heard from one of the assistant DAs that Harrington and d'Ortega had met with the U.S. attorney. Something was in the wind.

Unlike Claire's station, Kristina Collins's reception desk was immaculate. And unlike Claire's standard-issue green metal wastebasket and gray metal desk, Collins's rosewood desk glistened from constant polishing. Her word processor was the latest in electronic technology. The rich celery green broadloom complemented the heavy pecan-wood paneling. And as always, Claire couldn't avoid the imperious gaze of Cardinal Richelieu. The reception area was meant to be intimidating.

She tried the drawers to Collins's desk, but they were locked.

Then she rummaged through the wastebasket but turned up nothing of interest. She knocked lightly on Harrington's office door but
was greeted with silence. She turned the knob gently and was surprised when the door opened. The last two times she had tried the
same door, it had been locked solid. She pushed the burnished oak
door slightly open and peeked in. Like the reception area, the office was quiet and deserted.

Claire stood in the doorway for several seconds. The only sound
was the cleanup crew starting their evening chores in the outer
hallway.

There were several papers on Harrington's desk—she flipped
through them quickly—interoffice memos mainly, covering routine
assignments. A quick search of the wastebasket drew a blank. She
tried the center drawer on Harrington's oversized teakwood desk:
locked. The two side drawers were also locked, but surprisingly the
bottom drawer slid open. The first thing Claire Doherty spotted was
the large envelope marked U.S. ATTORNEY'S OFFICE: CONFIDENTIAL.

After a few moments' hesitation, she removed the envelope from
the drawer and pulled out its contents. Her eyes scanned the memo
with the professionalism of a speed-reader.

*OPERATION BLACKSTONE. Wiretaps of lawyer Daniel Sheridan's office,
home, and car phones were approved this date by U.S. Magistrate Shirley
Rae. . . .*

This was as far as she got. Feeling queasy in her stomach, she
looked around quickly, then slid the envelope back into the bottom
drawer, closing it quietly.

Dan Sheridan leafed through the Saturday-morning mail. He and
young Buckley, both attired in sweaters and blue jeans, were the
sole occupants of the office. Sheila O'Brien, the new secretary, had
volunteered to come in, but Sheridan had said that it was not necessary.

A letter marked PERSONAL AND CONFIDENTIAL caught Sheridan's
eye. No return address. He zipped it open. It was from Claire Doherty.

*Dan, please see me at one Saturday at the altar confessional of St. Denis,
near Chinatown. Urgent, Claire.*

Dan glanced at his watch: almost noon. He'd grab a quick sandwich and be there on time. It was only a fifteen-minute walk. Before, Claire had always telephoned. Could be that her husband, Al, has been drinking again.

Dan mounted the granite steps to the church vestibule. St. Denis was a moldering Gothic hulk that had seen palmier days. But it had been Claire Doherty's childhood parish and she still took time to attend Mass at least twice a week and sometimes got there on Sundays.

Dan blessed himself at the entrance font and made his way down the side aisle toward the altar. Except for a lone lady parishioner making the Stations of the Cross, the church was deserted. Near the altar rail, votive lights flickered their melancholy glow and Dan could make out the confessional, as silent as the rest of the church. He genuflected, then slid into a pew. For several moments, he just sat there, allowing his eyes to adjust to the dark interior. He noted an odd sculpture of the martyred saint above the confessional. St. Denis was not Irish, as Claire Doherty had always imagined, but Greek. When St. Dionysius had been decapitated by the Romans in the first century, he picked up his head, carried it in his hands, and proceeded to outdistance his assailants. Apocryphal or not, it was a good story. And there he was, ensconced in marble above the confessional.

"Dan." Claire's voice was a stage whisper. "Thank God you got my note." She slid in alongside him.

"I hope it's not too late," she said, apprehension creeping into her voice.

"Has Al been drinking again?" Dan kept his eyes straight ahead on the altar.

"He's always drinking." Claire eyed the old woman who was moving off toward the Tenth Station at the rear of the church.

"Dan, your phones are being tapped."

"Tapped. By whom?"

"The feds."

Dan looked over at Claire Doherty quizzically. "How do you know this?" he said.

"Don't ask me how I know. I just know. I'm frightened, Dan. I called you last week. If they connect me with you, I could lose my job, or God knows what.'' She began to sob, quietly.

Dan gave her a handkerchief from his suit coat and she dabbed her eyes.

"Okay." Dan patted her hands, which already clutched some rosary beads. "Thanks for the tip, Claire. I won't forget this."

Dan got up to leave and she handed him back his handkerchief.

"I think I'll stay awhile," she said. "I find real solace here. And Dan"—her hand grasped his arm—"be careful."

The sculpture of St. Denis, holding his severed head in his hands, came into Dan's view. It didn't augur well.

"Say a few for me, Claire." He patted her hand again, tapping the beads gently.

15

SHERIDAN pulled into the Howard Johnson's parking lot off I-95 a few miles from the Burlington town line, for a morning rendezvous with Manny Raimondi. They'd attempt to secure the town's police file, look at photographs, locate the witness who chanced upon the body, and check out the area where the victim was found. Maybe a mission impossible. Buckley had tried but hit a stone wall. During a homicide investigation, the police zip their files. Confidential. No disclosure, particularly to an attorney, more particularly to an ex-cop attorney. Sheridan knew the odds were less than zero. But he figured Sunday might be covered by a weekend police force, perhaps auxiliaries, maybe a woman or two, someone who could be reasoned with. He parked next to a fleet of tour buses and watched passengers stream out toward the restaurant. It was Patriots Day, and the new sprouts on birches and lindens lent a mint green softness to the land. There was a hint of summer in the air and the tourists seemed to be in a festive mood. The nearby battlefields of Lexington and Concord would soon be alive with bewigged redcoats and grizzled minutemen reenacting their annual duels.

Sheridan's mood was far from festive. Manny Raimondi pulled in and parked alongside, raising his hand in a mock salute.

"Let's skip the bacon and eggs," Sheridan said. "We'll take your car. There's something I think you should know."

Sheridan fastened his seat belt as they sped along the highway headed north. Raimondi sensed the lawyer's introspection. Neither spoke for several seconds.

"I just received a tip that my phones are tapped."

Manny kept his eyes glued to the road and moved into the high-speed lane. "Tapped? By whom?"

"Probably the FBI," Sheridan said grimly. "The U.S. attorney's office secured court approval."

"Do you know what phones?" Raimondi's mind began to click.

"Not exactly," said Sheridan. "Our office to be sure, perhaps my condo, maybe even my car phone."

"Why do you think you're being bugged?" Manny chanced a glance at his boss.

"I suppose it was bound to happen. We haven't exactly been representing the cardinal or Mother Teresa. I'm probably not the only one targeted. And somehow I think it has to do with Dillard and Sonny Callahan. I don't owe Callahan any favors, but Dillard is my client. I'll have to talk to the doctor, tell him to watch his phone calls."

"What about Callahan?" Manny slowed down as they approached the Burlington exit.

"That's going to be a problem," Sheridan said. "The less I have to do with his crowd, the better. Something doesn't smell right. Callahan tried to sucker me. He may be part of a sting operation. I'm not sure. In any event, get word to a friend of a friend of Callahan that his phones might be bugged."

"Will do."

"Tell me, Manny, can you get a wattage snooper or something that picks up the tap? Seems I read about these gizmos in *Soldier of Fortune* magazine. At least I'll know when and where the bugs are being activated."

"I can buy the techs at Radio Shack."

They left I-95's swarm of speeding traffic, circled the cloverleaf, and passed into the bucolic New England town of Burlington. It was another world: weathered clapboard houses, split-rail fences, fields enclosed by low stone walls where a few cows lazed in little ponds of piney shade. They passed a small cemetery; the lichen-covered headstones were tilted with age, the names and dates obliterated by wind and weather. The Civil War monument, a gray stone obelisk studded with granite cannonballs, guarded the entrance, tiny American flags fluttering at its base. At the far end of the village green, the bell of the white-steepled Congregational church tolled solemnly as its members decked out in holiday finery headed toward Sunday services. As they turned into an oak-lined road, Sheridan noted the ten o'clock Mass at the local Catholic church was competing fairly evenly for souls. Even the Presbyterians were doing a brisk business.

"You know, Manny"—Sheridan's grim visage eased for the first time—"we might be able to use these taps to our advantage."

"Like the Nixon tapes." Manny smiled. "Dick lathering it on

about altruism and humanitarian concerns when describing payoffs to his gang of break-in artists.''

"Once I thought a client was taping my conversation. He was on implement income from Social Security, SSI. You have to sign a form that you're practically destitute. Well, I settled a malpractice case for him for a hundred and fifty thousand dollars. 'What about Social Security?' he says. 'Should I report it?' 'Absolutely,' I said.

"Well, he wants his money in cash, no check. So the client's the captain of the case; he wants cash, he gets cash. He comes into the bank. The head teller is there with Judy and we count out one hundred grand. He stuffs it into two paper bags and goes on his way.''

Raimondi saw the redbrick town hall just ahead and slowed down.

"Two months later, he gets me on the phone. 'Dan, me boy,' he says in a chipper tone, 'I followed your advice. I *didn't* report it to Social Security.' He pauses. I figure he's recording my reply. I could have said, Hell, they'll never find out. Forget about it. This is what he wanted to hear. And nine out of ten attorneys would go along. But it's my ass, and my license.

" 'Listen, Bart,' I said emphatically. 'I told you to do the *right thing*. Report it tomorrow morning. That's the American way!' I sounded like Dick Nixon, all right. That's the last I heard from him. Probably hightailed it faster than you can say 'off-peak fares to Santo Domingo.' ''

The police and fire stations flanked the municipal building, which housed the town hall, and Raimondi parked next to a blue-and-white police cruiser. They entered through electronically triggered glass doors and made their way to the front counter. Two young police officers were talking about the Red Sox and an old-timer with glasses perched on the end of his nose sat hunched over a Teletype as it ticked away.

"Can I help you gentlemen?" She was matronly, late fifties, wore Ray•Ban mirror glasses, and had a no-nonsense "take no prisoners" sort of voice. Her hair looked like a scouring pad.

She was wearing a tan uniform blouse with a police department shoulder patch and a plain black tie and slacks—the acid test of a woman's figure. A test she flunked hands-down. A straight forty-five, Sheridan thought. Forty-five-inch bust, forty-five-inch rear end, and .45-caliber automatic strapped around her bulging waistline. Pinned to her blouse was a nameplate: K. BAXTER.

"Is Chief Dawkins in?" Sheridan asked politely.

"No. He'll be here tomorrow morning." She forced a smile, but it lacked invitation. Sheridan could see himself in the reflection of her sunglasses.

"May I ask who's in charge, ma'am?" Sheridan ventured.

"I am. I'm Deputy Kate Baxter."

"I'm Dan Sheridan, an attorney from Boston. And this is my associate, Emanuel Raimondi."

All nodded, no handshaking.

"I'm investigating a possible wrongful death case for a client," Sheridan began.

The two officers had departed. Sheridan could see their cruiser pulling out of the parking lot. The old-timer was still checking the Teletype as it spilled forth a staccato of data.

Baxter smiled. Tough to know if the smile extended to her eyes.

"What case are you boys looking into?"

"Angela Williams. Her body was found off I-Ninety-five."

Kate Baxter's smile suddenly evaporated. The old-timer at the Teletype looked up.

"That's all under wraps," she said tersely. "Now, if you'll excuse me."

Manny Raimondi thought of the extra C note in his wallet. But such a crazy move could land them in jail, if he was any judge of this broad.

"Okay. Just doing my job." Sheridan shrugged. He turned to go, then hesitated. "Say, would you be related to Tap Baxter? I think he coaches baseball at Lowell High."

"Used to." A glimmer of the smile returned to Kate Baxter's lips. "He retired to Sarasota two years ago. He's my uncle."

"Well, he was one helluva coach. I made the North Shore All-stars back in high school and Tap steered us to the tristate title."

"Oh, what position did you play?" As she leaned forward, her bosom seemed to splay out on the counter.

"Catcher." Sheridan grinned.

"My dad was a catcher," Baxter said, pushing her sunglasses up into her hair. Her smile extended to her pale blue eyes. "He did a stretch in the minors. Utica, mainly. Went up to Indianapolis one year—Triple A. Died three years ago next week. He and Tap were brothers.''

"I take it you like the game?'' Sheridan said.

"I still pitch softball—just weekends.''

"Say, how would you like some Red Sox tickets? I have four boxes I can't use for Saturday night. The Yankees are in town.'' Sheridan reached for his wallet.

She glanced over at the old-timer, who had returned to the Teletype.

"Why don't you boys step into my office.'' She extended her hand, palm outward, and nodded toward the enclosure.

"Here's an extra set of photographs,'' Baxter said as she spread them out on her desk. "Victim was found facedown. Not a bruise or mark on her. But of course it was night and the EMTs performed only a cursory examination.

"You can get this stuff through discovery anyhow, so might as well give it to you now. . . . But don't go flashing it around. Understand?''

"We do,'' Sheridan said solemnly.

"I hear the Boston Police have a line on some highfalutin society doc who may have done the poor kid in. . . . She was black, you know.''

Sheridan sidestepped both remarks and became engrossed in the police diagram. "Kate.'' He pointed to the Magic Marker X that indicated where the victim had been found. "Officer Turco's report says that the guy who found the body, Anton Kent-Smythe, went some seventy-five yards into the woods to take a leak.'' Sheridan looked at her quizzically. "That's almost a football field.''

"Yeah, that's what it says.'' Kate Baxter's smile had an all-knowing look to it.

"Here this Smythe guy stops to take a leak,'' Sheridan continued. "It's a truck stop. Says he's going home to Danvers. Danvers is north, yet he's in the southbound lane. He walks right past the comfort station and treks seventy-five yards into wooded underbrush to relieve himself, when two feet would have sufficed. Didn't Officer Turco think his story was kind of funny?''

"Not exactly." Baxter's grin now had a pixieish twist to it. Smythe said he had just left Buddy's Hilltop Lounge about two miles down the road. We checked it out and he was there, all right. Oh, we didn't quite buy his entire story. But he's not a suspect. We figured he was with some guy and they were giving it a go."

"A go?" Sheridan frowned.

"Buddy's is a gay bar and the truck stop is a cruising spot." Kate shook her head as she smiled. "Smythe is married. A banker. He should have cut out of there just as soon as he stumbled on the body. I guess his sense of citizenship got the better of him. He called us and stuck around—but not his pickup. That's a sleeping dog we'll let lie." Kate gathered up the documents and shoved them into a large brown envelope.

Sheridan removed the Red Sox tickets from his wallet. The exchange was simultaneous.

Sheridan surmised *Baxter* was her maiden name. In fact, she looked kind of butch. He thought he'd take his leave on a gracious note. "Going to take the kids to the game, Kate?"

"No. Never had kids. Never got married."

"Bet you broke a lot of hearts," Sheridan suggested.

"My own, mainly." Kate put on her sunglasses and walked Sheridan and Raimondi to the door. "But I think I'll take Stevie and his two children."

"Stevie?"

"He's my boyfriend."

16

THEY ASSEMBLED in the FBI's conference room at their Beacon Street headquarters. U.S. Attorney Norman Wright stood at the small rostrum. He adjusted the mike and then leafed through a sheaf of notes. Mayan d'Ortega sat in the front row next to Neil Harrington. A trim, distinguished-looking man dressed in a conservative gray tweed suit sat to the right of Harrington. He wore rimless glasses and his thinning frosted hair and slim white mustache gave him an air of scholarship. He tapped his pipe lightly on a nearby metal ashtray, inspected its bowl for a moment, then tucked it into an inside pocket.

There were fifteen others present, including Brian Loughlin and Sheila O'Brien. These were the untouchables, the Justice Department's elite strike force assembled for Operation Blackstone. This was strictly a federal show. No Boston or state police were included. These were the dedicated young professionals with top secret clearance, most of them legally trained. Their integrity and loyalty to the bureau were beyond question. Brimming with eagerness, they were like a family. But more importantly, they were imbued with the heady, seductive fever of esprit de corps.

Wright waved the group to order and their murmuring died down. "Sorry to get you out on a Sunday night," he said, "but two things prompted this meeting." He held up two fingers to form a V. "First, I thought we should meet and get the operation rolling. Some of you have worked together before. For others, this is a first assignment. And most of you are new to Boston. This can be a plus, but it also presents certain logistical problems that your unit chiefs will discuss as the operation unfolds." He nodded toward Sheila O'Brien and Brian Loughlin. "You'll have to get rid of your southern drawls and midwestern accents and start using broad A's—like parrk your cahr in the Harvahd Yaahrd."

The group erupted in good-natured laughter. Wright smiled, waited, then flicked his wrist upward and the laughter slowly subsided. "We're a team," he continued, "and we're out to bury a lot of thieving lawyers, attorneys who'd sell their own grandmothers to protect the mob. We know who they are. Operation Blackstone will rid this country of the worst kind of cancer.

"This operation is international in scope. Certain targeted lawyers are connected with international terrorist groups, Colombian drug lords, and plain old homegrown American gangsters. They're the consiglieri. They thrive on drug money. They sneak and hide and obstruct. Well, quite frankly, they are scum. And we're going to eradicate them."

"Reason number two." Wright again held up two fingers. "I have a surprise for you." He looked over at the elegant visitor seated next to Harrington. "I want to introduce Col. Hugh MacCallister, who served with the Third Scotch Highlanders in World War Two and is now chief of the United Kingdom's security forces, better known as the Strategic Air Services, the commandos of British intelligence. . . . Colonel MacCallister, would you come up and say a few words to the team?"

There was a smattering of applause. MacCallister rose, turned to face the group, and signaled Wright that he would speak from where he stood rather than use the dais.

"I want to commend all of you for getting involved in a dangerous mission." His voice was crisp, button-down British. There was a candid no-nonsense presence in his stance. The group hunched forward to listen.

"Our enemy is no longer communism, not even Iraq or Iran, but terrorism—terrorism aimed at women and children and legitimate business establishments, not only in our country but worldwide. I'm talking about the Irish Republican Army." MacCallister's gray eyes narrowed and took on a dark intensity. "Just last week, these killers bombed Victoria Station."

"Excuse me, Colonel." Brian Loughlin raised his hand. "Doesn't the IRA give ample warning, by a code that you people know is authentic, where and when a blast is to go off?"

MacCallister seemed startled. He glanced at Wright, who was still at the rostrum. Wright nodded. "Colonel," he said, extending his palm outward. MacCallister had been briefed that the task force was predominantly Catholic—many Jesuit college–trained. The gesture from Wright signaled that he went along with Agent Loughlin's interruption and the inquiry should be addressed immediately.

MacCallister, a tough, wiry Scotsman, had never graduated from Oxford or Eton, never attended the military schools such as Sandhurst or Cranwell. Untitled, without much formal schooling, he had originally served as a brevet sergeant in World War II. He won the Victoria Cross for gallantry at Dieppe and gradually rose through the ranks. Now a career officer, head of the secretive SAS, he quickly regained his military composure.

"What you say is partially correct. We get a lot of crank calls about bomb scares. If we responded to every one, we'd have to shut down our transportation system. The London subway is the largest in the world. The IRA has a code designed expressly for MI-Six, our international intelligence section. When a caller comes up with that code, we know it's the real thing. They tell us the approximate location but not precisely where the bomb is placed and generally give us thirty minutes' lead time. We clear the area. Hitler with all his bombers—sometimes a thousand a night, which eventually wiped out one-third of London—never shut down the London tubes. Now a handful of terrorists can tie up a city of fourteen million people. The economic cost is staggering, not to mention the loss of life."

MacCallister paused for several seconds. The drama of the moment hung in the air. "That's why I'm here tonight. That's why we're all here."

He reached down for a valise that he had placed by his chair, opened it, and removed a file.

"Here," he said, "I want to pass these out." He handed several photographs to Mayan d'Ortega. "Look through these," he said, his tone assuringly confidential, "then pass them along to the others.

"These are a series of photographs taken over the past several weeks at locations throughout Greater London. They could have been shot in downtown Sarajevo."

Mayan studied each photograph, shook her head in apparent disbelief, then passed them to Harrington.

"The destruction caused in Selfridges department store, Fortnum and Mason's in Piccadilly, and Green Park station is so much brick and mortar. These can be repaired, replaced. But look at the dead women and children. They were housewives, schoolchildren, youngsters who had parents and grandparents who doted on them.''

MacCallister spoke in soft, solemn tones.

"That's your lead time; that's your warning. These terrorists are planting one-hundred-pound bombs. The devastation and loss of life are unbelievable.

"We can't even send detonating crews in there. We simply clear the area and hope for the best. That's the lead time we get. Does that answer your question, Mr. . . . ?''

"Loughlin, Brian Loughlin.'' Loughlin stood up.

"Well, I'm glad you asked the question . . . and please resume your seat, Brian.''

Loughlin sat down just in time to receive the photographs from Sheila O'Brien.

"This isn't a question of religion,'' MacCallister continued. "It's a question of humanity, for individuals to be able to go about their everyday lives peacefully and without fear.

"Now these Irish terrorists are condemned by their own church; their members gain only an infinitesimal fraction of the electoral vote in national elections, and as far as we're concerned, they're demented killers!'' MacCallister folded his hands behind his back like a sea captain about to give an order in a storm.

He paused only briefly. "Okay,'' he said. "Where do they get the munitions, an arsenal of rockets, grenades, and blockbusting bombs? Mainly from South America—some Chinese stuff, of course—Libya, and, odd as it seems, from certain locations in France.

"And buying munitions costs money. We know the IRA has a budget of one million dollars a day and it comes mainly from the international drug trade.'' MacCallister's courtly voice was now taut with indignation. "That's why we're here,'' he snapped. "As Norman Wright said, it's a cancer, and you attack a cancer at its source. You wipe it out. That's what we intend to do!''

The applause, led by Brian Loughlin, was enthusiastic and prolonged. Wright had to rap for order.

They split up into teams. Mayan d'Ortega would work with Sheila O'Brien and Brian Loughlin on Sheridan, Dillard, and Callahan.

"We'll try not to keep you too long tonight,'' Mayan said. "I know it's late and as a new employee you have to be at work well before nine A.M." She looked at Sheila O'Brien.

"I've been assigned to Thomas Buckley," Sheila said. "Sheridan has a personal secretary, Judy Corwin, who runs the administrative show in the office. She keeps the books, fields some crazy calls, and acts as a buffer between nutty clients and her boss. From what I can gather in my short time there, he turns down a lot of cases."

"According to Hal Davis—he's the section chief at Justice," Loughlin said, "we're to determine if Sheridan leans toward any illegal activity. If we can show he's engaged in criminal conduct, then we can get court authorization to place electronic devices in his own office and conference room. This is where you come in, Sheila."

"I've already got a Sunday key." She smiled.

"People can be discreet on their own telephone," Loughlin said. "And by the way, the phone taps on all three, Sheridan, Dillard, and Callahan, are already in place."

"You people work fast," d'Ortega said, offering a professional compliment.

"And we've got another kicker." Loughlin had a boyish grin. "Every married guy who ever calls a girlfriend uses a pay phone— always pays cash for flowers or a fur coat. No record floating around. My father was a divorce lawyer in New York. MasterCard and telephone bills can hang you.

"Well, Justice wants the lobby phones where Sheridan has his office tapped, and the one on the corner of Tremont and Beacon, which is right down the street from Sheridan's office."

"You mean pay phones?" Mayan d'Ortega looked puzzled.

"We've been doing this since 1986, just after congressional authorization. We can plug into a pay phone without a court order. They're called roving taps."

"Has this been tested constitutionally?" Mayan asked.

"According to Davis, the Court of Appeals for the Ninth Circuit upheld the Electronic Communications Privacy Act of 1986 as constitutional. Bugging public phones didn't violate a person's Fourth Amendment right to privacy.

"It was the case of a mobster trying to muscle in on gambling at an Indian reservation. The mobster's lawyer brought motions to suppress the conversation gained through the taps. The panel voted three to zero against him.''

"So I work the inside," Sheila said, "and you guys listen to the tapes. But when do we put the voice bugs in Sheridan's office?"

"Well, here's the drill." Loughlin sounded as if he was calling a play in a huddle. He looked over his notes.

"Tomorrow at ten A.M., I'm calling Sheridan's office from a location in Dorchester. Who'll be on the phone?"

"I'm the receptionist as well as Buckley's secretary, so chances are I'll field the call. Unless, of course, I'm tied up and Judy Corwin answers."

"Well, try to be available. At ten-oh-two exactly, I'll call. My name will be Timmy Kelleher. Got that?"

Sheila jotted down some notes.

"I've been rear-ended by a truck. Accident occurred two weeks ago. My back hurts. I'm a self-employed plumber residing at One-six-five-five Talbot Street, Dorchester, age thirty-three. . . . You sure Sheridan handles automobile cases?"

"I've already talked to a few clients. They range from serious injuries to the whiplash variety."

"Okay. Here's the bait. I saw a doctor in the emergency room of Beth Israel. He had X rays taken. They were negative and he said I was okay. . . . But I need Sheridan to send me to his *own* doctor to build up the case over the two-thousand-dollar medical no-fault plateau. Think Sheridan will go for it?"

"He might—or he might refer it to Tom Buckley."

"Well, try to steer me to Sheridan. I'll come through with the necessary accolades about his reputation around Dorchester, and of course I'll give it my best Barry Fitzgerald imitation.

"The phone taps will pick up the discussion. If he bites and says he can help me and sets up an appointment, I think that'll be all we need to get court approval to plant a bug in his office.

"I understand we'll be using similar ruses on attorneys Bob Catalano, Steven Dragna, and Barry Ginsberg. Catalano and Dragna represent the mob and Ginsberg would take a hot stove; he's been mixed up in some shady real estate deals and has been skirting disbarment for years."

Sheila tried to contain her excitement as the meeting broke up.

At last she was part of an elite corps within the bureau—the cul-
mination of all of her hopes and hard work, from law school
through Quantico. She was exactly where she wanted to be.

"Hello, Mr. Buckley." Sheila O'Brien smiled at Tom Buckley as he
entered the small reception area. It was 8:35 and her bright smile
was a welcome tonic for a Monday morning, and also a welcome
change from Caitlin O'Malley, whose litany of complaints and tired
sighs never seemed to cease.

"God, you're in early." Buckley returned the smile. He noted
her glistening lips. Her eyes seemed full of life.

"Oh, I'm a morning person," she said. "Can I get you some
coffee? I have a pot brewing in the Xerox room."

"That'll be fine." Buckley nodded. "And call me Tom."

"Tom it is." Her voice tinkled like crystal. "Black or regular?"

"Uh . . . black, with a tad of sugar."

"Those letters you dictated Friday afternoon are on your desk
for signature," she said. "I'll get the coffee."

Buckley traced the lyric swirl of her honeyed hair, trim figure,
and shapely legs as she moved off down the hall. He emitted a
thankful sigh. What a pleasure she was, especially compared with
Caitlin and even Judy Corwin with her "Jewish mother" bossiness.

An hour later, Judy buzzed Tom to say that Sheridan wanted to
see them in the conference room, that it was important.

Buckley was in the middle of dictation but signaled Sheila that
things would keep. Sheila closed her steno pad and glanced at her
watch: 9:55.

Judy and young Buckley entered the small conference room,
which also served as a law library. Sheridan's jaw was taut as he
signaled both to have a chair.

"Would you like some coffee, Dan?" Judy asked.

"No thanks, Judy, maybe later. How long have we been together?" Sheridan began solemnly.

"Fifteen years this August." Buckley's face rolled into an easy
grin. "Seems like only fourteen."

"Well, what I'm going to say isn't good news. Our telephones
are being tapped."

"What?" Judy furrowed her brow. "When did you find this out, Dan?"

"I got a tip from a confidential source that the U.S. attorney's office secured court approval."

"Why in the world . . . ?" Buckley exclaimed.

Sheridan sighed and shook his head. "Somehow, I think it has to do with Dillard and that wheeler-dealer Sonny Callahan. I don't know what it's all about, but Raimondi's got his feelers out."

"So, big deal," Buckley said.

"Do you think we should tell the new secretary?" Judy inquired.

"No. It's liable to spook her. Right now, we'll play it as if nothing is happening, and if you guys want to leave . . ."

"Hey, for Christsakes, Dan," Buckley said, "what's a little heat?"

"You staying?" Sheridan looked at young Buckley.

"You're goddamned right we're staying!" Buckley answered for both of them as Judy nodded.

"Okay, I—"

"Excuse me, Mr. Sheridan." Sheila O'Brien's voice came across the conference intercom. "You have a call on line five, a Mr. Kelleher. He's been in an accident. Says you come highly recommended."

"Get his phone number. I'll call him back. . . . Never mind, I'll take it."

"Hey," young Buckley said as Sheridan got up to go back to his office, "at least we're in on it. And you know"—he had a bemused look—"maybe we can work it to a fare-thee-well, pretend we're just doing pro bono work for the downtrodden and giving free legal assistance to the Poor Clare nuns."

"I've thought of it," Sheridan said. He opened the door to his office, which connected with the conference room. "As of now, we've got to assume every call, coming in and going out, is monitored—so do it up brown."

"Hello, Mr. Sheridan, sir, me name is Timothy Kelleher."

"Yeah. What can I do for you, Mr. Kelleher?"

"Sir, me car was totaled April fourth by a Mack truck on the Southeast Expressway."

"Well, if you had damage only to your car, report it to your insurance company. You won't need a lawyer."

"No. No. You dinna understan', Mr. Sheridan, sir. Oh Jaysus, me back hurts. 'Tis wrenched out of place, it 'tis."

"Were you hospitalized?"

"Yes. Emergency treatment at Beth Israel. The doc took X rays, gives me an exam, and said nothin's wrong. Dinna even give me a prescription for me back."

"You mean you haven't seen a doctor since the emergency visit?"

"That's right. Some two weeks ago. These doctors dinna seem to care, Mr. Sheridan, sir. I dinna have Blue Cross, so they sent me on me way."

"Well, you got maybe two hundred dollars in medical bills. You have to incur two thousand dollars or more to make a personal-injury claim. That's our no-fault law."

"Well, that's why I'm callin', Mr. Sheridan. Ya gotta good rep roun' here. People say you could direct me to the right medics to goose the bills up over that silly limit."

Quickly, the gongs sounded. Might be legit, but it could be a bar association plant. And he'd have to assume the lines were wired.

"Look, Mr. Kelleher," Sheridan said slowly and deliberately, as if he was spelling it out. "We handle only legitimate cases here—for poor people mostly."

"I'm poor," the voice replied.

"Look, you may be hurt."

"I think a disk popped out. Me back is killing me."

"Don't interrupt me," Sheridan said curtly. "What you're suggesting is that I engage in fraud, send you to some doctor."

"No . . . no!" the voice stammered. "All I want is an appointment. You give me the name of the doc and . . ."

"Look. Hear me well, Mr. Kelleher. I think you want to engage in some kind of scam. We want no part of it. We're a law firm, not con artists."

"But no. Jaysus, may the saints strike me dead. I . . ."

"That they may do, Mr. Kelleher. Take your case elsewhere. Our conversation is ended!" If anyone was eavesdropping, the slamming phone would give him an earful.

*   *   *

Sheila O'Brien placed the receiver down gently and started to type
as Sheridan came out of his office. That little ploy hadn't worked.
And Loughlin had sounded so real. She looked up at Sheridan,
who seemed more than a little perturbed.

"Sheila," he said, "give all calls on new clients to Judy."

"I'm sorry." She smiled sheepishly. "I shouldn't have interrupted you."

"That's okay," Sheridan said. "It was just a guy who thought he
could get something for nothing."

"We won't be making up a case?"

"Not with stiffs like that. We have a few barkers around here, but
we're not taking on any mongrels." He smiled. It was an appealing
smile. She smiled back.

Brian Loughlin listened to the tape a second time. Sheldon Fine
and two FBI agents sat in stony silence. Mayan d'Ortega cracked a
small smile.

"Well, that little caper didn't get off the ground." He sighed.

"A call on one." An agent motioned to a blinking red light.

"It's for Callahan," Loughlin said as he flicked a switch on a
composite board. The group put on earphones.

"Hello, Mr. Callahan, Deegan speakin'."

"Oh, Mr. Deegan, so sorry to hear about ya poor cousin Paddy.
He was a foine lad."

"Nothin's wrong with Paddy. Did ye get me message?"

"That I did, Deegan, but I can't make it down Sunday because
me niece, Mary Twomey, is taking her final vows with the Maryknoll
Sisters."

"Oh, the boys'll be disappointed. That you can't make it down,
I mean."

"Well, I'll have Mary say a few for them all. . . ."

"You know, time is gettin' short."

"That I know, Deegan. I'll be in touch. And give me best to the
monsignor. Good-bye."

Loughlin took off his earphones and shook his head. "Not much
today," he said.

*   *   *

They listened for three days. Arcane legalese from Sheridan's office—interrogatories, deposition notices, the usual give-and-take between law firms. They seemed to be doing a lot of free legal work. "No charge for the will, Mrs. Patterson. Glad to be of service." Begorras and bejabers drivel from Callahan. "He'll be at the funeral—say hi to Father Matt. God bless." The call from New York was traced to a pay phone in the Bronx. No return call from Callahan. A call from Ireland—again condolences, invoking lost saints, Finbar, Columbkille. Say hi to Paddy Nolan! Again nothing. The call was traced to a pay phone in Galway.

Brian Loughlin wondered, Why pay phones just to pass the time of day? No calls from Dillard, in or out. Loughlin thought it strange. So did Mayan d'Ortega. They called Dillard. The caretaker answered.

"The doctor is on holiday. No, he took the family. Don't know where he went or when he'll return." Mayan d'Ortega thought she'd better check in with Harrington. Dillard might have skipped.

17

SHEILA fingered the delicate camera in her skirt pocket. Then she opened the morning mail and perused it rapidly. It was mostly junk: legal flyers, pamphlets, book fillers, bills. There was a letter from a Sal DiMatteo with a check for five thousand dollars, thanking Sheridan for services rendered. Then she matched the correspondence to the proper files and placed everything on Judy Corwin's desk.

"Hi." Young Buckley startled her as she was opening the file cabinet to look for Dillard's case.

"Oh!" She turned, catching her breath and placing her hand on her breast. "I didn't hear you come in." She patted her skirt pocket self-consciously.

"You should keep the lock on the door when no one else is here, Sheila, especially this early in the morning." Buckley checked his watch: 7:45. "Lot of creeps around. You put your pocketbook down and it's gone." He gestured to encompass the small anteroom. "This isn't exactly a brontosaurus-sized law firm where you've got to check your soul just to get past the green-marbled foyer.

"Come on in and have a cup of coffee and tell me a little about yourself." She liked his easy smile. He was like a puppy, friendly and eager to please. "It's too early to start grinding it out. Judy won't be in until nine and Dan's headed for the Chelsea District Court on an arraignment. Seems some kid was doing his Christmas shopping a little early. They found him in Bloomingdale's at three in the morning."

They sat facing the windows in the veneered conference room. The early-morning sun glinted off the Hancock Tower's wall of glass. From their vantage point, they traced the gray shawl of mist that hung over the Charles River.

Buckley reached into his pocket, extracted a crumpled packet of Camels, tapped it on the table, and two cigarettes popped up. "Smoke?" he said, pointing the packet toward Sheila.

"No thanks." She smiled.

"One of my bad habits," Buckley said, striking a match and holding the cigarette at eye level between his fingers. "That, and maybe I drink too much."

"All lawyers drink too much." Sheila shook her head in mild disapproval.

"Yeah, we drink when we win, drink when we lose. One of the great compensations of this crazy profession." Buckley's boyish grin had a hint of rascality in it.

"You're not married?" Sheila glanced at his naked ring finger.

"Was." He sighed. "In college. But that was long ago." His tone was dismissive, and Sheila was smart enough to let the subject fade.

"Dan Sheridan," she said, "I assume he's divorced. No wife or children call."

Buckley took a long drag on his cigarette and exhaled slowly, letting the smoke drift in lazy eddies toward the ceiling.

"Dan's wife, Jean, and his eight-year-old son, Tommy, were killed by a drunk driver three years ago," he said. "Dan still hasn't gotten over it. Been sort of a depressed limbo ever since. He's turned into a workaholic. I drink; he works. We get along just fine."

"Oh, I'm sorry." Sheila's voice was as soft as down feathers, her eyes deep blue pools of concern.

"Hey, let's not get maudlin." Buckley ground the cigarette into a black ceramic ashtray. "Christ, it's tough enough to keep up with Dan's mood swings.

"A little morning java to get a kick start." He pushed his plastic cup toward Sheila and she poured carefully.

They sipped quietly for a few moments. Buckley studied Sheila with measured nonchalance. Somehow, she seemed too smooth, too articulate, to be a junior secretary. Yet maybe he was weighing her against the bronchial rasps of Caitlin O'Malley. God, when he heard that Caitlin was knocked up, he had felt like sending the guy a case of scotch.

"Judy filled me in on your background," Buckley said, "tells me you were a drama major at Northwestern, then went to New York to take the Great White Way by storm."

"Well, she exaggerated." Sheila took a sip of coffee. "I realized early in the game, too many starvin' actresses and too many liaisons that led nowhere." Her eyes narrowed in mock scrutiny. "I learned to type back in high school, so I took a crash course to bone up on dictation and the word processor."

"Well, you're fitting right in." Buckley smiled. "Judy likes you. Sheridan's a bit gruff, but he thinks you're a gem. I can tell." Again there was a slight pinkening in Sheila's creamy cheeks. Buckley liked that. Damn, the girl's looks grew on you!

She doesn't handle compliments too well, he thought. Not like a lot of Irish girls he knew. Yet, there was a calmness about her, and when you spoke to her, she looked you in the eye and listened, as if what you were saying was the most important thing in the world. Again, unlike a lot of Irish girls he knew.

"Does Dan have a girlfriend?" Sheila asked as casually as she could manage. She was intrigued by her boss, and not entirely because he was a suspect, she realized. She liked his comfortable rumpled look, his combative face and stance. He had been pointedly courteous and formal with her, nothing more.

"Oh, he goes out with a few predators who'd love to tie the knot. But Dan's too straight to lead them on, so those relationships seem to die pretty quickly.

"He may have someone we don't know about." Buckley had a bemused look. He noticed the sudden little look of surprise on Sheila's face. "Every Wednesday or Thursday afternoon, he disappears and comes back to the office late. Judy thinks he's seeing someone on the North Shore. Could be a long nooner. Dan comes back all pumped up. But it's kind of a mystery. He never volunteers where he goes, and somehow we don't dare ask him."

"How about you, O'Brien"—Buckley waved his almost-empty cup in her direction—"any romantic entanglements?"

"The usual crushes," she said. "All the good guys seem to be married. And I'm not going that route."

Before Buckley could make his move, Judy Corwin poked her head in the door. "Good morning," she said. "You two discussing the verities of the law?"

"Hey." Buckley grinned at Corwin. "You know, it was so cold outside this morning, I saw a lawyer with his hand in his own pocket."

"No more lawyer jokes." Judy pursed her lips in feigned disapproval. "Come on, the shop whistle is about to blow. Dan's got that breaking and entering case over in Chelsea and the Fergusons are coming in at ten."

"Oh shit—excuse me, Sheila—almost forgot about them! Jesus, Judy, have you got their answers to the interrogatories prepared?"

"I have. Their depositions are scheduled for Friday at Cranston, Moore and Mudge."

"And Dillard is due in at noon," Judy continued. "If Dan's not back, take him to lunch at Lazzarie's and Dan will join you later."

Sheila gathered up the coffee cups and put the lid on the urn, pretending not to listen.

"Goddamned strange." Brian Loughlin took off his earphones. "Sheridan seems to be out to save the rain forest and Callahan's remembering everyone in his prayers. No one seems to be talking shop or making a living. . . . What do you think?" He looked quizzically at his two FBI associates. "Well," one said, "the other teams are hitting pay dirt. The mob lawyer Catalano tells a witness who's been subpoenaed before a federal grand jury to clam up, take a dive if necessary. We have it all on tape.

"And Barry Ginsberg fell for a sting involving flipping commercial buildings in the North End. Creating straw buyers to inflate market value, then securing hefty bank mortgages. The land appraiser was one of our guys. We got Ginsberg pretty good—bank fraud, RICO violations, wire fraud, laundering, you name it."

"We already secured the magistrate's approval to plant bugs in their offices. Sometimes over the phone"—Loughlin spread his hand and wiggled it—"*mezza mezza,* but the real stuff comes behind closed doors.

"You guys go on out for lunch," he said as he replaced the earphones. "I'll keep the watch. Hope Sheila's having more productivity than we seem to be getting." He waved as they left.

We'll nail Sheridan and Callahan, he said to himself. Just a matter of time.

"It says here his name is Sebastian Simeone and he's coming up from New York with the family papers on Angela Simeone Williams. Claims he's her brother and the family wants the body released for cremation." Kristina Collins delivered the faxed message to Neil Harrington.

"Well, we can't keep the body on ice forever," Harrington said.

"Have this guy and his papers checked out by Mayan. If everything is in order, tell McCafferty to release the body, but I want the cricoid cartilage and stomach preserved as state's evidence. Better still, have this Simeone guy see me rather than Mayan." Collins jotted the instructions in her notebook.

"I understand someone's en route to pick up Williams's cadaver." McCafferty took a last puff on his cigarette, then tossed it into a soapstone tub, where it sputtered, then died. "Been here over two weeks." He nodded toward the steel cases.

Karen Steadman was spraying the stone table with a small hose. A new body was due in fifteen minutes and she was getting used to the routine with much less apprehension. In fact, she was a veteran of five autopsies. And she seemed to be getting used to McCafferty, particularly his off-color stories. Some bordered on the macabre, but not without a touch of humor.

"If Harrington gives the okay, then we release the body to whoever calls; it's usually some local undertaker.

"We'll take the necessary forensic photographs and freeze the cricoid cartilage, stomach, and lower intestines."

"I read your report," Karen Steadman said quietly as she turned the spigot, shutting down the hose.

"I don't know how I missed that fracture, but I guess I did," McCafferty said, shaking his head. "Of course, the neck is the no-man's-land of the autopsy." He hadn't mentioned pathologist Gellis or the fact that he had gone along with Gellis's finding of petechial hemorrhaging in the neck musculature. Even now he harbored doubts that a fracture that small—less than half an inch—could be trauma-related. And there was no way to be sure the minute hemorrhaging predated or postdated the actual death. He gathered that the DA was basing his case on the lack of stomach contents. He knew Dillard only by reputation, but if Dillard was somehow involved, McCafferty doubted he'd been the perpetrator. That just didn't ring true. Every doctor knew of numerous ways to kill someone without leaving a trace. And there were methods of disposing of bodies so that they would never be found. Dillard was too smart to lie about the dinner. But then again, that wasn't McCafferty's department.

"Well, from what I hear, this Williams woman's boyfriend claimed he dined with her the evening she was found. In fact, he was the last one to see her alive."

Karen Steadman could fill in the details. She looked quizzically at McCafferty.

"Yeah," McCafferty said, "no evidence she had consumed anything that day or evening. They'll try to hang the boyfriend on that alone. And he has no alibi. They'll seek an indictment. Ever been to court, Karen?"

"Only for a speeding ticket back in Wichita."

"Well, Harrington's a shark when it comes to criminal prosecutions. And d'Ortega's a piranha.

"I don't think you'll be asked to testify, Karen, but I'll have to relate my findings, cause and time of death."

Again Karen said nothing. She tied her blue rubber apron around her waist and reached for her latex cap. She knew McCafferty had changed his report on the cause of death from cause unknown to asphyxiation by strangulation and it bothered her, but that wasn't her responsibility. She slipped on the cap. They could hear the gurney wheels squeaking along the corridor with the next case.

"This is a five-year-old"—McCafferty studied the chart—"battered child." He shook his head. "This won't be pretty."

The old queasiness returned to the pit of Karen's stomach.

"You okay, Karen?"

"Yes, I'm okay," she said grimly as she tucked her hair up into her cap. But it was no good. She knew she would always react like this. She thought about it. Maybe she could still switch fields. Yes. This would be her last autopsy.

Two hours later, Karen Steadman untied her rubber apron and tossed it into the white canvas receptacle. It had been a long day, but somehow she had weathered it. The last post had been brutal, a little boy, stabbed, beaten. She held her breath to choke back tears and nausea. McCafferty had gone. She glanced at the wall clock. It was 7:05 P.M. and she was about to snap off the lights and head for home, but she hesitated. Something continued to bother her. Why had McCafferty changed his report?

Karen walked over to the bank of steel drawers, unlocked the case containing Angela Williams's corpse, and slowly slid it open. Icy vapors seeped from the vault and billowed toward the floor.

The stillness was eerie. But the body, altered by McCafferty's postmortem, still possessed dignity and heart-stopping beauty.

She snapped on the overhead kettledrum lights and adjusted them to focus on Angela's body. Taking a scalpel and spreader from a nearby cabinet, she gently sliced open the neck viscera, following McCafferty's incisional lines. She peered into the neck musculature, poking around the scalenes, the sterno grouping, the longus capitus, longus colli. There was evidence of minute hemorrhaging, but this could have been caused by McCafferty's post. There was no evidence that this was traumatically induced, no other sign of tissue damage. She found the plastic envelope nearby in the freezer and inspected the glistening white thyroid cartilage, then the ring-shaped cricoid just below it. Sure enough, there was a small jagged fissure. She measured it—1.1 centimeters—less than half an inch. At most, it was a nick and could have been made inadvertently by McCafferty. Then returning to the body she resutured the neck and slid the case back into the vault and snapped the lock on the small steel door. Her memory was correct. There had been no visible sign of injury, no hemorrhaging of the eyelids or conjunctivae. There was nothing to support McCafferty's change of diagnosis.

But there was no getting around the fact that Williams was dead and someone had gone to a great deal of trouble to dispose of the body. As McCafferty had said, Williams didn't walk up there. She was dumped.

Karen put the knife and spreader in the sterilizer. She glanced at the rows of steel cases, tiered three deep, oddly satisfied with the work she had just completed. She was suddenly proud of her professionalism.

Well, someone has to do this, she thought. And the pay wasn't bad and she didn't have to hustle for patients. Maybe she'd hang in for a while, after all. Get her government loan paid off. And a new assistant was due in a few days—Stanford Med, good-looking. She'd spotted his picture on the bulletin board. But why would a Stanford grad settle for being a pathologist? Maybe he's a little crazy, too.

She left by the back way, climbing the narrow metal staircase.

Each step resounded with a thunking echo through the vaultlike basement. She sighed with relief as she pushed open the frosted glass door leading to the white-tiled corridor. It was deserted except for two nurses walking ahead, one pushing a medicine cart.

Karen stopped at a pay phone to call her roommate. A raincoated figure with his collar turned up appeared at the end of the hallway and made his way toward her. She turned to place a quarter in the slot and saw the man hesitate briefly at the basement door. Then he pulled it open and entered. Karen could hear the hollow reverberations as he descended the stairs that led to the morgue. She knew she had locked the door, so he wouldn't be able to get in.

She had only a glimpse of the man, but she was sure she'd seen him before. Her fingers did a little dance on top of the phone casing as she let the dial tone drone on. She searched her memory. Yes, she had seen that man in a recent photo. She wasn't certain, but she thought he looked like the district attorney, Neil Harrington. She continued to wait. Minutes went by. The man did not reappear.

18

NEIL HARRINGTON clicked on the switch under his desk, opened the middle drawer, and watched the spools on the tape recorder winding into position. He closed the drawer quietly. He enunciated slowly and clearly as he dictated the date and time.

"Tell Mr. Simeone to come in," he told Kristina Collins over the intercom.

Kristina entered, hesitating at the door. "Mr. Harrington, this is Mr. Sebastian Simeone from New York," she said briskly.

Harrington was signing some correspondence and continued for several seconds without looking up, leaving his secretary and the visitor standing at the door.

"Oh." Harrington raised his head, as if suddenly aware he had company. "Please, do come in, Mr. Simeone." He stood up and walked from behind his desk. "I'm awfully sorry." His voice was grave as he extended his hand. "I understand you were the deceased's brother," he said as they shook hands. Kristina backed away and closed the door quietly.

Harrington quickly assessed his visitor. He was not what he had expected. He looked Latin, in his midforties, with early-graying black hair and gray-blue eyes, a soft-featured, almost old-padre countenance. Impeccably attired, he could easily pass for Williams's brother.

"Here, sit down." Harrington gestured toward the burgundy leather couch.

"Thank you." His voice was soft, his English perfect, with a hint of Spanish courtliness.

"It was a tragedy." Simeone shook his head. "The family is . . . uh, well, you know. She was such a beautiful person."

"I'm sure," Harrington said.

"Well"—Simeone reached into a valise that he had placed on the floor—"I have all the necessary papers certified by Kings County Probate Court in New York, signed by her mother and Juan

Simeone, her father, in Roseau, Dominica, British West Indies. Of course, Juan is my father, too."

He passed Harrington several documents: birth certificate, baptismal certificate, all bound with a red ribbon, notarized by a queen's counselor in the British West Indies.

"Where did your sister get the name Williams?" Harrington studied the documents. "Your mother's maiden name was Chichari."

"She was my stepmother," Simeone said. "Pure-blooded Carib Indian. Only some six hundred are left. Almost all live on a reservation in Morne Diablotin, Dominica. My father came from Cordova, Spain. He fought against Franco."

"Okay." Harrington flicked his wrist, snapping his fingers against the papers and cutting short the genealogy. "The probate judge has certified that you are the legal administrator of the deceased's estate. I assume Williams was her—as we say in this country—her stage name."

Simeone nodded.

Harrington perused the documents for a few more moments. The embossed seal of the state of New York looked genuine.

"All right, Mr. Simeone. I think your papers are in order. Now, what can I do for you?" (Find Angela's killer. Give me ten seconds with him and I'll tear his heart out. This is what Harrington expected to hear him say.)

"If you could, Señor Harrington"—Simeone's use of Spanish was deliberate, the title a sign of old-world deference—"release the body of my sister to me so we can return her ashes to Dominica."

"Of course," Harrington said, relieved. "But just to make everything legal—because you know the death is still under investigation—please sign this release." He handed a document to Simeone, then a pen.

Simeone read it slowly, then nodded his assent and scrawled his signature.

"Why don't you get in touch with Clancy Brothers Funeral Home here in Boston. It's in the book. Give them the death certificate. Have them call Miss Collins, my secretary, tomorrow. Tell them to pick up the body—I mean, your sister. You'll have my okay."

Harrington eyed his visitor critically. "Tell me, Mr. Simeone, your business card lists you as Simeone Imports, Five-seven-five Avenue of the Americas, New York. You are the proprietor?"

"That's right." Simeone handed the pen back and slid the release form toward Harrington.

"What kind of imports do you handle?" Harrington picked up the pen.

"Artwork mainly—Roman, Grecian, Tang dynasty, the pre-Columbian Mesoamerican culture. If you're interested . . ."

"No. I'm afraid I go in for nonclassical antiques. Ship lanterns—cracker-barrel auction stuff is more my style."

Simeone gave a half smile.

"Your sister"—Harrington turned the pen slowly in his fingers, studying the point as if he was examining a rare jewel—"was she also engaged in the art trade?"

"Yes." Simeone nodded. "She was a junior curator at the Prado in Madrid for a year. Because of that experience, she had many international accounts." Simeone's eyes misted and he took out his pocket handkerchief, then dabbed gently. "I'm sorry," he said softly. "She was my only sister. . . . Have you any idea who might have done this?"

"I can't discuss the investigation, Mr. Simeone, but we feel fairly confident of an indictment and conviction."

Harrington picked up the probate documents and held them by the edges with the palms of both hands. He tapped the papers on his desk briskly, squaring the corners with his fingers. "I think things are in order. We'll have to retain certain anatomical structures for evidentiary purposes." Harrington pointed to the release. "It's all been spelled out."

"I understand." Simeone tucked the handkerchief back into his breast pocket.

Harrington put the pen back in the holder and glanced at his watch. Simeone took the hint and rose. They shook hands.

"I'll have someone from the funeral home call your secretary tomorrow."

The two men shook hands again.

Kristina Collins showed Mr. Simeone to the door. "Thank you." He bowed slightly. "You and Mr. Harrington have been most kind."

Harrington picked up the release that Simeone had signed by one of its corners, as if he was handling an explosive. In a way, he was. The paper was fully sensitized. Only Simeone's prints would be exposed. It would be immediately transmitted to the FBI lab in Washington, and if necessary, to Interpol and Scotland Yard.

Prints on Angela Williams had come back negative. But maybe they'd get a line on the courtly Castilian.

Dan Sheridan gave Manny Raimondi an envelope with five one-hundred-dollar bills inside. This was the walking-around money, petty cash, payments to be distributed on the street, which Sheridan never inquired about. A C note to Mrs. McGillicuddy, who happened to witness an accident, for example. She'd be credible. "The defendant was exceeding the speed limit when he hit Mr. Sheridan's client. I was just coming from the seven A.M. Mass at St. Brendan's," she said. "Had a clear view from the top of the steps. That fella was going lickety-split." Somehow the breezy slang sounded more persuasive in front of a jury than a precise "fifty-three miles per hour."

"Did you get the word to Callahan about the phone taps?" Sheridan asked.

"Sure did." Raimondi creased the envelope into his wallet.

"You have to make many calls?"

"Not a one." Raimondi smiled.

"Okay?" Sheridan looked quizzically at Raimondi.

"I cut out some newspaper print. 'Your phones are tapped. A friend.' Cost me a twenty-nine-cent stamp."

"Not bad." Sheridan grinned. "Remind me to tell Judy you're due for a raise."

Neither laughed. They knew they had some real problems.

"What about the Williams woman? What do you hear?"

"She was a high roller. I'm not so sure you want this case." Raimondi's eyes turned stony.

"Manny"—Sheridan returned the gaze—"the practice of law isn't always a piece of cake. Christ, Dillard is a defense lawyer's dream. If he's guilty, he goes to the slammer. If he's innocent, he walks. Either way, he pays us."

But both knew it wasn't quite that simple.

"Who in the hell was this woman?" Sheridan frowned.

"She was into the international arts trade. Greco-Roman—you know, Neptune brandishing the trident, Eros tapping Aphrodite on the shoulder. That's the veneer. But there's something else. It may be drugs—I'm not sure. I've got a contact down in Fall River—Portugee like me.''

"Do you think Dillard is mixed up in drugs?"

"That, I don't know. But there's something that bothers me about the Williams woman.''

"Something bothers me, too. She might have been the greatest piece of ass who ever lived," Sheridan said. "A lot of guys have sold their souls for less. But Dillard isn't that dumb. He *knew* Williams. He passed the lie detector. There's got to be something else.''

"I'll see what I can find out," Manny said.

"Okay." Sheridan clapped Raimondi's shoulder. "Those sensors you put on the phones are like ultraviolet. And here." Sheridan gave Raimondi an extra five hundred from his wallet.

"Boss, on the phones, just keep blowin' smoke up their ass." Raimondi smiled. It was Christmas in April.

"I'll be up at Lazzarie's," Sheridan said to Sheila O'Brien as she passed him a sheaf of messages. She noticed the knuckles on his right hand were bruised.

"Can I get you some ointment for that?" she said, pointing to his hand. "Maybe a Band-Aid?"

He grinned. "Oh, it's nothing. Bashed my hand playing racquetball the other day."

She nodded. Their eyes held for a moment. Sheridan picked up his briefcase. "Got to meet young Buckley for lunch," he said. "We have a new client who got himself into a little hot water."

"Is it Dr. Dillard?" Sheila looked at the diary on the reception desk.

"Yes, the famous Dr. Dillard. We'll be working with him quite closely over the next few weeks. . . . I'll be back by two."

Sheila O'Brien watched Sheridan depart. She liked his presence, the forward lean of his stride, the square cut of his jaw, even his pug nose—broken more than a few times in past encounters, she would guess. And somehow she knew the bruised knuckles hadn't come from racquetball.

*   *   *

"This is perfect," Agent Loughlin said as he took a peek through
the high-resolution video camera aimed at the eleventh floor of the
Tremont Building and Dan Sheridan's reception area. He could
see Sheila O'Brien clearly. She had tweaked the vertical blinds into
the open position. He had seen her chatting with Dan Sheridan,
could almost decipher their conversation. And if need be, by sophisticated computer, the FBI technicians could do just that.

They had leased a small office across the street with a commanding view of Tremont Street, from which they could monitor the
comings and goings. But the shots didn't include Sheridan's inner
office. For that, they'd need a court order. That would come.

Loughlin focused in on Sheila O'Brien. He watched her typing
on a word processor. Judy Corwin came into view. They seemed to
be chatting easily. Good. It was important for Sheila to fit in with
the rest of the staff.

Sheridan passed the headwaiter a twenty-dollar bill. "Dom," he
said, pointing to a rear booth where Tom Buckley and Dr. Dillard
were seated, "put a reserved card on the booth next to us. We have
a business meeting and we'd like a little privacy." Dom snapped his
fingers and another waiter appeared and led Sheridan to his table.
Dom trailed and immediately cleared the adjoining booth, placing
the reserved card in the center of the table.

Dillard looked disheveled. He was wearing a blue blazer, a polo shirt
open at the neck, and rumpled khaki pants. His eyes were puffy.

"I have a retainer here." Dillard reached into his inside coat
pocket, extracted an envelope, and pushed it toward Sheridan.
"Twenty thousand dollars."

Sheridan picked it up without looking inside, snapped open his
briefcase, and tucked it into a folder. "Fine," he said.

Dillard looked around. "Can't we hold our discussions in less
public surroundings? Your office, perhaps, or mine?" he asked.

"For the moment, this is probably as private as we can get,"
Sheridan said. "You know your telephones are tapped—probably
your home as well as your office."

The waiter appeared and they ordered drinks. Then Sheridan
waved the man away. "Give us a few more moments."

He left menus and discreetly withdrew.

"Your Mr. Raimondi gave me a note to that effect," Dillard said. "I haven't really used the phones for several days."

"Well, don't stop using them," Sheridan said. "All I know for sure is that mine are wired. But keep following a routine. If our phone calls suddenly dry up, that'll tip the snoopers that we're on to them. We're goddamned lucky we found out."

"But who's doing the snooping?" Dillard's brow furrowed with concern.

"I'm not going into the whole scenario—let's just say I found out."

Sheridan smoothed an imaginary wrinkle in the tablecloth, then looked at Dillard. "Where does Sonny Callahan fit in?"

"I'm friendly with Callahan," Dillard said. "He's a contributor to several Boston charities I support. In fact, we cochaired the Cardinal's Appeal for the Inner City last December. One of Angela's companies catered the affair."

"Look"—Sheridan buttered a piece of a roll but still eyed Dillard—"I might give this retainer right back to you. Why should I get mixed up with the feds?"

"The feds?"

Young Buckley took a good swallow of his scotch.

"Let me tell you what I think," Sheridan said. "I think Callahan is mixed up with the IRA somehow—I mean the hard-liners. He sends money—*real* money—to certain factions in Northern Ireland. Now where does Sonny Callahan get all this loot?"

"Well, what difference does it make what group he supports?" Dillard began.

"Let me finish," Sheridan said curtly. "Sonny doesn't make it all from his laundries or condos. Times are tough and Callahan has taken a bath, just like every other developer around these parts.

"No, I think Sonny makes it in the drug trade—cocaine, you name it."

"What makes you think that?" Dillard lowered his voice and looked around the room, which now hummed with activity.

"Oh, I don't imagine Sonny deals in it himself," Sheridan said. "He's too smart for that. Others do the actual trucking. Sonny keeps the books, skims his share of the proceeds, and sends the rest to the IRA."

"Well, how does this concern me?" Dillard looked puzzled.

"I think it has something to do with Angela Williams's murder," Sheridan said. "That's why your lines and mine are bugged—and maybe Sonny Callahan's. Williams was somehow mixed up with Callahan."

"Okay." Dillard issued a tired sigh. "Can I tell you something in strictest confidence?"

"What you tell us now," Buckley said, "is privileged—like the seal of the confessional."

Sheridan shook his head vigorously. "No, that's not entirely correct," he said. "You tell me you snuffed Williams or had her killed, I give you back your retainer and we walk out of here right now. We won't even pick up the bill."

"I understand that. First, let me assure you I didn't kill Angela. I loved Angela. I was like a father to her."

"Do you know who did kill her?"

"If I knew that, I'd take matters into my own hands." Dillard's confidence seemed to return.

"Well, let's suppose that Angela Williams was a courier." Sheridan took a deep swallow of bourbon. "She'd carry cash from point A to point B, from certain parties in this country, say New York City art aficionados, to certain organizations in Paris, for example, or Madrid, London, Amsterdam, whatever. She'd pay cash for a statue of Romulus and Remus or for an Old Master. Back it would come. How did she know it was a fake? Where the money went after the exchange wasn't her concern. She wasn't Mother Teresa."

"I understand what you're implying, Mr. Sheridan. You think I'm somehow mixed up with these transactions."

"No, I didn't say that. All I know is that Sonny Callahan came into my office with a satchel of bribe money. Thought somehow I could get to the DA and have things melt away.

"Here's the way I see it." Sheridan took another sip of bourbon. "You knew Angela Williams—okay, like a father. You weren't screwing her. You sponsored her. She knew you. You knew Callahan. She knew Callahan. She traveled. She dropped francs, pesos, pounds, and marks off at various locales. Then for some reason, she was scratched. Time of death, according to two pathologists, was nine P.M. Cause: asphyxiation. Manner of death: Someone put his hands around her neck slowly, compressing the carotid arteries. No external signs of injury. You and Callahan are charitable bedfellows.

Angela Williams was probably skimming. You have no alibi. You dined with her. No stomach contents."

Dillard started to speak.

"I know, I know," Sheridan said. "She was bulimic, like the old Romans. Tossed her cookies right after she saw you to the door. And you passed the lie detector."

"Well, maybe I should get other counsel." Dillard started to rise.

"Sit down, goddamn it! We're probably all headed for hell. But you're my client and I'll do everything within my power to defend you."

"Hey," Buckley said, "I think we'll see a few of our fellow practitioners down there."

Sheridan wasn't amused. He tapped Buckley's glass with a fork. "Call Harrington's office and set up a meeting. And listen, Doc, you do as I say from now on in. Got that?"

Dillard nodded.

"Get Steinmetz's affidavit," he said to Buckley. "It's time to cut a deal." He motioned toward the waiter and picked up the menu. "You know, this is a classy place; even the hamburgers have Italian names."

"I'll drink to that!" Buckley saluted with his glass and then downed the remainder of his scotch.

Sheila O'Brien watched Manny Raimondi as he stood next to the window and looked out at Tremont Street, straight into the building across the street. He was hunched forward, hands on the sill, arms splayed, and seemed to be surveying right and left, up and down. For a moment, she stopped typing.

He turned and noticed Sheila looking at him. Both were a little embarrassed.

"Great view from here," he said. "Down there in that plot across the street are Paul Revere, John Hancock, Sam Adams, even Mother Goose."

"Mother Goose? I thought that was a nursery-rhyme character."

"Well, that's what they tell me." Raimondi smiled, a cryptic, Portuguese, "don't trust anyone but your own kind" sort of smile.

"You're the firm's investigator," she said, more a statement than an inquiry.

"And you're Buckley's new secretary." The courteous smile broadened, revealing even white teeth.

"Raimondi," he said, extending his hand. She gripped it warmly.

"I'm Sheila O'Brien. I was hired by Judy Corwin."

"She has good taste," Raimondi said. "Sheeelah O'Brien," he said, drawing it out. "As we say in Portuguese, *Raios partam, os Irlaneeses, sao mais que muitos agiu.*"

"What does that mean?" She laughed.

"It's a little obscene." He grinned. "Something like, 'There're too many goddamned micks around here.' The expletive might be a little too gentle. Thank God for Judy Corwin."

Sheila liked the banter. Good-natured camaraderie. The practice of law in the trenches. A more easygoing world than the bureau. She thought about it. Would she miss the hard-edged excitement of the covert part of that world? She thought she would.

Raimondi returned to the window. Somehow she sensed he wasn't taking in the gravestones of Paul Revere and Mother Goose.

19

SHEILA called Brian Loughlin from the lobby pay phone.

It was Thursday. "Dan Sheridan just told me he'd be out of the office from one on. It's that mystery trip he takes. He cleared the diary. Buckley will handle the clients."

"We may be on to something. Do you think you can handle it, Sheila?"

"Certainly I can handle it," she said, a little annoyed.

"Sheridan's car is a red Le Baron, license plate K-one-zero-seven-five; he parks it in the Beacon Hill garage."

"Have a car left for me, telephonically equipped, at a parking meter on Tremont Street at the corner of State. Sheridan can make only a left turn there, so he'll have to come right by me."

"No problem with getting the afternoon off?"

"I told Judy Corwin that my aunt was coming in from Milwaukee and I had to meet her at one at Logan Airport. I've really been boiling the work out, so she even told me to take Friday off if I needed it. I've got carte blanche."

"Okay," Loughlin said, "you'll be driving a beige Ford Taurus, Mass registration eight-nine-six-five-three-one. Keys will be in the glove compartment. It'll be equipped with a telephone but no exterior antenna. Hit the buttons on the side—six-five-nine-zero—to open the driver's door."

"Six-five-nine-zero. Got it."

"You sure you don't want Agent Walsh to ride shotgun?"

"No, I'll just tail several car lengths back. If I think Sheridan is on to me, I'll speed by in the passing lane and discontinue. The registration—who's listed as the owner?"

"A fictitious name and address in Jamaica Plain. Sure Sheridan won't recognize you?"

"You should see the getup. I'll look like Mother Machree; Mae Craig hat, pinch glasses, the whole bit. Right out of central casting. Northwestern Drama pays off again!"

"Okay, just zero in on the general location, and don't do any-

thing rash. Keep checking with us. You could blow the whole operation, and there'd be hell to pay with Justice."

"I understand. I'll get coordinates today and you guys can take
over next week, assuming he sticks to his usual schedule."

"If he's meeting with some mob figures or guys on the DEA list,
this'll clinch the probable cause for the surveillance bug."

"What are you getting over the taps?" Sheila checked her watch:
11:35.

"That's what's odd," said Loughlin. "We're coming up with zeros."

"Well, I've got to run."

"Don't tail too close—just get the geography down. There'll be
a pair of binoculars under the driver's seat—strongest power we
have. You can see a fly blink its eyes a mile away."

"Okay, Bri, over and out."

Sheridan drove his red Le Baron from the underground garage,
turned onto Tremont Street, then headed for the Faneuil Hall Mar-
ketplace. The acacia trees lining the Washington Mall were sprout-
ing new spring greens and the pushcart vendors along the way were
doing a brisk lunch-hour business. Sheridan turned onto Atlantic
Avenue, then sped up the ramp toward the Tobin Bridge, headed
north.

Early-afternoon traffic was moderate and Sheila O'Brien eased
into the right lane some five car lengths back. She punched a green
button, which immediately programmed into Brian Loughlin's receiver. "I'm headed over the Tobin Bridge. Subject's car is in right-
lane traffic some five car lengths ahead."

"I'd give it a little more distance," Loughlin said. "Keep in the
same lane. Put several vehicles in between."

"Will do," Sheila responded. "Looks like we're headed toward
Saugus and points north."

"Check in every twenty minutes," Loughlin said.

"Roger." Sheila pressed the discon button, keeping her eyes
trained straight ahead. Sheridan seemed in no rush—forty-five mph
in a fifty-mph zone.

Fifteen minutes later, they were on Route 1's famous strip—a collection of Pizza Huts, used-car lots, miniature golf courses, cinder-block motels, bars, and strip joints, all squashed together in a garish roadside jumble.

Sheridan kept in the right lane, his Le Baron easily identifiable some fifty yards ahead on the four-lane highway. Almost twenty miles north of Boston, a green roadside sign spelled out BROOK-FIELD in white lettering. Sheila reported her position, noting that Sheridan was slowing to make a right turn onto Route 129, headed northeast. Sheila decelerated and dropped back about a hundred yards. Several cars also exiting from Route 1 passed her.

Route 129 was a rural roadway, two lanes, rather bucolic; small farmhouses and weathered barns and silos dotted the rolling countryside. Sheila dropped back still farther. Things could now get tricky.

She spotted another sign: BROOKFIELD TOWN CENTER TWO MILES. Sheridan's Le Baron was ahead by a good city block. Sheila reached under the seat and pulled out the binoculars to take a quick look as Sheridan's car eased around a gentle curve. The powerful magnification brought the image hurtling into her face and, startled momentarily, she almost hit the brake, thinking she would broadside Sheridan's car. It was as if she was riding in his passenger seat. She could even make out the crow's-feet near Sheridan's eyes and the slight bruise marks on his knuckles as he gripped the steering wheel. She fell farther back now, maybe two hundred yards. Five or six cars were in between.

Suddenly, Sheridan made a turn into a Texaco station. Sheila drifted ahead, maneuvering around a small traffic circle that housed a bandstand, and parked in front of a two-story clapboard building with a sign that read BROOKFIELD TOWN HALL. She kept the motor idling as she surveyed the gas station a couple of football fields distant. The binoculars brought the scene into pinpoint range.

Sheridan was talking to the attendant, who put a nozzle in the Le Baron's gas tank, then pointed toward the side of the station. Sheridan reached into the backseat and extracted a large duffel bag, then proceeded to what Sheila could discern was the men's room.

"This is O'Brien," she said over the cellular phone. "It's one-ten P.M. I'm parked in front of the Brookfield Town Hall, about twenty-two miles north of Boston. Sheridan has stopped for gas. He's gone to the men's room."

"Brookfield," Loughlin said. He paused a few seconds. "Okay, we've got it. Any problems thus far?"

"Negative. And, man, are these optics something. If I stood up, I could read the mileage on Sheridan's dash. This seems to be the rendezvous. I'll check in when Sheridan finally lands."

"Just get the street and address. Nothing further. Then discontinue." Loughlin's raspy voice was hoarse with concern. "We'll take over from there. Agents Kerry and Walsh are just turning onto Route One twenty-nine. They've been in on all these communiqués."

"They have?" Sheila was momentarily angry. "Nice of you to tell me." Did they think the little girl needed a bodyguard? Or a brain?

"I'll check in when Sheridan drives off. Over and out."

Five minutes grew into ten. The attendant had replaced the hose, popped the hood, checked the oil, wiped the windshield, and was propped up on a chair in the station when Sheridan reappeared. She lifted the binoculars again.

Sheridan was wearing a baseball uniform, red cap, pinstripes, red stockings, maroon warm-up jacket. Cleats were slung over his shoulder and obviously his business suit was packed in the duffel bag.

"What the . . . ?" she muttered to herself. She saw Sheridan's broad smile as he handed the attendant a twenty-dollar bill. "Keep the change." She could read his lips. The two men exchanged smiles. Sheridan threw his duffel bag into the backseat and tossed his cleats in on the passenger side, slid behind the wheel, and started off. He made a turn at the traffic circle and sped past her position. She quickly looked in the mirror and adjusted her gray wig and hat. Good God, she thought, he must be a Little League coach. And to have gone through all this!

She couldn't suppress a wide grin. They'd been playing cops and robbers over a perfectly innocent activity.

She eased into traffic and followed Sheridan as he made a right turn and continued several tree-lined blocks to a park where half a dozen cars had pulled up near the tennis courts. JOSHUA THAYER PARK read a weathered sign badly in need of paint. But the park itself was trim, with a football field off to the left and on the far side a baseball diamond, where several players were fielding ground balls and a few outfielders were catching flies launched by a practice hitter. Sheila pulled up alongside the tennis courts, where several women were volleying. She parked inconspicuously among a mix of Chevys, Fords, and station wagons. Then she spotted Sheridan, who had emerged from his Le Baron on the far side of the football field, jogging toward the diamond. This time, he was carrying a small canvas bag and a catcher's mitt.

She lifted her binoculars and homed in on the greetings. They were baseball players, all right, but this wasn't Little League. Sheridan looked to be the oldest, but the rest were at least college age, maybe older. Two umpires in blue were going over some ground rules at home plate. She thought for a moment that Sheridan was a manager. But no, he donned shin guards, buckled his chest protector, and proceeded to warm up a gangly pitcher. Several locals filtered into the stands. Sheridan whipped a toss to second base. "Play ball!" She could lip-synch the umpire.

A batter came out of the green wooden dugout, knocked dirt off his cleats, got in the box, and waved his bat a few times. Sheridan donned his mask, then squatted behind the plate. She could see two fingers signaling a curve. The lanky pitcher started his windup and Sheila O'Brien settled back to watch the Brookfield Giants battle the Gloucester Mariners.

Great fielding but not much hitting, although Sheridan had sent a long fly to deep center, then sprinted toward first base, until the fielder shagged the ball and sent him back to the dugout. Good legs, Sheila thought absently.

It was the bottom of the fifth before she finally remembered to check in.

"Sheila, for Christsakes! Where the hell have you been? We've been—"

"I'm sorry." She laughed. "It's ludicrous, really. Sheridan plays baseball. That's his big secret."

"What?" Loughlin didn't sound amused.

"He's a catcher on one of those semipro teams. Actually, he's quite good for a guy in his forties."

"Are you telling us this whole surveillance was a wild-goose chase?" Loughlin's voice was curt.

"That's what I'd call it." She almost giggled. As she spoke to Loughlin, she focused in with her binoculars.

Gloucester had a runner on second. No outs. He was a big rangy kid. Probably played linebacker in high school or college.

"Well, you could have told us where you were. Walsh and Kerry were scouring the place. . . . Are you telling us to discontinue?"

"Affirmative," she said as she twisted the binoculars' corrugated dial for a sharper focus.

The Brookfield pitcher seemed to groove it. The Gloucester runner was off and running. The thwack resounded along the football field and carried to the tennis courts. It was a line drive to center field. The runner charged around third, his cleats kicking up dirt.

It was a long throw from center—accurate, one hop, but obviously too late. She could see Sheridan blocking the plate, crouched and waiting. The runner churned it up a notch and put his shoulder down. There would be no slide. "The base paths belong to the base runner." Sheila recalled her father quoting Ty Cobb. Sheridan braced for the collision as the ball, the runner, and the crash came at the same time, but the runner missed the plate. Bowled over, Sheridan was stunned, but through some primal instinct he had held on to the ball. On his knees, Sheridan groped and put the tag on the runner, who was sprawled on the ground. The ump's thumb shot skyward. Then the runner lurched woozily to his feet, but Sheridan lay still. He was out cold.

Sheila felt her hands go clammy as they pressed against the grainy leather of the binocular casing. Her chest ached, tight and heavy, as if she'd gulped down too much ice cream too fast.

Surprised at the intensity of her reaction, she watched Sheridan's limp body until she heard the siren of an approaching ambulance. What was wrong with her? She was behaving like a kid with a crush. Sheridan was just part of her job.

She put the binoculars on the seat beside her and turned the ignition key.

Sheila followed the flashing blue lights of the ambulance to Brookfield Hospital, pulling up at the emergency ramp. She watched the

EMTs wheel Sheridan's inert form through the electronically controlled doors, then waited almost an hour before making a call on the cellular phone to inquire about his condition.

"He's listed as fair," came the nurse's voice. "He's been admitted. Dr. Thompkins is in charge. Right now, no visitors."

Sheila shrugged, pulled ahead through the emergency parking lot, and headed back toward Route 1.

"I'm okay, Doctor." Sheridan hoisted himself up in the bed and looked blearily at the three figures in white, addressing the one with the chart.

"You took quite a blow to the head." The doctor smiled. "CAT scans are negative. Babinski normal. No pathologic reflexes. A couple of days and you'll be up and around."

The doctor turned to the nurse. "Check vital signs every hour. Repeat CAT scans tomorrow morning. And here"—the doctor reached into his white smock and pulled out a baseball—"the boys said this was yours. I'll put it here on the tray."

"Doctor, many thanks." Sheridan blinked a few times as the figures came into focus. "But I'm really fine." He lifted the bedsheet. "I've got to get out of here."

"Not for a few days." Dr. Thompkins's face grew stern. "You have a cerebral concussion; you could have a delayed bleed, maybe a subdural hematoma."

"Where are my clothes?" Sheridan persisted.

"Hanging in the closet," a nurse said. "Your baseball gear is in your duffel bag—also in the closet."

"My car?"

"It was driven back to Boston by one of your teammates."

"Listen"—Sheridan swiveled his legs over the side of the bed—"I've an important case coming up tomorrow. I'm fine. Look." He spread his fingers out at eye level. "Five. I know where I am. I'll take a cab back to Boston."

"You should take it easy, Mr. Sheridan." The nurse tried to cajole him back into bed.

Sheridan stood up. "Look, no swaying. If I start getting woozy, I'll check myself into Mass General, I promise. It's a few blocks from where I live."

All of the professional courtliness seemed to drain from the doctor's demeanor. "I warn you, Mr. Sheridan. The risk is all yours. You'll sign out over my express objection."

"I understand." Sheridan walked to the closet and opened it. "Now, if you'll excuse me . . ." He pointed to his hospital johnny.

Dr. Thompkins emitted a long, exasperated sigh.

"Get him the release," he said to the nurse.

Manny Raimondi thought he'd spotted something on the eleventh floor, directly across the street from where he'd been talking to Sheila O'Brien. The vertical blinds seemed to rustle and there was a glint of something metallic. He knew the phones were tapped. Could be they were under other forms of surveillance, as well. He checked their own building's security and learned that the security across the street was serviced by Pinkerton and that the man now on duty was Jesus Santiago. He had lucked out.

"*Bon dea.*" Raimondi flashed a smile at Santiago. "I'm part of security myself," he said.

They exchanged greetings. Santiago was from Cape Verde, had a green card, hoped to become a citizen.

"Any office space available?"

"*Voce esta baincando?* Are you kidding?" Santiago shook his head. "We only got a few tenants. Glad I don't own the place."

"Anyone move in or out lately? We may want to pick up some lease that's gone belly-up."

"Just the other day—some movie guys moved in." Santiago checked his chart behind the control desk. "World Cinematics, Inc. Pretty good fellas. Hollywood types."

"Maybe I could get a job. Where are they located?"

Santiago checked his chart again. "Suite Eleven-oh-five. Suite— sheeet." He grinned. "It's only a small office fronting Tremont Street. They're the only tenants on the floor."

Raimondi checked the directory in the foyer on his way out. Sure enough, 1105 was occupied by World Cinematics, Inc. That left 1106 and 1104 vacant. He'd talk with Sheridan.

20

"OMIGOD!" Judy Corwin winced as Dan Sheridan entered.

Buckley poked his head out of his office. "Wow, what a shiner! Looks like you got whaled by a jealous husband!"

Sheridan managed a sheepish grin.

"Something like that," he said. "I was trying to make a fast getaway. Bumped into the car door."

He picked up his messages. Judy shook her head. Sheridan's reddened right eye was partially swollen shut, his cheek puffy with telltale blue-and-black splotches.

Sheila O'Brien came out of the file room.

"Oh." She appeared surprised to see Sheridan. "Are you all right?"

"Racquetball can get rough at times." He winked with his good eye. "Actually, my opponent whacked me pretty good, but I'll live. . . . Tom, can I see you for a few moments?"

Sheila watched them walk into Sheridan's office. When they had closed the door, she went into the photocopy room, walked to the window, and tweaked the blinds to the open position.

"My God," Judy Corwin called after her, "the boss looks like he got hit by a ten-wheeler. I don't know where he goes midweek, but I'll bet it has something to do with that black eye."

"At least he hasn't got any jury cases coming up," Sheila said, returning to the reception area.

"Well, thank God for that. But he has a few court appearances. In fact, here comes one now."

"Good morning." Judy turned and smiled at the two priests who were entering the reception area. Each wore a black suit and Roman collar and carried a gray raincoat.

"I'm Monsignor Flynn," the younger priest said, "and this is Father Duffy. Mr. Sheridan is expecting us."

"Please be seated." Judy Corwin took their coats. "I'll tell him you're here. It will just be a minute or two."

"Thank you," they replied, almost in unison.

Sheila O'Brien sized up the two men seated before her. Neither looked comfortable. The monsignor's lips were compressed in a look of grim concern. Father Duffy was ashen and his fingers drummed nervously on the arm of the brown Naugahyde couch.

"May I get you some coffee?" she inquired cheerily. She beamed at Father Duffy. He tried to force a smile in return, but it was wooden.

"No thanks," the monsignor answered for both.

Sheila nodded and resumed typing.

"Problems come in bunches." Sheridan looked in the mirror on the back of his closet door and dabbed his cheekbone with his index finger as he addressed Tommy Buckley.

"Our phones are tapped, so Raimondi dropped by last night. Thinks the feds got a shotgun camera across the street, aimed at our office. Wants to set up a listening post in an adjoining office. I gave him the okay."

Buckley merely nodded. They realized maybe they were getting in too deep. "At least we know about it. It's not as if we were defending whores and transvestites."

"Well, we've got a doozy coming in." Sheridan motioned toward his closed door. "Father Aloysius Duffy. Used to be a curate at Star of the Sea in Newburyport some twenty years ago. Seems he was giving extracurricular lessons to the altar boys. Now twenty years later, they're coming out of the woodwork. Auxiliary Bishop Dunn called me; wants us to do the best we can."

"Thank God it's not in Suffolk County. Harrington would bury us," Buckley said.

"Hey, Essex County isn't exactly the Land of Oz. The DA is Thad Hollingsworth—old Dartmouth grad whose seventeenth-century forebears burned witches whenever they got the chance."

"Is Duffy seeing a psychiatrist?" Buckley inquired.

"We'll soon find out."

"Judy." Sheridan buzzed on the intercom. "Have Monsignor Flynn and Father Duffy come in."

She appeared at the door and closed it quietly. "Here," she said, "put these on. Cost me six dollars at Walgreen." She handed Sheridan a pair of sunglasses.

"It's that bad?"

Both Buckley and Judy nodded.

Raimondi signed the lease for 1106, gave the manager a seven-hundred-dollar certified check for one month's rent.

"You have a five-hundred-dollar allowance for repairs and refurbishing," the manager said.

"That won't be necessary. We're an election survey group and we'll be moving out right after the city council primaries."

"You'll need lettering on your door."

"Fine!" Raimondi said. "But have the painter keep it simple. Ajax Surveys, just like it reads in the lease."

Raimondi took the elevator to the twelfth floor, then walked down to the eleventh. World Cinematics had no sign on the frosted glass door, but he could hear voices within. He unlocked the door to 1106 and stepped inside.

From the alcove, he could see a plain square room with fiberboard walls painted light green. Frayed beige broadloom carpeting ran wall to wall. Raimondi stuck a rubber attachment resembling a bathroom plunger to the wall, hooked on a stethoscopelike line, and placed the acoustical plugs in his ears. He fingered the wall. Probably only a sheet of plasterboard separated the two offices.

The voices were barely audible. He could only make out isolated phrases. "Got something coming in now." "Okay." . . . "No, things don't look right."

All male voices. No names. He continued to listen for the next hour. Nothing useful came across. He fingered the wall again. This wasn't going to work.

He checked the ceiling: waffled fiberboard squares, four feet by two. He stood on his tiptoes, pulled out a pen, and poked at one of the ceiling blocks. Sure enough, they were detachable. There was a square-grilled air duct in the ceiling near the wall, perhaps one by three feet. This weekend, Sunday maybe, he could poke around inside the ceiling. Maybe 1105 might have a similar setup. He'd thread the sneaky peeky through this duct and place it next to the one in 1105.

Raimondi left 1106 and was standing in front of the elevator door when Walsh and Loughlin came out of World Cinematics. All three tried to look nonchalant while waiting for the elevator to arrive.

"I forgot something," Loughlin suddenly said to Walsh, motioning toward his associate. They retreated toward Suite 1105 just as the elevator doors pinged open and Raimondi entered alone.

"Run the video," Loughlin said to the FBI technician.

They watched as the lens zoomed in on Sheridan's reception area. Sheila O'Brien sat at the computer. A man in a black leather jacket and dark corduroys was looking out of the front window. He stood there for several minutes—seemed to be looking right at their camera lens. He didn't look like a client, since at times he chatted with Judy Corwin and Sheila O'Brien. Then Thomas Buckley appeared and there was a further exchange before the man in the leather jacket entered Sheridan's private office, out of camera view.

"Run that sequence again, in still-frame," Loughlin said. The group watched closely.

Loughlin hunched forward as he sat at the control desk. He steepled his fingers under his chin.

"Hard to tell," he said to Agent Dave Walsh, "but that guy in the jacket looks a helluva lot like the man we just saw at the elevator." The technician backed up the tape and they viewed it again. "Dark hair, kind of dark skin," Walsh said. "Of course, the guy at the elevator had a gray suit, white shirt, blue tie. . . ."

"Who are the other tenants on the eleventh floor?"

"As far as I know, just us."

"Check to see if anyone has rented space up here," Loughlin said. "When we came in, the floor was vacant."

Judy Corwin ushered Monsignor Flynn and Father Duffy into Sheridan's office and laid a file on the desk.

"Monsignor, good to see you. Father Duffy . . . This is my partner, Tom Buckley." They shook hands.

"Sit down—and Judy, hold all calls." It was a sign of special courtesy, not lost on the monsignor. Father Duffy slumped in the chair, issuing a tired sigh.

"Monsignor Flynn gave me a narrative," Sheridan said. "As I understand it, Father Duffy, you were a curate at Star of the Sea in Newburyport—that was twenty-two years ago. And let's see, it was your third parish after graduating from the seminary."

"That's right." The monsignor spoke for Father Duffy.

"The other parishes—where were those?"

"St. Ann's in Quincy and Corpus Christi in Haverhill." Again, Monsignor Flynn answered for Father Duffy.

"I used to be an altar boy at St. Ann's," Buckley intervened. "Remember Father O'Connell? He was the pastor."

"A fine priest," the monsignor said. "Died of a broken heart, as we Irish say." A twinkle lightened Flynn's eyes. Even Father Duffy forced a wan smile. Both Buckley and the monsignor knew that Father O'Connell drank himself into oblivion, just after the cardinal replaced him.

"Any complaints at St. Ann's and Corpus Christi?"

"None so far," the monsignor answered.

"Where did you go after Star of the Sea?"

Monsignor Flynn spoke for Father Duffy yet again. "He was six years at Star of the Sea, then pastor for ten years at St. Theresa's in Fall River. He retired to St. Thomas's priest home in 1990."

"No other problems?"

The monsignor cleared his throat. "None that we're aware of."

"How old are you, Father?" Sheridan looked at the figure slumped before him.

The priest looked up. "I'm sixty-three. Sixty-four next week."

"Under any medical care?"

"I see Dr. Twomey over at St. Elizabeth's for my heart condition. Also, Dr. Kornberg for my . . . uh . . . psychiatric therapy."

Sheridan scribbled down both names.

"I'd like to get you over to Dr. John B. White. He's a Catholic psychiatrist whom I respect greatly," Sheridan said. "He understands these situations and knows the subtle nuances of our criminal justice system."

Both the monsignor and the priest nodded agreement.

"Your accusers," Sheridan said, "the former choirboys and one altar boy—they've waited twenty-two years to make charges. Any contact with any of them since you left Star of the Sea?"

Father Duffy shook his head. "No," he said quietly.

Sheridan had read the lurid accounts in the *Boston Herald*. The boys, now grown men, had feared to come forward earlier. They said their lives had been psychologically ruined.

"Can we talk quite frankly?" Sheridan looked first at the monsignor and then at Father Duffy.

"That's why we're here," said the monsignor.

"Are the allegations true, Father?" Sheridan signaled to the monsignor to let Father Duffy answer.

"I was foolish." Father Duffy's voice was halting. He cleared his throat. "Weak." His eyes were tear-filled.

"Were you under any medical treatment at Star of the Sea?"

"No," the priest volunteered.

Sheridan had all the information he needed.

"All right." He rose from behind his desk. "I'll see what I can do. Tom, give DA Hollingsworth a call. Tell him I want a meeting. "And"—he looked at the monsignor, then at Father Duffy— "call Dr. White today and make an appointment as soon as possible."

Sheridan walked over to Father Duffy. The old priest looked ten years older than when he had first come into the office. Sheridan clapped him on the shoulder. "We'll see what we can do, Padre," he said, his voice professionally confident—like an airline captain telling his passengers that they would soon encounter some bumpy weather.

Sheila O'Brien helped both priests on with their raincoats. She saw the residue of tears on Father Duffy's cheeks and surmised that the two clerics weren't in looking for a donation. It would be a tough case to defend, and unpopular. But Sheridan didn't seem to flinch from it. She wondered how he managed to juggle all the problem cases he seemed to attract. If they felt undermanned, neither Sheridan nor Buckley showed it.

"I'll take my lunch hour at eleven-thirty, if that's all right with you, Judy," Sheila said.

"Fine." Judy nodded. "Guess you saw the two padres. Father Duffy's got himself in a wringer. It'll be pro bono all the way. When the bishop sends over a piece of . . . distasteful law work, you find yourself knee-deep in quicksand. But you don't complain and you don't charge."

"I don't know how Mr. Sheridan and Buckley do it. One problem after another."

"That's the name of the game," Judy said. "If people didn't have problems, there'd be no lawyers."

Sheila had a cheeseburger at Wendy's, then called Loughlin from a pay phone. He was a little curt.

"It was a wild-goose chase all right, and we're coming up *bubkes* on Callahan and Dillard. DA Harrington wants to move on Dillard, but U.S. Attorney Wright talked him into a ten-day delay before convening the grand jury. Wants Sheridan to make his play. What do you get from the inside?"

"Oh, the usual trade. Clients in trouble. Nothing clandestine. No serial killers. No Don Corleones."

"Well, he's represented some drug dealers in the past. We may have to move on the bugs with or without court approval. I'm checking with Justice now."

Sheila said nothing.

"We're to meet with Hal Davis of Justice at seven P.M. tomorrow. Walsh and Kerry will be there, and Mayan d'Ortega. Room One fifteen, Holiday Inn, in Dedham."

"Got it," Sheila said.

Loughlin wasn't quite sure, but he thought her voice lacked its initial exuberance. She seemed a little distant. He dismissed it. He'd be seeing her tomorrow night and could get a better take on her then.

A little after 6:00 P.M. Sheridan came out of his office. Sheila stopped typing for a moment. "Are you all right, Mr. Sheridan?" she asked. He seemed to sway a little as his hand groped for the reception desk.

"Oh, I'll live," he replied, still leaning against the desk. He glanced at his watch. "You should be home at this hour," he said. "Judy wraps things up by five and young Buckley's usually down at his local pub by now."

"Had a brief to type. Just about finished. Buckley has to file it in superior court by noon Monday."

Sheridan sat on the edge of Judy Corwin's desk and studied Sheila O'Brien for a moment. She had an engaging way about her, fresh, upbeat, someone you would like to have around.

"Can I buy you a drink, Sheila?" he said. "I don't want to leave you alone here. This isn't the safest place in the world. There have been a few break-ins on the other floors."

"I'd be delighted," she said. She punched a button on the word processor and the pages started to spill out to form a neat bundle. "Let me wrap this up. I'll take it home and proof it this evening."

Brian Loughlin followed them through the video camera as Sheridan and Sheila left the building foyer and walked along Tremont Street. It was drizzling and both had turned-up raincoat collars. He watched until they disappeared from view.

"Well, Sheila's being escorted someplace by her boss." Loughlin clicked off the camera. "Probably to the Government Center subway station. It'll be interesting to get her report. We may have to move on those bugs by the weekend. Depends on what Hal Davis has to say."

Agents Walsh and Kerry took off their earphones.

"Nothing?" Loughlin said, more a statement than a question.

Walsh shook his head. "Nothing."

"The building manager told me some guy named Leslie Howard rented Eleven-oh-six—short-term, a pollster group."

"Leslie Howard." Kerry smiled. "What a crock. Shades of *Gone With the Wind.*"

"Well, we can't take any chances," Loughlin said. "Let's switch the phones back to HQ and clear out of here tonight. Call the bureau and have the technicians dismantle this stuff." He motioned toward the camera and telephonic gear. "We'll make it look as if we're still here. Won't even terminate the lease."

They sat at the far corner of the Parker House lounge. The piano player was spinning out a medley of Gershwin tunes: " 'S Wonderful," "They Can't Take That Away from Me," "A Foggy Day." Sheila sipped a glass of Chardonnay while Sheridan was working on his second bourbon. The waitress had left a tray of baby oysters wrapped in crisp bacon, saltines, and a cheddar cheese dip. The lights were dimmed and there was a genteel ambience, murmured conversation punctuated by the occasional clink of crystal.

"You're doing a great job, Sheila." Sheridan gave a little salute with his glass. "Buckley thinks he's died and gone to heaven."

The piano struck up "Lady, Be Good."

"I understand Caitlin O'Malley wasn't a speed demon." Sheila scooped some cheese dip onto a Ritz cracker and handed it to Sheridan. She then made one up for herself. Sheridan liked that. It showed consideration, natural good manners.

"Poor Caitlin." Sheridan sighed. "She did her best, but she really wasn't up to much more than hunt-and-peck. Buckley just couldn't bring himself to fire her. She'd been with us for five years and we were sort of used to her shortcomings. Then you came on the scene and, shazam! Buckley can't keep up with you."

Sheila accepted another Chardonnay and could feel her face flush slightly as she took a deep swallow of her wine. She felt relaxed and comfortable in Sheridan's company.

The piano player segued into "Soon," followed by "Someone to Watch Over Me," finishing the set with a light-fingered flourish. Sheila applauded and others in the room picked up her lead.

"I love that song, even if it does sound sort of sexist in the nineties," Sheila said, her hands folded in front of her on the table.

Sheridan grinned. "What's wrong with wanting to be looked after once in a while?"

Then the piano player winked at Sheridan and, forsaking Gershwin, swung into a bouncy rendition of "Chicago."

"That's for you," Sheridan said, throwing back the remainder of his bourbon.

"How in the world did he know?"

"You can always tell a Chicago girl"—Sheridan avoided her question to complete the bromide—"but you can't tell her much."

"Actually, I came from a hick town north of Chicago called Ebbing Corners." Sheila looked at Sheridan. "That eye looks like it's closing." Her lips were pursed with concern.

"I'll strap on a little beefsteak tonight," he joked. The waitress appeared. "And speaking of beefsteak, how about a bite? We can eat right here. The food is delicious."

"Sounds wonderful," she said.

They chatted easily. She gave him her history from the Benedictine nuns in grammar and high school to her years at Northwestern. As a drama major, she had played all sorts of roles, St. Joan to Sadie Thompson. What was she playing now? She flushed a little when she told him of her stage career in New York. She didn't lie easily.

"I had the nuns, too—Sisters of St. Joseph," Sheridan said. "Still have the scars." He looked at the knuckles on his right hand.

They both laughed.

The time flew by. When Sheridan looked at his watch, it was 10:30. "Can I drive you home?"

"I'll catch a cab," she said.

Sheridan didn't push it. He paid the bill, put a ten-dollar bill in the brandy snifter on the piano, and walked with Sheila to the cab stand on the corner.

"Thank you," she said, "and take care of that eye." She rolled up the window and the cab drove off.

She settled back in her seat as the cab made its way along Commonwealth Avenue. Hugging herself, she felt a familiar shiver of apprehension. She was falling for Dan Sheridan. That wasn't in the game plan. That wasn't in the game plan at all.

" 'Lady, Be Good,' indeed!" she said to herself.

Sheridan got his Le Baron from the garage and headed for Atlantic Avenue. The rain had picked up and he turned the windshield wipers up a notch. Suddenly he caught himself humming "Chicago, Chicago, that toddlin' town."

"Whoa," he said to himself. An office romance. Not good. NG, boyo, NG. How often had he heard the saying Don't mix butter with your bread?

He tried to dismiss Sheila from his mind, but she kept reappearing. "Chicago" was replaced by the sophisticated strains of "Soon."

Not good, he said again. Not good. Wasn't there also a song called "Beware"?

Sheila O'Brien pulled into the parking lot of the Holiday Inn on Route 128. She was still driving the Ford Taurus, but later she had to return it to the Boston Common underground garage. The rest of the time, she used the subway like an ordinary secretary saving money on gas and parking fees. She looked over the Holiday Inn parking lot: nothing unusual. Gathering up her shoulder bag, she was about to alight when she glanced in the rearview mirror. She tilted it down and studied herself for a few moments. She was a lawyer, member of the New York bar, single, twenty-seven, a special agent with the FBI, involved in an adventure. Handpicked by the supervisors for the special strike force. They trusted her. Yet something was gnawing at her. She could see it in her face, in the little lines denting the corners of her lips. They hadn't been there two weeks ago. Her present existence was built on subterfuge; and a con, however justified, was still a con. She thought of her father, a widower, still toughing it out in the Chicago stockyards, laboring with his hands. He had worked weekends painting houses or loading trucks to send four kids through Loyola and Northwestern. He'd been so proud of her when she graduated from Fordham Law, then the FBI School at Quantico. Only eight months ago. "Whatever you do in life, Sheila," he said, "always stand up for what's right." She smiled as she remembered her father's imperative.

This is crazy, she sighed. I've got an assignment. She smoothed her hair, opened the car door, and headed toward the Holiday Inn foyer.

Hal Davis was the quintessential government employee, his career spanning thirty years with the Justice Department—the world's largest law firm, as he liked to put it. A bachelor, with a fine house in Georgetown, he was conservatively dressed in a gray pinstripe suit, white button-down oxford shirt, and a gray paisley bow tie. His wire-rimmed glasses and thinning white hair, the color of dry ice, gave him a professorial look. He could cite case law and federal regulations in an instant.

They sat in the small room, Dave Walsh, Brian Loughlin, Sheila O'Brien, and Mayan d'Ortega. Bob Kerry cracked some ice and served the drinks—tap water, club soda, and tonic—and a bag of pretzels.

"For some reason, Mr. Loughlin, your team with all its advantages"—Davis looked at Sheila O'Brien—"has been the least effective. Agent Cartwright has successfully planted electronic surveillance in the offices of mob lawyer Catalano and Agent Driscoll has done the same with lawyer Barry Ginsberg. What we've got makes the Gotti tapes sound like a lesson in ethics."

The group stirred uneasily. Brian Loughlin took a long drink of water. Only Mayan d'Ortega remained unperturbed. This wasn't Harrington's operation. And she had opposed the delay in convening the grand jury.

"We know that Sheridan has defended some small-time hoods in the past, got them suspended sentences. He seems to have the knack for getting the right judges." Davis looked at Mayan d'Ortega. "That's state jurisdiction." Mayan d'Ortega returned his gaze with Indian-like stoicism. Not a spark or a glimmer revealed what she was thinking. Davis moved on quickly.

"That baseball caper was ridiculous," he said. "I had a helluva lot of explaining to do at Justice, but it's like yesterday's paper—old news."

"Do you think we should set up a sting operation involving some state court judges?" Loughlin interrupted. "You said Sheridan gets preferred deals."

"We've thought of that," Davis said, "but it may be premature.

"Dr. Dillard is connected to the murdered Williams woman, who was somehow connected to Sonny Callahan. We believe that Sonny Callahan steered Dillard to Sheridan."

"Why do you say that?" Loughlin asked.

"We have a tip from a pretty good source. In any event, British intelligence, MI-Six, tells us that Williams was a courier for the IRA. Her passport discloses visits to London on twelve occasions over the last three years . . . stayed in a flat in Mayfair. They've checked her phone calls from that location. No overseas calls. Local stuff—the hairdresser, the cleaners. She also went to Amsterdam twice, Paris six times—staying in an apartment near the Étoile—Berlin twice, and thirteen trips to Tunis. All are being checked. Whenever possible, she flew Aer Lingus, always stopping at Shannon on return trips to the States. She billed herself as an art dealer and apparently had some authentic credentials in that line.

"Her brother in New York, Sebastian Simeone, is also an art dealer. Born in Spain but a U.S. citizen. We're looking into his background now.

"I've been in touch with Mr. Harrington, and Simeone's fingerprints came up negative—nothing at the FBI, Interpol, or Scotland Yard. But like his sister—if in fact she was his sister—he does a lot of foreign travel. Again, we're checking his itineraries and phone calls. But if I had to wager, I'd bet we draw a blank. So we have two frequent fliers in the same business who don't use hotel phones. What does that tell us?

"If we have reason to suspect that Sheridan or Dillard or Callahan contemplate criminal activity," Davis continued, "we can plant bugs in Sheridan's inner office. We have access, so it doesn't involve any breaking or entering. We have a sophisticated device that can record a pin dropping on a broadloom, and then we'd install a hidden camera, perhaps in the light fixture. Do you have a Sunday key, Miss O'Brien?"

"Yes, I do."

"Okay, it's not like Dick Nixon's 'plumbers'—they actually committed a felony when they broke in. I was the counsel at Justice who recommended prosecution when everyone got the word to back off.

"When is Dr. Dillard due to come into Sheridan's office?" Again he looked at Sheila O'Brien.

"I don't know," Sheila said. "He's back in town, I know that. But they always seem to meet outside the office."

Davis took off his wire-rimmed glasses, removed a handkerchief from his lapel pocket, and with great ceremony proceeded to polish the lenses. "Okay," he said, "what have we got? Can anyone tell me?"

"Well"—Loughlin sighed—"a dead body, a target who'll probably be indicted, and a defense lawyer."

"Fine. But what are we missing?" Davis rapped his knuckles on the marble coffee table in front of the sofa where he and Agent Walsh sat.

"Perhaps the Callahan connection?" Kerry gave a hesitant response.

"Did it ever occur to you that Dillard, Sheridan, and Callahan anticipate our every move?" Davis addressed Loughlin. His voice was steely and his eyes narrowed.

"Certainly it's occurred to me," Loughlin snapped back. "That's why I discontinued the camera surveillance."

"Well, I hope you didn't lug that camera equipment around during daylight hours. But why should Sheridan's man have suspected you guys in the first place? You said you spotted him scouring the place from across the street. And Sheridan's telephone calls, and Callahan's—sheer puffery.''

"It's not that—'' Loughlin started to speak.

Davis flicked his wrist, cutting him short. "There's a leak someplace.'' Davis was aware of the uneasiness in the group. "Not with you guys or our people. Miss d'Ortega, it's got to be with state personnel. Maybe in your office or with the Boston Police.''

"That's a possibility.'' Mayan fixed Davis with a steady gaze. "Mr. Harrington and I are looking into the situation.''

"Well, cut us in on it,'' Davis said, a cynical edge to his voice. "We don't want to cover any more baseball games.''

"You'll be kept informed,'' Mayan said. "We know Sheridan represents Dillard. Dillard's a target for a murder indictment. Sheridan hasn't called us yet. He will. He'll want to set up a meeting. We think he's got information that didn't come from Dillard. When we meet, the room will be wired. If he's got information that was leaked from state sources, that in and of itself is a crime.''

"When do you plan to convene the grand jury?'' Davis unconsciously adjusted his glasses.

"In ten days. Sheridan will call before then.''

"That's it.'' Davis pressed his lips together in a smug smile. "Sheridan has received information he didn't get from ordinary legal channels of discovery.''

"When you give us the word, Miss d'Ortega, we move on Sheridan's office. Sheila, this is where you come in. We'll plant the acoustical fixtures on a Sunday. Any security then?''

"No. The building is locked.''

"Fine. Gentlemen, Miss O'Brien, Miss d'Ortega.'' Davis consulted his watch. "You people carry on. I'll call you tomorrow from Washington, Mr. Loughlin. You guys nail this one and we go nationwide!''

There was a general round of handshaking, old-boy bonhomie, a grab on the arm, a slap on the back.

Only Sheila O'Brien withdrew. Somehow, she couldn't share the group's enthusiasm. Brian Loughlin noticed.

21

It HAD BEEN easier than Raimondi thought it would be. He signed in with the Sunday guard, brought a small stepladder into 1106, and pushed the ceiling panel aside. Poking his head up into the space, he traced the heating and air-conditioning pipes. He could make out the air duct that serviced 1105. He attached the line and acoustical mike to a telescoping rod and unwound it so that the bug was still out of sight, perhaps a foot from the duct. Fine, he thought as he left the rod in place. He got down from the ladder and hooked the stethoscopic line to a tape recorder. He'd set the timer to switch it on at 6:30 the next morning.

He picked up nothing on the tapes all day Monday except the scratching of mice and the scutter of cockroaches. He listened at the wall. Not a sound. He went out into the hall and tried the door to World Cinematics. Locked.

"Moved all their equipment out on Saturday," Santiago, the security guard, told Raimondi.

"Have they terminated their lease?"

Santiago checked the card at the control desk. "Not that I know of. Must be out on location. You know these Hollywood guys."

"Obrigado, amigo. Fizecte muite por mim."

Raimondi walked across Tremont Street, knowing that somehow he'd blown it. Then it hit him. Sure, they'd spotted him in Sheridan's office and recognized him at the elevator. No telling where the cameras were now located. Better keep the blinds closed from now on.

Lt. Phil Riley propped his feet up on his gunmetal desk next to a partially eaten doughnut and a clutter of memos. He was drinking coffee from a plastic cup as he studied the list of tenants supplied by the manager of Hawthorne-on-the-Charles.

There was a Cougan and a Croci, but that was as close as any name came to Cooch or Cooz. Cougan was a matronly sixty-three, retired schoolteacher. And Croci was a librarian at Tufts University. Not even worth checking out. He stuffed the list into his bottom drawer and made a mental note to spot-check some of the tenants later.

"We have the DA's authorization to release Williams's body to a Mr. Simeone from New York. Says he's her brother." Captain Furlong came out of his glass cubicle office and addressed Riley.

Riley gulped down the last of his coffee and lobbed the cup at the green metal trash container at his feet. It bounced off the rim and onto the floor. Riley made no effort to retrieve it.

"I suppose Harrington's office knows what they're doing. I can't understand why they haven't moved on Dr. Dillard," Furlong added.

"I hear Dan Sheridan's going to represent Dillard." Riley threw out the information as matter-of-fact gossip, common on the street.

Furlong reached into his shirt pocket for cigarettes. He knocked the packet against his wrist, popped one up, extracted it. "Mind?" He pointed toward a Bic lighter on Riley's desk.

"Be my guest." Riley made no attempt to pass the lighter to his chief. Furlong reached over to palm the Bic, put the cigarette in his mouth, lit it, and took a deep drag.

"What else do you hear?" Furlong said, wanting to test Riley's sources.

"Same things you hear, Captain. The feds have taken over the investigation. We do the crap work, they grab the glory. The scuttle has it the feds got a team looking into Williams's background. Could come up with some interesting names."

"Where do you get your information?" Smoke was drifting slowly from Furlong's pudgy lips.

Riley gave a wry contained smile. "Oh, I hear things. Here and there. You know."

"Well, what the fuck do those guys know? Bunch of gray-flanneled Ivy Leaguers with law degrees. Let them play cops and robbers, as long as they don't interfere with the department."

Furlong dropped his cigarette on the floor next to Riley's desk and crushed it underfoot. "Got to see the commissioner. The mayor's got a fundraiser coming up. I'll see you get your allotment of tickets. And let me know how the feds are doing."

"Sure," Riley said.

"And you can kiss my ass," he mumbled after Furlong had sauntered off.

Funny—Riley propped his feet up on his desk again—why did Mayor Jimmy Kane's name crop up in Angela Williams's date book and who the hell was Cooch? There had to be a connection. Maybe he'd check the Williams apartment again on his own. And maybe he'd go for a few drinks down at Casey's in the South End. He laughed to himself. As Yogi Berra put it, You can observe an awful lot by simply watching. And that goes for listening.

The mail had arrived early and Sheila began to sort it. A nondescript envelope caught her eye. It was marked PERSONAL AND CONFIDENTIAL. Addressed to DANIEL SHERIDAN, ESQUIRE. Postmarked Boston. No return address. But written in a legible script. A woman's handwriting.

It was 8:30 A.M. and Buckley was already in his office. It was risky, but she took out her miniature camera and clicked off several shots of the envelope before slipping the camera back into her skirt pocket just as Buckley came out of his office. It was close, but she was sure he hadn't spotted her.

"Sheila." He had a brief in his hand that she had typed. "This is perfect. Case citations, index, chronology. The appellate judges might even read it."

"I double-checked the citations," she said. "It's an interesting case."

"You know, you fit in great here. Did you ever think of going to law school? Maybe nights to Portia Law. Dan knows the dean. Wouldn't even have to take the LSATs. You could work here during the day."

"I've thought about it," she parried uneasily.

"You know, Sheila, I think Dan likes you."

"Likes me?"

"Well, Dan's been upbeat since you've been here. Before, he was in . . . well, you know—sort of angry at the world. Took it out on a lot of snotty-nosed prosecutors."

"You've been with him fifteen years?" she ventured. "It's obvious you like the guy."

"Hey, I love the guy. He's the most decent man I've met in my life. I was Dan's best man at his wedding. I remember him when he came back from Vietnam."

"He was over there?"

"A marine sergeant. Wounded at Khe Sanh. Do you ever notice that he limps a little? His leg was shattered. But he never let it get him down. You know, he was a helluva baseball player in high school."

Sheila knew.

"A catcher. Made every all-star team in the state. The Cubs and the Pirates were looking at him. Even the Red Sox. Instead, he goes to state teachers college, then enlists in the marines.

"Whoosh." Buckley zoomed his hand forward. "Off he goes to Nam. Back he comes, almost in two pieces."

Sheila was curious. "Then what happened?"

"Dan finishes college, gets a job as a patrolman with the Boston Police, and goes to night law school at Portia."

Sheila wanted to know more, but she spotted Judy Corwin coming down the hall. So did Buckley, who retreated to his office.

"Good morning, Judy." Sheila smiled brightly.

"If you get any more pleasant"—Judy feigned a sarcastic grimace—"I'll swear your motives are entirely dishonorable."

"What?" Sheila's face flushed.

"Hey." Judy spotted Sheila's sudden discomfort. "As we say in Yiddish, only kiddling."

Sheridan opened the letter. "Meet me at St. Denis at 12:15, in the confessional." It was unsigned.

"Sheila." He buzzed her on the intercom. "I'm going to lunch. Be back at one. We've got Miss McGillicuddy coming in at one-thirty. She's the witness to the Doyle boy's accident. Have the blackboard set up in my office. We're scheduled to go to trial next Tuesday and Mrs. McG might need some fine-tuning." Then he added, "You might sit in on the workup. We don't tell our witnesses what to say, only how to say it."

*   *   *

"Bless me, Father, for I have sinned." Claire Doherty knelt in the darkness of the confessional, her rosary beads clutched in one hand.

The small door slid open.

"Claire." Sheridan spoke from the priest's seat. "I got your note."

"Here," she said, sliding an envelope beneath the door, "it's the final autopsy protocol.

"But, Dan, this has got to be it. I'm getting some strange vibes. I think they're on to me."

"All right," Sheridan whispered. "No more contact."

"Dan, be careful," Claire whispered.

"Okay, Claire. *Slan agut,* as our grandmothers used to say."

"*Slan ahbile.* Safe home," Claire Doherty replied.

"For you, Claire." Dan slipped her an envelope containing five one-hundred-dollar bills. "And for your penance, say three Our Fathers and three Hail Marys. You can skip the Act of Contrition."

Claire went to the back of the church and slid into a pew to say a decade of the rosary. As she blessed herself, someone at the far end of the aisle caught her eye. Somehow she sensed he wasn't there to say the Stations of the Cross. She blessed herself again and moved out of the pew quickly, almost forgetting to genuflect. The man, dressed in an ill-fitting Robert Hall suit, fingering a gray fedora propped over the pew in front, also got up to leave. She knew a plainclothes cop when she spotted one. It was too late to warn Sheridan. She blessed herself for a third time at the vestibule font, pushed through the glazed glass doors, and hurried down the steps. She walked at a fast clip toward the South Station underground, pausing briefly to catch the man's reflection in a plate-glass window. He stopped, too, and lit a cigarette. Thank God he hadn't caught Sheridan coming out of the confessional, she thought. Or had he?

22

Davis sat in a swivel chair in the conference room of the U.S. attorney's office and addressed agents Brian Loughlin, Dave Walsh, and Bob Kerry. Sheldon Fine stood at the side of the group, occasionally tapping a notepad on an open palm.

He was still steamed at the performance of Loughlin's team. "That Barry Fitzgerald caper"—referring to Brian Loughlin's imitation of so-called accident victim Timmy Kelleher—"was absolutely inane, and that baseball fiasco . . ." He shook his head. "A complete waste of the bureau's time."

"Okay, it's time to cut the bullshit and snare this guy once and for all," Davis said testily. "Now thanks to Agent O'Brien and Sheldon"—he and Fine exchanged nods—"I think we have the ultimate sting."

"Sheldon, you take it from here." Davis aimed a flick of his pen in Fine's direction.

Sheldon Fine laid his notes on the table, then put both hands on the back of a chair and hunched forward. "We checked Sheridan's bank statements over the last several months. He has an open line of credit for fifty thousand dollars at First National Bank, but that's now down, showing only a five-thousand-dollar balance. That's all he's got to run his office, and the bank won't augment the credit line.

"Now what does that tell us?" Fine surveyed the agents.

"Needs ready cash," Walsh answered, almost too quickly.

"That's right." Fine lowered his voice. "So we called Agent O'Brien and had her get a read on some moneymaker that Sheridan was working on. Seems he and his associate are preparing an auto accident case scheduled for trial next Tuesday in Suffolk Superior Court."

Loughlin sat impassively but listened carefully. He wasn't pleased to be hearing the plan for the first time—especially since Sheila hadn't called him. It was obvious to him that Davis and Fine felt his performance was below par.

"The case is *Doyle* vs. *Adams Apparel.* We checked the docket number. Had a chat with the defense attorney, who told us it was a no-pay case in spite of some severe injuries suffered by a kid named Doyle. As the defense attorney explained, the boy darted out between parked cars. The driver jammed on the brakes, but there was nothing he could do. In his summation, Adams's attorney is going to look at each juror—'Put yourself in the driver's seat,' he's going to say. . . . The empathy will be with the defendant."

"How is this going to help us?" Agent Walsh was curious.

"Adams's insurer is Boston Mutual. The claims manager is Arthur DuPree. My boss, Normie Wright, and DuPree were classmates at Yale Law School." A small smile crept into Fine's face.

"We approached DuPree. He's no Sheridan lover. Seems Sheridan has been whacking Boston Mutual pretty good lately, so DuPree agreed to go to Sheridan's office and offer to settle the Doyle case for damn close to what Sheridan's asking—seven hundred and fifty thousand—*provided* he gives DuPree a twenty-five-thousand-dollar kickback."

"I don't know," Loughlin said. "I don't think Sheridan will go for it. He didn't fall for Timmy Kelleher."

"That was crazy," Fine blurted. "DuPree said even a crumbum ambulance chaser wouldn't go for such a ploy. But DuPree knows that adjusters—even claims managers—are on the take. Done every day in Boston—sometimes a bottle of booze, sometimes a catcher's mitt for the adjuster's son, most often cash. DuPree's got the okay from his home office and Justice gives us the green light."

"Don't you think Sheridan will think it's kind of funny that Boston Mutual goes from zero dollars to seven hundred and fifty G's?" Loughlin was still skeptical.

"DuPree's got that figured. It'll be a private one-on-one meeting in Sheridan's office. He's sure he can bribe Sheridan. And of course"—Fine's small smile turned into a toothy grin—"DuPree will be wired. Once we hear the agreement, we march the tape up to Magistrate Rae and plant the bugs in Sheridan's office that night. We'll have Sheridan on criminal charges, but we want bigger fish to fry."

"Will Sheila be involved?" Loughlin looked up at Fine.

"Only to greet DuPree, hang up his coat, and give him the usual cup of coffee greeting."

"Does she know DuPree's a plant?"

"Absolutely," Fine said as he gathered up his notes.

Sheila O'Brien manufactured a smile as the tall, distinguished-looking Arthur DuPree gave her his business card.

"Oh yes, Mr. DuPree. Mr. Sheridan is expecting you. May I take your coat?"

"Thank you." DuPree merely nodded. He recognized Sheila O'Brien from Davis's description. She was on the team. "Play it straight," Davis had admonished. "Strictly business. No chitchat."

DuPree took the chair next to Sheila's desk and proceeded to flip through an old copy of *National Geographic*.

He had been seated only five minutes when Sheila saw the green button light up on her intercom. "Mr. Sheridan will see you now, Mr. DuPree." Again the plastic smile.

"So far so good." Loughlin looked at Agents Walsh and Kerry. Each unconsciously adjusted his earphones. Davis and Fine hovered nearby; Loughlin noticed the expectant sprinter's stance in both. Something was going to go down.

After a light rap, Sheila opened Sheridan's office door.

"Mr. Sheridan, this is Mr. Arthur DuPree. He's from Boston Mutual."

"Hey, Arthur." Sheridan jumped up from behind his desk, extending his hand. "How'n hell are you? It's been a long time!"

"Dan." DuPree flushed slightly at Sheridan's effusive greeting. "I've been paying Mr. Sheridan's rent for years." DuPree winked at Sheila O'Brien—a supplicant's deference. Sheila retired diplomatically.

"Who was that?" Judy Corwin asked Sheila. "The appointment's not in my diary."

"Call came in yesterday," Sheila said. "A Mr. DuPree from Boston Mutual . . . on the Doyle case."

"Oh, you mean the Holy Grail No Liability Anatomic Give You an Apple for an Orchard Any Day Casualty Company."

"Well, he's in there now. Maybe they'll settle."

"Settle what? He'll offer ten grand and you'd think he was paying it out of his own pocket. Believe me, Dan won't budge a cent from seven hundred and fifty thousand."

"How have you been, Arthur?" Dan's tie was loosened and his jacket was draped over a bronze statue of the goddess of justice, the uplifted scales serving as a convenient hook.

"Not too well, Dan." Arthur DuPree sighed audibly. "Wife's been diagnosed as a stage three ovarian cancer. Been at University Hospital for the past three weeks."

"Gosh, I'm sorry," Dan said. "I hope things will be all right."

"I certainly hope so, Dan. Trouble comes in bunches. Bad enough Ann has taken this hit—but the home office is forcing me into an early retirement. . . ." DuPree's eyes misted. He cleared his throat.

"Been there twenty years, Dan. Saved them millions of dollars and now those Young Turks down in the home office want to throw me out on the dump heap—with a pittance for a pension." DuPree slumped in his chair and shook his head.

"Well, I didn't come here to complain." DuPree straightened up. "I want to settle the Doyle case. It'll probably be my last official act for Boston Mutual. I'm here to offer you seven hundred and fifty thousand dollars."

Sheridan gasped. "What?" He shook his head in disbelief. "Am I hearing correctly?"

"You are, Dan. The home office fears a runaway jury. A kid with a fractured hip, permanent injuries. Suffolk juries have been known to give the store away.

"We must, of course, get the necessary releases and the court has to approve the settlement, the kid being a minor."

"Hey, Arthur," Sheridan said enthusiastically. "It's a done deal. We'll whack out the paperwork right away." He extended his hand to shake on the pact.

"One other proviso, Dan. And I'm a little embarrassed even to raise it." DuPree looked up, his eyes still moist.

"I'm broke, Dan. My wife's medical bills cost me sixty thousand over our group medical plan. Even though I'm the claims manager, they don't overpay me. My oldest kid, Henry, opened a French restaurant in the North End. Borrowed over a hundred grand from me and the whole enterprise is going belly-up."

"Boy, Arthur, I'm sorry. Sometimes we don't realize how fortunate we are. . . . How can I help you?"

DuPree took out his lapel handkerchief and dabbed his eyes, this time allowing the tears to flow. "I need twenty-five grand. A little set off from your fee. I'm not asking much, only a small percent. . . ."

The silence of a few seconds seemed to stretch into minutes. It was Sheridan who finally issued a loud sigh. He looked at DuPree, who slumped in the chair like a rag doll.

"Let me get this straight, Arthur." Sheridan's voice was low, cautious.

"Your offer to settle the Doyle case is contingent upon my giving you twenty-five thousand dollars in cash in an under-the-table envelope. Am I understanding you correctly?"

"That's about it, Dan. Christ, I'm up against the wall. . . . Believe me, I thought I'd never resort to this."

Sheridan should have become incensed and thrown DuPree out of his office. Instead, his tone was soft, almost conciliatory.

"Can't do it, Arthur. Never took a bribe in my life. Don't intend to start now. I'll forget I ever heard you say what you said." Sheridan shook his head.

"But your clients. Seven hundred and fifty thousand dollars. There's a quarter of a million fee in it for you!"

"Arthur, you're a member of the bar. So am I. . . ."

"Dan, it's done every day. A little grease. No one's hurt. You're not thinking of your client. You try this case, you're going to lose. You know that."

"Maybe. Maybe not. Might pick one of those runaway juries. They might think the whole thing's one big lottery."

Sheridan punched his intercom. "Sheila, Mr. DuPree is leaving. Please get his coat and show him the way out.

"Good-bye, Arthur. . . ."

"Dan, you won't reconsider? Make it fifteen thousand. . . ."

Sheridan shook his head again.

DuPree didn't extend his hand, but shuffled toward the door.

"Arthur," Sheridan said as DuPree reached for the knob.

"Yes?" DuPree looked back over his shoulder.

"I hope your wife will be all right."

"Sheila." Sheridan buzzed her on the intercom. "Please send some flowers to Mrs. Ann DuPree at the oncology ward at University Hospital . . . and tell young Buckley I'd like to see him."

Sheila knew the flowers would be returned. There was no Mrs. DuPree at University Hospital.

"Certainly," she said, knowing that this would be her first secretarial lapse.

Late that afternoon, Sheridan jabbed the intercom button to summon Sheila. "And bring your pad. Tom is trying a child pedestrian case in Suffolk Superior Court starting Tuesday morning . . . and get some coffee for Mrs. McGillicuddy. She's our star witness."

"Black or regular, Mrs. McGillicuddy?" Sheridan paused.

"Cream and two sugars." Sheila could hear the mouselike voice over the intercom.

"Got that, Sheila?"

"Got it," Sheila replied.

"It's going to be a tough case," Judy said. "Kid from the projects was hit by a delivery van. Happened four years ago in front of St. Brendan's Church at eight in the morning. Defendant driver claims the kid darted out between two parked cars. Says he applied the brakes but there was nothing he could do. Boy's name is Doyle, six years old at the time. Banged up pretty bad, fractured hip, still walks with a limp."

"Can't they settle a case like that?" Sheila asked.

"Not with Boston Mutual. Dan didn't tell me what Arthur DuPree wanted, but he did tell me they're not offering a dime."

Sheila finished stirring the coffee and shook the spoon gently.

"Mrs. McGillicuddy witnessed the accident. She was coming out of church at the time. But she's goofy and blind as a bat. She's in there now with Sheridan and Buckley. They're trying to remake her into Barbara Walters."

*   *   *

Sheila poured the coffee into a porcelain cup, added cream, dropped in two lumps of sugar, and handed the cup to the little old lady with the Fay Bainter smile.

"Thank you, my dear," she said from the depths of the leather couch, her voice squeaky and thin. She sipped the coffee.

"Very nice," she said with a smile.

There was an uneasy silence in the room. Sheila caught Sheridan's tense demeanor. Even the happy-go-lucky Buckley sat tight-lipped. Sheila figured that their star witness was dimming and the case was going down the drain. And she still had no idea what had happened with Arthur DuPree that morning. Sheridan had looked like a thundercloud ever since he'd left.

Mrs. McGillicuddy was wearing a fusty black dress with a white crocheted collar and cuffs. Completely oblivious to the consternation of the two lawyers, she seemed to be enjoying herself.

Sheridan, still wearing dark glasses, scratched his forehead with his thumb. "Marie," he said, "finish your coffee. You're really doing fine."

"I hope I can help your case," she said, smiling again at Sheila O'Brien. "My, you have such nice secretaries."

"Can I get you a doughnut or cruller, Mrs. McGillicuddy?" Sheila offered.

"Call me Marie. In fact, everyone calls me Auntie Rie. . . . No, the coffee's fine."

Sheila looked around. A chalkboard with a diagram was attached to the near wall. Next to that, on an easel, was a blowup photo of the accident scene, coursed by dotted lines, X's, outlines of automobiles, and Magic Marker imprints.

"Sheila, please take notes," Sheridan said. Sheila withdrew to a chair next to the leather couch and placed her steno book on her lap.

"Let's see what we have. . . . The Doyle boy was crossing the street here at the corner of Dorchester and Elm." Sheridan pointed to the enlarged photo. "He stepped off the curb, then bam!" Sheridan punched an open palm. "In the hospital for thirty-three days. Unfortunately, the kid remembers absolutely zilch about the accident. Can't testify where he was or what he was doing in the roadway. Of course, the defendant says the Doyle kid darted out between parked cars. That's where you come in, Auntie Rie."

Marie McGillicuddy took another sip of coffee and smiled again.

Young Buckley let out a tired sigh, let it out slowly, as though he'd been saving it for years.

"Okay." Sheridan pushed away from where he was sitting on the corner of his desk. "Let's go through it one more time. You ready, Auntie Rie?"

"I don't think I'm doing too well." She put the cup and saucer down on an end table.

"You're doing great," Buckley lied. "The jury will love you."

"I certainly hope so. I'm so nervous."

"You were coming out of the seven A.M. Mass at St. Brendan's," Sheridan said. "You take it from there, Tom."

Buckley looked at Marie McGillicuddy. "All right, you're on the witness stand. Pretend the jury is to your right, just where Miss O'Brien is sitting. Twelve good citizens. Just like you, Marie. They want to do the right thing by the Doyle boy. They need your help. Reach out to them. Look them in the eye. Ready, Auntie Rie?"

She sighed. "I guess so."

"Okay, I'm going to lead you in the right direction," Buckley continued. "You just tell me what you saw when you came out of St. Brendan's."

"Well, the seven ran a little late," Marie McGillicuddy began. "Father Murray was on the altar. He's pretty old. Should be retired. Dropped the chalice. Hosts went spilling on the floor."

"Okay." Young Buckley nodded impatiently. "Let's move ahead."

"No." Sheridan waved his hand. "Auntie Rie, explain it in your own words. Take your time. I'll cross-examine you."

"Cross-examine? Like in 'L.A. Law'?"

"Something like that."

"Well, as I was saying, Father Murray dropped the chalice. He got so flustered. The altar boys cleaned it up. Took a good ten minutes.

"Well, after Mass, I made the Stations. It was Billy McGillicuddy's anniversary Mass. He was killed a year ago. Hit a tree on Morrissey Boulevard. My brother Mike's boy . . ."

Buckley looked at Sheila and rolled his eyes. "What happened after you said the Stations?"

"Well, I blessed myself, said a little prayer for Billy and the Sisters of Charity, and then I walked out onto the front steps."

"What happened next?" Buckley urged.

"I saw the young Doyle boy crossing the street."

"He was walking, right, Auntie Rie, walking, not running?"

"Yes. He was walking. Then I saw the truck coming up Elm lickety-split. Then the truck hits the boy. He goes flying."

"Flying where?"

She shook her head. "I don't know. I was so frightened, I ran back into the church."

There were a few seconds of exasperated silence. Then young Buckley motioned toward Sheridan. "Your witness." It was a reluctant turnover.

"Let me cross-examine you, Auntie Rie." Sheridan had returned to his position, seated at the corner of his desk, his arms crossed against his chest. "I'm the bad guy, the lawyer for Adams Apparel's truck driver. The lawyer who isn't offering a dime to Mrs. Doyle."

"Not a dime?"

"Not a dime. Adams Apparel, can you imagine?"

"I'm not surprised. I returned a dress there last week. Didn't fit. Only wore it twice. They wouldn't give me a refund."

"All right. Marie, you're the only disinterested witness to this accident. You have no ax to grind. Adams's driver claims he was going only fifteen miles per hour."

"Fifteen! That's a crock! He was doing sixty!"

Sheridan liked that. She's pissed off. The defendant is lying.

"Now, don't get me wrong, Marie, I'm still playing the bad guy. We'll practice, and by the time you testify, the truth will prevail."

"Bad guy." Sheridan pointed to his chest. "You're still on the witness stand. I'm going to try to poke holes in your testimony."

Her lips were pressed thin as color drained from her face.

"Okay." She braced herself defiantly.

"Mrs. McGillicuddy, I see you need glasses."

"I do," she said. "At seventy-five, everyone needs glasses."

"Did you put your glasses away after you made the Stations of the Cross—say, in your purse?" Sheridan's voice was soft, benedictory.

"I believe so."

"So when you left St. Brendan's and you were at the top of the steps, you didn't have your glasses on?"

"I ... I'm not sure." Her defiance was ebbing.

"Can you see that picture on the far wall?" Sheridan pointed.

"Let me get my glasses." She reached into her purse, pulled out her spectacles, and put them on.

"Yes. It's a scene of Boston Common. There's George Washington on his horse."

Between scribblings, Sheila could see Mrs. McGillicuddy starting to come around. But it would take some honing.

"When you first saw the defendant's vehicle, where was it?"

"Up by that telephone pole." She pointed toward the blowup photo. "The far one."

"Where was the Doyle boy at that time? Go to the photo, Marie. Take this marker and put an *X* to mark the spot where you first saw him."

She took the red marker, then considered for several seconds. "I'd say right about here." She was about to put an *X* beyond the middle of the road when she suddenly realized the boy would be out of the defendant's line of travel. Confident now, she put an *X* halfway from the curb and the center line. "Yes, right about here."

"Did you have the defendant's vehicle in view from the time you first saw it until it struck the Doyle boy?"

"I did."

"How fast would you say the defendant's vehicle was going when it hit the boy?"

"Lickety-split!"

"Move to strike!" Sheridan turned to his vacant chair.

"Yes," Buckley said. "Just give us the speed."

"Sixty miles an hour."

"And from the moment you first saw the van up until it struck the Doyle boy, how much time elapsed?"

"Maybe a minute."

"Now that telephone pole, the far one where you first saw the delivery van, how far away was it from the point of impact—this *X* here—when the van struck the Doyle boy?"

"I'm not good at distances, you know, but I'd say forty to fifty feet, maybe more."

"Okay, Auntie Rie," Sheridan said, "let me show you where you're mistaken. And let me show you how, with a little work, you're going to be the best witness we've ever had.

"This telephone pole, where you first spotted the van, is a hun-

dred and fifty feet from that one near the crosswalk. We'll go down
to St. Brendan's tomorrow morning—you say there's a seven A.M.
Mass?"

"Yes. Father Clougherty's on the altar."

"So when you first saw the delivery van, it was a hundred and
fifty feet away, not forty to fifty feet. We'll pace it off so you'll
know."

Auntie Rie put on her glasses again. "You know, you're right."

"Now, I'm going to give you some calculation tables," Sheridan
said. "I want you to study them." He spread them out on the coffee
table. "See these diagrams. A car going fifty miles per hour goes
seventy-five feet per second. That's a scientific fact."

Auntie Rie nodded, then smiled. She could see the folly of her
prior testimony.

"If a minute went by," Sheridan said, "the defendant's vehicle
would be barely creeping.

"So from the moment you first saw the delivery van to the impact,
how much time elapsed?"

"A second and a half," Auntie Rie answered. She exhaled audibly
and crossed her arms.

"When the bad guy asks you that, just say a second, maybe two.
And look at the jury when you say it."

Auntie Rie nodded.

Sheridan continued. "The steps at St. Brendan's are steep,
Auntie Rie, are they not? Six steps made of concrete?"

"That's right."

"Your eyesight with glasses is what?"

"Twenty–twenty. Pretty good for my age."

"No question about it. So you had your glasses on when you
descended the steps of St. Brendan's. You didn't want to tumble,
maybe break your hip like the Doyle boy."

"You know, you're right. I always wear my glasses going down the
steps at St. Brendan's!"

And so it went. Sheila was amazed. A few more trial runs. Sheridan cross-examined. Auntie Rie hung in tough. There were no
parked cars in front of St. Brendan's. The Doyle boy was walking
across the street, just toddling along. She had a clear, unobstructed
view. The defendant was going fifty, maybe fifty-five miles per hour
in a fifteen-mile-per-hour zone.

"It's a wrap." Sheridan made an affirmative circle with his thumb and forefinger. "One last thing, Auntie Rie. It's eighteen and a half feet from where you're sitting to the far wall. How far do you say it is?"

"Nineteen, maybe twenty feet at the most." Auntie Rie smiled a demure "I'm not too good at distances" kind of smile.

"Tom, take Auntie Rie to the courthouse after the seven at St. Brendan's. Have her walk off certain dimensions. You know, witness box to the back of the courtroom. The defense attorney will try to win the case on geometrics. I happen to know the witness stand to the back of the courtroom is fifty-nine and a half feet."

"Oh, I'd say it's sixty, maybe sixty-one feet, give or take a foot." Auntie Rie gave a sly semblance of a smile.

"We don't tell our witnesses what to say, only how to say it." Sheila recalled Sheridan's forensic advice. Auntie Rie sure knew how to say it. And just coming from Mass. *God, Sheridan, and Buckley* vs. *Dewey, Screw'em and Howe.* Sheila laughed to herself. It wouldn't even be close.

DuPree must have really struck out, because clearly Sheridan was now loaded for bear. Had he sensed a connection?

Detective Riley approached the library of the Choate School. He paused momentarily at the massive latticed cathedral window and watched the young and privileged preppies sauntering toward their assignments. The leafy campus with its manicured lawns and Gothic fieldstone buildings was another world—a long way from Boston's South End, where his two children attended inner-city high schools.

He turned, then walked toward the library, nurturing his idea. When you needed background information on a person, particularly one without a criminal record, a good place to start was the high school yearbook. The bios beside the toothy young faces and underneath the caps, usually speckled with egregious puffery—"Bound to succeed." "A penchant for loud ties." "Ladies' man"—provided the embryo of a hunch, to be followed up or crossed off.

The Choate yearbook, *The Sentinel,* for 1956 showed a smiling, handsome Christopher Breckenridge Dillard with a quote from Socrates: "Know thyself." The bio was a well-written synopsis of a boy destined for success. "Nickname: 'Chris.' Headed for Yale and a medical career. Address: Bronxville, New York."

Riley surmised that there was a great disparity between the Bronx and Bronxville.

Yet there it ended. Not a hint as to who Riley's wily phantom might be. Breckenridge? *Breck?* Not even close to Cooch or Cooze. Who else to check out? No one. It was a long, dreary ride back to Boston.

Buckley called Sheridan from a pay phone. The red alert kicked the tape into action and Brian Loughlin put on his earphones.

"Dillard passed the lie detector one hundred percent," he heard Buckley say. "I've got Dr. Steinmetz's results in front of me now. Dillard had nothing to do with the Williams woman's death."

"Well, that's good news," Sheridan said. "Dillard's due in at one. He'll be heartened."

"Who did you say did the examination?"

"Professor Steinmetz of MIT," Buckley enunciated carefully. "He's the dean of polygraphic practitioners, has done over two thousand tests—CIA, federal government, private industry, you name it."

"He seems eminently qualified," Sheridan said. "Get me his CV and we'll march over to Harrington's office. Dillard tells me he received a letter telling him that his appearance date before the grand jury has been postponed but that he's under a continuous summons and they'll notify him of the new date.

"But you say that the polygraph results are inadmissible as evidence?" Sheridan added.

"Not entirely. There's a 1973 case involving a juvenile who was accused of manslaughter. He took a private test and passed. The trial judge said that if both sides, prosecutor and defense, agreed on a mutual test, then the results could be considered by the jury along with any other evidence. Of course, it does involve a waiver of the defendant's right against self-incrimination."

"Well, let's take it up with Dillard. We'll recommend the procedure. We'll insist the DA put that evidence before the grand jury. There's no way a jury will go against the lie detector, especially when there's no cross-examination."

"Okay," Sheridan said, "where are you now?"

"I'm taking some Dominican nuns to the Red Sox game. Seems Sister Mary Ignatius is related to Roger Clemens."

"You coming in after the game?"

"Yeah, I've got to get my trial brief together on the Doyle case. Sheila's proofing it now."

"Fine. I'm meeting with Dillard. We'll get his okay, then move on the DA's office."

"Hey, Dan, did you see where Harrington has been nominated for the Cardinal Cushing Medal as Catholic layman of the year?"

"Seems I read that someplace."

Brian Loughlin took off the earphones. He turned to Agent Dave Walsh.

"Interesting," he said. "Dillard passed a lie detector."

"Depends upon the examiner," Walsh offered.

"Whom does the bureau use in its more sensitive cases—testing within the department?"

Agent Walsh thought for a few moments. "There's a guy over at MIT. I think his name is Steinmetz."

Claire Doherty was on her way to the ladies' room when she spotted the detective who had followed her from St. Denis. She ducked behind a pasteboard cubicle and watched him enter Harrington's office. Claire said a quick prayer and made a promise to St. Brigid. If she rode out this storm, she'd never yell at Al again, not even when he was drunk.

"I think we're wasting our time with Claire Doherty." The detective looked up from his notebook at Harrington. "She's made personal calls on office time, but mainly to her sister in Chelsea. Really drivel."

"Any contact with Dan Sheridan, maybe with his associate, Buckley? And they've got an investigator—a guy by the name of Raimondi."

"Negative," the detective said. "Doherty seems to be in the clear. I even followed her to church last Monday. She visits St. Denis down in Chinatown. Went to confession. I almost went myself," the detective added with a toothy grin. "Of course, I haven't been since my first communion."

Harrington wasn't amused. "What do you know about Detective Phil Riley?" He studied his visitor carefully.

"Hey, I've known Riley for twenty years. He's a good cop. You're not suggesting . . . ?"

"I guess not," Harrington said.

Just then, Kristina Collins buzzed on the intercom. "Mayan would like to see you. She just received a call from Dan Sheridan. He wants to set up a meeting."

"Okay, Jim." Harrington signaled that the session with the detective was over. "Put a tail on that Raimondi guy."

"A tail on a tail." The detective's grin turned into a rictus. "That's pretty good."

Harrington gestured again impatiently.

"A couple of things." Mayan watched the detective depart. "Just got this tape from the FBI boys." She handed it to Harrington. "Seems Dillard passed a privately conducted polygraph."

"What? Are you sure?"

"It's a telephone conversation between Sheridan and his associate. They're going to try to have us okay a stipulated test with a mutually agreed-upon examiner."

"Christ, a private polygraph. These guys aren't regulated. Two weeks' training and they think they're expert psychologists. No, we're not that gullible. Dillard's a cardiovascular surgeon. The test registers cardiovascular responses. It doesn't smell right." Harrington paced the room.

Mayan d'Ortega waited a few moments. "Sheridan wants a meeting."

Harrington stopped and grinned at d'Ortega. "Well," he said, "we'll be wonderful hosts. Set it up for the Marriott. We'll have the room wired, audio and video. Sheridan's been getting information from somewhere. If we can prove he's getting it illegally, we'll have his ass in a sling."

She gave him a cool conspiratorial smile.

"I like it, amigo," she said.

23

RAIMONDI checked the wattage snooper on Buckley's phone when Buckley called from the Chelsea District Court. The taps were still on.

Just then, Sheila O'Brien walked into Buckley's office carrying an armful of files. They exchanged good-morning nods.

"Yeah, Tommy," Raimondi said into the phone, "I got all the summonses out on the Doyle case. 'Dancing Dan' Howe—the defense attorney—has a note, wonders if you'll ask for a continuance. Says he's ready to go."

"Dancing Dan"—Buckley laughed over the phone—"wouldn't tell you if your pants were on fire. . . . Yeah, I'll be back by noon. We're set to go. Pick up Mrs. Doyle and her boy tomorrow morning and take them up to Courtroom Eight-oh-six. We pulled Judge Tasha Black. Inner-city gal. Got some heart."

Raimondi checked the wattage again before hanging up as Sheila placed the files on Buckley's desk. He wanted to let Sheila in on the tap, but that was Sheridan's department. He felt it was only a matter of time before Sheridan took Sheila into his confidence. It was no secret that in the short time she had been with them, Sheridan had become a new person. His tight-jawed, driven demeanor had eased and he even joked about his black eye, which now was taking on a yellow-brownish hue. He had replaced Judy's six-dollar shades with Ray•Ban reflectors. And Raimondi had noticed the subtle exchanges between his boss and the new secretary. Discreet at first, but now easily discernible—especially to Judy Corwin.

"Ever been to a jury trial, Sheila?" Raimondi asked.

"No." She lied hesitantly, thinking of her law school years. "But I watched Buckley and Sheridan prepare their witness."

"Raw drama," Raimondi said. "Not what you see on TV. The real knack comes in picking the jury. Sometimes it's hit or miss. Then again, it's the art of playing hunches. The very person you challenge for superficial reasons—because he's self-employed or an accountant or just looks too stiff—is the very guy who would give the home office away."

"Don't you have a voir dire in Massachusetts? Can't you question potential jurors to discover bias?" Sheila asked.

Something clicked in the recesses of Raimondi's brain. It was the casual way she used the term *voir dire*. But he dismissed his suspicions quickly. She was, after all, a legal secretary. And damn efficient and easy on the eyes. Judy Corwin had told him that Dan couldn't do better. And she'd put her Jewish blessing on their attraction. "But if it blossoms," Corwin had said, "Dan will have to let her go." That was simply sound office policy.

Judy met Sheila at the photocopier. They watched as the machine sorted pages into a neat pile.

"Did Dan tell you about the reception?" Judy asked.

"No." Sheila, puzzled, shook her head.

"It's kind of an office outing," she said. "Dan bought tickets to the cardinal's annual garden party. Can you come? I'm going. Hope my rabbi doesn't excommunicate me. Buckley's taking a friend, so's Raimondi."

"Hasn't Dan got a friend?" Sheila looked at Judy quizzically.

"A few. But let me tell you something—and this is between us chickens—Dan likes you. He's been a new man since you've been on board. It may cost you your job. But Sheila, there's no finer man than Dan Sheridan. And that includes my late husband, Solly."

"Oh, I'm sorry." Sheila's voice was halfway between concern and amazement.

"Hey, Saul was a good guy. Died from a heart attack five years ago. Set me up pretty good."

"How much did it set Dan back for the tickets?" Sheila inquired.

"These are the Roman mucky-mucks; a thousand a ticket, that's the base price. Once you get there, the cardinal puts his ecclesiastical arm around you."

"Okay," Sheila said. "Count me in."

Phil Riley sat at his desk fingering twenty-five tickets, at a C note a throw, to Mayor Jimmy Kane's birthday party. Buddy Furlong had just plunked them on his desk. He'd have to buy five and get rid of his allotment as best he could. A lot of relatives would hate to see him coming. He tossed them near a stack of memos and proceeded to scour the list of phone calls made to and by Angela Williams over the past six months. Dillard had called often, yet Williams rarely made outgoing calls other than to the florist, Saks, or the Simeone guy in New York. He zeroed in on the last week of Williams's life. Four calls were charged from pay phones—two from Brookline, one from Wellesley Hills, and one from Boston. One of these had to be the one from Cooch that was on tape. And why so brief and cryptic? It didn't make sense.

He buckled on his service revolver, adjusted it to fit into the small of his back, then creased the telephone list into his inside coat pocket.

He was about to leave when Captain Furlong interrupted him. "Don't forget the mayor's tickets."

"Sure," Riley said sarcastically. "I'll probably need another dozen."

"Just get rid of your quota." Furlong smiled a mirthless plastic smile.

"I called Harrington's office and spoke with d'Ortega," Sheridan said to young Buckley and Raimondi as they huddled in the small conference room library. "I could tell from her tone that she expected my call. We've set up a meeting at the Marriott, Suite Ten forty-seven, for Monday morning."

"You know the room will be wired, set up with hidden video," Raimondi said. "Why not change the venue at the last moment, say to a room on the twelfth floor? I could arrange it."

"No. We still have the advantage. We may be the buggee, but the buggers don't know we know it," Sheridan replied. "I'll play it carefully, lot of self-serving stuff. Give them the results of the Steinmetz test, and if I can't cut some sort of deal, I'll specifically request a mutually agreed-upon polygraph."

"You know they won't be thrown into that brier patch," young Buckley said.

"I know"—Sheridan frowned as if he had just thought of some abstruse legal gem—"but I'll make the request anyhow. Spell it all out carefully and audibly. When the turndown comes, I'll make sure the guy who's listening gets an earful. I'll make a demand that Steinmetz's test be presented to the grand jury. At least then, d'Ortega will be on notice of some exculpatory evidence."

"Evidence that isn't admissible," added Buckley, shaking his head.

"Well, we play the cards we're dealt," Sheridan said.

"Somehow I think d'Ortega's after bigger game," Buckley said. "Like maybe Dan Sheridan." His hand formed a simulated pistol, pointed at his boss. "She'll want to know what evidence you have and how you got it. Like why you thought it was necessary to give Dillard a lie detector test?"

"I'll play Mickey-the-Dunce," Sheridan said. "In any event, I'll want her to give me a letter that Dillard's a target."

"Will Dillard be there?" Raimondi asked.

"He'll be in the bar downstairs, a phone call away—just in case we cut a favorable deal, like involuntary manslaughter."

"Think Dillard will go for that? It'll cost him his ticket."

"If I had to bet," Sheridan said, "the meeting will be brief. No deals. We'll be back to square one. Dillard's indictment is almost certain."

"Don't underestimate d'Ortega," Buckley said. "She'd love to add your scalp to her tennis bracelet."

"It'll be a busy week." Sheridan looked at both of them. "Monday d'Ortega, Tuesday you go out on the Doyle case, and Thursday it's DA Hollingsworth. Apart from the other fires we have around here, the *Globe* wants a statement on Father Duffy. Judy told them no comment and they weren't too pleased."

"Well, the practice of law is like a wild broad in bed." A grin added another crease to Buckley's face. "When she's good, it's great; when she's bad . . . it's still pretty good."

24

"THE CARDINAL looks a little on the tired side," June Harrington whispered to Mayan d'Ortega and her husband as they inched forward in the reception line.

"He comes across a little beleaguered," Neil Harrington agreed. "Can't say I'm surprised, considering all the problems he's had lately. Nuns picketing, schools closing, and priests running for cover on sexual-abuse charges. It's a tough job."

They moved up toward the cardinal, who, although gracious, looked as if he'd rather be on the golf course. There were telltale dark crescents under his eyes. And he was in for a long day.

Harrington caught a glimpse of Sheridan, together with Buckley and Raimondi, making their way toward the bar set up at the far side of the huge tent. He recognized Judy Corwin, Sheridan's secretary, and suppressed a smile when he saw her chatting with Sheila O'Brien and two flaxen blondes, their heads bent toward one another. Sheila seems to be in solid, Harrington thought. But even with such an edge, Sheridan was still proving elusive.

What if Sheridan and O'Brien...? The thought crossed his mind. No. Preposterous. Every lawyer knows an office romance is taboo. A sure way to get into a peck of trouble.

And Sheridan is too smart for that, so's O'Brien. He dismissed the idea as Monsignor Fitzgerald waved them into position.

The cardinal, dressed in a black tunic, a scarlet sash tightened around his waist, a red biretta clinging to the back of his head, greeted them warmly.

"Mrs. Harrington"—he extended his hand and June kissed his ring—"so nice to see you again."

"Your Eminence, this is my top aide"—Neil Harrington motioned—"Mayan d'Ortega."

The cardinal was smart enough not to extend his ringed hand. He had heard of d'Ortega, a pro-choice activist and not exactly a churchgoer.

"So nice to meet you, Miss d'Ortega." He smiled warmly. "I've heard a great deal about you."

Neil Harrington shook the cardinal's hand. "Your Eminence," he said, "this is a deep honor."

"It is, Neil, especially the Cushing Medal. And you'll make a fine senator, believe me. I'd vote for you twice, if I could."

They smiled at each other and turned to face a camera. A sudden flash captured the cardinal and his guests and then the Harringtons and Mayan d'Ortega moved on toward the canapes and iced lobster. They were quickly joined by their chauffeur, Declan Haggerty, who was balancing a tray of cocktails—scotch for Neil, vodka gimlet for June Harrington, and straight tequila for Mayan d'Ortega.

"Have you seen Sonny Callahan, Declan?" Harrington surveyed the crowd.

"He's here somewhere," Haggerty said as he handed the drinks around.

Mayor Jimmy Kane made his appearance, tall, tanned. "Salt-and-pepper handsome," as his admirers, even his detractors, would say. He was accompanied by Chief of Police Costello in chevrons and gold braid, a badly preserved forty-nine, with a paunch to prove it.

Sheridan eyed the clusters. The trappings of power, money, and society mixed easily in Catholic Boston.

"Something to see," he remarked to Sheila O'Brien, who nursed a Chardonnay and nibbled on a stuffed oyster.

"Fifty years ago, even in the late forties, the Irish couldn't get a decent job in Boston. If you were number one in your class at BC Law and your name was O'Brien or McNaught, you couldn't get in the front door of a Brahmin law firm unless you were delivering the mail."

"Times have changed," Sheila offered.

"It took a little doing." Buckley jumped into the conversation. "Like James Michael Curley, the lovable rogue. 'Vote early and often,' he used to say to his rabble. Talk about Robin Hood. But he put the WASPs in their place. And by the way, have you all met? This is Alexis Pamela Davenport . . . of the Scarsdale Davenports."

The flaxen-haired looker with creamy skin gave a slight smile.

"The Irish came over on the boats—'coffin ships,' my grand-mother called them. One out of five went to the bottom, and"—Buckley downed another good swig of scotch—"the Davenports owned the boats." He waved his glass in a slight salute toward his date.

"You know, Tom, you drink too much," she said. Her mouth formed a tight smile, but her eyes were as cold as lake water. Some-how Sheila knew that the icy beauty and young Buckley would soon be history.

"Ladies and gentlemen." Sonny Callahan tapped on a wineglass to signal silence. The room's chatty exuberance subsided. The enco-miums were brief.

"I give you His Eminence, the cardinal, who'll present this year's Cardinal Cushing Medal—honoring the outstanding Catholic lay-man of the archdiocese."

Sustained applause. The cardinal was effusive. Neil Harrington beamed self-consciously as the cardinal pinned the red-ribboned medal on his lapel.

"Now I would like the *next* senator from Massachusetts to say a few words." The cardinal gave a sweep of his hand toward Har-rington and stepped down from the rostrum.

Neil Harrington walked forward and adjusted the microphone. He was never at a loss for words or hesitant to seize the moment. And this was his moment.

Buckley signaled Raimondi to fetch more drinks. He figured it would be a four-scotch speech. Out of the corner of his eye, Sher-idan saw Callahan leaving the room. So the schism was there. Sher-idan began to put a few things together.

On the podium, Neil waited. Five, six, ten seconds went by. Like Adolf Hitler, Billy Graham, and Winston Churchill, Harrington had mastered the histrionic technique of arresting attention. Wait. Look about. Wait. The audience was on edge. You had them. Wait some more.

"My dear friends." Harrington began slowly. He looked down at the medal, then raised it between his thumb and forefinger. "All I can say . . ." He paused again. His eyes misted. A tear welled, then slid down his cheek. His voice was husky with emotion. "All I can say is thank you!" He nodded toward the cardinal. That was it. No silver-toned promises, no mandates. Just a simple thank-you. The applause was deafening. Even those expecting something profound clapped as if they'd heard the most elevating oration of all time.

"Harrington knows how to milk it," Buckley said, draining his third scotch.

"Tommy, I think I'd better drive," Sheila heard young Buckley's date say.

"You know"—Buckley shook his glass, jiggling the ice cubes—"the thing that's bad about a guy who doesn't drink is that when he wakes up in the morning, that's the best he's going to feel all day. I think W. C. Fields said that." He lifted his glass, signaling Raimondi to fetch a refill.

Sheridan took off his Ray·Bans, tucked them into his breast pocket, and stole a sideways glance at Sheila O'Brien, who was nestled comfortably in the leather passenger seat of the Le Baron.

The luminous green of the dash, the CD playing soft rock, and the three Chardonnays she had drunk during the evening gave her a sense of well-being. She felt secure. And the case seemed far away, in another dimension.

Sheridan's car thrummed over the Mystic River Bridge. The soft rock turned softer—sixties music: "Ain't No Mountain High Enough," "Dock of the Bay," "Leavin' on a Jet Plane." Neither spoke. A few turns, a pause at a red light, a left onto Meridian Street.

"Over there," she said, "the gray tenement."

Sheridan escorted her up three wooden steps. She fumbled for her keys.

They stood there in the velvety stillness. Only the wan light from the buzzer system illuminated the porch.

"Won't you come up?" she said, her eyes lingering in his. "My roommate's on a business trip. Won't be back until tomorrow night."

"I'll have to sleep on the floor." Sheridan smiled boyishly.

"You'll sleep with me," she replied.

Sheridan moved closer to Sheila. She tilted her face upward. The chemistry, the mood, the moment, were just right, even the stars. Only the rules were wrong. And Sheridan always played by the rules.

Their lips touched, gently at first, lingering, then came together with a hungry crush.

25

SHEILA PROPPED herself up in the bed and quietly reached for the pack of Carltons and matches on the night table. The numbers on her digital alarm clock winked: 3:37 A.M.

She peered down at Sheridan. He was wrapped in the tangled bedsheets, not stirring, sleeping soundly, like a giant child.

She lit a cigarette, blew out the match, and flicked it toward the bedside ashtray. The room was dark, punctuated only by the bright ember of her cigarette; the only sounds were Sheridan's deep breathing and the muted moan of a foghorn somewhere off in the distance. She took a long drag of her cigarette, savoring the taste, then let the smoke drift lazily from her lips.

She couldn't deny it had been good. By now misgivings should have been settling in, the ancestral guilt emerging. But she felt only a sense of contentment—the afterglow of great sex, the pure delight of intimacy. She knew it went against every grain of logic, let alone professional ethics. But sheer pleasure blocked out self-recriminations. They would come later.

And somehow she knew she couldn't write Sheridan off as a one-night stand. He had started slowly, gently, but the preliminaries soon ended. They slammed into each other like feral animals, crunching, grinding. It lasted and lasted and mounted to a furious explosion. Then peace. Neither spoke as Sheridan cradled her in his arms, muscular and lean, hardened by his years as an athlete. There was intimacy in the silence: The barriers were down and something within each of them reached out to the other. They drifted. The next thing she knew it was 3:30.

She continued to smoke. One cigarette, two. Sheridan stirred now and then but didn't awake.

Sheridan blinked his eyes. He could smell coffee brewing and bacon frying and then Sheila appeared in the doorway.

They smiled at each other.

"I hope . . ." he began.

"Shh." She came over to him, putting her fingers to his lips.

He had started to say he was sorry. But the way her eyes glimmered, her mouth a soft line of contentment, he knew it would sound insincere. And he wasn't sorry. Emotionally, this was the best he had felt in years. And he knew he wasn't going to end it.

He pushed himself up against the headboard. "You don't happen to see my skivvies around here, do you?"

"Wait," she said. She went to her closet, removed a white terry-cloth bathrobe, and tossed it at him.

"It's a unisex, a gift from the Chicago Hilton. One size fits all. . . . You like cream in your coffee?"

They sat opposite each other at the small table. The sun spilled through the window and over the broadloom like molten honey. They sipped their coffee. Sheridan, suddenly ravenous, ate six slices of toast and four eggs.

"I'm forty-six," he said finally. "Got a lot of scars. You're young, fresh." He shook his head.

"Hey," she said, "let's not get into that Irish-Catholic guilt stuff. I had my fill of that with the Benedictine nuns. If it's good, grab it and don't let it go. It comes so seldom in life. Sister Mary Ignatius, my drama teacher, gave me that line. Unfortunately, she broke her vows six years into the order." A soft smile played around Sheila's mouth.

Sheridan showered, put some Vaseline around his puffy eye, shaved with Sheila's razor, dressed, and straightened his collar.

She stood on her tiptoes and kissed Sheridan softly on the lips. She saw him out, watching him go down the stairs at a jaunty pace, then shut the door slowly. Then the implications hit her. She could endanger the entire operation, her whole career. Somehow she would have to stay close enough to Sheridan to bring off her part in the sting without getting more deeply involved on a personal level. She had worked too single-mindedly for too long to let some Chardonnay and a sexy stud throw her off course.

Then the phone rang and, flinging herself across the bed, she picked it up, unprepared for the dilemma her caller presented.

"It's me." She bolted upright in bed upon hearing Sheridan's voice.

"I'm in my Batmobile, headed for the Cape. My aunt Ginny has

a cottage down in Chatham. Clapboards need replacing. Got to
have someone hold the ladder. Can you be ready in, say, twenty
minutes?''

"I'll be ready in ten."

What the hell, she thought. If she refused, he'd be suspicious.
And she stood a good chance of finding out more about the case
the closer she stayed to him.

She made a quick call to Loughlin, who was torn between dis-
approval and approbation. She threw jeans and sweaters into a Le
Sportsac duffel and waited for Sheridan to buzz from downstairs.
What the hell, she mused again. A weekend romp. It could be fun.

Sheridan put the top down as they sped along Route 3 toward the
Sagamore Bridge. He wore a white Irish knit sweater and a plaid
scally cap. Adjusting his Ray•Bans, he stole a look at his companion.

Sheila's soft blond hair tumbled and tossed in the wind. She, too,
had on sunglasses, and she caught Sheridan's profile, his hands
firmly on the steering wheel—like a ship captain's on the helm.
They chatted easily as Sheridan took the bay route, passing through
leafy white-steepled towns—Sandwich, Barnstable, Yarmouth. Cape
Cod Bay with its spread of sandy vistas was always within view.

They stopped for lunch at a roadside jetty in Brewster. The sun
was warm, the weather clear. They could see the curve of the bay
as it hooked toward Provincetown. A few trawlers dotted the horizon, outlined against fat cumulus clouds.

Sheridan ordered oysters on the half shell for starters.

"Usually, I'm a beef-and-potatoes guy." He smiled as he mixed
horseradish into the peppery sauce, then shook in a few drops of
Tabasco. "But when I cross the canal, I turn into a crusty old salt.
For the rest of the weekend, unless I hear any objections, it'll be
littlenecks, quahogs, lobster, chowder, and ale. You like ale,
Sheila?''

"Hey." She scooped down her third oyster. "Cakes and ale," she
said, lifting her glass of amber Canadian in salute. But for a moment, she shuddered inwardly, masking her qualms with an exaggerated smile.

Sheridan returned the salute, taking a good swallow of Molson's.
"Aunt Ginny was my mother's sister. Virginia Dacey."

"Was?"

"My mother died several years ago. She left the cottage to Aunt Ginny, who never married. A saint, really."

"Will we meet her?"

"Ginny's off on a pilgrimage somewhere. Maybe Medjugorje or Lourdes. When she's away, I take care of the place."

Sheridan bought some scallops, three pounds of scrod, a bucket of clams, and two live lobsters.

"We'll cook these guys for our evening meal," Sheridan said, shaking the spiny crustaceans. "Hope you won't be squeamish when I stick them into the pot."

Again a cold shudder passed through Sheila, but it wasn't the thought of crustaceans being boiled alive. It was her misgivings about being tugged between two worlds.

"At this time of year, we've only got the natives," Sheridan said as he turned the car into a dirt lane, the tires crunching over crushed oyster shells.

They continued past weathered saltboxes half-hidden among crooked locust trees and windswept bayberry and heath, finally pulling up into the driveway of a small cottage surrounded by a split-rail fence.

As Sheridan unloaded the car, Sheila paused to take in the spectacular view. The little house was situated on a bluff overlooking Nauset Beach, some fifty feet below. She felt the rhythm of the breakers as they rolled in from the open sea, crashing into a giant froth on the sandy strand that stretched in both directions as far as she could see. In the distance, beyond the white pinnacle of a lighthouse, she could make out Monomoy Island, and farther still, almost against the horizon, lay the purple silhouette of Nantucket.

The cottage interior had a neat and tidy charm—braided rugs, beamed ceilings, pegged oak flooring, wicker furniture, maple end tables, ship lanterns, a cocktail table made from pockmarked cyprus lobster traps.

While Sheridan checked the refrigerator and the stove burners, Sheila looked at several faded photographs placed on the mantel above the stone fireplace. In one, she picked out a boy, perhaps ten years old, with a sheepish grin, surrounded by several other children and adults. It was Dan Sheridan. She saw the family resemblances between the Sheridans and the Daceys.

"Oh, that's the Sheridan brood—cousins and aunts and uncles,"
Dan said as he saw Sheila inspecting the picture. "That was taken
just out front on some Fourth of July—don't ask me the date."

In the late afternoon, they hiked along a deserted trail bracketed
with dunes rippling with bronzed beach grass. They sat and watched
the sunset as long streamers of clouds tinted in lavender caught the
last vestiges of daylight. In the tawny stillness, neither spoke. They
made their way back, this time along the beach. The only sound
was the crashing surf; the only movement was that of sandpipers
scurrying to catch small edibles flung onto the shore in the cease-
less ebb and flow of the tide.

Sheridan lighted a fire, the dry driftwood crackling and sputtering,
then roaring into life. Next he proceeded with the dinner, stuffing
the live lobsters into a kettle, dicing cucumbers and beets, mixing
a salad, heating up a loaf of French bread, and stirring a clam
broth. He poured two ales, cut open the now-pink lobsters, removed the tomalley, and coated the meat with drawn butter. They
sat on the floor in front of the fire, enjoying the meal. Then Sheridan cradled her in his arms and they watched the embers fade like
the dying sunset. For a long time, neither spoke. "I saw the photo
of you, your wife, and your son on Aunt Ginny's end table," Sheila
said, breaking the long silence.
  "That was taken three years ago," Sheridan said, sighing.
"Tommy was in the third grade and Jean was pregnant, about two
months along."
  "I'm sorry," Sheila said. "Buckley filled me in."
  "Yeah. It was pretty sudden. We thought we had it made. But
sometimes when you got all your ducks lined . . . you know." Sher-
idan's voice choked.
  "She was a beautiful woman," Sheila said.
  Sheridan merely nodded.
  "Do you have any brothers and sisters?" Sheila asked.
  "Got a younger brother and sister. Michael is a doctor down
in Connecticut. My sister Ann teaches English lit at Worcester
State."

Dan held her a little closer. "And what about you? Beyond your résumé, tell me about Sheila O'Brien?"

"Oh, Irish like you, Dan. Strict parents. Product of the seventies. Mother died in childbirth delivering my sister Joany. That was fifteen years ago."

"I'm sorry," Sheridan said softly. "Guess we've both had our share of misfortune.

"So you were a product of the seventies?" Sheridan kissed her lightly on her forehead.

"I was just a kid. It was the tail end of the flower generation. The old values were crumbling. We questioned our country, our parents—even the church. I really hated Sunday mornings when Mom and Dad would force us out to Mass and we'd listen to old Monsignor Devlin give us his archaic Bible stories. Here it was 1975 and he was telling us about devils with horns and forked tails.

"I never forgot one sermon. He told us something about some prophet going up into the temple to pray. 'And lo!' the monsignor says, 'Isaiah saw tongues of fire and seven dragons high in the sky.'

"I took a peek over at my dad." Sheila looked up at Sheridan, who had an amused smile on his face. " 'Dad,' I said, a little louder than I should have, 'do you believe this bullshit?'

"Well, he damn near hits me—there in the third pew of St. Barnabas.

"My sister and brother were giggling. Mother was mortified. I'm sure the monsignor heard me. He stopped for several seconds. Dad grabs me by the back of my dress collar and hauls me out a side door. He plunks me down on the lawn, glaring at me as if he was really pissed. 'No,' he says, 'I don't believe there were seven dragons in the sky. . . . There were only six!' Then he plops down beside me, laughing so hard, I thought our whole family would be excommunicated. He lights up a cigarette. We chat. He's really a good guy. Later he tells Mother that he gave me a good talking-to.

"Do you believe in the Divinity, Dan?" She again looked up at Sheridan.

He let out a contented sigh. "I think we're both products of Irish Catholicism. In Nam, I questioned a lot of things. My country, our Christian God. I saw death, brutality, mutilation, children actually burned to death—mainly from our firepower. But you know, Sheila"—he tugged her closer—"it was the Christian God that saw me through. . . . I guess it's the old saying, There are no atheists in foxholes.

"Now I don't know. If there is a divine being out there—a kind of supernatural wizard controlling black holes, galaxies, seasons, snowfall, rain, caterpillars—I hope he's got a sense of humor."

The more they talked—simple things, growing up, grammar school, nuns, little events that made a difference, big events that somehow weren't great when assessed in later years—the more the bonding grew. They went through their lineage, the funny stories, the bad. And even the bad seemed to have rounded edges. Sheridan stroked her silky hair, then buried his face in it, smelling its soft purity. Occasionally, their lips touched, lingered.

"You know what I think?" Sheridan tugged Sheila a little closer. "I hate to say it, but tomorrow morning we've got to put up the clapboards on the south side. Take a good four hours." Sheridan yawned. "I think we should turn in." Sheridan gave a soft nip on Sheila's earlobe. "You can have Aunt Ginny's suite. I'll just curl up on the couch and keep the watch."

The couch detail lasted maybe twenty seconds. Sheila, in striped cotton pajamas, poked her head around the corner.

"Sheridan," she said, "it's lonely in here." An impish grin crept into her face; her eyes smiled almost maliciously.

The next morning, Sheridan and Sheila went for a run along the beach. The water was cold, but they plunged in, tumbled by the charging waves, then laughing, toweling, running again.

Sheridan spent the remainder of the morning pulling out dilapidated clapboards as if he was a veteran carpenter. Sheila handed up replacements and in about four hours the windward side of the cottage was finished, the new wood contrasting starkly with the gray weathered boards.

"That'll keep Aunt Ginny snug at least for the summer," Sheridan said as he came down off the ladder. "Come the fall, I've got to work on the roof. It's in pretty bad shape."

*   *   *

They rented bicycles in town and rode the old Penn Central railroad bed through tunnels of greenery from Eastham to Dennis, stopping to explore cranberry bogs, salt marshes, hidden ponds, and shadowy lanes that led to crumbling foundations of a bygone day.

That night they sat on the lawn in front of the gazebo on the village green and with the locals watched the Chatham "Philharmonic" thump out a repertoire of Sousa marches, Strauss waltzes, pop, and country-western.

Late Sunday, they tidied up the cottage, put the rubbish in the bin, and packed the Le Baron.

Neither spoke on the trip back to Boston. Sheridan had a slight, satisfied smile. Behind her sunglasses, Sheila's eyes were troubled. The sex and the easy companionship made her alive, vibrant, but more than that, it was the bonding.

She knew a hell of a lot more about Dan Sheridan than she had two days ago. But she had nothing to add to the bureau's case against him. All she knew was that he seemed to be a fine lawyer, and a fine man.

Raimondi sat at the bar with Dillard. It was too early to drink, so Raimondi ordered a Perrier with lime, Dillard a black coffee. He had been briefed earlier by Sheridan about the meeting with the district attorney's first assistant. Something bothered Raimondi about Dillard. He should have been apprehensive, obsequious, hat in hand. Instead, he seemed in perfect control, imperious, not engaging Raimondi in conversation, sipping his coffee slowly and gazing off into some middle distance.

Upstairs in the Marriott, Sheridan and Buckley were ushered into Suite 1047 by a uniformed police officer.

Mayan d'Ortega rose from the Louis XIV–style sofa to greet them. Although Sheridan had heard about her, this was their first meeting. For a moment, he was taken aback. She's a beauty, he thought, jet black hair, amber skin, slanted eyes. Yes, it was the eyes—tiger eyes, sullen, watchful.

"I'm Dan Sheridan." He extended his hand. "And this is my partner, Tom Buckley."

D'Ortega shook Sheridan's hand, then nodded toward her associate. "This is Sheldon Fine."

Fine had button-black eyes like a stuffed squirrel, curly black hair, and a Tom Dewey mustache. He eyed Buckley and Sheridan cautiously for a moment. No one smiled. The handshaking was crisp, professional.

"Mr. Fine," Sheridan said, "are you Miss d'Ortega's associate in the district attorney's office?"

Fine was about to answer, but d'Ortega cut him short. There was no time for games.

"Mr. Fine is with the U.S. attorney's office." There was a peremptory edge to her voice.

"U.S. attorney's office?" Sheridan feigned confusion.

"Yes." D'Ortega motioned for all to sit down. "You asked for the meeting, Mr. Sheridan. . . ."

"Call me Dan."

Her lips tightened in annoyance but then relaxed.

"Mr. Sheridan, Mr. Buckley," she said, her hand unfolding outward, "the ball, as you Celtics fans like to say, is in your court."

Sheridan knew the preliminaries were over. Some warning frisson ticked at his consciousness. One thing was certain; he didn't like Sheldon Fine. Maybe he just didn't care much for thirty-year-old attorneys with mustaches. And he wasn't enamored of d'Ortega, either.

Sheridan stole a glance at the air-conditioning duct above his head, then came right to the point.

"I represent Dr. Christopher Dillard," he began, "a respected doctor who has received a summons to appear before a grand jury yet to be convened."

"What are you asking?" Fine broke in.

Sheridan grimaced in obvious displeasure. "My client was friendly with a lady by the name of Angela Williams."

"How do you know that?" Fine asked.

Even d'Ortega looked irritated at Fine's interruption.

"Hey, pal." Sheridan sucked in his breath. "Dr. Dillard is my client. He gives me his history. Tells me about the Boston Police, tells me about stuff you guys know all about, that's how I know that.

"And why is *he* here?" He nodded toward Fine. "What has the U.S. attorney's office to do with a death in Suffolk County?"

Fine was about to rise to the challenge. D'Ortega again cut him short.

"Let's start at the beginning." She smiled so as not to let her annoyance show, a tolerant smile. "What can we do for you, Mr. Sheridan?"

"For my client. I want you to assure me that he's not a target."

"I'm afraid that's impossible." The tiger eyes sized him up, cold, implacable. "Why should we be so accommodating?"

"Because he had nothing to do with the Williams woman's death."

"How do you know that?" She tried to draw him out.

Sheridan raised his hand, snapping his fingers. Buckley handed him the Steinmetz polygraph.

"It's all here." Sheridan slapped the packet. "My client took a lie detector test. . . . Bad metaphor," he added, "I should say truth indicator." He handed the dossier to d'Ortega.

"There were no charges leveled against Dillard," Fine cut in. "He wasn't arrested. There was no arraignment. Why did you find it necessary to give him a lie detector test? . . . And don't call me pal!"

Again, Sheridan glanced toward the ceiling. The meeting was deteriorating. He wanted to say, Okay, I won't call you pal, asshole. He counted to himself, three, four, six seconds, sheathing his anger. "Look," he said, his voice finally controlled, modulated, "we're all officers of the court. In the interest of justice, I'm here to see if we can reach some common understanding. I'd like a letter indicating that Dr. Dillard is or is not a target. And if he is a target, I'd like us all to agree on an outside polygraph examination."

D'Ortega examined Steinmetz's report. She studied each page— the etchings, blips, and squiggles.

"You are of course aware that a lie detector test is inadmissible as evidence in the Massachusetts courts."

"Not if we stipulate on impartial test results."

"Well, there'll be no such stipulation." D'Ortega's voice was dismissive.

"Okay," Sheridan said, "is my client a target?"

"He is."

"May I have a letter to that effect?"

D'Ortega reached into her small valise, removed a letter, and handed it to Sheridan. "Here," she said. It was addressed to Dillard.

*Please be advised that the Suffolk County District Attorney's Office, Common-
wealth of Massachusetts, hereby advises that you are considered feloniously
responsible for the death of Angela Williams, late of Suffolk County . . . You
should seek counsel to protect your interests.*

Sheridan handed it to Buckley, who scanned it quickly.

"Well, I guess the issues are joined," Sheridan said. "When are
you convening the grand jury?"

"Shortly. You and your client will be notified."

"I'm trying to avoid a grand jury appearance."

"Does he have an alibi?"

"No."

"Then he'll be indicted," d'Ortega said. "Does he wish to waive
an appearance?"

"Not really." Sheridan could see there was little to be gained, so
he threw out the lure. "Can we make some sort of deal?"

"What do you have in mind?" Fine said, the dark, bright squirrel
eyes focused on Sheridan.

"Involuntary manslaughter. No jail time. Community service."

"Why should we agree to that?" d'Ortega asked.

"Because *you* know you can't prove my client perpetrated the
crime of homicide, if in fact there was a homicide," Sheridan said.

"How do you know we can't prove it?" D'Ortega studied him
carefully.

"The burden of proof is on you," Sheridan replied. "How can
you prove it?"

"Look, we're wasting time," Fine said. "Here's the deal. Your
client pleads guilty to second-degree homicide. We'll recommend
a suspended sentence, the community service bit."

"Is that it?" Sheridan knew there was more.

"And he agrees to testify against James Callahan."

"Sonny Callahan?"

"Sonny Callahan."

"On what charges?"

"Drug charges, mainly. RICO violations. Money laundering. Ex-
tortion. Wire and mail fraud. Conspiracy in aid of foreign insur-
gents. Maybe a few more."

"Dillard will finish out his career at the Leavenworth dispen-
sary?" Sheridan said.

"He'll be granted limited immunity."

Sheridan looked quizzically at Buckley, then at Fine and d'Ortega.

"When do you need a reply?"

Fine checked his watch. "We understand your client is at the bar downstairs. Talk with him. We'll wait."

Dillard took the news dispassionately. He steepled his fingers under his chin and waited for Sheridan to finish.

"The lie detector test," he said. "Wasn't that fairly conclusive?"

"It would be if the prosecutor would go along, but she won't."

"Why are they willing to consider a reduced charge? Isn't that an indication they have a weak case?" Dillard looked at Sheridan.

"Perhaps," Sheridan said.

"Well, what is your recommendation?" Dillard took a sip of his coffee.

"Let me tell you how it'll all go down," Sheridan said. "You plead. The government keeps their end of the bargain. The judge accepts the plea. You'll get a two- to three-year suspended sentence."

"No jail time?"

"No jail time."

"I resume my practice?"

"That's up to the Massachusetts Medical Board. If you were a lawyer, you'd be disbarred for five years, maybe for life. You guys may have different rules."

Dillard was listening.

"That's the good news," said Sheridan. "The bad news is the publicity. But you're going to get that regardless. That's a given.

"Now you're going to have to testify in federal court against your charitable colleague, Sonny Callahan. I don't know how deep it goes, but it could get messy. Callahan is into everything that can turn a buck. The DA can't be fixed, that's obvious, nor can the feds. You'll be called before a federal grand jury, this time as a witness. They'll indict Callahan and you'll be kept on ice to testify at his trial."

Dillard was about to speak. "No, hear me out." Sheridan flicked his wrist forward. "I'm not into your IRA connection. I've heard some stories about Callahan. The feds are out to bring him down. I don't know what they have, but they need someone to tie it all together, and that's you." Sheridan pointed toward Dillard.

Raimondi and Buckley said nothing.

"Well, what do you think?" Dillard looked at Sheridan intently.

"Legally, I'd say go for the deal. But as one man to another and in the interests of longevity, I think it'll be your death warrant. Frankly, I'd rather testify against the Mafia than against Sonny Callahan."

Dillard unmeshed his fingers and sat up straight. "Tell the prosecutors no deal!"

"Are you serious?" Buckley knitted his brow in amazement.

"We're going to beat this thing, Mr. Sheridan!" Dillard's voice was strong and sounded optimistic. "Tell them I want total vindication. Maybe I'll even file a liability suit against the Commonwealth!"

"Okay," Sheridan said, getting up from the table. "It's your call. No deal."

They were ushered back into Suite 1047. Fine tried to read them, but Buckley and Sheridan maintained neutral expressions.

"My client says he's innocent." Sheridan looked first at d'Ortega, then at Fine.

"He's crazy," Fine exclaimed in disgust.

D'Ortega had somehow expected it.

"All right," she said, her voice revealing no emotion, "you have your target letter. We'll convene the grand jury one week from today. Your client will be notified."

"One week from today, got that, Tom?" Sheridan turned to Buckley, wiggling his finger above his head.

Buckley and Sheridan stood up to leave. No handshaking, just cool, abbreviated nods.

"Don't say anything flip like 'See you in court,' " Sheridan whispered to Buckley as they made their way to the exit.

Sheridan rapped on the door and the outside guard opened it.

"See you in court, pal." Sheldon Fine winked sardonically.

Buckley started to turn, but Sheridan's elbow punched him in the ribs.

*   *   *

Phil Riley checked the police file on Mayor Jimmy Kane. A few traffic violations, a DUI that had been nol-prossed. Nothing caught his eye. Kane, after all, picked the chief, and the chief did his bidding. There had been talk that Kane would get a slot in the President's cabinet, but that had failed to materialize.

He checked Kane's bio—press clippings, mainly. Kane was inner city, born in Dorchester, Dorchester High School '65, Boston University '69. Mother was Mary Hennessey, deceased; father, Michael Kane, longshoreman.

Riley knew the rest. Kane was Callahan's prat boy. City council, school committee until eight years ago, when he had bested incumbent mayor Henry Lameraux. It had been close, but Irish Catholic Boston hadn't been about to put up with another four years of a French heron choker—not if Sonny Callahan had anything to say about it, which he did.

Riley had checked the Dorchester High yearbook. It was unproductive. Kane had played football and baseball: all-city end, first base. Nickname: "Brother." "Brother Kane." Riley repeated it. "Brother?" A dead end.

26

SHEILA MET Agent Brian Loughlin at 10:30 in a small deli on Charles Street, not far from the Boston Common. They sat in a booth away from the window, where they drank black coffee and shared some English muffins.

"There's a leak somewhere, Sheila, on our end. We're putting all three, Dillard, Callahan, and Sheridan, under surveillance—even Sheridan's two associates, Buckley and Raimondi."

"Look," she said, "I think Sheridan's in the clear. Most of his clientele are simply victims, unfortunates on the downside of life. He represents those people because he's a lawyer. That's what being a lawyer is all about."

"Any clue that he's being tipped off?" Loughlin studied her carefully.

Sheila shook her head.

She thought about the unmarked confidential letter. It was in a woman's hand, postmarked Boston. She had photographed the envelope. The handwriting could be traced.

Loughlin thought the leak came from the Boston Police or the district attorney's office.

"You off again today?" He buttered the last English muffin, broke it, and offered a piece to Sheila.

"I'm due in at noon," she said.

Sheila raised the muffin halfway to her mouth, then paused. "Any inkling as to when Harrington's office is convening the grand jury on the Williams death?"

"D'Ortega and Harrington want to move forthwith. It'll crimp our investigation on Sheridan, but that Dillard guy will be indicted—that's a certainty. After that, the Callahan connection will evaporate. I understand Fine and d'Ortega are meeting with Sheridan and his associate Buckley right now at the Marriott. The room's wired. They're trying to smoke Sheridan out; they think he's getting information illegally from some source. That may be the clincher to get the magistrate's approval for a bug in Sheridan's office. We'll know today. If so, we'll go in Sunday around midnight. The techs tell me it'll take about an hour. You still have that Sunday key, Sheila?"

She gave Loughlin a nod.

Sheldon Fine didn't have to study the tapes of the meeting to realize that no U.S. magistrate would grant a court-ordered surveillance plant. "We'd look like idiots," Fine said to Mayan d'Ortega as they left the Marriott. "Somewhere down the line, this Sheridan guy will make a slip and we'll nail him. For now, I'd go ahead with the grand jury. Maybe after the indictment, things will heat up."

They both stopped at the cab stand.

"I have to fly to Washington to meet with Davis at Justice," Fine said. "We'll give you the nod on the grand jury."

Mayan d'Ortega didn't warm to Sheldon Fine, especially his authoritative attitude. Professionally, he was brilliant; she couldn't deny that. But she could see how Sheridan and Fine collided and she didn't like Fine dictating as to when she was or was not to present her evidence. She merely nodded and shook hands from a professional distance.

Sheila needed to reload her camera. When it was time for her lunch break, she headed for the ladies' room that served their entire floor of seven offices—small businesses like the Sheridan law firm. There were four stalls, each secured by a dead bolt and all empty. Sheila chose the one farthest from the front door. As she removed her camera from the pocket of her skirt and fumbled to release the used cartridge, she heard the outer door open and the *tap-tap-tap* of a woman's heels against the tile floor. Startled and clumsy, she dropped the tape cartridge and watched as it skittered across the floor, coming to rest outside the cubicle and beyond Sheila's line of vision.

It was an aching eternity before Sheila heard Judy Corwin's voice. "Who's there?" she called tentatively.

Sheila kept quiet, scarcely daring to breathe.

"Who dropped this?"

Still Sheila said nothing.

"Well"—Sheila could sense that Judy had shrugged—"if you want it, you can pick it up in Dan Sheridan's office, Suite Eleven-oh-one."

The outer door snapped shut. Sheila, trembling, waited a full minute, then bolted from the cubicle and ran down the service stairs, avoiding the elevator for fear of running into Judy.

She spent her lunch hour walking in the Common, trying to decide what her strategy should be. Denial, she thought, was her only recourse. If Judy mentioned the incident, she would feign curiosity—and innocence. Northwestern Drama School would be useful once again.

Judy held the small black cartridge between her thumb and forefinger. It was about an inch in length and at best one half an inch wide. Could be a roll of film, but Judy dismissed that notion—just too small. Not much bigger than a Tylenol capsule. She had never seen anything like it.

It was possibly valuable. Could belong to someone on the floor. She thought of the tenants. Not exactly first class. It was a building of whispers, a "Sam Spade building," as Sheridan put it—detective agencies, second-mortgage companies. She slid the cartridge into her desk drawer. Raimondi might know what it was or to whom it belonged. She'd ask him.

Raimondi walked down to the end of the hall to Molloy Associates, Private Investigations. The frosted glass door had a sign: BACK AT TWO. Raimondi knocked.

"Yes, what is it?" a voice answered.

"Skip, it's me, Manny."

The small peephole in the door frame moved and the door swung open.

"Manny, you caught me on my lunch hour. Come in."

They sat opposite each other at Skip's gunmetal desk in the one-room office.

"Want a beer?" Skip pointed to a small refrigerator behind his desk. "Maybe a sandwich?" Raimondi shook his head, noting that

Skip's lunch, a hero sandwich, french fries, and a Budweiser, was half-consumed.

"What can I do for you, Manny? Compromising photos is our specialty this week—extra Green Stamps."

Manny Raimondi was friendly with Jim Molloy, who had earned the nickname "Skip" from his ability to chase down recalcitrant witnesses and deadbeat dads. Raimondi had almost gone in with Skip, had even joined him on a few assignments—a workers' comp claimant with a feigned back injury got caught lifting bags of cement, stuff like that. But it wasn't Raimondi's shtick. He'd stayed with Sheridan.

"Ever used something like this?" Raimondi extracted the cartridge from his pocket and jiggled it in the palm of his hand, then handed it to Molloy.

"Not anything this small."

Molloy studied it, turning it over between his thumb and forefinger. "I use something similar. Catch middle-aged husbands coming out of motels with young chicks, sometimes with guys. In divorce proceedings, it gives my clients the edge."

Raimondi smiled. He knew how these things worked.

"Judy found it on the floor early this morning in the ladies' room. Probably nothing, but it's small-millimeter stuff. Not ours. I thought you might have lost it."

"Not in the ladies' room," Skip said, "but come on in the back to my darkroom. We may screw it up when we open it, but we'll see what develops. Could be a baptism, bar mitzvah, or, if we get lucky, an orgy."

"You got a darkroom?" Raimondi looked at Molloy quizzically.

"Hey, I even develop the stuff. I used to farm it out—and all of a sudden, I got a lot of partners. Come on in. Don't breathe or you'll disturb the shades and ruin the negatives. The room's that tiny."

Molloy switched on a thin red light, then took a penknife and peeled off the small cap on the cartridge. He placed the tiny roll of film in a solution and watched the pictures emerge. It took a good half hour.

He peered through a magnifying glass. "All gobbledygook to me,

Manny," he said, scrutinizing each picture. "Pics of some letter envelopes and what looks like shots of the interior of some office. Here, have a look." He handed the glass to Raimondi.

Raimondi studied the eight prints carefully. The views were a layout of their office. There was a letter addressed PRIVATE AND CONFIDENTIAL to Sheridan. It wasn't gobbledygook to Raimondi. "Can I have these?" he asked Molloy.

"Sure. I'll drain off the solution and put them in the enlarger."

"No, just the prints will be okay."

"You see something?" Molloy was curious.

Raimondi cocked his head as if he heard a door closing very far away. "I'm afraid so," he said.

27

WHEN SHEILA returned to the office after lunch, Raimondi smiled his usual Latin smile, white teeth flashing a welcome. Sheila noticed he was carrying a paper sack. She still hadn't figured out how to get the cartridge back from Judy.

"Brown-bagging it," he said, lifting the bag slightly. "The boss is two weeks behind in my pay."

"Dan will be back this afternoon," Judy said.

"Okay, I'll eat these munchies in his office." He hoisted the bag again.

Raimondi shot the inside bolt on the office door, took a screwdriver and a pair of pliers from the bag, moved a wooden chair under the air duct in the center of the ceiling, and stood on it. Safely balanced, he then proceeded to unscrew the protective grid, lifting it out of its groove. He poked his head into the void—nothing there but an air filter and corrugated tubing. He stepped down, extracted a coiled gadget resembling a charcoal briquette starter from the bag, plugged its wire into a wall socket, and climbed back on the seat of the chair. The Geiger emitted a slight hum as Raimondi poked it into the inner recesses of the cavity above.

Nothing there, he thought. Next, he pushed aside a fiberboard ceiling block, peered inside, then scanned with the Geiger. Nothing unusual.

He spent the next several minutes inspecting the room and its contents—the bookcase, law books, the corners of the chairs and the leather couch, underneath all the furniture. He lifted the rug, checked around Sheridan's desk, opened the windows, looked outside. He took the large painting of Boston Common down off the wall and inspected it, running his fingers around the edges. He unscrewed the recessed lightbulbs in the ceiling and repeated the process visually and checked the sockets with his Geiger. The room was clean—at least for now.

* * *

Raimondi walked down Tremont Street and mixed in with the late
commuters at Park Street station, keeping his eye on the entrance
of the building that housed Sheridan's office. He had a clear view.
When Judy Corwin departed with Buckley, it was 6:10 P.M.

He moved over to the steps of the Park Street Church and maintained his vigil, scanning the passersby. Then he retraced his steps
toward the building, stopping across the street at the Old Granary
Burial Ground. He checked to his right and left. No one seemed
to be tailing. He doubled back and reassumed his position on the
church steps.

At 6:35, he saw Sheila O'Brien emerge from the lobby. He knew
she lived in Charlestown and assumed she would be taking the
MBTA Green Line at Government Center, but instead she headed
right toward him. He ducked behind a fluted pillar. She continued
on her way, walking across the Common, turning her head now
and then to check over her shoulder. Raimondi trailed at a safe
distance. At the entrance to the Public Garden, she stopped, pulled
a hand mirror out of her purse, and fluffed her hair.

Raimondi slowed down by the softball diamond and pretended
to take in the game. It was near dusk, and the lights on the field
melted in with the glare of the late-afternoon sun. Raimondi took
in several players going through their warm-up pacings. Out of the
corner of his eye some two hundred feet ahead, he watched Sheila
O'Brien as she moved on.

He followed along, keeping Sheila just in sight.

Suddenly, she quickened her pace, crossing Beacon Street and
turning into the brick-lined sidewalk of the Charles Way.

Raimondi saw her enter a café-style bookstore. He had waited at
a discreet distance for several minutes, when a nondescript car
pulled up—maybe an '83 Nissan—two-door. A tall, good-looking
college type got out of the passenger side, then waved the driver
on as he stood for a moment, checking right and left. Raimondi
stooped, pretending to tie his shoe, and watched the man enter
the bookstore.

Raimondi recognized him—the same guy he had spotted coming
out of World Cinematics. He moved down the street to a drugstore
on the corner, where he took a counter seat and ordered a black

coffee. He could still see the entrance to the bookstore. Ten minutes passed before Sheila O'Brien emerged and hailed a cab. Seconds later, the World Cinematics guy came out as the same Nissan pulled alongside. He got in on the passenger's side and the car drove away. Raimondi memorized the license plate number as it sped past his position.

Raimondi called his contact at the Department of Motor Vehicles. L-5705 was registered to Patrick Casey, 2585 Commonwealth Avenue, Brighton. There were a raft of Caseys in the Brighton directory, several Patricks, but none listed at 2585 Commonwealth Avenue. He took a cab over to Brighton. What should have been 2585 was a sprawling Stop & Shop. The pieces of one part of the puzzle were coming together. Sheila O'Brien was a cop, probably FBI.

As Raimondi took a cab back to Sheridan's waterfront condominium, he felt a sickening knot tightening in his stomach. He felt lousy. He had liked Sheila. And he wasn't sure how he'd broach the subject to Sheridan. He was pretty sure Dan was gone on the woman.

Sheila O'Brien went to the underground garage and, as instructed by Loughlin, drove her assigned car out to a motel on the Worcester Turnpike, parking in the rear. She ate a light dinner—soup and salad—in the coffee shop, then walked to 25L and knocked on the door.

"Come in, Sheila." Agent Dave Walsh greeted her. "Brian will be along in a moment. I think you know Hal Davis from Justice, Agent Bob Kerry, and Assistant U.S. Attorney Sheldon Fine." She shook hands automatically and then everyone settled back to munch on pretzels and sip tonic water and diet sodas. Loughlin arrived a few minutes later.

"Sheridan's shrewd, real cute," Davis began. "Wouldn't you say so, Miss O'Brien?" He looked at Sheila.

"Yeah, cute," she said, her voice flat.

Davis blinked uneasily but continued. "The meeting among Sheridan, Fine, and d'Ortega produced nothing. Our team proposed a plea bargain, but that went pfft." Davis's hand cut the air. "We've decided to let you ease off on Sheridan for the moment," he said, nodding toward Sheila. "Just play secretary."

"Wouldn't it be better if I sort of . . . well, you know?"

"Resign?" Davis inquired sharply. "No. We've never had such an edge. Just lie low. No photographs. Nothing to draw attention. Watch the comings and goings. We'll get the three on tape yet."

"What three?"

Davis studied Sheila O'Brien for a moment, then spoke as if he was delivering a lecture. "We'll nail Sheridan with conspiracy to obstruct justice. It's the broadest federal statute we have. Tell a witness to say *A* when the attorney knows it's *B*. Maybe we've been concentrating on the wrong frame of reference."

"I'm not reading you," Sheila said.

"We offered Dillard a deal. He didn't bite. So far, he and Sheridan are stone walls. Sheridan's a goddamned maverick. But Callahan is another breed of cat. We can indict Sonny Callahan for attempting to bribe District Attorney Harrington. When we confront him with that fact, he may decide to swing."

"Swing against Sheridan? How?" Sheila furrowed her forehead.

"We know that Callahan visited Sheridan on behalf of Dillard," Fine cut in. "If Callahan says that he offered a bribe to find the right judge and Sheridan said okay . . ."

Sheila O'Brien felt sick. She looked at Davis, then caught the arrogant curl of Sheldon Fine's lips. She eyed Brian Loughlin, militant yet innocent, and Dave Walsh. Zealous, sure, but robots within the system.

"What do you plan to do?" Lost, Sheila tried to summon up courage.

"We got a tip that Callahan is heading for New York. We plan to bust him then," Davis said, permitting himself a thin smile.

Sheila was disturbed. Loughlin noted the almost-imperceptible shake of her head.

She had come to admire Dan Sheridan. He was decent, honorable. And she didn't want to see him get bagged by the likes of Sheldon Fine, who was not above resorting to entrapment to get to Sheridan and Dillard. But she had signed on to do a job.

"All right." She looked at Davis, then at Fine. "I'll go along. Just keep me posted."

*   *   *

"I can't fucking believe this!" Sheridan grabbed Raimondi by his shirt collar, almost hoisting him off the floor. Raimondi didn't resist, allowing Sheridan to vent his rage.

Sheridan was primed to push Raimondi back onto the sofa, but suddenly he relinquished his grip. "I'm sorry." He sighed, shaking his head. "I . . . I . . ." He fought to compose himself. "Finish your drink, Manny. I . . . Are you sure?"

"No, not absolutely. But the coincidences defy the odds of chance." He patted the photos that he had shown Sheridan when he had described the nuances that only an experienced detective would pick up.

Sheridan went to the window overlooking Boston Harbor and leaned forward on the sill. He saw nothing.

Raimondi could sense Sheridan's hurt. He didn't feel too good himself. But he would get a good night's sleep and wake up tomorrow to another day, another quest. He knew that his boss was totally devastated.

"Can you give me Sheila O'Brien's résumé? I'll take the eight o'clock shuttle for New York tomorrow morning," Raimondi said.

"Okay," Sheridan said, still hunched at the window, his voice a hoarse whisper. "Judy will give you the—see Judy."

Raimondi let himself out, glancing back at Sheridan just before closing the door. Sheridan hadn't moved.

28

"THIS'LL BE my last run," Sonny Callahan said to his son, Bobby, as he snapped his shabby leather briefcase shut.

"Dad, I think it's too dangerous. Our phones are tapped; you know you'll be tailed."

"Listen, laddie," Callahan said as he struggled into a battered raincoat, "there's only a million here." He patted the case. "Deegan expected this two weeks ago."

"Deegan and the rest would turn on you in a moment if it served their purpose. They'll leave you out to dry."

"Now don't be talking nonsense. Deegan and I go back a long way."

"I know, I know," Bobby interrupted, "but I'm getting sick of the whole enterprise. You've worked your ass off for years. Fifty years from now, we'll all be dead, and there'll still be killings in London and Belfast."

"That's the way life is; it's been going on for four hundred years. D'ye think Wolfe Tone and Daniel O'Connell dinna know that?"

"Dad, for Christsakes! Stop giving me that Gaelic bullshit! You're living in the fucking past, a past that's dead and gone! We're the future!" Bobby tapped his chest.

Sonny adjusted the brim of his rumpled hat and said nothing. He picked up the briefcase in one hand and a small grainy suitcase in the other and made his way to the door.

"Dad, be careful." Bobby's voice softened. "You want me to fly you to Providence? You could catch the train from there."

"They'd spot us easy." Sonny Callahan opened the door. "I'll drive to Boston. It's the top of the rush hour. Park the car at South Station. Take the train from there."

Agents Walsh and Kerry followed Sonny Callahan's '88 black Cadillac up Route 3 without difficulty. They called ahead on a special cellular phone to Agents Casey and Rierson, who picked up Sonny's car as he drove into the South Station underground garage.

Sonny seemed oblivious to the people around him as he rode the escalator to the station level. He stood in line for a round-trip ticket on the Amtrak Senator, then carried his two bags to the Track 5 platform. Agent Walsh, looking collegiate in a tweed sports jacket, gray slacks, and open-collared shirt, bought two round-trip tickets and signaled to Kerry.

Callahan rested his bags against his legs and watched the Amtrak train pull into the station. He unwrapped a cigar, lit it, and proceeded to puff with nonchalance as the disembarking New York passengers filed past. Kerry, in a gray business suit, stood a dozen yards from Callahan but kept him in view while pretending to read the *Wall Street Journal.*

"Amtrak train, the Senator, now boarding on Track Five," came the PA announcement. "Stopping at Providence, New London, New Haven, Bridgeport, and Penn Station."

Sonny Callahan took a last deep pull on his cigar, flicked it onto the cement platform, ground it out with his shoe, took up his bags, and walked several cars ahead. Kerry and Walsh followed at a safe distance, converging when they spotted Callahan storing his briefcase in an overhead compartment. Sonny took a seat, keeping the suitcase on his lap. Walsh took up his position some five seats in front of Callahan; Kerry sat down eight seats to Callahan's rear. If Callahan had any inkling he was being followed, he failed to show it. He extracted a tabloid newspaper from his suit pocket and began to read it as the train pulled out of the station.

They clicked along the Connecticut shoreline and Callahan seemed engrossed in the *Irish Echo*. At New Haven, the train stopped for fifteen minutes to exchange engines, diesel for electric. Sonny placed his *Irish Echo* on the seat, then went out onto the platform, carrying the suitcase. He set it down close to his right foot, then unwrapped another cigar. Kerry moved out onto the platform, mingling with passengers who sought to catch a breath of fresh air, but keeping an eye on Callahan. Walsh stepped onto the platform about fifty feet ahead, continuing a conversation with a young woman who had been seated near him. Several passengers left the train at New Haven—Yale students, mainly. Callahan waited until the last warning whistle, then picked up his suitcase and re-entered the train.

The Senator arrived at Penn Station at a little past noon. Callahan pulled down his briefcase, picked up the suitcase, and walked with other passengers to the up escalator that led to the Thirty-third Street level. To the agents' surprise, he checked both bags at Amtrak's storage room, then climbed up the stairs toward Eighth Avenue.

Kerry gave Walsh a quick nod to follow Callahan, then turned to confront the young black attendant who had checked Callahan's bags.

"FBI," he announced, flipping open his wallet. "I want to see those bags you just checked in. Those two on the floor with the yellow tags."

"Yes, sir," the attendant said, and lifted them onto the counter. "Is anything wrong?"

Kerry first looked at the briefcase. It was fastened with leather straps but had no lock.

"I just want to see the contents," he said to the attendant, his voice intimidating. He unbuckled the straps and pulled the flaps apart. He reached in and pulled out an Irish hand-knit sweater, socks, shaving kit, underwear, and a pair of shoes. He emptied the contents on the counter and ran his hand around the inside corners: nothing.

He unclicked the suitcase. More sweaters, socks, underwear, and a copy of the *Irish Echo*.

"Here, put these back!" Kerry snapped. "And . . . uh . . . here's a ten for your trouble. Okay?"

Kerry took the stairs two at a time and entered the brassy crush of Eighth Avenue.

"He's in there." Walsh motioned to a small bar where a sign on the frosted glass storefront spelled out IRISH ALEHOUSE.

Kerry shook his head, quickening his pace toward his partner.

"I think we've been had. There wasn't a goddamned thing in either bag but crap."

"What?" Walsh looked quizzically at Kerry.

"Sweaters, underwear, I can't understand it."

They waited outside the bar for almost an hour. They could see Sonny downing several shots of Jameson, conversing with the bartender, laughing with a few old Tads, setting up a round of drinks. Finally, he plunked what appeared to be a hefty wad of bills on the bar and made his way out.

Kerry and Walsh followed, watching at a distance as Callahan reclaimed his bags and got on the Shoreline Limited for Boston.

"What the hell is this?" Kerry said to Walsh. "Callahan takes the train to New York, hoists a couple at an Irish bar, then rides back. A nine-hour trip. Something's screwy!"

Sonny chortled when he called Deegan from a pay phone at South Station. Deegan was also at a pay booth, in the South Bronx. Callahan was calling at a designated time. Out of the corner of his eye, he spotted the two agents who had tailed him.

"Jaysus, Deegan, couldn't have gone better. Sean gets on at Providence, he did, looked like a fancy Ivy Leaguer in a Yale sweatshirt. The two bloodhounds follow me out at New Haven, see me guarding me suitcase like it was Fort Knox. Then Sean picks up the briefcase from the overhead bin, shoves it in his duffel bag, replaces it. Jaysus, Deegan"—he started laughing, almost in tears—"even I couldn't tell the difference. Sean gets off at New Haven, keeps going. I check me bags at Penn Station, then go have a few jars. I know they searched 'em. Put me *Irish Echo* on the top and later I find it on the bottom." Both men chuckled.

" 'Tis accounted for," Deegan said. "The lads will be pleased. You'll be given credit."

"We've got a bit of a problem, Deegan."

"I know, but it had to be done. I'm sure you appreciate—"

"Maybe I do; maybe I don't. I'm getting a little old, Deegan."

"So am I. You're not suggestin' now . . ."

"I'll be in touch, Deegan." Callahan gave an exasperated sigh.

Kerry and Walsh watched from across Atlantic Avenue. Callahan wanted to wave to them like the guy in the movie *The French Connection*. But he simply picked up his bags and headed for the underground garage.

* * *

Raimondi took a cab from La Guardia and checked in at the Burdett Secretarial School listed on Sheila O'Brien's résumé. It was housed in a business complex near Barnard College, up on Broadway at 128th Street. He took the elevator to the third floor and was directed to the admissions office.

Raimondi was wearing a dark blue suit, white shirt with cuff links, and a regimental silk tie. He had left his leather jacket back in Boston.

"Hello," he said pleasantly to a matronly woman who was shuffling papers at the counter separating the entrance area from the clerical offices. "Maybe you can help me, Mrs. . . . ?"

"Perkins." Her jelly-bean eyes danced behind her thick-rimmed glasses.

"I have here the résumé of one of your graduates, Sheila O'Brien. Got a certificate here—let's see." Raimondi laid a paper on the counter. "About a year ago. She's applying for a position in our law firm as a paralegal, and I was just checking up on her credentials."

"Sure," Mrs. Perkins said. "I remember Sheila O'Brien. Lovely young woman. Going to law school at the time."

"Law school?"

"I think she was in her last year. She was one of our best students."

"Do you know what law school?"

"I'm not sure, but I believe it was Fordham."

Raimondi thanked her.

He took a cab to Lincoln Center and got off at the Fordham alumni office there.

He settled down in a quiet alcove in the library. The young student librarian brought him copies of the university's yearbook, *The Quill,* for the last five years.

Nineteen ninety-two. There it was. "Sheila Kathleen O'Brien." A smiling, radiant picture. "*Law Review:* 2,3. Moot Court Award, 3. . . ." Raimondi whistled to himself. He had hit pay dirt. But it was pay dirt he had hoped he wouldn't find.

29

RAIMONDI TOOK the 7:00 A.M. shuttle from La Guardia, arrived at Logan an hour later, and took a cab to Sheridan's waterfront condo. On the sidewalk in front of the building he hesitated. Maybe I should skip it, he thought. He had to double back to Revere and pick up Mrs. Doyle and her boy. Buckley wanted them in court by ten, when they would start empaneling the jury.

No. Sheridan's got to know up front. He rang the doorbell.

Sheridan was in his bathrobe. He hadn't shaved and his left eye was still puffy and the skin around it had taken on a jaundiced cast. Raimondi recognized the grainy look of a sleepless night, the shadows dark as bruises under his disconsolate eyes.

"Come on in, Manny." Sheridan's voice was artificially jaunty. "Just about to cook some grub. . . . You eaten yet?"

"Had some rolls and stuff on the plane, but I could use a cup of coffee."

Raimondi and Sheridan sat at the kitchen table in front of the window overlooking Boston Harbor. There was an awkward silence. Raimondi took a few sips of coffee and looked glumly at the gulls floating and wheeling outside, their raucous cries muted by the thermal windowpane.

"Well?" Sheridan looked at Raimondi, his eyes hooded with melancholy resignation.

"She's a cop, all right." Raimondi let out a tired sigh. "Some of the stuff was legit. Business certificate. Got the secretarial skills, that's obvious. The Chicago bit, Northwestern, even the summer stock checked out.

"She graduated from Fordham Law about two years ago, even made *Law Review*," Raimondi said quietly.

"*Law Review?*"

"Number two in her class. Passed the New York bar exam on her first try."

Sheridan seemed to fold within himself. He kneaded his eyes with his thumb and forefinger but said nothing.

"You want Judy to handle it?" Raimondi cradled his cup in both hands. "She can say Buckley got soft—that Caitlin's coming back."

"No." Sheridan's voice was as far away as his gaze. "I have to do it. I'll see her today. I'll be in later.

"You'd better get going, Manny. You have to ferry the Doyles to court." He rose to his feet like a tired old man. "I might drop in to see how Tommy's doing."

Raimondi was feeling uneasy. In all their years together, he had never seen Sheridan so openly overwhelmed, not even when his wife and son were killed. He always had an inner toughness that sustained him regardless of the adversities they had faced. And they had faced them often. The liaison with the O'Brien woman must have gone deeper than Raimondi realized.

"Can I do anything, Dan? Want me to swing by and pick you up after Tommy gets going?"

"No, stay at the courthouse. Tommy may need you. . . ." His voice trailed off.

Raimondi abruptly drained his cup and stood up. "Hey, Dan"— he grabbed Sheridan's shoulder and gave it a little shake—"she's not worth it. I don't know what gets into broads these days. You're better off solo."

A trace of the old Sheridan surfaced. He cocked his head to one side and gave Manny a sardonic grin, full of rue and self-knowledge.

"I just feel like such a goddamned fool," he said. "I thought I was beyond all that adolescent mooning and yearning. But the fact is, the girl got to me and I let myself get suckered."

"Yeah." Manny clapped Sheridan on the shoulder again. "Broads." He shook his head. "They're like streetcars. One comes along every five minutes."

Phil Riley made a call to Hawthorne-on-the-Charles. He wanted to recheck the Williams woman's apartment. Maybe there was something they had all overlooked, something that would identify Cooch.

Schofield, the manager, told him the place was vacant.

"Several moving vans were here last week," he said.

"I'd like to see it anyway," Riley responded. He wasn't quite convinced Schofield was leveling with him.

Schofield unlocked the door with "I told you so" annoyance, gesturing with his hand as he swung the double doors open.

Riley could hardly believe it. The living room was completely vacant. The center of the floor where the fountain had once gurgled was a lead-lined depression. Even the decorative rocks had been removed.

Everything was gone—drapes, rugs, furniture—only a phone and answering machine sat on the barren parquet flooring.

Riley went from room to room, Schofield trailing behind.

"Who authorized all this?" Riley's hand swept in an outward arc.

"Why, you guys did." Schofield's face had an amused smile. "The movers had a letter from your district attorney's office."

Riley knew he appeared foolish. Best to say nothing. But he had to have the authoritative last word. "Ever see anyone besides Dr. Dillard going into Miss Williams's apartment?"

"Lieutenant." Schofield's voice was pinched with displeasure. "The answer is *no*. I didn't even see the doctor. I'm the manager, not some busybody landlady. Now, if you'll excuse me . . ."

Riley drove back toward headquarters. Whoever cleaned out Williams's apartment couldn't have been more thorough. He'd call d'Ortega. Somehow the district attorney's office wasn't letting the Boston Police in on certain aspects of the investigation.

Sheila O'Brien was in the Xerox room when Dan came in just before noon.

"Good morning, Dan!" Judy said, trying to emulate Sheila's ebullient personality.

"Good morning, Judy," Dan said huskily as he removed his sunglasses and tucked them into his breast pocket.

"Your eye looks thirty-three and a third percent better, as we legalites like to say. The morning mail and messages are on your desk. Want Sheila to bring you in some coffee?"

"No." Dan seemed to avoid Judy's eyes. "Give me ten minutes to go through the mail and stuff. Then send Sheila in."

Dan didn't smile. Unlike him.

"Oh," she called after him, "Monsignor Flynn called. Wants you to call him right away."

Judy could tell from the lights on her telephone that Sheridan was making a call on his private line. Even she couldn't listen in.

A few moments later, he buzzed her on the intercom.

"Judy, have Sheila come in. It's almost lunchtime, but could you hang in for a while? Buckley and Raimondi won't be back until close to five."

Judy signaled Sheila, then returned to her conversation. "Dan, Raimondi called from the courthouse. They've seated a pretty good jury—six blacks, two Hispanics, and four Caucs." Her voice was upbeat. "Things look good."

Dan did not respond. The shrug of her shoulders had ancient origins.

"Can I bring you coffee, Mr. Sheridan?" Sheila hesitated at the door with her steno pad.

"No. No, thanks." Sheridan looked up from the correspondence on his desk. There were tight parentheses at each corner of his mouth, a serious edge to his voice.

"Sit down." He motioned with a pen. "I think you and I have to talk."

Sheila sensed that he was deeply upset. She sat in the client's chair.

Dan remained silent as Sheila became increasingly apprehensive.

"I have to let you go," he said at last.

"Why?" She furrowed her brow. "I don't understand."

He avoided her gaze, concentrating instead on the point of his pen, which he twirled between his thumb and forefinger.

"We have to take Caitlin O'Malley back. Seems she's found a live-in baby-sitter and needs the money."

Still he did not look at her.

Sheila knew there had to be more. Caitlin's coming back didn't ring true. Had Judy given him the damn film?

"Is it because of us . . .?" She tried to read him.

"No, nothing like that," he retorted. "I rather enjoyed it." The remark was meant to sting.

"You're not leveling with me!" Sheila bolted from her seat, her eyes suddenly furious. "I think you owe me an explanation!"

In that moment, their eyes collided, then held. Sheridan's blue stare was as cold as Siberia.

"You want an explanation, Sheila? Here!" He tossed the tiny film cartridge toward the front of his desk. She made no attempt to catch it as it rolled onto the floor. She slumped back into the chair like a rag doll, limp and defeated.

Sheridan sat unmoved.

"You're an FBI agent." His voice was now whispery deep. "Fordham Law, number two in your class, member of the New York bar. Who's not leveling with whom?"

She absorbed the spite and hiss of his anger.

Sheridan felt like saying something else cruel, something more to wound her. Was getting me in bed part of your assignment? he wanted to ask, but he wasn't sure he wanted to hear the answer.

"I think you should go—right now. Clear out your desk. Judy will send you two weeks' severance pay." His voice was mild but held an icy undertone.

Sheila jerked forward in the chair, then dashed for the door.

Sheridan sat at his desk, not moving for several minutes. Then he picked the small cartridge up off the floor and tossed it into the wastebasket.

He opened his closet door and checked in the mirror. He looked drained, exhausted. He straightened his tie. He had to put this all behind him.

"Dan." Judy's voice came on the intercom. "What was that all about? Sheila just left. Said she was fired. What happened? She's the best secretary we ever had."

Sheridan paused for several seconds. "I'll tell you all about it. But now get ahold of Essex County District Attorney Hollingsworth up in Salem and tell him to forget the Father Duffy prosecution."

"Forget it? He's not going to buy that."

"He'll have to. Father Duffy hung himself in his room about an hour ago."

"Oh my God! Bad day, Dan."

"Yeah, Judy, not good."

30

MAYAN D'ORTEGA sipped her early-morning coffee as she scanned the stories in the *Boston Globe* and *Herald*. There were pictures of lawyers Barry Ginsberg and Bob Catalano, hands cuffed in front, heads bowed, as they were being hustled by FBI agents into the federal courthouse.

"Sting operation nets two prominent Boston barristers," the caption began. "Both arraigned before federal magistrate Shirley Rae. More arrests expected."

It was strictly a federal show. There was no mention of the Williams case, although it was noted that a special grand jury was being convened by District Attorney Harrington's office. It added that Harrington was calling a press conference for 10:00 A.M. the next day. "He is expected to announce his candidacy for the United States Senate and to endorse his first assistant, Mayan d'Ortega, to complete his term of office. She will be the first woman to be so appointed in the Commonwealth."

Mayan's intercom button blinked red.

"Miss d'Ortega," Kristina Collins said, "Mr. Fine is here with Mr. Harrington and several federal agents; if you could find the time, he would like you to come over."

It was a polite request.

"I'll be there within five minutes," Mayan replied, "and would you remind Miss Doherty to start preparing summonses for the Burlington police officers and the other witnesses. She knows what to do. And put a call in to Dr. Myron Gellis in New York. I want to speak with him personally." She paused. "One other thing. Have Dr. McCafferty see me in my office at five this afternoon."

Of the talent gathered in Harrington's office, only Harrington appeared relaxed. Brian Loughlin nodded a grim hello. Sheldon Fine looked as if he had bitten into a lemon.

"Hey, it's not the end of the world." Harrington clapped Fine on the back. "We can get Sonny Callahan on just my tape alone."

"Callahan pulled a fast one on us," Agent Walsh said. "Have to hand it to him. Somehow, somewhere during the trip to Penn Station, someone made an exchange, probably when we followed him out at New Haven."

"Both of you left the train?" Fine's expression hovered between exasperation and disbelief.

"Hey," Walsh said testily, "we had our man, carried out our assignment. He duped us. We're going to nail that son of a bitch, believe me!"

"I believe you," Fine replied, his voice heavy with sarcasm.

"For Christsakes," Loughlin cut in, "we've got to stop this goddamned bickering! We're all on the same team. Right now, we've come up with a lot of zeros. But, as Yogi Berra would say—"

"Screw Yogi Berra," Sheldon Fine cut in. "And how's the Sheridan connection doing? . . . Agent O'Brien?"

"That might be the one ace we've got," Loughlin said. "I'm seeing Agent O'Brien tonight. We just need a scintilla of evidence"—Loughlin signified with his thumb and forefinger held a hair apart—"and we plant the bugs. Could catch the three of them—Sheridan, Callahan, and Dillard—in one net: conspiracy to obstruct justice."

Harrington sat on the edge of his desk, secretly amused by the discordant attitudes of Fine and the federal agents, each side wanting the glory. Let them fight it out.

"I think it's time to execute our basic plan." Harrington seized the moment. "We start presenting evidence to the grand jury next Thursday. No need to run over the protocol. Miss d'Ortega will handle the case." There was a slight acquiescent nod exchanged between Harrington and his chief prosecutor. "Dillard will be indicted, no question about it."

"What about the lie detector bit?" Sheldon Fine tried to regain the momentum he seemed to have lost.

"What about it?" Harrington said, still sitting on the edge of his desk, his arms crossed.

"Don't you have to put exculpatory evidence in front of the grand jury? The good with the bad?"

"Exculpatory evidence, yes." Harrington's voice took on a professorial timbre. "Lie detector—no! That's like a target defendant trying to read a letter from his mother to the jury. You were there, Fine. Miss d'Ortega shut that crazy pitch down cold!"

Sheldon didn't like being called by his last name, especially in front of federal agents, and he didn't appreciate Harrington's lecture.

"What do you say, Mayan?" Harrington again nodded toward his chief prosecutor.

Mayan d'Ortega, too, recognized the dissension among the feds. Their part of Operation Blackstone had fizzled. And strangely, she had come to feel a nagging respect for Dan Sheridan. It may have been just the first impression, but he seemed to be a straight shooter. She kept this to herself.

"We take the case in segments." Her voice was calm, disciplined. "Williams was murdered. Motive?" Mayan d'Ortega's forefinger drew a question mark in the air, signed with a dot.

"We have some ideas. She was a courier for international terrorist groups—the IRA, mainly. Maybe she skimmed. That's probably why she was hit. We haven't yet linked her with stand-up evidence to the IRA. For our purposes, we don't have to. We linked her with Dillard. . . ."

"Hey, we know all this," interrupted Fine, looking perturbed. "You indict Dillard for Williams's murder. What then? . . . What about the big picture?"

Harrington smiled inwardly. He disliked Fine. Tact wasn't one of the federal prosecutor's strong points. He watched Mayan d'Ortega respond.

"Sheldon," she said as her fingers did a little dance on the tabletop, "my job at the moment is to present sufficient evidence to the grand jury so that they will return an indictment. Down the line, there'll be a trial. I don't underestimate my adversary, Mr. Sheridan, nor should you. Right now, the big picture, as you put it, is of little concern to me."

"All right, look," Harrington interrupted diplomatically. "You guys keep up the surveillance. We turn up the heat. Don't move on Callahan just yet. He'll contact Sheridan or Dillard. Then you guys know what to do. Okay?"

"Okay, Mayan," Loughlin said, "the case is all yours. We'll set up surveillance around the courthouse, like a Mafia don's wake. Check the comings and goings."

Harrington glanced at his watch. Sheldon Fine and the feds knew the meeting was over.

* * *

Harrington flicked a switch near his rich walnut credenza and the top slid into a recess in the wall, revealing the concealed bar. He cracked some ice, poured two fingers of Dewar's for himself, and measured out straight tequila for Mayan, lacing it with a lime segment.

"To you, Mayan," he said, handing her the cocktail glass. They toasted each other, the crystal glasses clinking.

"Did you read the morning *Globe*?"

"You mean about Barry Ginsberg and Bob Catalano?"

"No, I'm referring to the bit about you becoming the first woman district attorney in the Commonwealth." Harrington tipped his glass in her direction, then took a good swallow of scotch.

"Where I come from"—Mayan gave a wry smile—"on an occasion like this, I pour salt on my thumb, lick it up, and toss the tequila straight down."

"I'm out of salt." Harrington gave her a wicked grin.

"Salud!" she cried, and downed the tequila.

"Salud!" Harrington responded, and drained his scotch.

"This will be my last major case as district attorney." Harrington jiggled his ice cubes. "Want a refill?"

"No thanks, Neil. I've got to get summonses out, and Bernie McCafferty is coming in at five."

"Bernie McCafferty." Harrington poured himself another scotch. "A drunken sot. I saved his ass more than once. You know, five years ago he was the number one orthopedic surgeon in the city— sports injuries, hip and knee replacements, you name it. The booze and the bro—señoritas did him in."

Mayan suddenly looked pensive.

"Neil, I'm a little bothered about the case, particularly the feds attempting to entrap Sheridan."

"Don't let Sheridan fool you." Harrington stirred his scotch. "He's an ex-cop. I almost nailed him once."

"What happened?"

"Long time ago. I was an assistant DA. Sheridan's uncle was a bookie—longshoreman, a drunk to boot. I presented evidence to the grand jury, targeting the uncle for illegal bookmaking. They returned a No Bill. It was absolutely ridiculous. Several witnesses recanted stories they had given the police. I couldn't prove it, but I know Sheridan had a hand in it. I ran into a stone wall."

"Do we need this fight with Sheridan now?"

"Perhaps not," Harrington said. "We indict Dillard. That's our prime job at the moment." He looked at his glass again. "Then let the feds have their field day.

"I'll be relinquishing my office in June to go after the Democratic nomination. That's when you take over. Your appointment has been arranged with Mayor Kane and Governor Stevenson."

"Stevenson's a Republican." Mayan looked at him quizzically.

"Believe me, Mayan, I've got it arranged. If Stevenson appointed one of his own blue bloods, we'd force an election. Jesus Christ couldn't get elected in Boston if He was a Republican. You'll be a good appointment from our standpoint. And oddly, from the governor's. A woman, Latino, talented, and most attractive."

Mayan wasn't completely taken in by the blandishments. All that Irish blarney wasn't her style. And sticking people in jail was beginning to get her down. She had seriously thought of joining the legal staff of the Civil Liberties Union before the DA's office opened up. That was a plum too rich to refuse.

"And once I get to Washington, I'll be appointed to the Judiciary Committee. It's a six-year term. Who knows? We might have even bigger things on the docket."

Mayan was sure he believed that.

"Nice to see you again, Miss d'Ortega," Bernie McCafferty said as the secretary ushered him into the chief prosecutor's office.

"Dr. McCafferty." Mayan came out from around her desk and shook his hand. "Please sit down."

"Mind if I smoke?" He coughed slightly, shielding his mouth with the back of his hand, his eyes mawkish, imploring.

"Go right ahead. . . . I hope you brought your autopsy protocol."

He lit a Carlton with a quivering hand, waved the match in the air until it was extinguished, and placed it in an ashtray on the small conference table. He took a drag, then let the smoke billow upward.

"The autopsy notes and photographs are all here." He patted a manila folder resting on his knees.

"The grand jury will be convened Thursday morning. It's an old room; there are about thirty chairs placed in a semicircle. Looks like a town meeting hall."

"I've testified there many times, Miss d'Ortega. I've always thought the antiquity of the place sort of overawes the jurors."

"Tell me, Doctor . . ."

"Call me Bernie."

"Tell me, Bernie, how many autopsies have you done in the last five years?"

"Oh, I'd say about five hundred, give or take fifty."

"Then you're eminently qualified. You'll have no problem there. How many courtroom cases have you testified in?"

"Civil and criminal, I would say at least two hundred."

"So you know the ropes as an expert witness."

"You bet."

"You know, before the grand jury, there'll be no cross-examination of your testimony. What you say, as far as the jurors are concerned, will be gospel. But the grand jury minutes will be available to defense counsel."

"I'm aware of that." McCafferty pulled his documents from the folder and began spreading them on the table.

"Time of death"—Mayan fixed him with her implacable gaze—"how can you be so sure?"

"It's all here." He gestured toward the pages arrayed before him.

"You say it was between eight-thirty and nine P.M., give or take fifteen minutes?"

"That's what'll cook Dillard." McCafferty was eager to please. "He says he left at ten. Had a full dinner. No stomach contents, nothing in the duodenum or bowel to indicate she had eaten, not even lunch."

"We'll get to that," Mayan said. "But time of death. The grand jury will buy your opinion without question."

"And the same for Dr. Gellis," McCafferty added.

"Okay," Mayan said. "So the jurors buy it. But why should I?"

"Why should you *what?*" McCafferty looked up at her from underneath his shaggy eyebrows.

"Let me put it this way." There was a cynical edge to her voice. "From what I've read, estimation of time of death based on biological factors alone is at best guesswork. We don't want to be giving the jury any pseudoscience."

"Okay, let's analyze it." McCafferty ran his hand through his thinning hair. "Dillard last saw her alive at ten P.M. He has no alibi, before, during, or after.

"And don't overlook his claim that they had a full gourmet meal. I have Dillard's statement right here. They had the works!"

"Couldn't the food contents be digested, say, by nine? The body was found at ten minutes before midnight. You started your post about five A.M. Couldn't the food contents, even blood alcohol, have been completely eliminated by that time?"

"The answer is emphatically *no!* And I can base that on my experience, the medical literature. And Dr. Gellis will back me up."

"Yet the lack of food contents doesn't help in establishing the time of death," Mayan d'Ortega persisted. "What made you and Gellis zero in on eight-thirty to nine?"

"Gellis has considerably more experience than I do as a forensic pathologist. He's done over twenty thousand autopsies and his book *Forensic Pathology* is in its tenth edition. It's the bible in the field.

"Look, Mayan, I can state with reasonable medical certainty that she had *no* dinner that evening, contrary to what Dillard claimed, and that she was not alive when he claims he left at ten P.M." McCafferty was beginning to look flushed. He took another long drag on his cigarette.

Mayan wasn't pleased to see that her office was taking on a smoky haze. "Why couldn't the time of death have been ten-fifteen to eleven P.M., sometime *after* Dillard was seen leaving the premises!"

"You want to nail the guy, don't you?" McCafferty challenged, grinding the cigarette into an ashtray.

"I want to see that justice is done!"

"Well, time of death is sometimes controversial. But the body was found at eleven-fifty P.M. The pictures here"—McCafferty shuffled through the papers—"indicate she was found facedown, fully clothed, in a wooded area. It was cold, environmental temperature fifty-three degrees, according to the Burlington Police.

"When I started my post, the body was cold. Rigor mortis was present, but that's after all night in the cooler. Rectal temperature was sixty-five degrees. Assume normal temperature at ninety-eight point six. I subtract four degrees for each hour. That gets us back to about eight-thirty."

"You obtained your thermal reading at what time?"

McCafferty looked at his notes. "Five-ten A.M., before we started to cut."

"You base all your conclusions on the assumption that she had a normal temperature about nine P.M.?"

"Well hell, Mayan, we have to have a starting point. A normal healthy individual such as the Williams woman walks around with ninety-eight point six."

"Wouldn't it have been more helpful if the EMTs who recovered the body had done a rectal temperature, or Dr. Supples at Boston Memorial when the body was delivered at twelve-thirty-six A.M.?"

"Sure. But that wasn't done, so you've got to go with my findings. . . . And that's not the only factor. Rigor mortis hadn't set in at Boston Memorial. So the death was recent. I measured the potassium content of the eyeball, the vitreous fluid. It was up over normal values. I can draw a graph indicating how this helps to estimate time of death. It's consistent with eight-thirty to nine P.M. And again Gellis will back me up." McCafferty's voice had the whine of frustration. He was sure that if he ever performed an autopsy on Mayan d'Ortega, he would find ice water in her veins.

"When it comes to trial, Sheridan will counter with his own expert pathologists," Mayan said.

"Look, Mayan, there are a lot of whores out there who'll preach pseudoscience, to use your phrase. That's where your cross-examination comes in."

"Do you know Sir Howard Lawton, professor of forensic medicine at London's Guy Hospital, and past president of the International Congress of Legal Medicine, Pathology, and Toxicology?"

"I've heard of him."

"I have his book here." Mayan went to her desk and picked up a large green volume and carried it to the table. McCafferty watched with annoyance as she leafed through several pages in a leisurely way.

"Here," she said. "Let me quote: 'The rate at which the body loses heat after death is a good example of the number of variable factors which make it impossible to arrive at any accurate conclusion on a standard formula as to time of death.'

"Oddly, Doctor, you found the deceased's rectal temperature to be sixty-five degrees. Using the same temperature of sixty-five degrees, Lawton compares six different cases where forensic pathologists estimating the time of death based on thermal loss disagreed, varying from two and a half hours to nine hours."

"May I take Lawton's book?" McCafferty said. "I'll bone up on it."

"Bone up on this part," Mayan said. She spread the book open. "I'm reading from page four ninety-six. Quote: 'At present all that an experienced pathologist can give is an estimation during which death could have occurred. Any estimation presented definitively within narrow limits must be viewed with suspicion. Any estimation down to the hour of death, to say nothing of a fraction of an hour, cannot be made with any degree of exactness.' "

She closed the book with an authoritative thud and handed it to McCafferty.

"You didn't mention finding any cricoid fracture or neck hemorrhaging when you were reporting to Harrington." Mayan's eyes fixed him with a steady dark gaze.

"It was early in the morning. I was a little . . . well, bushed. It was my third post in forty-eight hours. When I heard Gellis was coming in, I rechecked." Perspiration started to stipple McCafferty's forehead.

"Did you arrive at your additional findings before or after Gellis did his post?"

"Before, of course. Gellis and I later agreed."

"Do you know Dillard's attorney, Dan Sheridan?"

"Sure I know him. He's got a way with juries. I have to hand it to him. He's a winner, but he has had his share of tragedy. His wife and son were killed in an automobile accident three years ago; as medical examiner, I viewed the bodies and signed the death certificates."

"Oh? I hadn't heard." Mayan frowned.

"Sheridan's a damn good lawyer, Mayan. But there's no love lost between him and Harrington."

For a moment, Mayan looked thoughtful. Then she shook her head. "I know." She managed a trace of a smile.

McCafferty emitted an inward sigh of relief. The "spic" is a goddamned tough competitor, he said to himself.

He had heard about these Mexican women. Tear you apart in bed. He wondered whether Harrington was humping her. He suppressed a smile. Probably not. Harrington couldn't risk a scandal if he wanted to thrive in the political arena.

"Sheridan never got over the deaths," McCafferty continued. "Poured all his energies into the law. He's a little obsessed."

Mayan, as Harrington had done, gave a dismissive glance at her wristwatch.

McCafferty took the hint. As he got up to leave, he turned on his Gaelic hat-in-hand charm.

"Mayan," he said, wanting to ingratiate himself, "I understand you're going to be Suffolk County's next district attorney."

Mayan merely nodded.

"Congratulations. And *buenos días, señorita*," McCafferty said, as he gathered up his documents. "It's going to be nice working with you."

"*Buenas tardes*," she replied, her dark tiger eyes now liquid, slightly tranquilized.

McCafferty headed for the door.

"You forgot something," she said.

McCafferty turned. "I did?"

"Dr. Lawton's book." She held it up.

The secretary buzzed Mayan d'Ortega that Dr. Gellis's daughter was on line five.

"Yes, this is the district attorney's office in Boston."

"I'm Natalie Gellis, Dr. Gellis's daughter. Is there something that I can help you with? My father had a mild stroke last Thursday. He's now a patient at Mount Sinai Hospital."

"Oh, I am awfully sorry to hear that. I met the doctor in Boston. He performed a postmortem on a homicide victim here and I was going to tell him that the case was coming up before the grand jury tomorrow and that I would like him to testify about his findings on Friday."

"He told me about it," the daughter said. "He got a message from District Attorney Harrington about a week ago and he made arrangements to be there. Unfortunately, he can't make it. I am sure you understand."

"I'm awfully sorry to hear about your father. Please extend our get-well wishes." Mayan d'Ortega clicked the receiver button off and reflected on the turn of events. McCafferty seemed to rely a great deal on Gellis. McCafferty would now be on his own.

31

SHEILA MET Brian Loughlin at a singles bar near Harvard Square in Cambridge. It was late, 10:30, and unusually crowded for a weeknight. They sat in a corner under a dimmed Tiffany lamp. Ferns spilling from polished oak boxes gave them partial protection from the predatory swirl of Harvard students sizing one another up.

"You look a little frazzled," Brian began as he looked over the menu. "Let's get something good to eat."

"Just a cup of coffee, Bri, and hold it for a few minutes."

"What is it?" Loughlin looked quizzically at Sheila. He sensed something was wrong.

"I blew the assignment," she said with manufactured calmness.

"You what?" Loughlin put down the menu.

"I dropped a film in the ladies' room, the one from my mini-camera."

Loughlin studied her as she spoke. She looked drawn and her skin was pasty.

"Judy Corwin found it. They had it developed. It had interior shots of the office, files, correspondence. Sheridan and the investigator, Raimondi, must have done some checking. They know I went to Fordham Law, that I'm an FBI agent. Sheridan confronted me about it earlier today."

"And?"

"I didn't deny it. He fired me on the spot."

Loughlin let out a soft whistle. He made a steeple of his fingers and peered over them. Several seconds passed.

"How in hell did they link you to the film?"

"Who else would be taking pictures of our office? Who had access? No. Raimondi was always suspicious. I could tell, little things."

Loughlin emitted a loud sigh.

"Okay, Sheila, these things happen. It's no big deal."

"I'll have to tell Davis," she said. "It's not going to be easy."

Loughlin felt sure that after the Callahan fiasco, Davis would be furious—even mad enough to get her dismissed. But he would try to protect her.

"Leave Davis to me. I'll tell him Sheridan felt he had to cut down, or that the old secretary needed the job and had to be rehired."

Sheila seemed confused.

"I'll handle it." Loughlin picked up the menu. "I think you need a drink, Sheila. I think we both do."

Loughlin looked at her again. She was silent and seemed very, very far away.

He signaled a waitress hovering nearby. "Two neat scotches."

It should have been good news. Young Buckley stormed into the office. "The defense threw in the towel; we just settled for eight hundred and fifty-eight thousand dollars."

"What?" Judy wrapped her arms around Buckley and embraced him with a nonmaternal kiss straight on the lips.

"Eight hundred and fifty-eight thousand big ones!" Raimondi yelped as he entered just behind Buckley. "Let's all take the rest of the week off!"

"I'm so proud of you, Tommy." Judy was almost crying. "And that poor Doyle family. God, they must be delirious."

"Dan! Where's Dan?" Buckley looked as if he was going to jump in the air like the salesman in the Toyota commercial.

"You heard?" Judy Corwin lowered her voice. She nodded toward Sheridan's closed door. "He's been in there all morning."

"I heard," Buckley said, still riding a high.

Suddenly, they came down to earth. "Raimondi told me. I still can't believe it." Buckley now spoke in a subdued tone. He shook his head. "Sheila O'Brien, all-American girl," he drawled.

"Well, let's not judge her too harshly," Judy said—as always, the peacemaker. "She had a job to do, just like us."

"Come off it, Judy," Buckley said tersely. "How in hell can a girl like that do a number on a guy like Dan?"

"She wrote him a letter." Judy's voice had a conciliatory tone. "Came in this morning. Personal and confidential. I opened it."

* * *

Sheridan sat there, feet propped up on his desk, and reread Sheila's letter.

"Dan," it began, "I know you are angry. I don't blame you. I offer no excuses. It was a job I was assigned to do. Maybe you, having been a marine in an unpopular war, might understand.

"In the short time I got to know you, I came to like and admire you—unfortunately for me. . . . Sheila."

Dan crumpled the letter and was about to slam-dunk it into his wastebasket, but he hesitated. Maybe it was still a con. He wasn't going to get burned by the same flame twice. Into the basket it went.

He punched the intercom button. "Judy"—his voice had regained its old martial timbre—"come on in, and bring your pad. We've got to file a motion forthwith to suppress statements made by Dillard and petition the court for an independent lie detector test."

"Good news for a change, Dan," Judy said. "Young Buckley and Raimondi just came in. They settled the Doyle case."

"An apple for an orchard?"

"No, close to nine hundred thousand."

"Nine hun . . . Judy, you'll get paid this week."

"That's what I keep telling myself."

"What time is it?"

"Almost noon."

"Close the shop. Tell the guys to head up to Lazzarie's. You and I will meet them there in, say, half an hour."

"Now you're talking!" Judy said.

Sheridan called Clerk of Courts Johnny Flaherty on his private line. Funny, he thought. This is exactly what Sonny Callahan had recommended. Call Johnny Flaherty. File a motion to suppress. Johnny will steer it to Judge Israel Katzmann. Sheridan recalled how he'd almost thrown Callahan out of his office for suggesting such an inane maneuver. Now here he was following Callahan's subtle orders to a tee.

"Johnny?"

"Yes."

"Dan Sheridan here."

"Danny, me boy, what can I do for you?"

"It's a long story, Johnny, and I won't go into the scenario. I represent a Dr. Christopher Dillard, who finds himself in a bit of trouble."

"Christopher Dillard, the cardiovascular surgeon?"

"The same. He's a target defendant about to be summonsed before a special grand jury on Thursday."

"I know. I'm making up the jury lists right now."

"Well, my guy passed a lie detector test, but he made some damaging statements to two Boston Police detectives that will croak him."

"Was he informed of his rights?"

"No, that's why I'm calling. I'd like an immediate pre–grand jury hearing before an emergency judge—a motion to suppress and a petition for an independent lie detector test for my client."

Oddly, Johnny seemed to know exactly what to do.

"You got to give the DA's office immediate notice," he said. "Fax your petition to Mayan d'Ortega; she's handling the prosecution's case. And I'll try to get it assigned before Judge Katzmann, ten A.M. Wednesday morning."

"Will do, Johnny. It's practically on its way."

Judge Katzmann. Sheridan reflected back on Sonny Callahan. It was a ridiculous motion. Mayan d'Ortega would shoot it full of holes and Katzmann would broom it out of his session. Or would he? Sheridan remained motionless for several seconds.

He pushed the intercom button. "Judy, I have to do a rush petition."

"Be right there," she said. "Buckley and Raimondi have headed up for Lazzarie's. . . . Did you see Sheila's letter?"

"Obviously you read it before I did," Sheridan said with some newfound humor.

"Don't judge her too harshly, Dan."

"I'm sure that's what Duncan said about Lady Macbeth. No, Judy. Some things you don't forgive."

*   *   *

"I've set up the hearing before Judge Katzmann in his chambers tomorrow morning at ten o'clock," Clerk of Courts Johnny Flaherty told Sheridan on the phone. "D'Ortega filed a written objection and counterbrief to your motion. I wish you luck."

"Thanks, Johnny. We'll need it. Somehow I think I'm pushing a car uphill with a rope. But you never know, Johnny."

"Yeah, you never know, Danny, me boy," Flaherty's voice echoed.

Dan Sheridan sat in the conference room with young Buckley, studying their motion to suppress. The euphoria from the Doyle settlement had started to abate, but Judy Corwin and Buckley sensed that Dan was regaining his old drive.

"You know, Tommy, I've got a funny feeling about this motion. I didn't tell you, but when Sonny Callahan came into my office making his pitch for Dillard, he was the one who mentioned Judge Katzmann. Told me to file a motion to quash, all the legal gobble-dygook—said Johnny Flaherty would set it up."

"Hey, Dan, we have about as much chance of winning this motion as the Red Sox winning the pennant, which is nil. They're six and a half games back and the season's just started."

"I agree. But why did Flaherty steer this case to Katzmann? The thing that bothers me is that I'm doing exactly what Callahan told me to do. You don't think . . ."

"Come off it, Dan. Israel Katzmann is one of the finest judges in the Commonwealth. Right down the line. Been on the bench for twenty years. Gave up a good practice as a trial lawyer, so he knows what it's like to be in the trenches. He isn't a political hack, like some appointments."

"I know." Sheridan still seemed concerned. "There are guys wearing the robes who couldn't judge a dogfight." He looked at Buckley. "I'll argue the hell out of our points of law. It'll be interesting to see how d'Ortega reacts. That lady is one cool papaya. I still hope nothing funny's going down."

"I was sorry to hear about Sheila." Buckley got up to leave.

"If I had to guess," Buckley said, "she was getting disenchanted with the spooky stuff. She had too much class. Maybe she was falling in love with you, Dan."

"Hey, for Christsakes!" Sheridan's voice was taut with indignation. "It's bad enough that Judy reads my personal mail. I don't want the whole goddamned office bouncing it around!"

"Look, Dan, I know how you feel. . . ."

"How do you know how I feel?" Sheridan fumed.

"Yeah, you're right." Buckley was smart enough to let the subject drop. "I have the Doyles coming in to sign releases. Good luck on your motion, Dan."

Sheridan sat in the bar enclosure and tried to keep the butterflies quiet. Courtroom veteran that he was, he never quite got used to it. The adversary system was just that; you were in there alone trying hard to survive and the opposition was trying just as hard to dismember you. A judge could make or break. He wasn't merely the third man in the ring enforcing the rules of legal propriety. Given the right judge, one sympathetic to your cause, you could prevail. Given one not so inclined, you were in trouble. The real art of advocacy was in the selection, cultivating the clerk or the assignment judge. You learned the ins and outs of courtroom roulette. If an assignment judge suddenly held the case himself and he was particularly deferential to your opponent, you sensed it would be an uphill battle.

A few attorneys filed into the enclosure, nodding Sheridan's way. He looked around. A sickening feeling that he would win his motion strengthened his surmise. There were certain clues.

The clerk told him the records were impounded. The matter would not be heard in open session, but in Judge Katzmann's chambers. No newspaper reporters had checked in: Fletcher Porter of the *Globe*, Pat Nolan of the *Herald*, not even Susan Zabilski of the *Beacon Underground*. And she had a way of knowing when something was going to break. The media wasn't on to things. So far, no leaks from Harrington's office. It was nearing 10:00 A.M. and no Mayan d'Ortega.

The grand jury was convening on Thursday and usually checked in on a Wednesday. That was today. He noticed nothing more than the usual flow of civilians in the three regular jury sessions. Sheridan was getting queasy. Was the fix in? If it was, it was a motion he wouldn't be proud to win.

He rechecked his notes. The lighting was poor, always had been. The courtroom was hoary with age—dust on the floor, the rust-colored linoleum squares lumpy and turning up at the edges. The oak railings had long ago lost their burnish and the jury enclosure was pitted and stained.

Sheridan squinted in the dim light, studying his brief and formulating some mental notes to present to Judge Katzmann. It read well. Black letter law. If needed, it would be persuasive.

Mayan d'Ortega arrived a few minutes before Judge Katzmann was due on the bench. Sheridan eyed her carefully as she glided through the swinging doors and made her way toward the bar enclosure. The coterie of lawyers looked her way. She wore a tweed suit, gray with a hint of purple, tailored exquisitely, and a white silk Spanish shirt with a high collar and strings of dark purple. Her Ferragamo boots of soft Moroccan leather were a subdued shade somewhere between gray and purple. She gave a slight toss of her raven hair and it reflected the harsh lighting with a silken gleam.

Sheridan rose and faced her.

"We meet again, Mr. Sheridan." She extended her long, tapered fingers, as brown as the dark oak jury railing, framed by a white ruffled cuff. He shook her hand lightly.

"Delighted," he said.

She smiled warmly. "Thank you. Me, too." Again the toss of the hair. "I'll be representing the Commonwealth in these proceedings."

I'm sure you will, Sheridan thought to himself. And you'll blow some easy layups. He could not imagine that she would concede on any point without a fierce fight.

"Here," she said with professional dexterity, reaching into a stylish lizard case and handing Sheridan some official-looking papers, "our counterbrief. . . . I was impressed by your case authority. It should be an interesting morning."

"Thank you. It will be."

Sheridan started leafing through the six pages, continuing the pretense.

There is that short interval before the bailiff tolls his intonations that is almost sacred. The cynicism and the doubts are suspended in the moment. It happens in every courtroom in the United States, from Macon, Georgia, to Santa Fe, New Mexico. It goes back to Runnymede field, to Thomas More, to Bellarmine, Brandeis, to

Holmes, Cardoza. And as a lawyer sits there in that brief instant before the judge in his black robe of impartiality ascends the bench, suddenly he is proud of his profession, proud for the American system of justice. The moment is not forgotten easily. Sheridan wondered whether Mayan d'Ortega experienced the same thrill, the same sense of honor. He glanced over at her.

"All rise!" boomed the bailiff. Judge Israel Katzmann entered with a dignified stride from his chamber. There was a muffled clack in the courtroom and thirty or more lawyers stood. Sheridan's flesh tingled.

"Court is open. Be seated!" the bailiff cried.

It was time for Judge Katzmann to dispense justice (or to dispense *with* it). Sheridan still wasn't quite sure.

Several matters were called and decided. Lawyers wandered in and out. An hour later, only Sheridan and d'Ortega remained in the now-vacant courtroom. Judge Katzmann peered down from the bench.

"In the matter of *Dillard* vs. *the Commonwealth*, I'll see both sides in my chambers."

Judge Katzmann greeted them warmly. The bailiff helped him off with his robe and hung it in the closet.

"Sit down, Miss d'Ortega, Mr. Sheridan." He motioned toward a sagging wine-colored Naugahyde couch in front of a battered oak-veneer desk.

Katzmann looked like a judge—silver hair, high forehead, benign scholarly face with just the proper weathering. A few crow's-feet crinkled the corners of his soft gray eyes. He looked impartial, fair, and wise. A shade under six feet tall, trim and fit, he looked younger than his sixty-five years. His voice was seasoned with concern. Katzmann was probably the most competent jurist in the state. And this made Sheridan uneasy when he assessed the situation.

"I've read the documents," said the judge. "I felt it best to have them impounded. That's within my discretion."

"Have you read Mr. Sheridan's petition and supporting brief, Miss d'Ortega?" To Sheridan, the query was ridiculous, which strengthened his suspicion. Of course she had read it.

"I have, Your Honor," d'Ortega responded.

"Mr. Sheridan?"

"Yes, I've seen the Commonwealth's brief."

The judge leaned back in his squeaky chair. His custom-tailored white-on-white shirt and his eighteen-karat scales of justice cuff links, a gift from the bar association, caught Sheridan's eye. Judge Israel Katzmann, respected by all sides of the bar—plaintiff, prosecution, defense. A judge's judge. A lawyer's judge. Even-tempered, fair-minded, sensitive to the plight of those appearing before him, treating lawyers with utmost courtesy. It was difficult for Sheridan to imagine that the scales of justice on Katzmann's cuff links might belong to the finest judge whom money could buy. Paradoxically, he hoped the scales weren't tipped too heavily in his favor.

"Your motion and petition is extraordinary, Mr. Sheridan. I'm not sure the court has jurisdiction to grant it." Katzmann tilted farther back in his chair.

"The circumstances are extraordinary, Judge. A renowned individual is being unjustly linked to a sordid affair." Sheridan's voice was wooden. He droned. His heart wasn't in it.

"I've cited two cases analogous with my proposition, Your Honor," he continued, trying to get back on track. "Of course, you're familiar with *Arizona* vs. *Miranda,* where the Supreme Court enunciated the principle that a suspect has a right to remain silent and the right to counsel."

"Sound law," said the judge, looking thoughtful, adjusting his glasses. "I don't think anyone quarrels with that. Right, Miss d'Ortega?"

"No quarrel, Your Honor. The rubber hoses in the back rooms went out with the Lizzie Borden case. But with all due respect, Your Honor, Mr. Sheridan has missed the basic principle of *Miranda,* which incidentally was a five-to-four decision. Regardless, it's the law of the land, and rightly so." She had the judge's attention, and even Sheridan listened to the liquid flow of words as she took the play away from him. The judge slowly regained his upright position.

"*Miranda* addressed itself to a *custodial* coercion, where the suspect was actually under arrest, brought to the station house and deprived of his freedom and ability to communicate with the outside world. The Boston Police Department scrupulously adheres to constitutional principles. Even gives a list of attorneys to indigent defendants."

"Judge," said Sheridan, getting irritated, "I know that." He glanced frostily at d'Ortega. If it was all rigged, as he suspected, his opponent had the early going. "I'd prefer to argue my own case," he said curtly, "cite my own case law, and develop it without interruption. This is the only real shot my client has. . . .

"*Miranda* does address itself to custodial interrogation following arrest. But let's not miss the mandate of *Miranda*. It was a major breakthrough in protecting constitutional rights; the due-process clause of the Fourteenth Amendment guarantees the right to counsel, and the Fifth and Sixth amendments guarantee one's right to remain silent and to be advised of one's privilege against self-incrimination. That's before any questioning even starts. No more star-chamber stuff.

"And incidentally, *Miranda* was only decided in 1972, five centuries after the Magna Carta."

Mayan d'Ortega had an amused half smile, Sheridan noticed.

"What *Miranda* did was to make the one accused totally aware that he is embroiled in the adversary system and that persons interrogating him are not acting in his best interests."

"Again, Judge," d'Ortega interrupted, "Mr. Sheridan's interpretation of *Miranda* has absolutely no application here. *Miranda* expressly refers to *custodial* investigation, where one's freedom has been significantly restrained. May I suggest to Your Honor that this is clearly pointed out on page seven twenty-one of the Supreme Court's decision." D'Ortega didn't have to refer to notes. Katzmann scribbled. Sheridan did a slow burn.

" '. . . Any statement given freely and voluntarily without compelling influences is, of course, admissible in evidence.' Justice Black specifically says at page seven twenty-six." D'Ortega continued to quote from memory. " 'Volunteered statements of any kind are not affected by our decision today. . . .' "

Sheridan tried to regroup. He shot a sideways glance at d'Ortega, waited a few seconds, then started again. "Well, *Miranda* set the environment, Judge. I know we're not talking about a station-house interrogation. I'm taking issue with the word *restraint*.

"Please note my case *People* vs. *Allen*, where the New York court held Miranda warnings had to be given *before* an arrest was made, the court indicating that the *police questioning* was the new standard and defining *compulsion* as simply *any* questioning in *any* setting when a criminal fact might be elicited.

"Now, two police detectives showed up at Dr. Dillard's office and flashed their credentials. The interrogation carried its own badge of intimidation.

"In *State* vs. *Thomas*"—Sheridan again squinted in the dim light and read from his brief—"three years after *Miranda*, the New Jersey court held that welfare recipients were entitled to Miranda warnings on interrogation by welfare investigators seeking statements that might be used in prosecution for welfare fraud, even though the interrogation was carried out in the recipient's *home*.

"And in *Mathis* vs. *United States*"—Sheridan's voice rolled with regained authority—"it was ruled that self-incriminating evidence given to IRS agents without warnings was inadmissible in prosecutions for filing a false tax return.

"By the way, Miss d'Ortega," he put some sting in his voice, "that was the same Justice Black of *Miranda* fame, now speaking for the majority of the Court, who rejected the government's claim that it was merely a civil tax investigation. In fact, Judge, IRS agents now give warnings of a person's constitutional rights."

Judge Katzmann seemed to be listening. Cupping his hands, he rested his chin upon them and furrowed his brow as if weighing the law carefully. Sheridan sounded persuasive. Katzmann turned to Mayan d'Ortega, signaling that it was her turn to argue.

D'Ortega proceeded to pick Sheridan's cases apart. In her cool, modulated voice she was eloquent, methodical, convincing. "In *Mathis* vs. *United States*," she said, "the defendant was *already* in prison.

"Please note the later case of *Beckwith* vs. *United States*, where our same Court held that IRS agents investigating potential criminal tax violations were *not* required to give Miranda warnings in an interview in the taxpayer's *home*, where he was not in custody or restrained in any way. In questions of interpreting the federal Constitution, it's axiomatic that state courts such as New Jersey, as cited by Mr. Sheridan, *must* defer to the U.S. Supreme Court.

"Mr. Sheridan's argument in his brief that he understands certain incriminating letters were seized without a search warrant in Miss Williams's apartment, which were the property of Dr. Dillard, is without merit.

"Your Honor"—d'Ortega had a half smile on her lips—"love letters from time immemorial are the property of the recipient. I don't think case citations are needed on that point. . . . As to the claim of illegal search and seizure, no warrant was required to enter Miss Williams's apartment. She was not accused of any crime. She was a person dead under homicidal circumstances. A warrant would have been necessary to search Dr. Dillard's office or home. No such search was conducted.

"Finally, a lie detector is still an occult science, not admissible in either civil or criminal cases in Massachusetts. The Commonwealth will not agree to a so-called independent testing. We are only following the letter of the law.

"Now the district attorney's office has the right—indeed, the duty—to convene the grand jury when an unexplained death is involved and someone might be responsible. It's the jury's investigation, not the district attorney's, and they return a bill of indictment or No Bill. When the detectives from the Boston Police interviewed Dr. Dillard, he was not a suspect. He hadn't been charged, accused, detained, or even arrested, merely asked to answer questions about Miss Williams. He's been subpoenaed before the grand jury. He is now deemed a suspect; Mr. Sheridan was given a target letter a few days ago. He can, of course, invoke his constitutional privileges against self-incrimination before the grand jury."

Judge Katzmann removed his horn-rimmed glasses and chewed on a stem thoughtfully.

"When was he deemed a suspect?"

"About a week later, following the autopsy findings and the forensic investigation of the deceased's premises," d'Ortega answered. "Certainly *not* at the time of Dillard's initial interrogation."

"When is the grand jury convening?" asked the judge.

"Tomorrow morning at ten."

"Thank you, Miss d'Ortega, Mr. Sheridan. Both of you have indeed done your homework. I'll check the law carefully, evaluate both briefs, and give you my decision before then."

D'Ortega smiled graciously. Sheridan started filing his notes into his briefcase. He was peeved. He had been outmaneuvered and beaten at every turn. A different feeling settled into the pit of his stomach. He might need all the help he could get. So would Dillard. If it was all a charade, the Ice Maiden was doing a pretty good job of making it look like the real thing.

It didn't take long for Judge Katzmann to file his decision. Young Buckley went over to the clerk's office as soon as Sheridan got word on the telephone that the opinion was in. It was a terse one-liner.

"Upon due consideration of argument and briefs submitted by counsel, the petitioner's motions are denied."

No explanation. Sheridan read it with a wry smile. Sonny Callahan could reach a clerk of court, maybe even a judge—but not Katzmann. Perhaps not even Johnny Flaherty. Certainly not Mayan d'Ortega.

32

SHERIDAN sat at Lazzarie's bar watching Neil Harrington's televised press conference. The cameras zoomed in first on Harrington's wife and two of his younger children as they stood next to a speaker's podium. Mayan d'Ortega could be seen in the background, conversing with several associates.

"Now, from the historic Parkman House on Beacon Hill"—a Channel 5 reporter cut into view—"we bring you an important announcement from the Suffolk County District Attorney."

Neil Harrington entered amid sustained applause, accompanied by Mayor Jimmy Kane.

The preliminaries contained no surprises. Harrington paid tribute to the citizens of Boston and the surrounding communities, enumerating them carefully—Chelsea, Everett, Roxbury, Revere. . . .With self-deprecating charm, he recalled his accomplishments of the past ten years. Next came accolades to his staff, particularly to Mayan d'Ortega. "More on that later," he promised.

Sheridan sipped his bourbon slowly as he looked up at the TV overhead.

"Today I am announcing my candidacy for the Democratic nomination for the United States Senate." Harrington paused. The applause followed the script—heavy, sustained, dying reluctantly. He tilted toward the viewers.

"Since the effort in behalf of the people will be one of total commitment, I am resigning the office of district attorney as of June first. . . ."

There followed a pat string of clichés about the importance of renewing access by and to the people, fighting drugs, keeping the lid on taxes, providing health care, jobs. He poked a less than courtly gibe at the incumbent, then introduced his wife and children, mentioning that two others were away at college. Finally, he introduced Mayan d'Ortega, "who," he said, "is to be appointed to fulfill my remaining term of office."

It was official. Harrington's run, rumored for months, was now a certainty. He'd have little opposition in the primary. Unless Crimmins could silence some ex-girlfriends and get Mother Teresa's endorsement, the senior senator would be back practicing law where he had started a decade ago. But it would be no cakewalk. Crimmins still had statewide visibility, the patronage and clout of two terms in office, and a high legislative profile. Even Harrington was aware that winning would require workers and money and political promises and a great deal of negative press coverage aimed at his adversary.

Sheridan wondered where Sonny Callahan fit into the picture. Callahan hadn't been able to get to Harrington, at least not in this case. But then again, maybe he and Harrington had already cut a deal. Stranger things had happened in the world of Boston politics. Enemies became bedfellows; allegiances could shift, sometimes overnight. Was Sonny Callahan a plant, after all? Why the phone taps, the FBI surveillance, Sheila O'Brien?

Sheridan took another sip of bourbon as he thought of Sheila O'Brien, especially her note. "I came to like and admire you—unfortunately for me." He tried to dismiss her from his mind.

Between sipping the bourbon and half-watching the political blandishments, Sheridan remembered that among O'Brien's pictures there were several shots of Claire Doherty's confidential envelope. Claire's handwriting hadn't been disguised. If Sheila had turned in the film, Claire no doubt would have been exposed. Sheridan realized he had placed an old friend at a dreadful risk.

Dillard's indictment would take only a day or two. The police detectives would relate Dillard's conversation. "He claims he left Williams at ten P.M. and she was alive and well." One little problem—the medical evidence. *Williams was stone dead at nine.*

Was Dillard being thrown to the wolves? Abandoned by Sonny Callahan and those he had served for over a decade? Could be, Sheridan thought. He wouldn't have been surprised if Callahan, who always backed a winner, had switched sides and turned to Harrington. The next few days would tell.

Despite Senator Crimmins's peccadilloes, it would take big bucks to topple him, and supporters to man the campaign. Sonny Callahan, the Machiavellian power behind more than one throne, could produce both in spades. It was hard for Sheridan to imagine that a consummate politician like Harrington would buck Callahan head-on.

"What do you think?" Sheridan addressed Tony the bartender as he put a twenty-dollar bill on the counter to cover his tab.

"Gutsy guy," the bartender said, snapping up the check, then totaling it out. "We need someone like Harrington in Washington. Law and order. Fuckin' people are going around crazy. Crimmins gave us ten lousy years of suckin' up to niggers and spics."

"Oh, he had some good points, Tony," he said, and drained his glass. "Women's rights, welfare, AIDS research."

"Yeah." Tony picked up Sheridan's glass as Sheridan signaled he didn't need a refill. "When he wasn't screwin' bimbos. And you know, Dan"—Tony leaned closer to Sheridan—"I hear he's now into guys."

"Keep that to yourself, Tony. Also the change."

Judy jotted down Sheridan's last-minute instructions before leaving for the day. Dillard would be coming in about six. Buckley and Raimondi were still celebrating. He'd given them the evening off.

"Oh, Fletcher Porter of the *Globe* called. I said you'd call him tomorrow," Judy said.

"Boy, the leaks have already started."

"Not yet. He wanted your comment on Barry Ginsberg and Bob Catalano."

"Okay, Judy, I'll call him tonight. Best to keep him on our side."

He'd hole up with Dillard alone. It was obvious to Sheridan that the Dillard indictment would rocket Harrington into political orbit. The press would seize on the privileged doctor bit, then stress that all defendants are equal under the law. Harrington would ride the case to the political moon. And then the thought crossed Sheridan's mind: As much as he disliked Harrington, he'd probably vote for him.

As he waited for Dillard in his silent office, he tried to sort out the jumble of events over the past weeks. Sonny Callahan, Dillard, Sheila O'Brien. Something gnawed at him. Among the kaleidoscopic shards, there was something that didn't fit. He couldn't quite put his finger on it. Something didn't figure.

"I came to like and admire you—unfortunately for me."

He hadn't heard that in more than twenty years. Even his wife, Jean, had never let down her hair. It was a reserved marriage, nothing hell-raising, nothing lustful. Nothing like the Vietnamese girls. His mind drifted into the evocative twilight of twenty-five years ago.

It was 1969, a year after the Tet offensive. He was a rawboned twenty-year-old marine sergeant based at Quan Tri just north of the huge naval base at Da Nang. Even then, despite the Seventh Fleet offshore and nonstop bombings of Hanoi and Haiphong harbor, Sheridan felt it was an unwinnable war. The enemy seemed everywhere. They'd engage in a firefight, inflicting heavy casualties, then stealthily withdraw into the jungle. The pine boxes from Khe Sanh, Cam Lo, and Gio Linh were wheeled past his position daily. Then on patrol one fateful morning, his squad was ambushed. The captain and the lieutenant were dead, and so were half the men. Sheridan, his right leg shattered, kept firing his M-16, expecting that they would soon be overrun. But then the staccato bursts of AK-47s and mortars suddenly fell silent. And while helicopter gunships overhead strafed the edge of the jungle, two choppers landed and medics quickly removed the wounded. The dead were left on the battlefield.

His life had almost ended then, but in a way it was just beginning. She was like no other woman he had ever known, a nurses' aide, the French nun said; her name was Vi Quoc Toan. She was sixteen, with large, liquid brown eyes, bronze skin, a single braid that hung between her shoulder blades. She was part Vietnamese, part French. She spoke halting English, but her long tapered fingers were sensitive and tender. She touched Sheridan gently, bathing his feverish cheeks and injecting penicillin and mild opiates. But it was her presence that nursed Sheridan back to health. She'd ride her bicycle daily to the hospital at My Tho, south of Saigon.

They walked in the garden, as he gradually recovered. Sundays she would dress in white: the traditional *ao dai*, white sheath with a high-collared neckline over loose white pants, a purple plumeria lacing her dark, shining hair. She brought him laughter; told him stories of dragons, of ancient folk heroes, spirits, and fairies; and taught him French words of endearment—words that flowed into words of love, as the lingering touches became more meaningful. Like no other woman he had ever met, she gave him the hint of immortality.

One day it ended. He had received his orders to return to the States. Somehow she knew. She never appeared at the hospital again. He made frantic efforts to locate her. The French nun said she'd gone back to her tribe in the Central Highlands. Even after the war, his attempts to find her were futile.

The abrupt drone of the telephone jolted him back to life.

"Dan, Chris Dillard here," came the voice. "I'm just coming over the Mystic River Bridge. Be there in, say, fifteen minutes."

"Fine, Doctor." Sheridan checked his watch. "We've got a lot to go over."

"I appreciate what you're saying, Dan, but I insist on testifying tomorrow." Christopher Dillard seemed a bit on edge.

Sheridan paused for a few moments.

"You won't be believed," he said matter-of-factly. "Don't underestimate the prosecutor. You take the stand and she'll hit you with all sorts of stuff, probably about things you haven't even told me."

Sheridan wanted to mention the surveillance and Sonny Callahan. D'Ortega wanted Dillard's testimony against Callahan as part of a plea—but now he wasn't sure that option was even viable.

"No, Chris, you just give them your name, rank, and serial number. Everything else"—Sheridan's hand cut the air—"it's the Fifth Amendment."

Dillard shook his head. "Why can't I testify about the polygraph?"

"Because I tried that angle. In fact, I tried to get your conversation with the police thrown out . . . your letters to Williams."

"And?"

"It was no go. Right now, we're being dealt from a stacked deck. So what do we do? We don't play. We bide our time, don't create any record that we might find untenable down the stretch, and we find out the exact testimony of the government's witnesses, particularly their medical experts. Time and cause of death can be crucial."

"Then I've got to explain that Angela was bulimic; you seem to stress that lack of stomach contents somehow is medically damaging."

"You give the jury that story and the pathologists will testify that the esophagus wasn't inflamed, didn't even show signs of irritation. Whether it's true or not, whether they even looked at the esophagus, isn't the point. They'll testify they did, and your credibility will be zero.

"No, Chris, you do what I say. We don't red-flag any defenses. We lock in their witnesses, not ours. We get the grand jury minutes, then we map our strategy."

"But I'll sure as hell be indicted."

"I told you from the outset that the grand jury is a one-way street. If the prosecution's evidence is unexplained or uncontradicted, then the presiding justice as much as charges the jurors to return an indictment.''

"Then this whole grand jury business is one big charade.'' Dillard's voice was midway between indignation and frustration.

"No question about it,'' Sheridan agreed. "But the Fifth Amendment of the Constitution guarantees that no one has to answer for a capital offense unless on an indictment . . . so here we are.''

"Some guarantee.''

"Chris, we live in an imperfect world. Some states have done away with the grand jury. Some have preliminary hearings sifting evidence pro and con, even allow cross-examination. Unfortunately, Massachusetts isn't one of them.''

There were a few seconds of silence. Sheridan jumped into the gap. "We'll enter the grand jury room probably about noon tomorrow. There'll be twenty-three inquiring faces. They will have heard the Boston Police, the witness who found the body, the Burlington Police. The prosecutor, Mayan d'Ortega, will work you in between lay testimony and the pathologists. She'll already have the jurors in her back pocket before you're called. It could be over in a day. We'll handle the arraignment when we get to it.

"Wear a conservative blue suit, white shirt, sober tie, no cuff links. You turn to me with each question. Follow my advice even if you don't want to.''

Dillard sat there without saying a word or revealing a fathomable expression. Sheridan wondered whether he was really getting through to him. "Okay, Chris, see you tomorrow.''

Sheridan called *Globe* columnist Fletcher Porter from his car phone. The feds would be listening; might as well give them an earful. He got through on the second ring.

". . . No, Fletch, I hate to see any lawyer bite the dust. With all the crime in the country—drugs, killings, you name it—the feds have enough to do without inventing crimes. And that's just what a sting operation is. I've known Catalano and Ginsberg for years. They're both diligent practitioners. Always did their best for the client. That's all one can expect. . . .''

This seemed to satisfy Porter. Sheridan could hear the pencil scratching down his comments.

"One other thing," Porter said, as if it was an afterthought, "I hear you're representing a famous Boston physician who has been targeted in a homicide investigation."

"Oh? Where did you hear that?"

"I have my sources. Tell me, Dan, I understand he's to testify tomorrow before the grand jury. Care to comment?"

Sheridan thought for a few moments. Best to sidestep Porter rather than put him off.

"Fletch," he began, parroting Dillard, "the grand jury is one big charade. It's an archaic, outmoded fetish of yesteryear, an expensive anomaly. Even in England, where it was born at Runnymede, it's been abolished. Today it's just a convenient tool for the prosecutor, too often used solely for publicity. Any experienced prosecutor will admit he can indict anyone, anytime, for almost anything, before any grand jury."

"Can I quote you on that, Dan?"

"Certainly. But attribute the remarks to the proper source. That came from Judge William Campbell of Chicago, a revered jurist who has been handling grand juries for thirty years."

Loughlin reached Sheila O'Brien at her apartment a little after 8:00 P.M. "Sheila, we lucked out. I cleared everything with Davis; you'll be staying here in Boston. In fact, you'll be on duty tomorrow morning at the Suffolk County Courthouse."

Sheila said nothing for several seconds. She was seriously thinking of resigning. Deceit wasn't in her makeup. And her whole relationship with Sheridan was based on deceit. So was letting Loughlin cover for her.

"Okay, Bri," she said, her voice flat, lowered into a kind of resignation, "what's the drill?"

"We're to check the traffic at the Suffolk County Courthouse around the grand jury room. The techs have already set up the cams covering the corridors and entrances. We mingle, see who's coming and going. We're to be in District Attorney Harrington's office at eight A.M. tomorrow. Agents Walsh and Kerry will be there and we're being joined by Diane Blakemore from the Phoenix office. Get a good night's sleep, Sheila. Take a cab up to the courthouse."

33

PHIL RILEY went out on the porch to pick up the morning paper. At 6:00 A.M. it was still dark. His kids had the day off from school—St. Anselm's Day—and they went to St. Anselm's Academy. Marge and the kids would still be in bed when he left for the courthouse.

He made the coffee and fried two eggs over several strips of bacon. The toaster was on the fritz, so he buttered two slices of bread, then popped them in the oven for several seconds.

Riley loved the solitude of a quiet breakfast. The early-morning turmoil, the kids vying for the one bathroom, Marge yelling like a banshee, was not his idea of how to start the day. It would soon end, he hoped. His daughter, Callie, was interested in an Italian kid from East Boston, and as much as he hated *gambinos,* as he called them, especially from Eastie, he was all for the arrangement. There would be less confusion, and Italians had a sense of family. That he'd have to admit. His son, Sean, of course, would ship off to Notre Dame—that's if Riley could afford it.

He ate slowly, savoring the fresh-brewed coffee as if it were a straight shot of Jameson, and propped the *Globe* up against the sugar bowl. First came the sports pages. The Sox had lost another. Jesus, he swore to himself, Clemens gets no goddamned support; imagine losing 1–0. Fourth one-run loss this year. And to think an ex-Sox, Wade Boggs, whacked in the Yankees' winning run.

"Fuckin' Yankees," he swore again, out loud this time. Next came the Irish sports page—the obituaries. Sister Mary Fagan, Francis Coughlin, Father Leo Devaney, Monsignor Barton Gillespie, City Councillor Joe Mulligan, others. Riley shook his head. Some were even younger than he was—especially the AIDS victims.

Strange, Riley thought. Not a word if someone cashes in from alcoholism. Died after a long illness, it says. But the *Globe* pulls no punches when the terminal event is AIDS.

As he turned the pages, he savored the peace and quiet. Thank God for St. Anselm, he thought, his eyes arched toward the ceiling, if you're really up there.

He next perused the front page. Usual stuff—Iraq, Israel, the President's upcoming summit meeting. Five more Americans killed in Bosnia.

Inside on page 5 was a puff piece by Fletcher Porter on Neil Harrington—a full-page spread. He knew the Boston Police would be first in line for Harrington's upcoming run. Riley read it just as slowly as he sipped his coffee. As he was about to bite into a piece of toast, his hand stopped in midair.

Harrington has been an athlete since high school days at St. Ignatius High, where he starred in baseball and football. Harrington is the son of Padrig Harrington and Tempesta Cuchinella, immigrants from Ireland and Italy.

Cuchinella. Cuchinella, Cuch . . . Riley turned it over in his mind. "*Cooch—*"

"Jesus," he swore aloud. "It can't be! Holy Christ! That is fuckin' crazy!" A shiver went through him, although the kitchen was quite warm.

He went into the den, unlocked the cabinet housing his service revolver, and extracted the tape.

He lit a Camel, then inhaled, letting the smoke slowly drift from his lips. He clicked on the recorder and turned up the volume.

"I think we have to let things ride for a while. Wait until November. Things will be different. We'll have a future."

Williams's response, the subtle threat: "I am your future."

He wasn't quite sure. The tape quality wasn't that bad. He played it again as he strapped on his .38 revolver.

The shiver of moments ago turned into a cold sweat. Mother of God, it can't be!

Riley played the tape a third time. If he hadn't known it was impossible, Riley would have sworn that Cooch sounded a hell of a lot like Neil Harrington.

"Wait until November." That was election time. No, it's preposterous, he said to himself.

He flipped the recorder's off button and struggled into the jacket of his blue dress uniform with the chevrons and citations and slipped the tape into his side pocket.

A horn beeped outside. He checked through the window. Captain Furlong was seated in the backseat of the chief's oversized black sedan.

"Just testify about the doctor's conversation when we confronted him," Furlong said. "You might add that he looked nervous, kind of like he was hedging. In fact"—Furlong pulled a cigar from his inside pocket—"he wouldn't look me in the eye. I'll put that in."

Riley said nothing. Maybe I should throw the tape away, he thought. He could get in a peck of trouble. But this was an unexpected turn of events. For Christsakes—Neil Harrington. Neil Harrington, Catholic Layman of the Year, Laetare Award from Notre Dame, Holy Name Breakfast speaker. Jesus. He sighed to himself again. Holy Mother of Christ. No, forget it; it's unthinkable!

"This Dillard guy really do it?" Riley looked over at Buddy Furlong, who was unwrapping his silver-foiled Mecundo cigar.

"Probably did." Furlong groped for a pack of matches, lit the cigar, took a deep puff, and then let the smoke curl slowly from his lips.

Riley cracked his side window open and settled back for the ride to the courthouse.

"Whether he's guilty or not isn't really our concern. We investigate; the rest is up to brass tits d'Ortega."

"Phil, let me tell you something." Furlong glanced momentarily at the rookie chauffeur, then turned confidentially toward Riley and studied the tip of his cigar for several seconds. "Chief Costello is resigning within the next sixty days. Going to take a job in D.C. with the National Chiefs' Bureau Association. I'm telling you this in strictest confidence. Keep it under your hat." He flicked the ashes onto the car floor. "Mayor Kane is nominating me as chief."

Riley had heard the rumors and wasn't surprised.

"Gee, Buddy, that's great!" He feigned enthusiasm. "I suppose your captaincy will be opening up."

Furlong sidestepped Riley's inquiry. "How many tickets have you sold to His Honor's birthday party?" Furlong gave Riley a sideways glance.

"Enough."

"Well, I sold four thousand dollars' worth."

"At a hundred dollars a pop, you got to have a lot of relatives," Riley said sarcastically.

"Listen, I plunked down three grand myself. Your ducats total two thousand, and I suggest you turn in the receipts by Friday. Monday at the latest. Buy at least a grand." Furlong took a long drag on his cigar and sent the smoke billowing around the interior of the car. "It's a good business investment." The words were not lost on Riley.

Furlong leaned toward the driver. "Turn in here and let us out. We'll buzz the department when you're to pick us up."

Furlong joined the federal agents in Neil Harrington's office. There were introductions and handshakes. Congratulations were extended to Harrington and Mayan d'Ortega while Kristina Collins brought in the coffee and doughnuts.

"Lieutenant Riley will be here shortly," Furlong said to Mayan d'Ortega. "He's down at the clerk's office."

Brian Loughlin noticed that Sheila O'Brien seemed somewhat reserved. She smiled politely when introduced to the new agent, Diane Blakemore, but other than the usual salutations, she didn't join in the banter. Her nods were distant.

"We'll position ourselves in the corridor," Loughlin said. "The grand jury sits in Room Twelve-oh-six. At the far end of the hall, there are two courtrooms where I understand a couple of civil trials are in progress, so there'll be a lot of activity. Our cameras are focused in the vicinity of the grand jury room. You all have your service hardware." Loughlin patted a side pocket of his gray parka. Only Neil Harrington and Mayan d'Ortega were appropriately dressed for the occasion, both wearing corporate gray. The agents were well disguised—some looking like litigants in loose-fitting suits, with rumpled collars. Diane Blakemore had on a tattered blue sweater that could have been a Goodwill reject. Even Sheila O'Brien melded in with her stonewashed jeans and maroon Boston College sweatshirt.

"Johnny." Phil Riley entered the clerk's office, catching Flaherty, his feet propped on his desk, nibbling a sugar cruller and studying the *Racing Form.* "What looks good in the fifth?"

Flaherty made no attempt to disguise his early-morning gold-bricking. He lowered the paper a notch and peered over it.

"Phil Riley, as I live and breathe. And look at you, all those medals and shiny braid. Jaysus, you look like Marshal Göring. Sit down." Flaherty lowered the paper another notch but kept his feet propped on the desk. "What can I do for you?"

"Gotta testify before the grand jury. It's that Williams homicide. . . ."

"Oh yeah. That's Mayan d'Ortega's gig, isn't it?"

"That's right. Buddy Furlong and I are here to bury a key suspect."

"So I've heard. Dan Sheridan's client—a Dr. Dillard. The newshounds were calling me all day yesterday. Sure will be crowded out there in the corridor."

"Tell me, Johnny. You went to St. Ignatius High about the same time as Neil Harrington. . . ."

"He was a couple of years behind me, but we were in the same general fold. I ran around with the hubcap snatchers from Dorchester. Harrington was a little more upper-class—Jamaica Plain."

"He was a pretty good athlete?"

"Sure was—helluva third baseman. I remember we beat Eastie for the title. Cooch hit a three-run homer . . . last of the ninth."

"Cooch?"

"Oh, it was a crazy nickname. His mom was Italian; she hung the label on him. He chucked it when he went further up grade to Harvard. And if I were you and the boys over at HQ, I'd get on Harrington's bandwagon . . . like right now. Early money, Phil. That's when it counts. Gotta be in at the beginning. I've kicked in five grand already."

"Strange, Johnny"—Phil smiled—"that's exactly what my investment counselor told me just about an hour ago. Well, gotta get back to the compound." Riley gave a two-fingered quick salute. "Anything look real good? Something I should put a twenty on?"

"Neil Harrington, to win, place, and show."

They both smiled. Johnny Flaherty lifted the *Racing Form* and resumed his study.

Riley rode the elevator to the twelfth floor. The pieces to the puzzle were beginning to come together. Harrington couldn't afford even the slightest scandal. His whole professional life was built on moralistic propriety. A black girl, no less. Bill Clinton had been able to ride it out, even explain a tape recording. But Boston was still a puritanical village. The press would love nothing better than an old-fashioned stoning.

Still, he couldn't quite believe it. He fingered the tape in his jacket pocket. He held the key to Harrington's political future. There were ways this could be done. Money would change hands. He wouldn't have to be involved. Blackmail to save a career—save a soul. Blackmail to hide a murder. Hell no! He swore at himself for even harboring the thought. *I have to get this tape to someone. Maybe to Brian Loughlin or to that O'Brien woman.* Then he thought of Dan Sheridan.

"I'm sorry there aren't enough chairs to go around." Johnny Flaherty addressed the overflow crowd, some standing in the grand-jury holding area on the fourth floor. "But the bailiffs will try to make you comfortable. We hope to call twenty-three of you within the next hour. That should free up some seats."

It was a moment Johnny Flaherty relished. A rotund, animated man with a quick smile, today he sported a bright green tie, vivid against his double-breasted gray glen plaid suit.

He stood at the mounted rostrum and peered down at the expectant faces. "Ladies and gentlemen, you are especially privileged today, because those of you chosen will make up the grand jury." He paused for several seconds. "You, today, right now, are the investigative body of the great Commonwealth of Massachusetts. Now, as I call your names, answer 'Here.' The first thirty selected will go into Grand Jury Courtroom A. The next twenty-three will be on standby. About noontime, we'll dismiss the rest of you. But let me say this." Johnny smiled a leprechaunish smile. "Your lunch will be on the Commonwealth. Not Locke-Ober's, mind you. But the bailiff will take you to a nice luncheonette on Beacon Hill. It has the best clam chowder in the city."

The prospective jurors milled around uncertainly in the assembly area. Some read the morning *Globe* or *Herald;* others worked crossword puzzles, knit, or tried to chat with their newfound neighbors. Some just sat, staring vacantly. A grammar school teacher, Thalia Shapiro, leaned against the wall of the jury-pool area, her raincoat folded over one arm as she balanced a paperback in the other hand. Clumsily, she dog-eared a page and put the book in her coat pocket. She had tried to be excused from jury duty, as had others, but Barbara Chang, the presiding judge who would handle and charge the grand jury and field any legal questions they might have, was unsympathetic.

One potential juror, a dentist, said he couldn't afford to take time off—even three or four days. He told the judge that he had many patients and was booked well in advance.

Another had three children; she was divorced and couldn't get a baby-sitter.

A black man with fuzzy white hair, his trim beard flecked with gray, was a professor at Boston State College of Arts and Sciences. He had to prepare an important lecture.

Others had sick aunts, an indisposed wife, or feared they couldn't be impartial, especially in a criminal case.

Judge Chang listened patiently to the litany of excuses.

To the man who said he couldn't be impartial, she replied, "Try." She advised the professor to work well into the night. "I'm sure you'll mesmerize your audience. . . . We need good citizens like you."

Only those with genuine hardships—a pregnant woman one week overdue, another scheduled for surgery, a grandmother with hearing problems—seemed to move the judge.

Barbara Chang was Governor Stevenson's most recent appointee to the bench. There were ranklings among the bar and judicial nominating committee that she was unqualified, had never tried a case, and had graduated from a third-rate law school. Her father was David Chang, owner of several Chinese restaurants, who had kicked in $100,000 to Stevenson's campaign. For the governor, that was qualification enough. But in fact, she was one of his best appointments. Young, hardworking, and even-tempered, she quickly established herself as one of the Commonwealth's best trial justices.

Sheridan had watched her on several occasions. He would often sit well back in the spectators' enclosure, catching the nuances of how a particular judge wanted a case tried. Some judges were autocratic, domineering, treating litigants and lawyers shabbily while fawning on the jurors. Others manifested their dislikes in subtle ways: "If you want to believe the defendant, that's up to you!" one cantankerous old judge had remarked to the jury. Perfectly good charge. What didn't get into the record was the way the judge arched his eyebrows and looked toward the ceiling. Barbara Chang was like none of these. Her black robes signified impartiality, the scales of justice evenly balanced. Yet she was not a pushover. More than one litigant and lawyer had felt her judicial heel when they misread her sensitivity.

Sheridan recalled watching her sentence Genovese Baldinaro, a Mafia don, to fifty-five years in prison.

"Judge," Baldinaro spoke in a raspy voice, "I gotta wife who's sick. I'm a tired old man, age sixty-seven. I gotta bad heart—Judge, fifty-five years! I'll never make it."

Judge Chang looked down at the aging don and frowned with concern. "Do the best you can," she said evenly.

It took the remainder of the morning for Judge Chang to screen twenty-three citizens out of the thirty sent over from the jury pool, but she did so methodically and carefully, at all times listening patiently to individual complaints and reservations. Those not selected were discharged subject to call as jurors on civil or criminal cases.

"Ladies and gentlemen," the judge addressed the group. She had a benedictory smile. "You have been selected to form the grand jury of the county of Suffolk to conduct an investigation into the death of one Angela Williams, late of Boston. Various witnesses will appear before you. They will be administered the oath to tell the truth. The examination of witnesses will be conducted for the Commonwealth by Assistant District Attorney Mayan d'Ortega.

"Now keep in mind that the grand jury in our Commonwealth is deemed to be an informing and accusatory body rather than a judicial tribunal. You are to conduct an investigation into an untimely death. It is your investigation, not the district attorney's. As you listen to the testimony of witnesses, you may at any time ask questions of any witness. You are entitled to clear, lucid answers. If at any time you need clarification, either of the procedure itself or of the witnesses' testimony, you should ask Miss d'Ortega for such clarification.''

Judge Chang paused. ''Any questions so far?''

It was an obedient, slightly overawed group—the dentist, the housewife, the professor, Shapiro, and others. They shook their heads in unison.

''Fine.'' The judge took a drink of water from a plastic cup.

''If questions do arise, the prosecutor will undoubtedly provide you with the correct answers. She is most experienced. I will not be in the grand jury room, but I will be in my chambers and on the bench to render what wisdom I can to clear up any difficulties.

''Now, as I said before, this is not a trial. There is no cross-examination such as some of you have seen on 'Perry Mason' or 'L.A. Law.' '' Again the slight smile.

''You are twenty-three individuals coming from all walks of life.'' The judge glanced down at the jury sheets. ''Some of you are schoolteachers, plumbers, accountants, lecturers''—she nodded toward the black professor—''housewives, and some of you are simply unemployed.

''Think for a moment.'' Judge Chang's voice had a melodic ring. The jurors sat up straight, attentive—like the first day of school. ''You are an eclectic mix; that's the beauty of all this—it's a cross section of the community. And you are the collective conscience of this community. Perhaps that's what the founding fathers had in mind when they met in Philadelphia two hundred–some years ago and guaranteed that no one should be indicted for a capital offense unless by a grand jury of his or her peers.''

The jurors sat in rapt attention. Judge Chang's delivery was captivating. She didn't lecture or pontificate, but it was as if she was talking to them over the back fence or chatting over a cup of tea.

She went on to tell them their duty—again in simple nonlegalistic terms, sprinkled with practical analogies, wit, and kaffeeklatsch wisdom.

''You bring with you the collective experience of twenty-three individuals. In your everyday experiences, you have met salesmen who knock on your door, politicians running for office, people at the checkout counter at Stop and Shop, or some relative looking for a loan. You inquire. You weigh their responses. Your collective experience in dealing with people, with life itself, gives you that great intuitive perspective; you know where the truth lies. You know when someone is trying to pull the wool over your eyes.

"Now, after hearing the testimony and viewing what evidence Miss d'Ortega presents to you, you are then to decide if anyone might be criminally responsible for the death of Angela Williams. If you decide in the affirmative, you are to sign the ballot and return the indictment. Only twelve out of twenty-three must agree to return an indictment. If twelve do not vote, if you decide that the Commonwealth has not produced sufficient evidence to indicate criminal responsibility, you are to return a No Bill. That means no indictment. . . .

"Now, if you return an indictment against some person, that does not mean that he or she is guilty. An indictment is not a conviction. After all, an individual—or individuals, as the case may be—who is indicted has not had his or her day in court, hasn't been allowed an opportunity to test the credibility of the Commonwealth's evidence by cross-examination of witnesses or by offering exculpatory or rebuttal evidence or witnesses in his or her own behalf. It means only that you find sufficient evidence to hold that person or persons for trial. Any questions so far?"

Again the collective shaking of heads.

"To sum up, at the conclusion of the testimony, you are to decide one thing: Does the evidence, if unexplained, indicate that someone is responsible for Miss Williams's death? If so, you are to return an indictment. If not, you are to sign a No Bill, meaning no indictment is returnable."

"That's about it." The judge brushed an imaginary speck from her black robes. "But let me leave you with this last thought. You are about to fulfill the highest civic duty you'll ever be asked to perform in our free society. You've witnessed or heard about justice or forms of justice in Bosnia and in Africa." The judge shook her head. "But right here in Boston, today, *you* are the *law;* you, the grand jury, have tremendous power. Your power exceeds that of the Court, even that of the Commonwealth. Use it wisely. Use it with a sense of honor and duty.

"And keep in mind that your deliberations are secret. I can't impress this upon you too much. You will not be sequestered. You will go home at night to your spouses, your friends and associates.

But I pledge you to absolute secrecy. You are to discuss these proceedings and deliberations with absolutely no one. If our justice system is to function, ultimately to lead to justice, no juror is to talk about the proceedings or what happens within the confines of the grand jury room, even with a spouse or dearest friend.

"All right, Mr. Coyne." The judge nodded to the bailiff. "It's now one-ten. I think these jurors are in need of nourishment."

Several jurors smiled and nodded.

"Please take them to lunch. Now it's not the Ritz-Carlton, is it, Mr. Coyne?" The judge looked appropriately amused.

"More like The Beacon Hill Deli, Your Honor."

34

THE JURORS were led by the bailiff, Mr. Coyne, who wielded a long white staff tipped with brass. They had enjoyed a frugal lunch at the Beacon Hill Deli—clam chowder, spinach salad, rolls. Those who didn't like spinach salad were served extra rolls. It had been a long walk up Beacon Hill, past the Statehouse, with a right jog off Joy Street, taking them almost to the cobblestone walk of Louisburg Square. The professor had remarked to the schoolteacher that the place seemed out of the way and that the clam chowder was padded with diced potatoes and there were not enough clams. Also, they had passed several delis and coffee shops that had seemed more inviting and perhaps less expensive for the taxpayer.

"How about going down to Cheers?" a ruddy-faced juror asked. "Maybe we can meet Ted Danson."

The service at the deli was expeditious and Peggy Flaherty, the owner-manager, who just happened to be Clerk Flaherty's sister-in-law, quickly collected the chits. Flaherty would see that she got paid the next day. It was a nice family enterprise, with a guaranteed flow of patrons.

Like a drum major, the bailiff strutted along Beacon Street with his group of twenty-three, herding them back toward the courthouse. He paused at strategic intervals to ensure that the group was intact.

"Here is Nathaniel Hawthorne's house," he said, throwing in a free history lesson. "He wrote *The Scarlet Letter* in that room you see up there," he added, pointing with his staff. "You all remember Hester Prynne? We could use a little more of that puritanical discipline these days, believe me! And Henry Wadsworth Longfellow lived for a time in that building with the grillwork." Again the staff was used as a pointer.

The group shuffled along, bathed in soft sunlight. The Boston Common to their right was alive with the pastels of spring. Pink and white dogwoods, creamy pale magnolias, red azaleas, and pur-

ple rhododendrons were in full bloom. Kids were skateboarding
and throwing Frisbees and the three-card monte players were picking the pockets of novice and naïve gamblers. Coyne stopped again.

"Follow the cards, pick out the black queen!" barked a disheveled youth whose handwork seemed rather inept. One man feign-
ing to be an onlooker pointed correctly and walked away with
twenty dollars.

"Another winner!" cried the dealer.

"Hell, I could have picked that one out," the professor said to
Thalia Shapiro.

"You got a license for your roving card game?" Coyne growled
at the kid. The boy noticed the bailiff's black uniform with brass
buttons. He folded his game quickly and moved on.

"That so-called winner was just a shill." Coyne smiled all-
knowingly to his troop. "I've seen some college kids get taken for
three or four hundred dollars by those scam artists."

They continued on, past the gold-domed Statehouse, where rows
of sprightly yellow and coral tulips were ranked up the terraced
lawn leading to the structure's fluted columns and pediments.

To the left of the main entrance loomed a statue of Fighting Joe
Hooker, who surveyed the group from astride his bronze horse,
gray-green with a soft patina. This illustrious son of the Commonwealth, leading the Army of the Potomac, had taken a shellacking
at Chancellorsville.

"Take a moment." Coyne stopped in front of the seated figure
of Mary Dyer, a Quaker hanged on Boston Common in 1660 for
her religious beliefs.

"The flamboyant Fighting Joe to the tragic Mary Dyer," Coyne
remarked, still acting like a tour guide. "Representing two ages in
our history where intolerance ruled. We killed our own. . . ."

"Frankly, I think this guy's getting a little boring," the professor
whispered to Thalia Shapiro.

"Well, we only have to put up with him for two or three days,"
she replied, "but I think the testimonial to Mary Dyer is touching;
I'd like to study her life a little more. Imagine a woman being
hanged for her religious beliefs."

"I can check on her history at the college library. Would be glad
to Xerox what I find for you and your children."

"I'm not married." She smiled slightly.

"Neither am I. . . . Say, maybe when our service is over I can buy you a real lunch. I know this delightful Russian place in Brookline."

She looked at him: distinguished, articulate, available—and black. Shapiro, she thought, are you crazy?

"Maybe," she said, hedging.

"Okay." The bailiff banged his staff on the concrete sidewalk. "The judge wants us back by two-thirty." He checked his watch, then hoisted the staff as if it was a baton. The group marched on, briskly now as they neared the courthouse.

Phil Riley had to talk to someone. He felt as if he were going to a lynching where an innocent victim was being strung up by the guilty party. But he still wasn't sure. Could Harrington be that stupid? In the newspapers and on television news, Harrington was always playing softball with his kids, skiing with his kids, or riding horseback on some hidden trail in Vermont—again with his kids. That was the posturing revealed by the news clips. He was a public figure. Funny, though, all the family pictures Riley had viewed didn't seem to include his wife. But then again, she had stood beside him at the Parkman House as the political platitudes were played out, a patrician Hillary Clinton look-alike.

Strange, he thought, Harrington's name didn't make Williams's green book. Mayor Kane did. Also Cranston, director of the CIA. That was mind-boggling. Why Cranston? Why Kane? If she had something going with Harrington, why was his name not included? He pulled out the small green date book from his vest pocket. Kane's private number was listed as 426–1750. Just on a hunch, he'd give it a ring.

He stopped at the pay phones next to the clerk's office and dialed the seven digits. The number had been disconnected. Next he called a contact at New England Telephone.

"Gert, Phil Riley here. This is a semiofficial request. Two things. Will you get me Mayor Kane's unlisted home number? And check out four-two-six-one-seven-five-oh. It's been disconnected. See if you can run it down—find out who it was issued to and when it was taken out of service."

"Piece of cake," the contact said. "Take about an hour. Are you calling from headquarters?"

"No, I'm at the courthouse. It's now two-oh-five. Let me call you—say, about four-thirty. Okay?"

"Okay, Phil. Talk to you then."

Bailiff Coyne led the jurors into the vaulted grand jury room a little after 2:30. The group, who had chatted amiably during their trek to the courthouse, now grew somber, as if they were entering a church or temple.

A converted courtroom, the chamber resembled a small amphitheater where some thirty wooden chairs were fanned out in elevated rows, facing the focal point of a witness stand and two plain wooden tables stacked with documents. On the institutional green plastered walls hung portraits of past jurists. Their sideburns, goatees, and walrus mustaches, illuminated by harsh light coming from green-shaded fixtures hanging from the ceiling, gave a touch of antiquity to the place, adding to the seriousness of the moment.

"Please take the seats as you approach them," the bailiff said, his voice now almost funereal. Gone was the jauntiness of the stroll along Beacon Street. They did as instructed and waited in contemplative silence.

The court stenographer, a middle-aged woman with short gray hair, her glasses perched on the end of her nose, entered and began to set up her recording equipment at a small table adjacent to the witness stand. The bailiff came over and whispered to her while she plugged various cords into sockets. She tapped the machine lightly several times and nodded to the bailiff that things were in working order.

Seconds dragged into minutes. Each juror felt a tingling sense of awe and apprehension—almost like the sensation before the curtain rises on a great drama. But this was no play. No actors would strut through make-believe roles. This was serious business. And they were a part of it.

Mayan d'Ortega entered unobtrusively, pushing open the main door. She stopped and spoke briefly to the stenographer, again in whispers. She had on a light gray silk suit with a strand of coral at her neck and a speck of coral in each small white stone earring. She looked elegant as she walked to the counsel table and began to sort some papers into neat piles. Then she nodded to the bailiff, who moved forward to lock the doors. The bolt clicked ominously into place.

Mayan d'Ortega faced the jurors, leaning slightly back against the table. She studied them for several moments, looking up to their elevated level. All eyes were riveted on her.

"Ladies and gentlemen of the grand jury," she opened slowly. "In behalf of the Commonwealth of Massachusetts, let me welcome you. My name is Mayan d'Ortega. I am an assistant district attorney, and it is my job to call various witnesses"—she nodded toward the witness stand—"who are to testify as to their knowledge of facts concerning the demise of one Angela Williams, who died on April second of this year."

Now in crisp, clear tones, d'Ortega related the events surrounding the Williams death and outlined the evidence that would be presented. There was a calmness about her as she looked them in the eye, her voice reassuringly confidential. At times, she permitted herself a slight, benign smile. The jurors hunched forward, drawn by her magnetism.

"As Judge Chang told you during your inauguration as grand jurors, it is *your* investigation. I am merely the vehicle, so to speak, to place testimony before you. You can interrupt me at any time. Ask any question you deem relevant, either of me or of any witness.

"As the judge impressed upon you, these proceedings are private. I don't have to tell you how important this is. This case will be heavily covered by the media. I pledge you to absolute secrecy. You are not to discuss the case with anyone. No phone calls, nothing. If a member of the media calls—and they might—you have no comment. The work of this entire grand jury can be destroyed by just one leak."

She let several seconds go by; after the histrionic pause, she asked, "Any questions?" The jurors exchanged blank looks, like recruits asked by the general on the first day of boot camp. "Any problems?"

"Do I raise my hand when I want to ask a question?" the college professor said, obviously aiming to lead the group.

D'Ortega left her position at the table and walked partway up the aisle. "Please do. I will recognize you. Your question has to be germane and relevant to the interrogation. If there is any confusion, we can suspend and refer the problem to Judge Chang."

In that moment, d'Ortega and the jurors became a team, the women taking pride in the prosecutor's gender and competence, the men succumbing to her quiet demeanor, her poise, maybe even her obvious beauty.

The college professor ventured a whisper to Thalia Shapiro. "I understand she's to be our next district attorney."

"It's about time," she whispered back.

The acoustics were like those in a Greek theater. Mayan d'Ortega remained impassive, but her eyes radiated sheer pleasure. The jurors noticed, not without some amusement. At that moment, the predatory tiger eyes softened, almost into Audrey Hepburn eyes— almost.

By prearrangement, Dillard met Sheridan in the parking lot of the Museum of Fine Arts on Huntington Avenue. Fletcher Porter and a reporter from one of the tabloids had camped in Sheridan's office. Buckley engaged them in aimless chitchat and Judy served coffee while Sheridan made it through the conference room and slipped out a side door.

Dillard had followed orders; he was wearing a conservative blue suit, white oxford shirt with button-down collar, and a maroon-and-gold regimental tie. No cuff links or stickpins. His only jewelry was a plain gold wedding band. He looked weary and apprehensive. They left their cars in the parking lot and took a cab to the back door of the courthouse.

Sheridan checked his watch. "We have time for a cup of coffee, Chris. D'Ortega doesn't know whether she'll get to us today, but she agreed to let us use the back elevator at four P.M. and to wait in the prosecutors' room just outside the jury room. Nothing's been in the papers yet, but this will change. How is Mrs. Dillard holding up?"

Dillard looked at Sheridan with a vacant stare. "Fine . . . I guess. She's in Philadelphia with her parents. Seems her father is sick. I told her I'd join her as soon as this thing is over."

"I wouldn't make any definite arrangements, Chris," Sheridan said as they walked under the street passageway connecting the Statehouse to the state office building. "The jury could return an indictment sometime tomorrow. There'll be an arraignment and the matter of posting bond. In a capital case, your freedom might not be that easy to arrange."

"You still insist I plead the Fifth Amendment?" Dillard's voice was edged with frustration.

"Absolutely." Sheridan glanced at his client. In the back of his mind was the thought that they still might be able to make a deal before entering the grand jury room. But at this twelfth hour, he doubted that Harrington would go for it. After the good PR from his press conference and the fluff piece by Fletcher Porter, the district attorney would skewer Dillard on the equality-under-law hearth and serve him up piece by piece until the fall election.

The twenty-three jurors eyed the first witness, Sebastian Simeone, as he entered the room. He was impeccably dressed in a tailored blue serge suit and a white Dunhill shirt, plain burgundy tie, and gold cuff links. With his dark hair flecked with proper gray at his temples, he resembled a youngish Cesar Romero.

Always lead with your best witness was an old adage closely adhered to by trial lawyers. Never save the best wine for the last. It may be too late.

"Please take the witness stand, Mr. Simeone," Mayan d'Ortega directed, pen in hand. Her eyes had lost their fawnlike glimmer. The hunt was on.

After Simeone was sworn to tell the truth by the bailiff, d'Ortega led him through his relationship with the deceased. Her questioning, in direct examination, was lucid and persuasive. Simeone recounted the formative years of his half-sister's life, her humble beginnings, her fortunate adoption by Simeone's father, her schooling at Academia San Cristóbal in Spain under the Dominican nuns, her studies at the Beaux-Arts in Paris, and her work at the Prado in Madrid. She was twenty-nine years of age when she died, an international art dealer who worked on occasion for his import firm as a consultant and freelance entrepreneur. She was single, had never married as far as he knew. As the administrator of her estate, he had claimed the body and seen to it that her remains were given a Catholic burial after cremation.

D'Ortega now turned from the prosecutor's table and walked to the witness box. She first looked at Simeone, then at the jurors.

"Did you identify the body of Angela Williams at the morgue of Boston Memorial Hospital?"

Simeone bent toward the small microphone jutting from the ledge of the witness box.

"I . . . I . . ." He cleared his throat as tears began welling in his eyes. He removed the handkerchief from his breast pocket and dabbed the corners of his eyes.

D'Ortega waited. Simeone's breakdown was effective.

"Would you like some water, Mr. Simeone?"

"No." He cleared his throat again. "I'll be all right."

"Did you identify the body as that of your half-sister, Angela Williams?" D'Ortega now eyed the jurors, watching their reaction.

"I did." Simeone shook his head. "She was so vibrant, so full of life . . . a young sparrow knocked down on the fly."

He straightened his shoulders into a manly stance and looked squarely at the jurors. "I hope you bring the person who did this to justice."

The effect was electrifying. . . . "I hope you bring the person to justice!"

D'Ortega had planned to introduce photographs of a smiling, beautiful graduate in cap and gown receiving honors from a university provost and a confirmation picture, rosary beads clasped in hands folded in prayer, white crinoline dress beneath a gauzy veil, as angelic as the victim's name implied. But she would let those go. No more drama could be squeezed from the moment.

"Thank you, Mr. Simeone." She turned toward the witness. "You may be excused."

He nodded, replacing his handkerchief in his breast pocket.

"Excuse me," d'Ortega said, almost as an afterthought. She looked at the jurors. "Are there any questions?"

No one dared invade the moment. The jurors shook their heads in unison. No questions.

D'Ortega knew then, as she always knew, that it was her show. The hunt continued, the prey within sight.

"Please bring in Officer Turco," she said to the bailiff as he accompanied Sebastian Simeone and unlocked the door.

Phil Riley called Gert Trudeau from a phone booth in the corridor outside the grand jury room.

"Phil, you lucked out," she said. "What are you up to?" Gert was paying off some chits. Several months ago, Riley had put the fix in on Gert's son's drunk-driving charge.

"Four-two-six–one-seven-five-oh is not Hizzoner's number." She was not a Kane fan. "His private home number is two-three-five–eight-four-two-one, or Celtic-one. Can you believe that ego? What a crock!"

"What about one-seven-five-oh?" Riley leaned into the booth, which was only semiprivate. At five o'clock, the corridor was still jammed. He noticed the FBI cameras on the walls near the ceiling. The grand jury was in session and he knew the video cameras were still covering the entrances. He noticed the FBI agents, even Assistant U.S. Attorney Sheldon Fine. What the hell is *he* doing here? he thought. No Sonny Callahan, no Irish terrorists. But he had heard a disturbing rumor from one of his fringe informants. Sonny Callahan's days were numbered.

"Yeah, Gert." He cupped one hand over the mouthpiece and scribbled the information down in his notebook. "Four-two-six–one-seven-five-oh is registered to N. Cuchinella. Yeah, I got it."

Great Mother of Christ, he swore to himself. Jesus, Mary, and Joseph! Three twenty-one Beacon Street, the Revere Estates. He jotted it down. "Phone disconnected April fourth, you say?

"Hey, Gert," he said. "You're a peach. How's your boy doing?"

"Straightened himself out. Going to Northeastern, studying criminal law." Gert knew that favor for favor, it was now a wash.

"Keep in touch, Gert," Riley said.

Simeone followed the bailiff to the side door of the grand jury room. Reporters and spectators filled the corridor to the main entrance, but they were in the dark as to what was going on behind the locked door.

Mayan d'Ortega used the remainder of the afternoon to elicit testimony from the officers of the Burlington Police, from Anton Kent-Smythe, who had found the body, from the emergency ambulance technicians who had transported the body to Boston Memorial Hospital, and from Dr. Supples, who had pronounced Williams dead on arrival at 1:04 A.M., April third.

The testimony of each witness kept the jurors on the edge of their seats. Although everyone had been provided with a notepad, no notes were needed as they were carried along by the dramatic cadence of d'Ortega's interrogation.

The Burlington Police introduced blowup photographs of the rest area and a topographical chart with various dimensions depicting the locus where the body had been found. Photographs of the body were passed for each juror's inspection.

Kent-Smythe testified that he was heeding a call of nature when he stumbled upon the body. He explained how it scared him half to death and he immediately phoned the Burlington Police from the kiosk phone booth. D'Ortega didn't question him as to why he went seventy-five yards into the woods, nor did any juror ask.

Dr. Supples set the stage for more exacting medical testimony by explaining his medical findings in simple lay terms. "Cyanosis," explained the doctor, "is a condition in which the normal skin color is replaced by a bluish tinge. It indicates that there is not enough oxygen in the blood, for it is well-oxygenated blood that gives skin its usual flesh color. The lack of oxygen in the blood may result from an insufficient supply of air to the lungs, as when the throat is obstructed.

"Rigor mortis," he continued, "is rigidity or stiffening of muscles, and hence stiffening of the body, after death. It is due chiefly to an accumulation of lactic acid in muscle tissue. The rapidity of onset and the duration of rigidity vary with the condition of the muscle prior to death with regard to activity, with temperature of the environment, and other factors. The onset, beginning with the small muscles of the face, progresses thereafter to the legs and feet."

He had found no evidence of rigor mortis, meaning that death had occurred within a few hours.

About 4:30, d'Ortega sent word to Riley and Furlong that they would not be needed until 9:00 A.M. the next day. A message also went to Sheridan, asking him to have Dillard available at two

o'clock. Again they were allowed to use the rear elevator, avoiding
the press and spectators. Sheridan knew the old courthouse like
the back of his hand. He got off in the basement, followed a
bricked-in corridor lined with overhead pipes, and led Dillard out
through the maintenance entrance, where they hailed a taxi. At
least for the day, they had escaped the dagger quills of the Fourth
Estate.

Riley declined Furlong's offer of a ride back to headquarters, instead taking a cab to his house.

He changed into plainclothes, a gray tweed suit, hid his service
revolver in the small of his back, and folded the *Globe* article with
Neil Harrington's picture into his inner coat pocket. He hailed a
cab at the corner and at about 5:30 arrived at the office of Revere
Estates.

"Hi." He smiled at the secretary who was starting to wind down
the computers. "I'm Detective Riley, Boston Police." He flipped
open his wallet to display his picture and gold badge. "Is the manager in?"

"You mean Mr. Bennett," she said, then paused. "He's in his
office. Is anything wrong?"

"Not really. I'm just checking up on a tenant. Would you tell
him I'm here. I'll only take a few minutes of his time."

"Just a moment," she said. She rapped lightly on the walnut-
veneered door, then slipped inside.

She reappeared almost immediately. "Mr. Bennett can see you,
but he has to make a six o'clock appointment, so if you could please
make it quick."

"What can I do for you, Mr. Riley?" Bennett, a short, pear-
shaped, middle-aged man, stepped out from behind his desk and
smiled apprehensively.

Again Riley flashed his badge. "Does N. Cuchinella have an
apartment here?"

"Yes. He was in Six B, facing the river."

"Is he still here?"

"No. Had another six months to go, but he terminated."

"I assume the apartment's vacant?"

"Yes. Everything was moved out."

"Did he pay his rent by check?"

"Nope. Always cash. Three thousand dollars a month, due on the first."

Riley could scarcely believe his good luck.

"One last thing, Mr. Bennett. Did Mr. Cuchinella leave any forwarding address?"

"No. He just moved out. Paid two months' rent as a penalty under the lease-termination clause."

"Can you tell me what the guy looked like?"

"Handsome, I'd say forty-five to fifty, trim, athletic build. Maybe a foot taller than me." Bennett gestured with his hand above his head.

Riley reached into his inside pocket and pulled out the *Globe* article folded to Harrington's picture.

"You recognize this man?"

Bennett adjusted his owlish glasses and squinted. "Yes," he said, "that's Mr. Cuchinella."

35

RILEY CAUGHT Gert Trudeau just as she was leaving work. She agreed to stay on for a while to check out calls made from 426–1750 for several weeks before it was disconnected. She called him back within the hour. At first, nothing had seemed unusual, she said. Routine domestic stuff—the neighborhood liquor mart, Speedy Pizza, a local cab company. No calls to Williams. Gert had learned that four calls to Williams's apartment during late March had originated from a pay phone just outside the Revere Estates building. This had to include the taped call that Williams had kept. Smart, Riley thought. The pay phone, which every married guy since the days of Alexander Graham Bell had used to call his girlfriend. Couldn't be traced.

Then BINGO! She found three calls from 426–1750 to the district attorney. Harrington, alias Cuchinella, calling his own office. Stupid! Riley said to himself. Plain stupid. But sometimes convenience overrides caution. He thought of Sol Wachtler, the chief judge of the New York Court of Appeals, who had made a harassment call to his ex-lover from his car phone while driving from Albany to New York City—and the FBI with their computer triangulation had been listening. Scratch one judge.

He checked his watch. Marge and the kids were out at a school meeting. They wouldn't be back for another hour. He snapped open a can of Budweiser and took a few good swallows as he flipped through his notebook. He had the Williams-Harrington connection, no question. Harrington and Williams had been lovers. Legally, a pretty good inference. Motive? Williams was a big burr under the DA's political saddle. But would Harrington resort to murder? Would he have had it done?

Riley finished the Bud and popped open another can. His mind seemed flooded with unanswered questions. Was there a connection between Harrington and Dillard? Perhaps even with Callahan? Certainly Williams could tell no tales. So what did he have? Harrington screwing Williams. Williams threatening to blow Harrington out of the water. Dillard telling him and Furlong that Williams was alive and well when he left at ten, having been in her company since 7:30 on. Williams dead at nine, according to the medical report. Could Dillard have been with both Williams and Harrington that fatal evening?

If only Gert had come up with a phone call between Dillard and 426–1750. But she hadn't. The *O* in *BINGO* was missing.

"Karen," Dr. McCafferty surprised his assistant, who was dictating into a hand recorder. "How come you're working so late? It's after ten."

Momentarily startled, Karen Steadman looked up from her Spartan metal desk and clicked off the recorder. A gooseneck lamp cast a thin pane of light on her scratch pad and she could barely make out McCafferty's features, his shape silhouetted against the steel cases containing the day's supply of cadavers. "Oh, just finishing up," she said, regaining her composure. "Did a post on that drowning case they fished out of the harbor and now I'm dictating my report from my notes."

"Well, it's kind of spooky and damp down here. At this hour, you should be out having a little fun."

"I'll be closing up shortly," she said, giving her recorder a little shake.

McCafferty went over to the wall and flipped a switch. The overhead fluorescent lights fluttered, then came on.

"You know, Karen"—he fumbled in his vest pocket and removed a pack of cigarettes—"the beauty of pathology is that it's the easiest of the medical disciplines. Except for the occasional forensic and cancer case, it's nine to five. And best of all, no pain-in-the-ass patients.

"Smoke?" He had popped two Camels out of the pack.

Karen shook her head. She folded her notes into her white tunic pocket, then looked up at her boss as he lit his cigarette, watching him puff for several seconds.

"You testifying tomorrow?" she asked.

He sent a lungful of smoke billowing toward the ceiling, then held the cigarette between two fingers, almost at arm's length, cocking his head at a self-satisfied angle. "Scheduled for ten tomorrow morning. I rather enjoy the courtroom. You can pick up some real money testifying in civil and criminal cases, Karen; that's one of the fringees to our trade.

"Reminds me," he continued, "gotta get the slides and Williams's anatomical parts. And there's a plastic model of the upper thorax around here someplace. The jurors love that demonstrative evidence stuff."

"Are you going along with the strangulation bit?" She eyed him carefully.

"Hey, Karen, that's the whole ball of wax. We're going to nail Dr. Blue Blood. Christopher Dillard's next clinic will be the infirmary at Walpole prison."

"You're really going to testify that there was hemorrhaging of the neck musculature and a fracture of the cricoid cartilage?"

McCafferty's cigarette stopped halfway to his mouth. He didn't like the tone of his intern's voice. "What are you talking about?"

She paused momentarily. "Doctor," she said curtly, "when you cut into the thorax of the Williams woman, I bent down as close as I could. There were no external marks on the neck, no indentations, no bruises, no hemorrhaging of the neck musculature, and *no* fracture of the cricoid cartilage!"

"Look, Karen, sometimes you miss things first time around." McCafferty flicked ashes onto the floor.

"I didn't miss a thing, Doctor, nor did you. You specifically told me you couldn't determine the cause of death, remember?"

"Hey!" He wiped his brow with the back of his hand. "Don't mess with me. I spotted hemorrhaging and a fracture! Period! That's in my official report and that of Myron Gellis!" His voice was a throaty growl.

She eyed him coolly, gauging the depth of his fabrication. "You really know what you're doing?"

McCafferty said nothing for several seconds. He took one last drag on his cigarette, then dropped it on the cement floor and left it to smolder there. "You stick to learning the basics of pathology, Dr. Steadman, and don't meddle in police work. Leave this to me."

Karen sat motionless, digesting the subtle threat. During the past week, she had regained the zest she feared she had lost. The new intern from Stanford had invited her to lunch—even if it was only the hospital cafeteria—and they seemed to hit it off. Now the old misgivings were beginning to reappear. She didn't doubt Mc-Cafferty's competence; she could even get used to the booze on his breath. But now she doubted his integrity. That made the situation unacceptable.

McCafferty spent the next ten minutes gathering his equipment—slides, anatomical parts encased in containers with formaldehyde, the plastic anatomical model—then stuffed it all in a large leather bag.

"You coming, Karen?" He paused at the door.

"I've almost finished my dictation," she said with manufactured brightness. "I'll lock up."

"Okay." His lips pursed into a tight smile, but somehow the droopy beagle eyes weren't smiling.

Karen could hear McCafferty ascending the metal stairs. The echoing *thunks* grew gradually fainter, then disappeared. Several seconds passed before she picked up her mike recorder. She enunciated carefully:

This is Dr. Karen Steadman, intern in Pathology at Boston Memorial Hospital.

She related the date and time.

I am dictating this memo because of certain irregularities I observed in the pathological opinion of my superior, Dr. Bernard McCafferty, chief of Pathology.

On April 3rd, I assisted Dr. McCafferty in a postmortem examination on the body of one Angela Williams, late of Boston, who was pronounced dead on arrival by a Dr. Supples here at Memorial at 1:04 A.M. said date.

Dr. McCafferty and I conducted a thorough eight-hour post. Nothing was overlooked. At the conclusion of the post, Dr. McCafferty was of the opinion that the time of death was between 8:30 and 9:00 P.M., April 2. I had serious reservations about that estimate at that time and still have today. As to cause of death, Dr. McCafferty said, and I quote him, "I haven't got the foggiest idea. There's not a goddamned thing wrong."

I am aware that a Dr. Myron Gellis from New York did an additional post and reported that he found hemorrhaging of the neck musculature and a fracture of the cricoid cartilage. Dr. McCafferty told me that he also did an additional post prior to that of Dr. Gellis and his findings coincided with those of Gellis.

I did not see any hemorrhaging in the neck musculature. There were only Tardieu spots—natural blood clots caused by the postmortem. Drs. Gellis and McCafferty's joint report indicated cause of death was due to neck strangulation causing hemorrhaging and a fracture of the cricoid cartilage.

I did not, let me repeat, I did not see any fracture of the cricoid cartilage during the initial post. My view of the thorax cartilages was unobstructed. I was within six inches of the dissected area and viewed, as did Dr. McCafferty, the subject area.

I understand that someone is suspected of being criminally responsible for causing Williams's death.

On my own, I reexamined the subject. Although there was a minute crack in the cricoid cartilage, this was not evident upon the initial post.

I want to record my observations and conclusions, since I feel a grave injustice is about to be perpetrated. . . . I also have a feeling my own safety and well-being may be endangered.

She clicked off the recorder button, gathered up her notes, and slipped the recorder into her tunic.

"Would you get that, Sheila?" Brian Loughlin motioned toward the telephone ringing in the assistant director's office, which adjoined his station. "Probably some nut who spotted Fidel Castro lurking around the John Hancock Tower with sticks of dynamite. These nocturnal calls are usually kook cases." It was 10:30 P.M.

Sheila glanced at Brian Loughlin hunched over the FBI intercept. Agents Bob Kerry, Dave Walsh, and Diane Blakemore, equipped with air force–type headphones, seemed engrossed in luminous squiggles that trucked across the fluorescent screen, hoping to trap a call that would give them some sort of lead.

Sheila nodded, went next door, punched the blinking button, and picked up the phone.

"Federal Bureau of Investigation."

The female caller was hesitant at first, perhaps expecting a male voice. "Hello, am I speaking with the FBI?"

"You are. I'm Sheila O'Brien, agent in charge for the evening."

"I need to talk with you, Miss O'Brien."

"Certainly, but can you give me some idea what you want to talk about? And may I have your name, please?"

"My name is Karen Steadman." The voice now seemed reassured. "I'm a doctor, a Pathology intern at Boston Memorial Hospital. It concerns a recent death."

"Does this concern violation of federal law?"

"I don't know. Perhaps we'd better meet. I'm not too sure I should be discussing this over the phone."

The young voice had a cry of urgency but otherwise seemed coherent. Sheila sensed this wasn't a crank call. She reached for the assistant director's memo pad and pulled out a pen from his desk set to take down the caller's name, address, and telephone number.

"Perhaps you could meet me at noon tomorrow," Sheila said. "I'm on duty during the morning, but there's a coffee shop, the Iron Kettle, in Government Center. It's got a large teapot over the door, actually hisses steam."

"I know where it is. I'll be wearing a gray suit."

"Meet you out front at exactly twelve noon. I'll be wearing jeans and a Boston College jacket."

"Wait a minute!" Agent Walsh signaled his associates. "Got a call coming in to Sheridan's residence."

Sheila O'Brien had just hung up and had come back into the electronics room. She watched as Brian Loughlin put on his headphone.

"Hello, Mr. Sheridan. I'm Detective Phil Riley of the Boston Police."

"Oh, uh . . . uh, Mr. Sheridan isn't in. I'm his houseboy. Give me your number and I'll have Mr. Sheridan call you when he gets back."

"I'd better call him. Can you tell me when he's due?"

"No. Let me get in touch with him. We'll get back." There was an audible click.

"That's the goddamnedest conversation I've ever heard!" Brian Loughlin said as he and the agents took off their headphones. Sheila O'Brien moved closer.

"Phil Riley," Bob Kerry said, knitting his brow. "Isn't that the detective who was in Harrington's office this morning waiting to testify before the grand jury?"

"Sounds like the same, unless they've got a few detectives named Phil Riley."

"And the one answering," Loughlin said. "That's Sheridan's voice all right. He gives Riley the houseboy bit because he knows his phones are bugged."

"Do you think Riley . . . ?" Kerry looked quizzically at Loughlin.

"No, obviously Riley was unaware that we had Sheridan tapped or he wouldn't have called. Riley has info he wants to impart, that's for sure."

Sheila listened as the agents discussed the sudden turn of events.

"Here's Riley investigating the Williams death, speaks with the key suspect, and on his own wants to talk with the suspect's attorney," Loughlin continued. "Doesn't smell right."

"Do you think we should call Sheldon Fine?" Kerry asked. "Maybe even Mayan d'Ortega?"

"It's after eleven o'clock." Loughlin checked his watch. "We'll wrap it up for the night, put the tapes on auto. We're scheduled to be in Harrington's office at eight A.M. for the day's briefing.

"They didn't reach Riley yesterday, but I understand he's scheduled to testify, along with Captain Furlong and the medical examiner, sometime tomorrow.

"We'll clue in Fine and d'Ortega first thing in the morning, maybe go for a surveillance of Riley and a tap on his phone.

"What do you think, Sheila?" Loughlin suddenly glanced at his associate, who had moved closer to the group. Momentarily sidetracked by Loughlin's remark, she hesitated for a few seconds. She wanted to impart the information about the telephone call from Dr. Steadman, but she held back.

"Oh, it does seem a little unusual. . . ."

"A little unusual," Kerry scoffed. "I think the Boston Police are playing footsie. We may have our first good break."

Sheila merely nodded. Coming from the veteran Kerry, a special agent for twenty years with an enviable record of major busts, it was a mild but testy rebuke.

"Okay," Loughlin said, noticing Sheila's reticence. "Let's cut out for the night.

"Sheila, can I give you and Diane a ride home? I've got the bureau's wheels for the evening."

"I'm heading for Brookline," said Diane Blakemore. "That's in the opposite direction. I'll grab a cab."

"I'll cab it, too," Sheila said quickly. "I think the bureau can afford it."

"Nonsense!" said Loughlin. "We live in the same vicinity. Come on! There's an all-night diner on the Revere Beach Parkway. I could go for some ham and eggs."

"No, I'll see you at eight tomorrow." Her smile was as distant as her voice. "Diane," she said, "I'll take the elevator down with you."

Loughlin knew something was wrong. Maybe she was still sulking over the Sheridan fiasco. He wanted to talk with her, maybe pick up a clue as to what she was thinking.

Then he remembered the ringing phone. "What was that call all about?"

"What call?"

Even Kerry was now aware that Sheila O'Brien seemed to be in another time zone.

"The telephone call—the assistant director's office," Loughlin snapped.

"Oh, some nut . . . just a crank call." She hesitated. "Said he spotted John Dillinger going into the Biograph Theater with Baby Face Nelson."

"Hey, that's a new one." Kerry grinned and turned to pick up his briefcase.

"Hold it!" Walsh signaled toward the electronic tote board winking its fluorescent squiggles. "Sonny Callahan's line."

The group, including Sheila O'Brien, rushed to put on headphones.

"Hello, is Mr. Callahan in? I'm Detective Riley of the Boston Police Department."

"Just a minute," came a woman's voice. There were several moments of mumbling in the background. Then the woman's voice came back on the line.

"I'm sorry, Mr. Riley. He's sound asleep. I'll ask him to give you a call in the morning."

"Tell him to call me at six A.M. tomorrow at my home in Dorchester, four-two-six–one-one-six-six. It's very important. Are you Mrs. Callahan?"

"I'm his daughter. Wait until I get a pencil and paper." There were several seconds of silence. Again a muffled conversation. "I'm sorry, Mr. Riley." The voice came back on the line. "He has to fly to Washington early tomorrow morning. He'll be in touch."

"That's it!" Brian Loughlin's thumb and forefinger formed a circle, his fingers extended as he took off his headphone. "I think we've got enough to set the bugs and peepers up in Sheridan's office. Sheldon Fine says all we need is a link between Sheridan and Callahan. I think we just lucked out.

"You still have the duplicate key to Sheridan's office?" He looked at Sheila O'Brien.

"Yes," she said reluctantly. "It's at home."

Sheridan drove along Storrow Drive. It was well after midnight. He pulled into an emergency island, stopping in front of a telephone booth. After calls to several Rileys listed in the telephone directory, he finally made the connection.

"Mr. Riley? Mr. Phil Riley?"

"Yes," came a sleepy voice.

"I'm Dan Sheridan. I think you called me earlier."

"Mr. Sheridan. Yes, about ten-thirty, but your houseboy . . ."

"Yes, he told me you called. Is there anything I can do for you?"

"I understand you represent Dr. Christopher Dillard, who's due to testify before the grand jury tomorrow."

Sheridan's sensors were all in the red. This conversation was undoubtedly being taped from Riley's end.

"I'm afraid I can't talk to you, Mr. Riley. Code of ethics, you know. Your interests are really adversarial to me and my client."

"I've got some information about the case I think you should have. It's vital. Can we meet, Mr. Sheridan?"

Sheridan sensed a trap, but somehow Riley seemed sincere. And ethically, he could justify it. His duty was to his client and he had an obligation to investigate, even to listen to the other side, to find out every scrap of information they had, short of stealing the prosecutor's file.

"Okay, I'll be in the prosecutors' room on the twelfth floor of the courthouse with my client for most of the morning, maybe all day."

"I know where it is, Mr. Sheridan. Sometime tomorrow I'll make contact."

36

MAYAN D'ORTEGA listened intently as Sheldon Fine related the substance of Phil Riley's calls to Sheridan and Callahan.

"Well, you guys do what you have to do," she said. "I'll use Riley as my first witness. If I have any inkling that he's changing his testimony or suppressing anything, I'll suspend immediately. If I accompany Riley out of the grand jury room, that's the signal for you and your agents to make the arrest."

"Riley's the key," Fine said. "To save his hide, I think he'll roll, implicate Sheridan and Callahan—perhaps Dillard. But that's down the street."

"I've allowed Sheridan to use the prosecutors' room," Mayan said. "He agreed to have Dillard available at any time, so they'll both be there."

"Exactly where?" Loughlin asked.

"You come out of the grand jury room, take ten steps to your left, you'll see a door, unmarked. That's the prosecutors' room. Sheridan and Dillard will be there from nine o'clock on.

"You've done a fine job, all of you." She scanned the group, taking in Brian Loughlin, Bob Kerry, Dave Walsh, Sheila O'Brien, and Diane Blakemore. "I've got a call in to Neil Harrington. He'll be here shortly." She nodded toward Sheldon Fine. "It looks as if this conspiracy went a little deeper than either of us thought."

"Ladies and gentlemen," Mayan d'Ortega addressed the members of the grand jury, "yesterday you heard the testimony of Anton Kent-Smythe, who found Miss Williams's body, the testimony of the Burlington Police who responded to Mr. Kent-Smythe's call, the emergency technicians who transported the body to Boston Memorial Hospital, Dr. Supples, who gave you his initial findings and pronounced Miss Williams dead on arrival, and Sebastian Simeone, who identified the body as that of his half-sister, Angela Williams, who until the time of her death resided at Hawthorne-on-the-Charles here in Boston.''

She spoke slowly, lucidly, with a measured cadence. Thalia Shapiro, the black professor, the dentist, and the other jurors hunched forward with rapt attention.

The early-morning sun filtering through the grimy east windows homed in on the prosecutor, who looked attractive in a gray two-piece suit with a splash of lavender chiffon at her throat. She paused several seconds to embellish the unfolding drama.

''Bailiff,'' she said, ''please call Lt. Philip Riley of the Boston Police Department.''

Riley, impressive in formal blues, gold chevrons and citations arrayed across his chest, was administered the oath and took his seat in the witness box. He unconsciously smoothed his graying hair, then adjusted the small microphone in front of him and nodded at Mayan d'Ortega.

Mayan picked up a folder from the prosecutor's table, then walked several paces and positioned herself just to the right of Riley's shoulder, turning slightly to face the jurors. If Riley was going to blow, she wanted to be certain he understood her clearly, that the stenographer, and more particularly the jurors, caught the exchange.

In answer to her opening question, Riley recounted his background, his years with the homicide unit, the numerous cases that he had investigated over the years. Next came the specifics of the Williams case. With Captain Furlong, he had searched Williams's apartment the evening after she was reported dead. He detailed the lab techs' investigation. Photographs of the interior of Williams's apartment were passed to the jurors.

Mayan waited as they reviewed each photograph. She studied their individual reactions.

''Thank you,'' she said to Thalia Shapiro, who had been elected forelady, as she collected the last photo. She could see that the jurors were overawed. Williams was a high roller. Even in glossy black and whites, the place looked like something out of *Architectural Digest.*

Next she picked up a small parcel and returned to her position at the witness stand. So far so good. Riley was following the book. No waffling yet. She fixed him with her dark steady eyes.

"Lieutenant Riley, I hand you a packet marked Commonwealth's Exhibit Five. Do you recognize this package?"

"I do."

"Would you explain to the ladies and gentlemen of the grand jury what this exhibit is?"

"These are letters that Captain Furlong and I found in Miss Williams's apartment on the evening of April third."

"How many letters are there?"

"Eight."

"Where were they found?"

"In a drawer in a table in Miss Williams's bedroom."

"Were they wrapped in the same blue satin ribbon that encases them today?"

"The same."

"Tell me, Lieutenant Riley"—Mayan's voice took on a crisp nononsense timbre—"to whom were these letters addressed?"

"Angela Williams."

"By whom were these letters sent?"

"They were all signed 'Chris.' We learned later that they were sent by Dr. Christopher Dillard."

"How do you know that?"

"We, meaning Captain Furlong and I, talked to Dr. Dillard at his office at St. Luke's Hospital in Boston."

"When was that?"

"The next day, April fourth."

"Did you and Captain Furlong identify yourselves?"

"We did."

"Were both of you in uniform?"

"No, we were in plainclothes."

"Was anyone else present?"

"Just Captain Furlong and me."

"Did Dr. Dillard admit that the signature was his and that he had sent these letters?"

"He did."

"All eight letters?"

"All eight."

"Lieutenant Riley, would you kindly read to the grand jury a letter dated March seventeenth."

"Yes." Riley untied the blue ribbon and sorted out the letter.

"Go ahead, please." Mayan d'Ortega again sized up the jury. No question about it: They were front row center at the year's best drama.

Riley cleared his throat. " 'Dear Angel,' " he began to read. . . .

"Excuse me, Lieutenant Riley, is this the most recent letter you found in the packet?"

"It is."

"There were no other letters subsequent to that date?"

"That is correct."

"Did you find any letters from anyone else addressed to Miss Williams?"

"None."

"Not even a postcard?"

"Not even a postcard."

"Please continue with the letter."

Riley studied the letter for a moment, then began to read it aloud:

I do hope plans for the restaurant are going well. I am proud of you for taking this bold step and will support you in any way I can.

I trust your recent trip went well.

Now for serious business.

There are some discrepancies that we must talk about. As you know, our people have invested in you quite heavily. They will not tolerate even the slightest irregularity. Believe me, I know.

I'll see you at your place, 7:30, April 2.

Today is St. Patrick's Day. Ironic, isn't it? But as they say in Gaelic, Ta fior graw agam duit, ta is agat sin! Act ar mait duinn beirt, ta suil agam nac bfuil se ro deanac.

                                                                    Chris

P.S. I trust you will destroy this letter.

Several seconds went by.

D'Ortega now faced the jurors directly—a veteran trial lawyer's technique. Her interrogation, although directed at Riley, would be strictly for the panel's benefit.

"Dr. Dillard admitted to you and Captain Furlong that he had sent the letters to Miss Williams?"

"He did."

"Did you question him about the contents of any of these letters?"

"Only about the letter of March seventeenth, which I just read."

"Ladies and gentlemen of the jury, you are probably wondering about the contents of the other seven letters. Our next witness will be the county's medical examiner, Dr. Bernard McCafferty. He will be followed by Capt. Charles Furlong, who will read the remaining letters. All will be placed in evidence so that each of you can read them at any time you may deem appropriate. Okay?"

All nodded agreement.

She was still unsure of Riley, but she continued, keeping the jury firmly in view. "Why did you question him about that particular letter?"

"Well, the Williams woman was dead. The March seventeenth letter set up a meeting between Dillard and Williams for April second, the day she was *murdered*." Riley supplied the emphasis.

The jurors were now filling in the pieces to the mosaic. *Murder. Dr. Dillard.*

"And," Riley continued, "there were some subtle threats in that letter, the implication that 'the boys don't like the way things are going.' And, of course, we also found cocaine on the premises. We couldn't overlook a possible connection."

"Now the letter concludes with a Gaelic expression." Mayan d'Ortega pronounced it flawlessly. "A difficult ancient tongue, one that goes back four thousand years before English. Wouldn't you agree, Lieutenant?"

"Most certainly."

"I take it you're Irish, Lieutenant Riley?"

"Irish-American. My grandparents came from Ireland."

"This expression in Gaelic, did you ask Dr. Dillard what it meant?"

"Captain Furlong did."

"What did Dr. Dillard say?"

"He said it was an old expression he learned from his Irish grandmother."

"Do you know what it means?"

"I didn't at the time. I remember my grandfather speaking Irish, but it was all Greek to me."

Several of the jurors laughed. Mayan d'Ortega forced a smile. Prosecution of a homicide case was not "The Tonight Show." There was no room for humor. She'd tighten her interrogation.

"Did Dr. Dillard say what the expression meant?"

"He said it was a term of endearment."

"Did he elaborate?"

"He did not."

"Now, at the time you and Captain Furlong questioned Dr. Dillard, you had no idea what the expression meant?"

"That's correct."

"Nor did Captain Furlong?"

Riley nodded in agreement.

"You must answer for the record, Lieutenant."

"That's right. We had no idea literally what it meant. It's a strange language."

"I agree." Again the slight smile at the jurors. "Did you subsequently determine what it meant?"

"I did."

"How did you do that?"

"I gave it to our linguistics expert, Dr. Liam Cahill, who is also chairman of Irish Studies at Boston College."

"Did he interpret it?"

"He did."

Mayan d'Ortega again repeated the Gaelic expression.

"Dr. Dillard said it was a term of endearment. Was he correct?"

"Partly."

"Partly? You mean he wasn't telling the entire truth?" She now focused on Riley.

He didn't hesitate. "That's right."

"Why do you say that he wasn't telling the truth?"

"Well, the first few words"—Riley looked at the letter, then at the jury—"*were terms of endearment.* Literally"—Riley stumbled through the tongue-twisting phrase—"according to Professor Cahill, it means 'I love you dearly, you know that.'"

Mayan d'Ortega left her position near the witness stand and walked toward the jurors.

"What did the rest of the expression say? . . . What does it mean?"

"It translates, 'For your sake and mine, I hope it's not too late.'"

" 'For your sake and mine, I hope it's not too late.' " Mayan looked at the jurors, repeating it slowly, carefully, dramatically.

Again she fixed Riley with her steady, deep gaze, brow furrowed quizzically.

"Lieutenant Riley, why the Gaelic? Why in your opinion did Dr. Dillard resort to Gaelic?"

Now came the hearsay—unobjectionable in a grand jury presentation. The floodgates were about to open. Riley responded. He detailed the ledger accounts of cocaine sales, trips to Europe, Tunis, Madrid, London, Berlin, various locales in Northern Ireland.

"As a result of your investigation, Lieutenant Riley, what in your opinion was Miss Williams's occupation?"

"In my opinion, she was a courier for a certain European terrorist group."

"Any particular terrorist group?" D'Ortega studied Riley carefully. He didn't hesitate.

"The Irish Republican Army."

Several jurors stirred uneasily. Simeone had portrayed his half-sister as an art dealer, cultured, with a burnished background of fine schools and jobs. Things were now turning sinister.

Mayan d'Ortega now had no reservations about Riley's testimony. He was going right down the line. His forceful delivery, his eye contact with the jurors, forensically and histrionically neared perfection.

Riley put the letter back into place, retied the packet, and handed it to Mayan d'Ortega with a courteous nod.

"Thank you, Lieutenant," she said.

She looked up into the semicircle of faces, again the dramatic pause.

"Following the conversation wherein Dr. Dillard acknowledged writing the letters, did you have a further discussion with the doctor?"

"We did."

"Would you tell us what you and Captain Furlong said and how he, Dr. Dillard, answered?"

"May I?" Riley held up his notebook.

"Certainly, if it will refresh your recollection and help you to testify as accurately as possible."

"It will."

"Please proceed."

"Well, Captain Furlong did most of the questioning. Mind you, at that time Dr. Dillard was not a suspect."

"All right," Mayan d'Ortega interrupted quickly. "Please give us the verbatim conversation."

"The captain asked him where he was that night, meaning April second. He said he had had dinner at Miss Williams's apartment, arrived a little after seven P.M. They had a few drinks. Miss Williams prepared a gourmet dinner with wine, a rich dessert, and brandies.

"Do you want me to keep on reading all this stuff?"

"Please."

"He then said—I quote his words: 'I took my leave about ten P.M.'"

"Now, Dr. Dillard said he was in Miss Williams's presence from a little after seven until ten P.M."

"Yes."

"And during that time, he said, they had a full gourmet dinner, with wine and after-dinner brandy."

"That's correct."

"And Dr. Dillard said he left at ten P.M."

"About ten."

"And she let him out the front door."

Riley knew being let out the front door was an assumption. But he went along. It was a logical assumption.

"Yes," he said.

Mayan d'Ortega turned from the witness and looked directly up at the jurors. "He left at ten." She strung it out, letting the phrase linger.

"Yes." Riley also looked at the jurors. "He said he left at ten."

"Thank you, Lieutenant," she said as if she had been delivering a sermon and was closing the book on a final biblical quotation. "You are excused."

"Bailiff," she said, turning toward Coyne, "kindly escort the lieutenant out and please bring in Dr. Bernard McCafferty."

The twelfth-floor hallway was jammed with reporters, municipal clerks, FBI agents, cameramen, plain citizens, and curious courtroom buffs with time on their hands.

The grand jury proceeding was secret and would remain so for its duration. But somehow the story had been leaked. The FBI cameras were hidden, but those of Channels 5, 7, and 4 and CNN were obviously in place. Something important was going on. True-life drama—the best kind.

"Please, please." The bailiff pushed the crowd back forcibly as Riley emerged.

The cameras whirred; a mike was thrust into Riley's face.

"Is it true that a famous Boston doctor killed his girlfriend?" A reporter barged forward through the jostling crowd.

"No comment," Riley said repeatedly as he made his way to the bank of elevators. "No comment."

"Hey, Lieutenant!" yelled Fletcher Porter. "You know that after you testify you're allowed to comment. There's no legal prohibition against a witness telling what went on in there."

"No comment." Riley lowered his head and pushed the elevator's down button.

Brian Loughlin's stiffened hand cut the air, a prearranged signal to the agents spaced strategically throughout the crowd. The move on Riley was off.

Behind the closed door of the prosecutors' room, both Sheridan and Dillard could hear the commotion.

"Let me see if I can get a word to the bailiff to try to find out when we're to be called," Sheridan said. He opened the door and stepped out into the hallway. For several seconds, he went unnoticed. The cameramen and others still jostled around Riley as he stood patiently waiting for the elevator.

Then Sheila O'Brien, positioned across the hall, turned almost instinctively. Their eyes met and held, then moved away quickly, almost guiltily. Sheridan felt a pang of sorrow, regret. He still wanted her, wanted to be with her, and in that split second, he believed she felt the same way. When he raised his eyes, she was gone, swallowed by the crowd that now surged toward him.

"Johnny," he collared Flaherty, "would you get me a read on when d'Ortega is going to call my client? That cubicle we're sitting in—must be a hundred and ten degrees in there."

"I'll see what I can do." Flaherty motioned for him to step back inside. Almost too late. Fletcher Porter, brandishing his notepad, was between Sheridan and the door.

"Care to give me your side, Dan?"

"Just put this down, Fletch. A man is innocent until proven guilty. And you can quote me . . . and Thomas Jefferson."

With that, he dodged inside the room and closed the door.

"Christ Almighty," he said to Dillard, who was seated ramrod-erect, both hands gripping the arms of his chair.

"Goddamned mob scene out there. I got to the clerk to say that we want to be called next."

Dillard merely nodded. The shadow of melancholy had displaced his earlier jauntiness. Sheridan for the first time recognized the glint of fear in his eyes.

"Might have some good news." Sheridan tried to be buoyant. No sense in saying he had bad news and worse news.

"Oh?" Dillard suddenly came alive.

"Do you know a Boston Police lieutenant named Phil Riley, homicide unit?"

"Only that he and a Captain Furlong questioned me the day after Angela's death."

"Is he a member of your organization? The Sonny Callahan connection?"

"Look, Dan!" Dillard's face suddenly became white with indignation. "You're not going to get me to plead and turn government witness against Callahan. Now we've gone all over that stuff. And to answer your question, other than the time he talked to me at my office, I never saw Riley or spoke to him before in my life."

"Okay. You know my phones are bugged by the FBI . . . yours, too. Same for Sonny Callahan. The FBI even planted an agent in my office."

"God, I never knew that!"

Sheridan made an impatient, dismissive gesture. "Don't worry. We were on to it early. And don't ask me how I found out about it . . . but last night I got a late call from this Lieutenant Riley. I know a lot of Boston cops, even Captain Furlong. But Riley is kind of an outsider. He tells me he has important information about the Williams case."

"You think you were being taped? Maybe set up?" Dillard's death grip on the chair's arms suddenly relaxed.

"Maybe. I happen to know the hallway out there is crawling with FBI agents.

"Jesus!" Sheridan suddenly jumped up from his chair, putting his finger to his lips. He had never questioned d'Ortega's generosity in offering them use of the prosecutors' room. Son of a bitch, he swore to himself. Why had he been so stupid? He stood on a wooden chair and unscrewed the light fixture, inspected the window air conditioner, the beat-up walnut-veneer desk. He checked everywhere: under the worn rug, in the lavatory, the artificial flowers in a ceramic vase. Nothing. "Okay." He breathed a long sigh. "I think the place is clean. Maybe d'Ortega has a code of honor, after all."

Then came a knock on the door. Dillard's face looked as if he were embalmed.

"Mr. Sheridan." Dan recognized the voice of the bailiff, Coyne. He opened the door a crack. "Your client, Dr. Dillard, is slated to testify immediately after the medical examiner. Maybe in about an hour."

"Thanks, Dermie. We'll be right here."

Sheridan would try a psychological tack.

"We got an hour, maybe two. I understand you were a naval officer in Korea."

Dillard looked at Sheridan quizzically.

"Tell me," Sheridan said, "what was it like over there?"

Sheila O'Brien slipped away from the courthouse, her absence unnoticed even by Brian Loughlin.

"Hello, Dr. Steadman." Sheila greeted the young woman standing in front of the Iron Kettle sandwich shop. "I'm Special Agent Sheila O'Brien."

"You're the agent I talked to last evening?" Karen asked apprehensively. As promised, she was wearing a gray suit, over a pink turtleneck. She looked dubiously at Sheila's jeans and Boston College jacket.

"Yes. You have to excuse my appearance. I'm on assignment. We

don't wear sharkskin suits anymore, not even baseball caps and
SWAT team jackets." Sheila's voice and smile were pleasant.

"Here's my ID." She pulled a wallet from her jeans pocket and
flicked it open.

Karen Steadman seemed reassured. "The coffee shop is a little
crowded. Do you mind if we walk?"

"Good idea," said Sheila. "Let's head across the plaza and you
can fill me in."

They started off toward the fountain at the far side of Government Center Plaza. To their right, the granite and brick mix of City
Hall looked like a giant upside-down cake. Street vendors with push-
carts were doing a brisk business hawking everything from T-shirts
to hot cross buns. Several jugglers were tossing rings and balls in
the air and the three-card monte players were extracting money
from tourists.

"It's sort of strange you called," Sheila said. "We're investigating
the Williams case. In fact, we are covering the courthouse where
the grand jury is in session."

"I don't know what's involved," Karen Steadman said. "I did the
autopsy with Dr. McCafferty, who is scheduled to testify—I believe
today."

"That's my understanding," Sheila said.

"Here," Karen said as they approached the fountain, "put these
on." She pulled out a small pair of earphones attached to a Walk-
man. "It's a tape I made last night."

Sheila sat down on the fountain steps, put on the earphones,
turned on the recorder button, and listened.

Several seconds after handing the set back to Karen Steadman,
Sheila finally spoke.

"Would you mind coming with me to the courthouse? I think
we should have a talk with Dr. McCafferty before he testifies."

37

SHEILA O'BRIEN and Karen Steadman arrived at the courthouse too late to get to McCafferty before he entered the grand jury room. The noise in the corridor outside was reaching bedlam proportions. Clerk Flaherty had threatened to clear out everyone but those on legitimate court business. The media could stay, but the curious would have to go.

"For Christsake, this is getting out of hand!" Flaherty blurted to one of his bailiffs. "I want you to clear the area."

"Everyone?" one of the assistant clerks asked.

Flaherty exhaled audibly. "Get rid of the goddamned stragglers." His lips were pursed in an authoritative scowl.

All eyes were focused on Dr. Bernard McCafferty as the bailiff escorted him into the grand jury room through a side entrance. Coyne carried a black leather satchel that looked like a lawyer's trial bag and McCafferty had a manila folder tucked under his arm.

Mayan d'Ortega was standing at the prosecutor's table.

She greeted him as he approached. "Good afternoon, Doctor."

McCafferty, wearing a gray tweed three-piece suit, white button-down shirt, and blue rep tie, returned the salutation, then asked Coyne to set the bag on the table and to secure an overhead projector and screen in case they were needed for demonstrative purposes. Coyne promptly complied, wheeling the projector into place and setting up the screen at an oblique angle to the jurors.

Despite his florid color, McCafferty seemed composed. His eyes, often half-closed, were now clear and alert. A brace of pens jutted from his breast pocket, adding the proper touch to his professional demeanor, as Coyne administered the oath.

"Do you swear to tell the truth, the whole truth, and nothing but the truth, so help you God?"

"I do," McCafferty responded, his right hand raised, his voice mild, but with a somber undertone.

Mayan d'Ortega waited as McCafferty opened his folder and spread his notes on the small shelf in the witness box.

"Do you mind?" He looked toward the prosecutor as he extracted a small black beeper from his vest pocket, holding it aloft
for all to see. McCafferty wasn't expecting a call, but it was an old
courtroom ploy he always used to impress a jury—the "busy doctor" bit.

"No. I know your time is valuable, Doctor." Mayan d'Ortega unconsciously went along.

The preliminary interrogation, medical background, qualifica-
tions, honors, credentials in surgery and in pathology, provided a
crisp dialogue between the prosecutor and the chief medical examiner for Suffolk County. Mayan d'Ortega held a hand microphone and positioned herself near the first row of jurors. It was as
if she were their extended voice, that the inquiries were their inquiries.

"Dr. McCafferty, did you perform an autopsy on the body of
Angela Williams during the morning hours of April third?"

"I did."

"I show you six photographs taken by the Boston Police at Boston
Memorial Hospital at approximately"—Mayan looked at the date/
time stamp—"twelve-forty-five A.M. on April third, of the body of
Angela Williams. Would you kindly look at these, Doctor, and tell
me if these photos show the body of the woman upon whom you
performed an autopsy."

McCafferty studied each picture, then looked at the jurors. "They
do. These are six views of the unclad body of Angela Williams taken
just prior to Dr. Supples's preliminary examination."

"These views depict what?"

"Well, two are full supine views. The body was faceup on the
examining table. Two are prone views with the face, stomach down,
the back viewed by the camera.

"Two are lateral views, the body positioned on its, I believe, right
side, the front of the body facing the camera." He studied the
pictures again. "The other shows the body positioned on its left
side, back to the camera."

"Now, these photos are in color, Doctor, are they not?"

McCafferty held one up for the jurors to see. "They are."

"Do any unusual marks or bodily disfigurement appear in those
photographs of Miss Williams?"

"Yes. They are most evident in what we call the prone view."

McCafferty shifted his gaze toward Coyne, who was seated in the bailiff's chair to his left, against the wall. "If I could use the projector."

Coyne, who had been dozing, suddenly scrambled to life. He quickly plugged in the projector and adjusted the portable screen so that it gave the jurors a clear view.

"Can you all see the screen?" Mayan d'Ortega inquired.

They gave a collective nod.

Coyne pulled the shades, then dimmed the lights. McCafferty took what looked like a pen from his breast pocket. When he pulled on it, it telescoped into a thin steel pointer. He was center stage, the chief of Pathology as lecturer, a moment he relished.

"Now these photos may make some of you a little squeamish," he said. "They reveal the unclothed body of Angela Williams. But they're not grotesque or morbid. She was a beautiful woman, really, as you'll see in a moment.

"There were no outward signs of trauma—but here, let's look at these together." He stepped down from the witness stand and slid the photographs into the projector frame.

Mayan d'Ortega moved to sit in a vacant seat next to Thalia Shapiro.

"Exhibit Six A"—McCafferty clicked on the projector—"is the supine view of Angela Williams."

There was a collective gasp, then an eerie stillness settled on the courtroom. The only movement was dust eddying in the projector's beam like an old-time movie.

"You see here"—McCafferty pointed to the front of the body— "there are no marks. This is important, because the body was found facedown in the prone position by the Burlington Police at eleven-fifty-eight P.M. If Miss Williams was killed at the scene where she was found—the wooded area off I-Ninety-five—there should have been blood pooling at the dependent portions of the body—the front of the body, at the thighs, the abdomen, the breast area, even at the cheeks and throat. We recognize this pooling as dark splotches. In pathology, we call this livor mortis.

"Now this is the first important clue as to what happened to this unfortunate young woman."

McCafferty was in his element—smooth, erudite, yet talking the jurors' language. No questions were needed from d'Ortega.

He flicked the automatic projector button. "Exhibit Six B is a prone view. Note the purplish splotches on . . . Miss Williams." He thought it best now to personalize; he'd eliminate the term *the body*. "See Miss Williams's buttocks, the back of her knees, calves, shoulders. That's blood. When the blood ceases to circulate, it stagnates in the vessels and begins to drain and pool in large venous cavities of the body in the direction of the pull of gravity. It drains and settles in a recumbent area. So we know from this phenomenon that Miss Williams was *killed* elsewhere, then transported to the spot where she was found."

"Where the hell have you been?" Brian Loughlin looked at Sheila O'Brien, quickly taking in Karen Steadman.

Inwardly, Sheila smarted at the rebuke but sheathed her anger.

"I've been working on the case," she said, "and I think I have something. Is Dr. McCafferty in there now?"

"Been testifying for almost an hour. Should be just about finishing up." Loughlin's voice reflected irritation. He had bailed out Sheila and now she was going off on another tangent. As he had confided to Dave Walsh, "She's like a golf ball hitting cement."

"I want you to meet Dr. Karen Steadman," Sheila said to Loughlin. "She did the Williams autopsy along with Dr. McCafferty."

Brian merely nodded. Somehow, Steadman looked too young to be a doctor—and, with her blond hair and Nordic features, too good-looking.

"Is there someplace we can have a private talk?" Sheila said. "I want you to hear what she has to say."

Loughlin motioned to Dave Walsh, who joined the group. "You know this courthouse better than anyone, Dave. We need to huddle."

"Take the stairs one flight up. The law library. Go to the Vermont alcove. You could hide there forever. The last person to check in was Daniel Webster."

McCafferty completed his demonstrative testimony, clicking off the projector. Bailiff Coyne opened the shades and turned up the overhead lights. It was a short intermission, with the jurors murmuring among themselves.

Mayan d'Ortega remained standing at the first row of jurors, next to Thalia Shapiro and the black professor, unlike her position during the examination of Lieutenant Riley earlier.

"What do you think?" The professor leaned over toward Thalia Shapiro.

"We're not supposed to discuss this," she whispered back, "but I think this Dr. Dillard is as guilty as hell."

"Please." D'Ortega turned abruptly, giving her mike a slight slashing movement. "If you have a question or comment, please direct it to the witness. Don't discuss this among yourselves until all the evidence is finally in." Then she turned to Dr. McCafferty. "Would you please resume the stand?"

McCafferty permitted himself a self-satisfied smile. As an old pro, he could feel the vibes. He pushed his pointer back to pen size and replaced it in his pocket.

Mayan d'Ortega had decided to reduce her presentation to simple, understandable terms. She would sidestep McCafferty's medical esoterica—glycogen levels, cerebrospinal fluid changes, blood enzymes—and get to the heart of the medical problem: *cause of death and time of death.*

"Dr. McCafferty," she said, "at what time did you commence your postmortem examination of Angela Williams's body?"

McCafferty didn't have to refer to his notes. He looked directly at the jurors. "Five-ten A.M."

"Were you assisted by any other pathologist?"

"By Dr. Karen Steadman, a pathology intern at Boston Memorial."

"Was it a meticulous examination and autopsy?"

"The most thorough I've ever done. We went eight hours, concluding at about one P.M."

"Now, Dr. McCafferty, as a result of the postmortem examination of the body of Angela Williams, based upon your experience as chief medical examiner and based upon reasonable medical certainty, what, in your opinion, was the *cause* of Miss Williams's death?"

McCafferty readjusted the microphone. He paused for several seconds, then looked out at the jury.

"Death by asphyxiation. Someone compressed the carotid arteries of her neck until she ceased to breathe."

"The carotid arteries—where are these located?"

"Let me use the blackboard." McCafferty pointed to one on wheels next to the bailiff. Again, Coyne was quick to respond, wheeling the blackboard into place.

"For the stenographic record"—Mayan d'Ortega dotted the *i*'s and crossed the *t*'s of legal propriety—"would your use of the blackboard and any sketches you make assist the grand jurors in understanding your testimony?"

"It would."

"Please proceed."

Again, McCafferty was in his element as physician-teacher. With white chalk, he drew a sketch of the upper torso, heart, aorta, the brain, the arteries leading from the aortic arch. He colored the aorta and arteries in with yellow chalk.

"Now, human life—in fact, any animal life—is dependent on the breathing in of oxygen and its distribution to and use in tissues of the body. As long as the oxygen cycle is maintained, tissue cells remain viable, metabolism is normal, food and water can be ingested, absorbed, and excreted, and locomotion is possible. So every organ of the human body, even the little toe, depends on oxygenated blood in order to remain alive and functional. Cut that supply off, the organ dies. We call that necrosis. Comes from the Latin word for 'death.' So cut off the blood supply to the little toe and it dies.

"That's what happened to Bo Jackson." McCafferty shifted his gaze to the black professor. "Aseptic necrosis of the hip. The blood supply to the hip was shut down.

"Now, the carotid arteries are these two kind of wishbone-shaped arteries shooting off the aorta, this big artery here.

"The heart is essentially a pump. Envision a sort of box as big as your fist. It receives oxygenated red blood in this little chamber here"—he pointed to his illustration—"then the heart contracts." He held up his hand and clenched it. "Like this. And when this happens, the nice fresh blood is squeezed up into the aorta, up into the carotid arteries here, and up into the brain. Now, you see, the carotid arteries run through the neck. They and the vertebral arteries coursing through the neck are the only channels allowing blood to the brain. It's like stepping on a garden hose. You prevent the water from reaching the grass. Step on it long enough, the grass withers and dies. Compress the carotid arteries for two to four minutes, the brain starts to die. And in the brain stem, right about here, just off the basilar artery"— McCafferty again pointed to his illustration—"are control centers, little buttons that control life itself. Shut off the blood to these buttons, life ceases. That's what happened to Angela Williams."

"In other words, Doctor, she was strangled?"

McCafferty didn't hesitate. "She was strangled to death. . . . Rather slowly," he added.

Mayan d'Ortega would now fill in the blanks. *By whom?* The jury had a pretty good idea. She waited several seconds as McCafferty brushed some chalk dust from his lapel and then resumed the witness stand. He hunched forward, both hands on the rail.

"What is the basis for that opinion?"

He now had free rein. "Well, as a result of my examination and autopsy, I knew Miss Williams did not die from natural causes. She had no heart disease, no evidence of any demyelinating disease, such as multiple sclerosis, no history of diabetes or other diseases such as epilepsy, so we eliminate these conditions as causing her death. There was no evidence of poisons, toxins, drugs, medications, or alcohol. So we eliminate these possibilities.

"When I opened the neck area, I noticed minute hemorrhaging. These were little blood clots a pathologist sees when the neck area has been compressed traumatically. There was no gross hemorrhaging, mind you, which is sometimes found in hanging deaths, which led me to believe that the victim's neck was compressed slowly, leaving no outward marks on the throat. Then I discovered a small fracture in the cricoid cartilage. . . . If I may, I have an anatomical model of the upper thorax in that bag on the table."

"Certainly, Dr. McCafferty," Mayan d'Ortega enunciated for the legal record. "Again, would the use of an anatomical model aid you in explaining your testimony and assist the jury in understanding this testimony?"

"It would."

McCafferty left the witness stand, reached into the trial bag on the prosecutor's table, and unwrapped a life-sized upper torso complete with lungs, rib cage, sternum, and trachea with its attendant cartilages.

"Let me place this on this chair in the first row so you all can see. Okay?"

"That will be fine, Doctor."

Jurors seated in the back of the room partially stood as McCafferty went through his forensic paces. Again he took out his penlike instrument and extended it into a pointer.

"You can see the trachea here," he said, indicating the grayish tubelike structure coursing between the lungs.

"This is what we call the windpipe. It allows us to breathe. Sometimes we get a piece of food or some water caught in the trachea. I'm sure you've all experienced it. It can be extremely uncomfortable until you cough it up. It can even be life-threatening. Then you use the Heimlich maneuver—you put a bear hug around the victim and press upward with both arms." He clasped his hands and jerked them forward to demonstrate.

He had everyone's attention. Even the bailiff remained wide awake.

"Now the thyroid gland is this pinkish ring just below the cricoid cartilage and the thyroid cartilage. This is where I found the fracture in the cricoid cartilage . . . in front. It measured one point one centimeter in length by point one centimeter at its widest aperture. This is a little less than half an inch." McCafferty indicated with his thumb and forefinger. "Now that's not large, but it's significant, since the cricoid cartilage is quite resilient. So again this fracture demonstrates that a lot of pressure was exerted in the neck area to cause, first, disruption of the blood supply to the brain and, second, a crack in the cricoid cartilage."

"Does anyone have any questions of Dr. McCafferty?" Mayan d'Ortega had been standing near the wall next to the bailiff. She walked to the prosecutor's table and looked up at the row of jurors.

There were no hands raised, only mute and negative shaking of heads.

"Let the record show," she said, "that the jurors have no questions of Dr. McCafferty at this time." The doctor returned to the witness stand.

"Dr. McCafferty, there is evidence or will be evidence before the grand jury that the last person to see Miss Williams alive was Dr. Christopher Dillard.'' She paused and turned from the jury as if deep in thought, then faced the panel directly. ''He told Lieutenant Riley and Captain Furlong of the Boston Police's homicide unit that he was with Miss Williams from about seven P.M. until ten P.M. on the night of April second, the night she died.''

McCafferty leaned forward in the witness stand and nodded.

''Dr. Dillard said that they had a festive dinner that evening, including wine and brandy. Now, when Miss Williams's body was discovered by Mr. Anton Kent-Smythe, it was facedown. The Burlington Police transported the body to Boston Memorial Hospital, where Dr. Supples pronounced Miss Williams dead at one-oh-four A.M., April third. He testified that rigor mortis had not set in. Now, based on these facts and based upon your autopsy of Miss Williams's body, would you tell the jury at *what time,* in your expert opinion, Miss Williams actually met her death?''

''The time of death according to my estimation and that of Dr. Myron Gellis, who also did a postmortem on Angela Williams, was approximately eight-thirty P.M., April second, give or take a half hour.''

''By that you mean it could have been as early as eight P.M., or nine P.M. at the latest.''

''That's correct.''

''Now, Dr. McCafferty, you mentioned a Dr. Myron Gellis. Who is this doctor, and what is his position in this case?''

''Dr. Gellis is the former chief medical examiner of New York City. His book *Forensic Pathology* is the bible in the field.

''Dr. Gellis flew in from New York at the request of the district attorney's office and conducted an independent examination.''

''Did Dr. Gellis find hemorrhaging in the neck musculature and a fracture of the cricoid cartilage?''

''He did.''

''Now, Dr. McCafferty, how did you arrive at your estimation that Miss Williams died at eight-thirty P.M. on the evening of April second?''

''It's rather complicated, but I'll try to boil it down into simple language. The body was found at eleven-fifty-eight P.M. It was still warm, so death was fairly recent, perhaps three hours earlier.

''When I did my post, commencing at about five-ten A.M., I took a rectal temperature. This registered sixty-five degrees. Normal body temperature is ninety-eight point six. I subtracted four degrees for each hour. That gets us back to about eight-thirty P.M.

"Another indication of the time of death came from my examination of the vitreous humor. That's the fluid of the eyeball.

"In death, especially a recent death such as that of Miss Williams, the potassium content of the vitreous humor is elevated. Without confusing you with plotting potassium values of normal individuals against the time of death and factoring one mathematical square and slope intercept, I can reasonably say from the thermal factor and elevated potassium content that Miss Williams died at approximately eight-thirty P.M. on the night of April second."

"One last question, Dr. McCafferty. Dr. Dillard told Lieutenant Riley and Captain Furlong that he left Miss Williams at ten P.M. and that between his arrival at seven P.M. and his exit, he and Miss Williams had eaten a full gourmet meal." Mayan d'Ortega glanced down at her notes. "Duck à l'orange, gratinéed potatoes, crêpes Bayaldi, a bottle of Chardonnay, and after-dinner brandies.

"Did you find any evidence of food in the stomach, internal organs, or digestive tract of Miss Williams?"

"I found none."

"Nothing at all?"

"Absolutely nothing."

"Any evidence of alcohol in the blood?"

"None whatsoever."

"Did you check for alcohol?"

"I did. I was looking for some toxic substance, alcohol or drugs in particular. I found nothing."

"What did that indicate to you as chief medical examiner?"

"That Miss Williams had nothing to eat and did not drink alcohol that evening. Her most recent meal was perhaps a light breakfast."

"Thank you, Dr. McCafferty. You have been most helpful. Mr. Coyne, it's now after one o'clock. The jurors have been extremely patient and are perhaps hungry. Would you kindly escort them to lunch."

McCafferty put his equipment into the trial bag while recording the nods of approval from several jurors as they filed out.

"You were excellent, Bernie," Mayan d'Ortega said. "Direct and emphatic. The case should be a lock by four o'clock."

*   *   *

McCafferty needed a stiff drink, but felt he should check in with Neil Harrington first. After his impressive testimony, Neil would probably slip him a C note or two. And he needed it, what with his wife's attorney breathing down his neck for overdue alimony payments. The old days when surgery could generate $500,000 a year were long gone. It was hard to manage as medical examiner on the county's budget of $65,000. Maybe Harrington could recommend a raise or bonus.

As he stepped into the corridor, the media zoomed in, brandishing their mikes and cameras and notepads. The bailiff tried to hold them back as McCafferty, who inwardly enjoyed the limelight, waved them off with a professional "No comment."

"Doctor McCafferty." Suddenly a woman's voice came out from behind the cameramen. "Dr. McCafferty, I think we have to talk."

"Karen . . ." he stammered, "what in hell are you doing here!"

He lunged for the elevator, but she squeezed past the bailiff, who held his arms outthrust to hold back the crush of reporters. The door pinged open and McCafferty bounded in, quickly followed by Karen Steadman.

Calmly, she pressed the lobby button. "I think we'd better talk," she repeated.

"It's too late." He sighed and rubbed his hand across his forehead as the old beagle eyes drooped in dismay. He shook his head. "Listen, Karen, that doctor killed that girl." Suddenly he stopped. "I've nothing more to say."

"You can go back in there and set the record straight," she said.

"It's too late," he said again, and pushed the third-floor button.

He'd see Neil Harrington. And what the hell, he thought, if worse comes to worst, it's my word against hers. Surely the lack of stomach contents would carry the day.

The first-floor door opened. "I'm getting off here, Dr. Steadman," McCafferty said testily. "I told the truth in there. That's what you'd better do, too, if you know what's good for you." He bolted out. Somehow he felt that Karen Steadman was wired. The meeting at the elevator went beyond coincidence. She was in cahoots with someone, maybe Dan Sheridan. He'd have to tip off Neil.

* * *

Neil Harrington listened impassively as Bernie McCafferty told of his encounter with Karen Steadman. He sat at his desk, twirling a letter opener, idly examining the point of the blade.

McCafferty stammered and stuttered as perspiration stippled his face.

"She's a loose cannon, Neil. Someone's got to talk with her."

"I want you to handle it, Bernie," Neil said.

"She won't listen to me, believe me!"

Suddenly, Neil's voice became glacial. "You do what you have to do, Bernie."

"Neil," he said, desperation revealed through the whine in his voice, "I think I nicked that cricoid cartilage on my follow-up autopsy."

"That's your problem. I've bailed you out too often. You handle this one!" He rose from behind his desk and leaned forward on both arms.

McCafferty understood the stance. Harrington was calling in all the chits.

"When Gellis called it a fracture, I sort of went along." McCafferty tried a desperate plea.

"Listen to me well, Bernie. You're a drunk who makes sixty-five grand a year because I keep you on the payroll. Understand that! Don't give me any crap about the cricoid cartilage. You'll jeopardize the entire indictment and put everyone in the soup with that bullshit—Gellis, Mayan d'Ortega, the department. Mayan has already sent down word that your testimony was the best medical testimony she ever heard. Now, you go back into the grand jury room to correct your testimony because some little hay-shaker broad is making noises and admit to perjury, that'll be the end of Dr. Bernard McCafferty." Neil Harrington cut the plane of his neck with the edge of his hand. His voice suddenly softened as he reached into his trousers pocket. "Here," he said, "here's a C note." Harrington put the bill on the table next to where McCafferty was seated. "Go over to the Parker House, order a lobster dinner, and have a few good snorts on the county."

"Yeah, sure." McCafferty sighed as he picked up the money. Beaten, he made his way out.

*   *   *

Still perspiring and shaken, McCafferty rode the escalator down to Government Plaza. He crossed Beacon Street and stopped in front of the iron-grilled enclosure of the Old Granary Burial Ground. He had passed this way a thousand times but never actually paid attention to who was buried there. Now he noticed the tilted headstones, darkened with lichen, grotesque skeletons with angels' wings sculpted on most.

"I understand Mother Goose is buried here. Would you know where her grave is?"

For a moment, he was startled. The young blue-jeaned blond girl with a knapsack strapped over her shoulders looked like Karen Steadman.

"Mother Goose?" Had there really been such a person? McCafferty didn't know.

"Let me see," he said, glancing aslant at the open Nordic face, the guileless blue eyes. "Your guess is as good as mine, but let's take a look."

They walked together under the leafy elms, through the pale spring light, past markers for Samuel Adams and John Hancock, until they came to a plaque encased in granite.

McCafferty read aloud.

" 'Here lies Elizabeth Goose, better known as Mother Goose.' "

"Lovely," said the girl.

"Those were simpler times." McCafferty sighed. "Nothing's that cut-and-dried anymore."

"I don't see why not," she said. "You can always tell what's right or wrong. Can't you?"

McCafferty felt a melting of resolve, a loosening in his chest. He looked at the girl more closely.

"Where are you from?" he asked. He would not be surprised if she said Neptune.

"Minnesota," she replied cheerily. "Studying American mythology at the state university there."

"American mythology? Can you make a living at that sort of stuff?"

"Of course not." She laughed. "But I like tracking down Paul Bunyan, the runic stone, Bigfoot—and Mother Goose. Eventually,

I'll marry some nice dependable guy my parents approve of and live happily ever after."

On impulse, McCafferty reached into his pocket and pulled out Harrington's one-hundred-dollar bill. "Here," he said. "Please take this. Have a few chocolate malts on me and Paul Bunyan."

She waved it off. "No, please. I don't need it. See that old woman outside the gate?"

McCafferty looked. A bag lady sat holding a plastic cup on the cement sidewalk just beyond the compound.

"Give it to her," the girl said.

"God bless you!" The old lady's gin-racked eyes sprang to new life as she examined the benign face of Benjamin Franklin and quickly slid the bill under her shabby shawl.

McCafferty wondered at the variety of human beings. Two women, one young, exuberant, with not a care in the world. Money? She scorned it. The other was destitute, friendless, with no expectations. Yet suddenly, she had hope, at least for a day or two.

He said good-bye to both of them and walked down State Street toward Atlantic Avenue, mulling over Neil Harrington's words: If you admit to perjury, that'll be the end of Dr. Bernard McCafferty. He glanced at his watch: 2:30. Mayan d'Ortega would be questioning Dillard.

Then he thought of the girl from Minnesota. "You can always tell what's right or wrong. Can't you?"

He turned and headed back toward the courthouse.

38

A SUBDUED jury filed in and took their seats. Bailiff Coyne tried to joke with them, but they failed to respond. The case was becoming too serious for even the slightest levity. There was no murmuring, no shuffling. They sat in silent anticipation, awaiting the appearance of Dr. Dillard.

Mayan d'Ortega entered by the side door. She gave a slight welcoming nod to the jurors, but her determined stride reflected the gravity of the moment. She was on a mission.

"Mr. Coyne, please bring in the next witness, Dr. Christopher B. Dillard." Her voice was taut, prosecutorial.

Bailiff Coyne rapped on the door to the prosecutors' room.

"Yes?" Sheridan asked.

Coyne poked his head inside.

"Dan, your client is next. We've cordoned off the area so you won't be harassed."

Dillard entered the courtroom first. He had been in tight spots before, even looked death in the eye in wartime and never shifted his gaze, but somehow today was different. Today he faced a scandal, the possibility of being a fallen hero.

"Do what I say, regardless of what happens," was Sheridan's last-minute instruction. "No exceptions. You're a navy officer, understand? A different breed. You'll handle it. We start to prepare our defense immediately after you testify."

Dillard walked with erect bearing but was not oblivious to the icy stares of the jurors. He and Sheridan sat at the witness table adjacent to d'Ortega, who was shuffling some papers. She failed to acknowledge either man. The jurors could not help but notice.

"Ladies and gentlemen of the grand jury," she addressed the panel, "following the testimony of Dr. Dillard, the Commonwealth will present one last witness, Capt. Charles Furlong, detective from the Boston Police Department's homicide unit. He will essentially corroborate the testimony of Detective Lieutenant Riley.

"Dr. Dillard, do you wish to take the witness stand or remain with your lawyer at the table?"

"We'll stay right here," Sheridan said as he adjusted both microphones, then removed a yellow legal pad from his briefcase and laid it on the table. He glanced up at the jurors. He knew what they were thinking. His client was aristocratic, a man of privilege who had gone to fine schools and was inordinately wealthy. Life's pluses would now be detriments. Mayan d'Ortega would get into his academic and social background. His fine war record and dedicated practice of medicine would never surface, and there was not a thing Sheridan could do or say about it. He was not allowed a rebuttal or cross-examination. There would be no defense before this forum.

Mayan d'Ortega took the hand mike and positioned herself in front of the jury box, facing Thalia Shapiro and the black professor.

"Would you kindly rise and be administered the oath."

Sheridan nodded toward Dillard. Bailiff Coyne went through the formalities as the doctor promised to tell the truth. Sheridan gauged the jurors. He could sense their skepticism. He knew Dillard was dead in the water.

Mayan d'Ortega started at the beginning. "May we have your name, please."

"Christopher B. Dillard."

She carefully led Dillard through his formative years, the Choate School, Harvard College, Yale Medical, then his background as a surgeon, stressing the glamour of his profession, the high fees, without mentioning the backbreaking work and long hours. Sheridan didn't even nod toward Dillard, but he knew d'Ortega's rhythm. The smooth, lulling dialogue would soon be abandoned. Dillard would have to face a barrage of pointed questions and hide under the Fifth Amendment. Sheridan knew it was going to be rough.

"Are you married, Dr. Dillard?"

"Yes."

"Children?"

"Four."

"You and your wife still live together?"

"Absolutely."

"Now, Dr. Dillard." D'Ortega's voice took on a derisive timbre. "Did you know the deceased, Angela Williams?"

Dillard glanced toward Sheridan. Not a signal.

"I did."

"How well did you know her?"

"How well?"

"Yes. Socially, intimately? Tell the jurors about your entire relationship with her." D'Ortega glanced toward the jurors. "How did you meet Angela Williams?"

Sheridan leaned toward his client and shook his head.

"On advice of counsel, I respectfully invoke my right under the Fifth Amendment to the United States Constitution and under the Massachusetts Declaration of Rights and decline to answer your question on the grounds that what I say may incriminate me or tend to incriminate me," Dillard said quietly. He turned toward the jurors but seemed to be staring off unfocused into some remote distance.

"How would your answer tend to incriminate you?" Mayan d'Ortega stood at the prosecutor's table, turning slightly toward Dillard and Sheridan.

Dillard seemed flustered, knitting his brow quizzically. Again Sheridan gave a negative nod.

"On advice of counsel, I invoke my right . . ."

The afternoon went quickly as d'Ortega's interrogation became rapid-fire.

"Were you in the company of Angela Williams the evening of April second from seven or seven-thirty P.M. to ten P.M.?"

Again Sheridan's negative nod. Again the Fifth Amendment.

"Did you dine with Angela Williams the evening of April second?" D'Ortega enumerated the evening menu, right down to the after-dinner brandies.

"On advice of counsel . . ."

"Did you have a conversation in your office at approximately one-forty P.M. on April fourth, of this year with Detective Lieutenant Riley and Capt. Charles Furlong of the Boston Police's homicide unit?"

Dillard looked haggard. He wasn't weathering the storm too well.

The jurors sat in stony silence, but Sheridan could read the mounting anger in their grim faces.

The black professor raised his hand. "May I ask the doctor a question?"

Mayan d'Ortega feigned surprise and appeared to think for a moment.

"Yes," she said. "It's your investigation."

"Dr. Dillard, with the aid of your lawyer, you've been dodging simple questions all afternoon. Let me ask you this. Did you kill Angela Williams?"

No sign from Sheridan.

"I did not."

"Do you know who did?"

"Keep it simple," Sheridan whispered.

"No."

"Any suspicions?"

"No."

"Dr. Dillard, why do you answer my questions and not Miss d'Ortega's?"

Dillard was about to speak, but Sheridan cut him short.

"Invoke the Fifth," he said.

"On advice of counsel . . ."

"One last question, Dr. Dillard." The juror's voice registered anger and disdain. "A Boston Police detective testified earlier. He said you told him that on the evening of April second you had your gourmet dinner with Angela Williams, soup to nuts, whatever, but the pathologist told us that there wasn't a trace of alcohol found in Miss Williams's blood, nor food found in her stomach or intestinal tract. How do you explain that?"

Dillard cupped his hand and whispered to Sheridan. "Let me tell them about her bulimia."

"That defense comes later. Right now, the jurors wouldn't believe that story even if it was true. And we don't want to open up the conversation. You plead the Fifth."

Even Dillard looked exasperated.

"On advice of counsel . . ."

The juror shook his head in disgust. "Is that the way you want to leave it, Dr. Dillard?"

"Don't even answer that," Sheridan said in a whisper, behind his hand.

"Any further questions of this witness?" D'Ortega addressed the jury.

They looked at one another and shook their heads.

"All right, Dr. Dillard. You may be excused. Mr. Sheridan, according to our agreement, your client will remain with you in the prosecutors' room until today's adjournment."

"We'll be right next door," Sheridan said. He slipped the yellow pad into his briefcase. He had taken no notes.

The jurors, the bailiff, and Mayan d'Ortega watched them leave. Sheridan could see the irate stares, sense the group's lynch mentality, their outrage.

"Bailiff." Mayan d'Ortega motioned toward Coyne. "Please call Capt. Charles Furlong."

The black professor suddenly stood up. "I think I speak for all of us, Miss d'Ortega," he said. "No further witnesses are necessary. I think we know what we have to do."

It didn't take long, perhaps twenty minutes. Thalia Shapiro, the black professor, the dentist, and the remaining twenty were unanimous. They sent for d'Ortega. They would sign a true bill indicting Dr. Christopher B. Dillard for the first-degree murder of Angela Williams.

There was a light tapping at the prosecutors' door. For a moment, Sheridan thought it was Lieutenant Riley. It was now 4:30 and he still hadn't been in touch. Perhaps Riley had been spooked by all the media coverage.

"Mr. Sheridan, I'm Dr. Bernard McCafferty. Please let me in. There's an awful crowd out here."

Sheridan wasted no time. He forcibly pulled McCafferty into the room, then slammed and locked the door. He knew Fletcher Porter and the other scribes outside were aware of the intrusion. They were hovering like jackals. Somehow they had gotten wind of the fact that the jury was ready to return an indictment.

"Dan, we've never met. . . ." McCafferty looked guardedly at Dr. Dillard.

"It's okay. At this stage, we share confidences."

"With due respect, Doctor, I'd prefer to talk with your counsel alone."

"Okay," Sheridan said. "Chris, can you step outside for a few minutes? Tell the bailiff you have to use the men's room."

McCafferty's ruddy face was now a pale pink. He waited until Dillard left before he spoke.

"You don't know me, but I knew your wife Jean and your son Tommy."

"How?"

"I mean, sort of. I was on call in surgery when they were brought in. Your little boy was gone, but I tried to pull Jean through. I later did the post on both."

"I remember," Sheridan said softly.

McCafferty sighed a tired, agonized sigh.

"I think I'm going to need you . . . down the road, I mean. I perjured myself in there today."

"You what?"

Both were standing by the window overlooking the parking lot. "Mind if I sit down?" McCafferty said. "I'm a little winded. Practically ran up here all the way from Atlantic Avenue."

Sheridan sat on the edge of the metal desk and McCafferty flopped onto the sagging Naugahyde couch. It *whoosh*ed beneath him as he landed.

"Doctor," Sheridan said cautiously, "why are you coming to me? You should be addressing the court or the district attorney."

"I've been to the district attorney."

"D'Ortega?"

"Harrington. He told me to keep quiet. Said it would be my ass if I breathed a word.

"I'm in a real jam," McCafferty continued. "Do you have the autopsy report, the joint report from me and Dr. Gellis?"

"Not yet," Sheridan responded with a white lie.

"Well, I did an eight-hour post. There wasn't a thing I could put my finger on as causative of the Williams woman's death."

"What did you tell the grand jury?"

"I said Williams had been strangled, asphyxiation by strangulation. One of her neck cartilages, the cricoid, had been fractured. I told them I found hemorrhaging in her neck musculature."

"That was in the autopsy report?" Sheridan asked in the form of a question, not wishing to look too well informed.

McCafferty nodded. He was starting to breathe heavily, his voice becoming husky.

"Dan, there was no hemorrhaging, no fracture. The fracture Gellis saw was an inadvertent nick from my scalpel. I . . . I was sort of goaded into these findings."

"What else did you say?"

"I cooked your client. I placed the time of death as eight-thirty P.M., nine at the latest. The police told the jurors that Dillard claimed he left Williams at ten P.M."

"What are you saying?"

"I lied about the fracture. And time of death, I stretched it. I gave the jury a lot of medical gobbledygook, elevated potassium of the vitreous humor, thermal cooling. You would have cross-examined me right out of the courtroom on that one. No pathologist could have pinpointed the time of death down to the half hour like I did. For all I know, she could have died at eleven or eleven-thirty, well after your client said he left her apartment."

"Did Harrington know all this?"

McCafferty's pink color had now faded to a sick gray. He merely nodded an affirmation.

"How about d'Ortega?"

"I don't know. I only told Harrington. He could have passed it on to her. I just don't know."

There came another rap at the door. It was Coyne.

"Jury's returning an indictment, Dan. First-degree murder. I have to take them before Judge Chang now. Thought I'd let you know."

The gears in Sheridan's head meshed quickly.

"Can you stall them for several minutes? I'll make it up to you, believe me. The Indians are in town Friday night."

"See what I can do, Dan."

"And can you round up d'Ortega and tell her I want to meet with her in front of Judge Chang in about five minutes?"

"Can you get four ducats, Dan? My brother-in-law . . ."

"Sure . . . sure." Dan closed the door.

He turned to McCafferty. "Are you willing to repeat what you've just told me to Judge Chang?"

Suddenly, the color returned to McCafferty's face.

"It'll be my license, Dan, my livelihood."

"Maybe not. You came to me. You came forward immediately. You were intimidated by Harrington. I'll represent you down the line. There can be mitigating circumstances."

"May I talk to you, Miss d'Ortega?" Sheridan caught up to the prosecutor as she stood at the counsel table watching the jurors file into the courtroom. Judge Chang, in her black robe, waited patiently on the bench. She would take the jury's decision. She had a pretty good idea what it was.

D'Ortega noticed Bernie McCafferty seated behind the counsel rail. What was he doing here?

"The grand jury is about to return a first-degree murder indictment," she said curtly. "I'll speak to you after the judge takes the bill."

"You'll speak to me now!" Sheridan leaned down into her face. "Before we all make complete assholes of ourselves!"

Mayan d'Ortega's eyes flashed in defiance. For a second, Sheridan thought she would kick him in the balls. But then she remembered McCafferty. She realized something was wrong.

Suddenly, she arched her eyebrows in a parody of professional conceit. "What do you want to tell me?"

"Can we step outside? Tell Judge Chang we need about five minutes."

They stood by the watercooler. Bailiff Coyne had diverted the press, and save for a couple of attorneys toting briefcases, at 5:00 P.M. in the afternoon the courtroom corridors were practically deserted.

"McCafferty just told me he lied."

"What? What are you doing, tampering with a government witness!"

"Listen, Miss d'Ortega. He came to me. I'm trying to salvage a situation that's bad for you and me both."

"Don't lecture me!" Her voice cracked like a pencil snapped in two. Sheridan took a step backward, as if she'd spit at him.

"Mayan," he said softly, "you . . . me. First, foremost, we're officers of the court. We've got to do the right thing, regardless of what side we're on."

"Listen," she hissed, "we're not here to discuss the verities of the law."

"That's for sure. But your star witness is going to tell Judge Chang that he lied. He's going to purge himself. He wants to go back in before the grand jury."

There was a short silence while d'Ortega assessed her position. It wasn't good.

"Okay," she said finally, "what are you asking?"

"We file a joint motion before Chang to suspend the grand jury presentment, reconvene next week. Let them hear McCafferty. Maybe you'll discharge the jury, nol-pros the case."

"Are you crazy, Sheridan?"

"Sometimes I think so."

"You'd better be leveling with me." Her voice softened only slightly. "I'll do you one better. I'll tell Judge Chang we have an additional witness. We'll go back into the grand jury room. If what you say is true, it's McCafferty's rear end. You know that. He knows that."

They turned to go back to the courtroom.

"Did Harrington know about this?" she said as her eyes locked with his.

"I'm afraid so. McCafferty told Harrington. Harrington told him to keep quiet."

She shook her head; a slight smile flickered across her beautiful face. "Gringo"—she exhaled—"we sure got us quite a ball game!"

The cameramen had picked up their gear. The media and attorneys, sensing an indictment was in the offing, had crowded into Judge Chang's courtroom on the sixth floor. They had just missed d'Ortega's motion to reconvene the grand jury for an additional but important witness, a motion that Judge Chang summarily granted. The judge agreed to remain available in her chambers until 9:00 P.M. if necessary.

Bailiff Coyne herded his twenty-three citizens into two elevators, and when they arrived at the twelfth floor, the corridor was deserted. D'Ortega, Sheridan, and McCafferty took the stairs. Except for McCafferty's heavy puffing, the climb was made in silence.

"You can't come in here," d'Ortega said to Sheridan at the door to the grand jury room. "Only McCafferty. That's the Supreme Court rule."

"I know," Sheridan said. "*Massachusetts General Laws.* I can even give you the chapter and section. But I now represent Dr. Mc-Cafferty, and as his attorney, he has the right to have me in attendance. I think that's Subsection H."

She studied Sheridan for a moment. He was a pain in the legal ass, to be sure, but inwardly she was beginning to like him—his gray-blue eyes; his pugnacious face had a mischievous, boyish look. But it was a face devoid of guile. And somehow in that brief moment when they stood outside the jury room, she sensed that more than one career would be dashed into oblivion. McCafferty for sure. Harrington? It was his word against McCafferty's. She'd be back with the Civil Liberties Union. She thought about it. Maybe that's where she belonged. And she realized she had committed a grave legal error: She hadn't questioned McCafferty or Harrington before agreeing to speak to the judge. She'd be winging it, flying by the seat of her pants. Maybe she trusted Sheridan more than she trusted Neil Harrington. Maybe through some ancient Indian intuition, she had a pretty good idea what McCafferty was going to say.

There was now murmuring, shuffling of feet, glances at watches. Bailiff Coyne rapped his staff on the floor for silence.

"We have had an unusual development"—Mayan d'Ortega faced the jurors—"one that demands your immediate attention.

"You have met Daniel Sheridan, who is counsel for Dr. Christopher Dillard." She stretched her hand to where Dan and Dr. McCafferty were seated.

"And this morning, you heard the testimony of Dr. McCafferty. By some strange turn of events, Dr. McCafferty has asked Judge Chang to allow him to readdress your membership. The judge has granted his request. Mr. Sheridan has been retained by Dr. McCafferty as his counsel. That's why he is in here again."

"Is this necessary?" The black professor spoke up, glancing at his wristwatch.

"It's necessary," d'Ortega said in a voice that brooked no argument.

"Dr. McCafferty, will you please resume the stand. Remember, you took an oath earlier today to tell the truth under the penalties of perjury." She hesitated. "Do you know the penalties for rendering false information before a grand jury, Dr. McCafferty?"

McCafferty, too, hesitated before he stepped into the witness box. "I understand the penalty can be severe." McCafferty faced the jurors so that there was no mistaking his stance.

"It can get you seven years in prison. Do you understand that, Doctor?"

"I understand," he said firmly.

Lieutenant Riley got word through the courthouse network that the grand jury had been ready to indict Dillard. He also got word from Johnny Flaherty that Neil Harrington wanted to see him. It was more a directive than an invitation.

Riley left the clerk's office and wondered what in hell he was going to do. For a moment, he wavered. Was he stupid? Neil Harrington could break or make anyone in Boston—in the whole of Suffolk County, for that matter. Secreting evidence constituted obstruction of justice. Why hadn't he turned in the tape? He might end up directing traffic at the corner of Beacon and Tremont—that's if he was lucky. He could be stripped of his badge and his pension. He thought about that, too. But his conduct was ingrained. Perhaps it came from the Dominican nuns at Blessed Sacrament grammar school, the arcane Irish Catholic theology, the parables—basics learned so long ago. Truth. He took the stairs to Harrington's office.

39

LIEUTENANT RILEY was ushered into Harrington's office by State Trooper Cataldo. He didn't suspect anything was wrong until he entered and was greeted by a tight-lipped group. Harrington, looking tense and grim, stood behind his desk. Brian Loughlin and Sheila O'Brien leaned against the far wall. And State Trooper Boyle had unsnapped his holster; his hand rested on the butt of his service revolver.

"You're under arrest, Lieutenant," Harrington said almost matter-of-factly, but his eyes were coldly furious.

"What?" Riley stammered. "What in hell are you talking about?"

Trooper Cataldo also unsnapped his holster.

"This is what I'm talking about." Harrington held up a tape cassette. "Offering information to defense attorney Sheridan on the very case you were investigating! We have a recording of your phone call."

Riley flushed, but he remained silent for several seconds. "What are the charges?" he finally asked.

"Don't play cute, Riley.

"Conspiracy to obstruct justice, conflict of interest, bribery, violation of departmental regulations, and maybe the U.S. attorney can throw in a few more." Harrington moved out from behind his desk. "Let me have your shield and weapon!"

Riley slowly unpinned his badge and handed it to Cataldo. He unbuttoned his blue jacket.

"Hold it!" Cataldo said as he moved behind Riley and reached in and removed Riley's gun and laid it on Harrington's desk.

"Do you want to be read your rights or do you wish to cooperate and just tell us about it up-front? We also know you tried to contact Sonny Callahan, even though you knew he was part of the federal investigation."

Riley's face was beet red, but he was smart enough to keep his mouth shut.

Harrington picked up Riley's .38 and checked to see that the

safety was on, then opened his desk drawer. He had activated the
tape button as soon as Trooper Cataldo had ushered Riley into his
office. As he placed the gun inside the drawer, he could see that
the recorder's spools were still turning. The entire conversation
would become Exhibit A.

"I'm surprised at you, Riley." he said. "You've disgraced your
uniform and the public trust. You've been on the force longer than
I've been DA. But before the press gets wind of this mess, maybe
you can purge yourself. We can still use you with Dan Sheridan and
Sonny Callahan."

Riley's mouth tightened, but still he said nothing.

"I understand you've got two kids in high school."

Startled, he asked, "What are you suggesting?"

"You keep your date with Sheridan. Feed him programmed
info about the Dillard case, maybe a few other cases he's handling. I understand he now represents Barry Ginsberg, who's just
been arrested. He'll pay you, of course. When he does, we'll
move in."

Sheila O'Brien wasn't sure how she was going to play her hand.
She still hadn't heard that McCafferty had gone back into the grand
jury room. Riley's conduct was another matter.

"I'm standing on my constitutional rights to remain silent and I
need an attorney."

"Why not get him Dan Sheridan?" Trooper Boyle chuckled sarcastically.

"Riley." Harrington's eyes narrowed. "I'll give you just five
minutes to reconsider. You have two kids in parochial schools;
twenty-five years on the force—that's a lot of retirement built up.
You're done on the force, that's for certain, but I may be able to
salvage your pension. You play ball with us and I'll go to bat for
you."

Harrington threw it out, a tiny branch anchored on the edge of
a black abyss.

"Mr. Harrington." Kristina Collins's voice interrupted over the
intercom. "Bailiff Dempsey is here, says it's urgent. Can you step
into the outer office for a moment?"

"All right. . . . You have exactly five minutes, Riley," Harrington
said, glancing at his watch. "When I get back, for your sake and
your family's sake, you'd have better made the right choice!"

* * *

The bailiff, gray-haired, paunchy in his tight-fitting blue uniform, paced nervously. Kristina Collins sensed that something was wrong.

Harrington showed brief displeasure as he emerged, but then he noticed Dempsey's worried look.

"Mr. Harrington, can I talk to you alone? It's very important." He looked guardedly at Kristina Collins.

"Kris, could you excuse us for a few moments."

"I'm on my way," she said brightly as she flipped a smile at the bailiff and headed for the door.

"What is it, Jerry? We've got a difficult situation inside." Harrington nodded toward his polished oak doors.

"Mr. Harrington, sir," the bailiff said, "I was assigned to Judge Chang's session when word came down that the grand jury was returning an indictment against that Dillard fellow."

"Yes?"

"Well, Chang was on the bench and the jurors filed in and Miss d'Ortega was about to make her presentation when in comes Dan Sheridan with Dr. McCafferty, kind of like they weren't expected."

"What are you trying to say?"

"Well, Miss d'Ortega and Sheridan step outside. I sort of moseyed out toward the clerk's office, since Coyne was the bailiff assigned to the jurors. I seen them talking, d'Ortega and Sheridan. Kind of intense, it was.

"Then d'Ortega tells the judge that she wants to reconvene the grand jury to hear another witness. Out they go, the jurors, d'Ortega, Sheridan, and McCafferty."

"McCafferty?"

"Just before Coyne locks the jury room door, he tells me McCafferty wants to correct his prior testimony."

"Son of a bitch!" Harrington swore through clenched teeth. "That drunken ingrate!"

"McCafferty's in there now before the grand jury. And the odd part is that Sheridan's in there, too."

Harrington quickly assessed the situation. It could be disastrous.

"Okay, Jerry. Get word to d'Ortega to suspend immediately and see me at once.

"And here." Harrington withdrew a one-hundred-dollar bill

from his wallet and handed it to the bailiff. "Take the missus out to dinner."

McCafferty faced the jurors from the witness stand, his hands gripping the rail, his shoulders hunched.

"I understand, Dr. McCafferty, that you wish to recant your prior testimony, am I correct?"

McCafferty leaned forward into the microphone.

"That is correct."

There was a murmur among the jurors, then a dead, expectant hush.

"Excuse me, Miss d'Ortega," said Coyne, "the white light is blinking." Coyne pointed to the small bank of lights on the podium next to his station.

"Okay." She nodded to Coyne. "See what the interruption is.

"Ladies and gentlemen," d'Ortega addressed the jurors, "there's a message that must be important. Please remain seated, and remember, no talking among yourselves."

Coyne unlocked the grand jury door, opened it a crack, and received a note from bailiff Dempsey. He nodded, relocked the door, and handed the note to d'Ortega.

"Suspend at once. Lieutenant Riley has been arrested. He's been supplying info to Sheridan. Don't let McCafferty testify."

D'Ortega paused for a long moment, then folded the note and tossed it on the prosecutor's table. She picked up the small microphone and faced the jurors, positioning herself between Thalia Shapiro and the black professor.

"Dr. McCafferty, I understand you wish to change your testimony from that which you gave this morning."

"Yes."

"Tell the jurors in your own words what you now wish the jurors to hear. . . . Just go ahead. I won't interrupt your testimony."

McCafferty hunched forward even farther, his shoulders almost touching his ears. He looked up at the jurors, his eyes steady.

"I gave all of you a lot of false and misleading information this morning," he began. He shook his head. "I've come back in here to try to right the record. A man's life is at stake.

"There was no fracture of the cricoid cartilage. I didn't find hemorrhaging of the neck musculature. Those were minute spots of blood, which we call Tardieu spots. They gather even after a natural death. I inadvertently nicked the cricoid cartilage on my second postmortem. I couldn't come up with a cause of death. My associate, Dr. Steadman, who did the initial post with me, is right outside. She'll verify what I'm saying.

"As to time of death, I . . ." McCafferty's voice cracked. He cleared his throat. "I told you it was eight-thirty P.M., or nine at the latest.

"That was only a guess on my part and not a very good one. That thermal stuff, counting back at a four-degree loss in body temperature per hour, just isn't accurate. And that elevated potassium— maybe Quincy on the old television show could get away with that pseudoscientific hogwash, but that's what it is—hogwash. That girl could have died at eleven to eleven-thirty P.M. that night, even around midnight.

"So, cause of death? I don't know the cause. Time of death? Perhaps closer to midnight."

"Dr. McCafferty, so that there'll be no mistaking what you are *now* saying"—Mayan d'Ortega glanced over at the court reporter, who was diligently catching every word on her steno machine—"is it fair to state that you lied to the grand jury when you testified earlier?"

McCafferty didn't hesitate or equivocate.

"I lied," he said firmly.

D'Ortega knew he was destroying himself.

"You committed perjury?"

"Yes," he said softly.

"Why are you changing your testimony at this time, Dr. Mc-Cafferty?"

The eyes of the jurors as well as those of Mayan d'Ortega focused intently on the witness. He didn't flinch.

"I knew I had caused the crack in the cricoid cartilage. I explained all of this to the district attorney, Neil Harrington, only hours ago in his office. I told him I really didn't find traumatic hemorrhaging of the neck musculature and I explained my reservations as to time of death."

The jurors sat in stunned silence.

"Please continue," d'Ortega said, her voice calm despite the bizarre revelations she was hearing.

McCafferty again cleared his throat. "The district attorney told me to keep quiet. I probably would have."

"What made you change your mind?"

"Conscience, Miss d'Ortega, conscience at last." He lowered his head, covered his face with his hands, and wept.

It took only five minutes on a show of hands for the jurors to reach a unanimous vote: no indictment. Thalia Shapiro as foreperson and Mayan d'Ortega as prosecutor signed the necessary document indicating a No Bill.

"All rise," intoned the bailiff.

"Please follow me," he said. "We're to appear again before Judge Chang. We'll use the side exit and take the elevators to the sixth floor."

"I'll join you in a few moments," Mayan d'Ortega told the bailiff as they filed past.

She looked at McCafferty, who was slumped like a rag doll in the witness box, his head buried in his folded arms.

Then she turned to Sheridan, who sat at the counsel table, not moving, hands clasped, no sign of triumph on his face.

"Well, you win, gringo." She stepped into the awkward silence. Their eyes met—Mayan d'Ortega's still defiant, intense, proud; Sheridan's soft gray-blue, understanding, even a little unsure.

Sheridan broke contact, putting his scratch pad into his briefcase. For several seconds, he said nothing. "I hate to see it end with a broken career." He nodded toward McCafferty.

"There's more than one career on the line," she said. "No doubt word has gotten back to Harrington. He'll deny it, of course, but the media jackals will tear him apart."

"How about you?" Sheridan said, knowing she had done the right thing but realizing that her image would be tarnished. She'd probably fall along with Harrington.

She started to sigh, then caught herself. "Hey, hombre"—she gathered up her notes—"maybe Monday I'll be over looking for a job. Might be interesting keeping people out of jail, for a change."

"You're too classy to come with my ragtag outfit," he said. "And don't be too sure that the DA office is a goner."

"It's a goner," she said quietly. She extended her hand. Sheridan shook it, clasping hers in both of his. She smiled at him, her dark eyes now less defiant, almost tender. Then she turned and was gone.

The amber beams of the late-afternoon sun filtered through the dusty windows, draping the burnt umbers and antique browns of the old courtroom like tones in a Caravaggio painting.

"Come on, Bernie," Sheridan said to the doctor, who was still slumped in the witness stand. "We'll take the side door. It's time to mount our defense."

When Harrington reentered his office, he quickly assessed that Riley wasn't going to make a deal. Trooper Boyle had handcuffed the detective's hands behind his back.

"He say anything?" Harrington inquired of Brian Loughlin.

"Not a word."

Harrington glanced at his watch. "Your time has run out, Riley. Maybe you'll come to your senses down at the station."

Riley shook his head.

"Tell Sheldon Fine to get the magistrate's okay for electronic surveillance in Sheridan's office," Harrington said, addressing Loughlin. "And I want Sonny Callahan picked up!"

Suddenly, Kristina Collins's voice broke in over the intercom. "It's Jerry Dempsey," she said. "He's got some bad news."

"Bad news? Okay, Kris, give it to me up-front," Harrington said, forgetting the exigencies of the moment.

There was a long pause.

"McCafferty testified," she finally said, her voice unsteady.

"What in hell! . . . Where's d'Ortega?"

"She's down in front of Judge Chang. The jury refused to indict Dillard.

"And Fletcher Porter of the *Globe* is here," Kristina continued, "and Pat Nolan of the *Herald*. Seems McCafferty said you told him to keep quiet!"

He realized what he had to do. React with audacity. It was McCafferty's word against his. A perjurer, a drunk. Then it flashed in his mind. The goddamned tape, he thought. He yanked open his desk drawer and clicked a lever on the tape recorder. There was a squeaking, squirreling noise. He punched off the intercom button.

In an instant, Riley knew what was happening. "The tape!" He jerked his head toward Harrington's desk. "The conversation with McCafferty, it's being erased!"

Sheila reached under her loose-fitting jacket and whipped out her Glock 9-mm semiautomatic. She pointed it first at Trooper Boyle, then at Cataldo. "Hold it right there! Don't anyone do anything foolish!" Her voice was deadly serious.

"She has no authority here!" Harrington yelled as he reached for Riley's gun in his top drawer.

Sheila fired a shot into Harrington's desktop. It shattered like matchwood, sending splinters flying about the room.

Cataldo and Boyle reached for their guns, but Brian Loughlin already had both covered in the sights of his .44. "As the woman says," Loughlin said sharply, his body coiled, both hands on his automatic, trigger finger ready to squeeze, "don't do anything foolish!"

As Harrington bolted back from his desk, Sheila calmly turned off the recorder button and just as calmly picked up Riley's .38. She noted the safety was still on, so she tucked it into the belt of her jeans.

Now Riley saw his chance.

"I have a tape," he blurted. "It's in my jacket pocket." He motioned with his handcuffed wrists. "The Williams woman is threatening a guy named Cooch. Cooch is Harrington. It's Harrington's voice. I've got a positive ID."

He looked directly into Harrington's eyes. "I don't know how you did it, but you killed Williams and you had the perfect fall guy. If McCafferty hadn't blown, come November you'd be sitting in the U.S. Senate and Dillard would be marking time on death row!"

"Have all of you gone haywire?" Harrington was stunned, but there was still a window, a way out.

"These agents have no jurisdiction here! Riley's under arrest! What these two are doing is preposterous! I'll have them both—"

"This is our jurisdiction!" Loughlin nudged the air with his .44. "And before anyone gets hurt, I want you two to keep your hands away from your sides!" Again he pointed his automatic toward Boyle and Cataldo. With a coolness that belied the moment, he removed the state troopers' revolvers, tossing one, then the other onto Harrington's leather couch.

Sheila O'Brien pointed her gun at Trooper Cataldo. "Unlock them," she said, motioning toward Riley's handcuffs.

"For Christsakes! They're faking!" Harrington stormed as beads of sweat stippled his forehead. "Do you know what's going on here?"

Suddenly, Boyle and Cataldo had heard enough. They changed sides.

Cataldo unlocked Riley's handcuffs. Riley rubbed his wrists for a few moments, then reached into his jacket pocket.

"Here it is. Williams threatening Harrington and vice versa." He handed the tape to Loughlin.

In that moment, Harrington felt abandoned, conspired against. They had all jumped ship: McCafferty, whose life and career he had salvaged; d'Ortega. Had she read his note and deliberately disobeyed him? Troopers Boyle and Cataldo were sniveling cowards. Suddenly, he paled, feeling nauseated. He thought he was going to vomit.

"We've got a tough situation here!" Loughlin said, his voice taut, FBI militant. "I'm going to get Sheldon Fine on the phone. . . ."

In that instant, he knew both he and Sheila could be in trouble. He hadn't listened to Riley's tape. But he had heard what Dr. Steadman had to say. And his gut instinct was to go along with Sheila.

"Neil Harrington," Loughlin said grimly, "you are under arrest for violation of U.S. Code, title eighteen, conspiracy to compound a felony, obstruction of justice, and as you say, maybe the U.S. attorney can throw in a few more."

Harrington staggered and held on to the edge of his desk. Everyone noticed that he looked ill.

"I'm getting sick," he said weakly. "I have to use the . . ." He gestured toward his bathroom.

Loughlin merely nodded.

As Harrington closed the door, Loughlin gathered up the revolvers belonging to Cataldo and Boyle. Those two men had been neutralized. Loughlin could read it in their eyes. It was a bizarre scenario. He had supported Sheila O'Brien to the hilt, without question. But everything could backfire. It could be both their asses. Although somehow he sensed that Sheila had it figured all along. He was staking his career on it.

They waited—Cataldo, Boyle, Loughlin, O'Brien, Riley. They heard the toilet flush.

Then a shot rang out. They looked at one another. They were all law-enforcement officers. There was no mistaking what had happened. When the men crashed down the bolted door, they found Harrington sprawled grotesquely on the floor, scrunched over like a sack of wet cement, a gelatinous blob where his head had been, splayed out in gray and scarlet against the white tile floor.

40

IT WAS TWO days after Harrington's death. The legal world, fueled by Fletcher Porter's full-page spread in the *Boston Globe* and Pat Nolan's lurid details in the *Herald,* was stunned by the bizarre turn of events.

Everyone seemed to jump to judgment.

They now saw a hidden dark side to Neil Harrington. He was a loner, said some. An overachiever. Little detractions began to surface, small things. He'd been known to cheat at poker. Petty, but enough to tarnish the image.

Dillard was throwing a goodwill get-together at the Ritz-Carlton. Sheridan's invitation came by special messenger, together with a grateful note and a certified check for $100,000.

"These are the kind of invites I like." Judy Corwin smiled at her boss as she handed him the opened envelope. "It's a black-tie affair," Judy said. "You deserve it, Dan. It was a great victory."

Sheridan had his feet propped on his desk and was reading the *Herald.* He tossed the newspaper into his wastebasket, took the invitation and check from Judy, studied both for a moment, then handed them back.

"Thank the doctor for the check," he said without a show of emotion, his feet still on his desk, "but tell his secretary I'll be out of town. Send my regrets. . . ."

Judy was smart enough not to ask questions. Something was bothering Sheridan. It may have been the media's praise for Sheila O'Brien. Her yearbook picture from Fordham Law was prominent, even in the *New York Daily News.*

"Fletcher Porter would like an exclusive." Judy thought she'd back out of the office on a high note. "And"—she glanced at her notebook—"CNN, the 'Today' show, and Connie Chung all want interviews in New York City. Even got calls from Fox and several Hollywood producers. We'll push the Menendez brothers onto the weather page."

"I should have advised our client against holding a victory party,"

Sheridan said dryly. "It was just a nonindictment. Lots can still happen. Things change."

"Well, I'll hold all the goodies at bay." Judy winked. "I think it was Mae West who said there's no such thing as too much of a good thing." She tapped the check against her notebook. "Oh, by the way, Raimondi reports that the bugs are off the phones, including your car and condo."

Sheridan merely nodded.

Judy grimaced and went out into the secretarial station, where Raimondi and Buckley were sitting on two of the desks, drinking straight Glenlivet.

Judy held up the check.

"One hundred big ones," she said with manufactured cheer. She was troubled by Dan Sheridan's lack of response. "Hey, you can pour me one, Manny!" She bunched three fingers together.

"What's with Dan?" Buckley asked. "We finally hit the jackpot and the big fellow's acting like he's about to join the Trappists. . . . You don't think it's all that press that Sheila O'Brien got?"

"Could be," Judy said. "Dan was wounded pretty deep."

"Well," Raimondi said as he poured the scotch into Judy's cup, "here's to all the nice Jewish girls—may I never marry one, if you know what I mean."

"And that goes for the Irish girls," Buckley responded. "Did I ever tell you the story . . . ?"

"Only about nine hundred and five times." Judy narrowed her eyes in mock dismay. "And listen, Raimondi—nice Jewish girls are just as passionate as Portugee girls. Just give us some shopping time and we'll do anything."

"Salut!" shouted Raimondi.

"I'll drink to that!" Buckley replied.

"*L'chaim!*" Judy raised her paper cup.

"*L'chaim!*" they choroused. And like friends of the groom at a Ukrainian wedding, they consumed the scotch in one gulp and tossed the cups at the watercooler.

At least *they* were able to celebrate.

Sheridan sat at Lazzarie's bar, downing a bourbon and looking up at the TV. Governor Stevenson was holding a press conference.

Suddenly, he was not alone. "Dan." An upscale State Street attorney clapped him around the shoulder as if he was a lodge brother. "Can I buy you a drink?"

"No . . . uh . . . I already have a drink." Sheridan winced at the forceful grasp. He fumbled for a name.

"Elliot Peabody. Wright, Frobisher, Peabody and Somes."

"Wright, Frobisher." Sheridan closed his eyes momentarily and thought, Why in hell can't some Princetonian just say, Hey, Dan. Call me El.

"Of course," Sheridan apologized, "I'm just watching the governor's speech. Seems he's going to appoint a new district attorney for Suffolk County."

"It's Gretchen Wilder," Peabody said, holding out his hand.

Dan extended his own and Peabody shook it as if Sheridan were the last survivor of the Scott expedition in Antarctica. He still had his other arm around Sheridan's shoulder.

"Wilder?" Dan looked up at him. Peabody had a chubby boyish face and black curly hair. He was sporting a slight mustache at perhaps the age of twenty-seven. "Never heard of her."

"Never heard of her? She's over at Cartwright, Devens, Moore and McCauliffe. Grandfather was Sinclair Weeks, of Weeks Publications, close adviser to Franklin Roosevelt, former president of MIT. Her father, Grafton Weeks, helped to develop the Patriot missile."

"The Patriot missile?" Sheridan pursed his lips and nodded.

"Hey, buddy!" Peabody yelled to the bartender, his arm still locked tightly around Sheridan, "another round!" He made a circling motion with his finger.

Sheridan glanced over his shoulder. Suddenly at 5 P.M. Lazzarie's bar was crowded. Gray-suited lawyers and some media types were lined three deep behind them. Sheridan was certain of one thing about his newfound celebrity. He wouldn't have to pay for a drink that evening, perhaps for the remainder of the week.

"Sorry." He stood up, glancing at his watch. "I'm late already."

The group parted reluctantly. He tossed a ten-dollar bill on the counter, then looked over his shoulder at Peabody.

"Let me know how Gretchen Wilder makes out."

Back at his condo, he took the telephone off the hook, poured a light beer, and caught the seven o'clock news. The Harrington suicide and the dramatic events in the district attorney's office occupied the first ten minutes. Most people believed that Harrington had killed Williams because she'd threatened his chance for a Senate seat, and the tape Riley provided had only confirmed that view. The media suggested that given Harrington's grim struggle for success and respectability, he could not bear to face a life of disgrace and ignominy. Dillard held a press conference, and although Sheridan had advised against it, the doctor seemed to relish the limelight and got quite chatty with the newscasters. It was still a sordid affair.

Riley had no comment, but Troopers Boyle and Cataldo, like Dillard, seemed to bask in their newfound notoriety. Sheila O'Brien and Brian Loughlin deferred to Assistant U.S. Attorney Fine, who lost no time in grabbing the headlines.

Next came Mayor Jimmy Kane, saddened by the events, of course, but assuring the city that it was now a time for rebirth, for moving on. He announced that he would resign as mayor in June to seek the Democratic nomination for the United States Senate. Then he threw out as an aside that Gretchen Wilder would be the new district attorney for Boston and Suffolk County. He and Governor Stevenson had agreed on the appointment.

Sheridan snapped open another Bud Light, then watched Mayan d'Ortega parry questions while a battery of mikes was thrust in her face.

She deferentially praised Neil Harrington. She had worked with him closely for five years. No, she had not suspected that Williams was Harrington's girlfriend. No, she had never had a romance with Harrington; their relationship had been strictly professional.

"Why do you think Mayor Kane and Governor Stevenson picked Wilder over you to fill the office of district attorney?"

She masked her annoyance by brushing a strand of hair back from her forehead.

"I really don't know," she said simply. "Maybe you should ask the mayor and the governor."

"Any ideas?"

"Not a one."

"Are you quitting the district attorney's office?"

"Yes."

"What does the future hold?"

"I believe I'll hang out my shingle."

On Sheridan's instructions, McCafferty refused to be interviewed.

Sheridan clicked off the TV, then gathered his baseball gear for tomorrow afternoon's game. They'd be playing up in Newburyport and he had heard that the Yankee Clippers had a new left-hander who used to play for Pawtucket in the Eastern League before he became a stockbroker—and he could really smoke the ball. Sheridan liked that: Curveballers were his nemesis, but guys who fired the high fast one were a piece of cake.

It was close to midnight when he decided to make the call. He had been reading Professor Pierre Collett's handbook on polygraphy.

"Dr. Leventhal, I know it's late, but I want to make an appointment with you . . . at your convenience. There are a few things I'd like to get clear about that new psychotropic drug Amitofanil."

"Dan, this isn't a malpractice case, is it? Or product-liability litigation? I never testify against a fellow practitioner—it's a code of honor."

More like a conspiracy of silence, Sheridan mouthed to himself.

"And let's face it. The pharmaceutical biggies keep me in business."

"Nothing like that, Doctor, and I'll pay you for your time—three thousand dollars up-front."

"Well, in that case, how about Friday at two? My office at University Hospital."

"Two P.M., Doctor."

He was about to click off the light. It was late, but what the hell, he thought. One more call. He dialed Sheila O'Brien's number. On the second ring, he hung up. No, this is crazy, he thought.

Suddenly, he was tired, bone-weary. Thoughts of his late wife, Jean, and his son, Tommy, washed over him. The events of the past three weeks—Sheila O'Brien—came crowding in.

He got out of bed, made his way to the bathroom, and looked at himself in the mirror. He was beginning to appreciate the price he had paid.

Brian Loughlin received a terse call from Davis at Justice. They weren't pleased by what had happened. The entire operation had to be scuttled. Sheila O'Brien, Sheldon Fine, and he were to be in Washington the next day. There was a lot of explaining to do. There were stories to get straight. Image and PR had to be worked on. There was to be no further discussion with the press or on television except interviews authorized by Justice and only through U.S. Attorney Norman Wright.

Sheila had typed her resignation and tucked it into her purse. A government car picked her up at her apartment and whisked her to Logan Airport, where she was driven to a private runway. Brian Loughlin and Sheldon Fine were standing there beside a twin-engine Piper Otter, waiting for her.

The trip to D.C. took some two hours. No one spoke. Sheila sat directly behind the pilot, watching him click dials and levers, adjust trim and power settings, occasionally checking in on his telecommunicator. The steady drone of the props and the gentle rocking of the wings imparted a strange sense of well-being, as if she was now certain, finally, of where she was heading. And it wasn't to Washington, D.C. She glanced back at Sheldon Fine and Brian Loughlin, who occupied seats apart from each other. Brian was peering out of the starboard window. The Long Island shore came into view. Sheila also gave a look. The towers and prisms of Manhattan, thrusting through the early-morning smog, looked as fictive as Emerald City.

Brian Loughlin knew his service with the bureau hung in the balance. It could go either way. He could be deemed too impetuous, incapable of command, relegated to dog soldier status, given the mean assignments. It would force his retirement. In a way, he envied Sheila O'Brien. Her options seemed unlimited. Whatever happened at the upcoming meeting with Davis, she could just say *sayonara.*

But then, things could bounce the other way. He and Sheila had turned a debacle into a win-win situation. They had guessed right. They had weeded out a dark player. Brian Loughlin didn't know which way the cards would fall.

For Sheila, even if Davis pinned the Medal of Honor on her with full military pomp, she was gone from the bureau. She glanced at Sheldon Fine. He was buried in paperwork, flipping pages, shuffling notebooks, checking, scribbling, pondering, canceling, jotting furiously, a slight, bemused smile on his face. Of the three, he was the one most certainly in the catbird seat. He looked up and caught Sheila O'Brien staring at him. He smiled invitingly. She simply nodded, turned, and rechecked the Manhattan skyline, picking out familiar landmarks—the Empire State Building, the Chrysler spire, the

World Trade Center, the UN, Central Park. Then, as she thought of her upcoming meeting with Justice, she realized that for once in her life she was holding the high cards. She didn't give a damn.

Riley was a hero of sorts. He could even read it in the resentful eyes of Buddy Furlong. Mayor Kane had canceled his birthday party, saying, "The good people of Boston shouldn't be lighting candles for politicians." The ad guys, the scriptwriters, and the prat men were in place. Even though it left a lot of small fry—including Buddy Furlong—high and dry, it would play well in Roxbury, Dorchester, Hyde Park, Chelsea, the neighborhoods.

There was talk that Mayor Kane might appoint Riley as police commissioner. After all, he had cracked the case while the others, the FBI, Furlong, the U.S. attorney's office, were going around in circles. The impropriety of secreting evidence was soon overlooked.

"Let me speak to Dan Sheridan!" Sonny Callahan said into the phone, his tone authoritative.

"He's in court right now." Judy Corwin delivered the white lie, recognizing Sonny's voice. "Can someone else help you?"

"I want to make an appointment. It's about my aunt's estate in Roscommon. Involves substantial property. Mr. Sheridan comes highly recommended."

"I'll see that he gets back to you, Mr. . . . er . . ."

"Sean Canavan. I'll be in touch."

The small deceptions were not lost on Judy, nor on Sonny Callahan.

Sheldon Fine, Loughlin, and O'Brien were met by a plain black Ford and driven from International Airport over the Fourteenth Street Bridge to the Justice Department on Constitution Avenue, the world's largest law firm.

From the underground garage, accompanied by the driver, they rode the escalator to the gray-marble foyer. They were waved through a metal-detector doorway by security and rode another escalator to the next landing. There they were met by another security guard and escorted down a long gray-tiled corridor.

Sheila sensed something important was in the offing. She was correct.

They paused momentarily in front of a mahogany-veneered door. The guard inserted a card in the electronic lock. A slight click and the door swung open. They entered an outer office, where two secretaries greeted them with pleasant smiles.

"Come this way," one said. She turned the brass knob on the polished oak door and ushered them into the office of the attorney general of the United States.

There in the massive office, behind a modest walnut desk, sat the newly appointed cabinet member, Dwight Jensen. Jensen, a youngish law professor at the University of Wisconsin, had been the President's third choice. His long blond hair and choirboy good looks seemed an incongruity, especially for the country's chief legal officer.

Davis, who had been standing next to a window with a commanding view of Capitol Hill, moved forward to greet them. Jensen flashed a kind midwestern smile, putting the trio immediately at ease. What tension they harbored dissolved in this moment as Davis danced through the introductions.

Jensen moved out to greet them. "I'm most impressed with all of you, as is the President. Sit down." He gestured toward his leather couch.

Davis, in a total reversal, was almost tripping over himself as he heaped praise on the trio from Boston.

"We're creating a new department here in Justice." Jensen sat on the edge of his desk. "It's to be headed by Hal." He nodded toward Davis and smiled at the assembled group. "You three will be in on the ground floor; you'll be the nucleus. You demonstrated the stuff the department needs. . . ."

"Excuse me, Mr. Jensen." Sheila dug into her purse. "I mean no disrespect, but before you continue, especially as it concerns me, I must give you this. As of this moment, I'm handing in my resignation." She presented an envelope to Jensen.

Davis gave her a withering glance.

Jensen said nothing. He opened the dated letter and read it. It was simple, no encomiums, no platitudes, no bullshit.

As of today, I hereby resign from the Federal Bureau of Investigation.
Respectfully,
Sheila O'Brien

* * *

Davis was upset at O'Brien's defection.

"I never was quite sure of O'Brien," he later said to Jensen, denying every hope he'd had for the young woman's talents.

"Hey"—Jensen nodded pragmatically—"these things happen."

Sheila took a cab from Justice to International Airport and caught the eleven o'clock shuttle to Logan, arriving a little after noon.

She called the Brookfield Town Hall. The Giants were playing up in Newburyport at 2:30. She rented a car from Avis and headed up I-95. It was a warm spring day; the scent of summer was in the air, a great day for baseball. She approached the Newburyport turnoff and had second thoughts. Was she crazy? With his injuries, hell, Sheridan might not even be playing. She eased up on the gas pedal.

He'll be playing, she decided with renewed resolution. She had no doubts. She pressed her foot on the accelerator.

Sheila had little difficulty finding the town field adjacent to Newburyport High School. The first-base side of the diamond fell away to a boggy marsh, making foul balls virtually impossible to run down or even retrieve. Deep center field backed up into another playing field, where a high school soccer game was in progress. Behind a wire mesh backstop, only a handful of people sat in the splintered wooden stands watching the old town teams go through their paces. In fact, there were more spectators at the soccer game.

Sheila parked by the high school gym and remained in her car. She noted from the makeshift scoreboard that the teams were locked in a scoreless tie at the bottom of the sixth.

Newburyport's pitcher, tall, husky, wasted little time and mowed down Brookfield with three strikeouts. He had blazing speed but an odd delivery. He would almost stumble with every pitch.

Little changed over the next two innings. Sheila watched Sheridan behind the plate, arguing with the umpire, stopping a few wild pitches, calling a conference at the mound, warming up a new pitcher, catching a Clipper in a rundown, chasing a pop foul right into the marsh, splattering into the weeds and bulrushes but hanging on to the ball.

Finally, she left the car and moved across the running track to sit behind the backstop, next to an old-timer.

"It's a squeaker," he said. "We need a couple of runs." He smiled at Sheila as she sat down. "This Hurley kid's been zappin' Brookfield all afternoon, got a two-hitter going, twelve strikeouts, but he can't do it all."

"Must be pretty good," Sheila said.

"Good! I've seen Roger Clemens, even Bob Gibson. Know who Bob Gibson was?"

"St. Louis Cardinals," Sheila said. "I saw him beat the Cubs once."

The old-timer studied her for a moment. "You must have been just a toddler," he said admiringly. Too bad it was into the late innings, he thought. We could have exchanged some baseball lore.

"Hurley's a real fireballer," he continued. "Used to play for Pawtucket, you know. That's when he lost his leg."

"Oh?"

"Yeah, car accident up in Seneca Falls. Cost him a professional career, but he can still smoke 'em. Wears a wooden contraption."

Just then, Sheridan, swinging two bats, approached the plate, tossing one away as he stepped into the batter's box.

"How's that Sheridan guy doing, the Giants' catcher?" Sheila asked.

"Hurley's got his number. Struck him out three times. Funny. Hurley usually just rocks back and fires away. But with Sheridan, he gives him lazy curves."

Hurley served up the slow roundhouse again. Sheridan waited and whiffed. Waited and whiffed again. This time, Hurley knew he'd gone to the well once too often. Sheridan would have his timing down—he'd kill the lob. The pitcher started a slow sidearm maneuver, then cocked his good leg and fired, hard and fast. Sheridan had figured that was exactly what Hurley had in mind.

High inside. Sheridan connected. The center fielder watched the shot rise over his head and yelled a warning to the soccer players. Everyone scuttled for cover as Sheridan trotted around the bases. Brookfield was up 1–0 going into the bottom of the ninth.

The Clippers went down one, two, with nobody on base. Hurley, the pitcher, stepped into the batter's box.

"He's not a bad hitter," the old-timer said to Sheila, "but I guess this just isn't our day."

The Brookfield pitcher fired two strikes and the game appeared to be a wrap. The Newburyport manager started rounding up the bats and balls.

The next pitch was low and inside. Hurley laid down a perfect drag bunt toward third. Sheridan whipped off his mask and pounced on it like a panther, scooping it up and turning to fire toward first. Hurley was gimping as fast as he could, but Sheridan had him beaten by fifteen feet.

Then, to everyone's amazement, Sheridan held the ball. He knew that it would have been a clean single in any league.

The rest was anticlimactic. Hurley was replaced by a runner on first. A moose of a kid lined the first pitch just where Sheridan had socked his home run—deep center into the soccer game. Both runners loped around the bases. The game was over.

"Well, I'll be damned," said the old-timer. "Never seen nuthin' like that in sixty years, 'cept maybe Bonehead Freddie Merkle failing to touch second. Cost the old New York Nationals the World Series."

Hurley came over to Sheridan and shook his hand, as did all of the Clippers. There was no rancor, even among Sheridan's teammates. They swapped good-natured jibes, rounded up their gear, and headed toward their parked cars. After all, it was only a game. Sheila now saw a new side to Sheridan's tough veneer, one she had always suspected was there.

Sheridan had spotted Sheila just after running down a Clipper between third and home. He saw her cross the running track and out of the corner of his eye he watched her take a seat behind the backstop. He noted her again as he packed his gear. He wondered what she was doing there, how she knew he would be playing. He thought of Raimondi's message that the bugs were off. Could be an FBI ploy. Like Hurley trying to sucker him into the final slow-breaking curve. He didn't acknowledge her presence, but she was still sitting in the stands as he drove off.

He wanted to call Raimondi on the car phone. No, things didn't feel right. Why was O'Brien still trailing him? She had gotten under his skin, no question about it, but not enough to make him careless.

"Amitofanil has been approved in France and the United Kingdom as an antidepressant." Dr. Melvin Leventhal sat behind a desk cluttered with anatomical knickknacks—plastic kidneys, livers, lungs; a model of the heart—all supplied by drug companies eager for his endorsement. He looked like a sitcom physician in his white lab coat, the obligatory stethoscope dangling from a pocket.

"The extract comes from the koaki frog, a South American denizen found only in the Mato Grosso jungles of Brazil.

"The Yugani, the Curangi, the Negro Blacenda, and a few other tribes have been using this toxin for a thousand years, well before the Spanish and Portuguese explorers."

"I understand," said Sheridan, "it's not all that acceptable to the honchos in the FDA."

"Side effects," Leventhal said. "A euphemism for dire complications, adverse reactions. It's a great sedative, beyond a doubt. Give this to a guy who's going to jump off the bridge over some broad and instead he'll go to Mass every morning and give his life savings to the Sisters of Mercy. It's a potent drug."

"Can you prescribe it, Mel?"

"No, not publicly. But I've taken a few tablets. Believe me, it's the ultimate relaxer.

"If I would normally fight with my wife when I get her bills from Bloomingdale's, after one of these babies I would tell her, 'Hey, I think you're scrimping.'

"Believe me, Dan, if the drug gets marketed in the United States, invest in Lord & Taylor, Bloomie's, the May Company."

"I take it," Sheridan said, "this is the ultimate opiate and inhibitions are tossed to the winds."

"Well, I'm an internist, not a psychiatrist, but—you pop a few of these little greenies and you're so laid-back, you'd screw a snake."

"Er, uh . . . I'd rather pay the monthly tab at Bloomie's.

"Seriously, Mel, how does it work? What's the chemical or physiologic impact on the human mind or body that can produce this artificial buffer?"

"It's not artificial at all." Leventhal pressed his fingers together. "The animal body has reacted since time immemorial to stress. Fight or flight. A hormone is produced by that little pea-shaped gland at the base of the brain. Then depending on the influences on or emitted by the adrenals, we beat a retreat from a bad situation or attack ten thousand antagonists, euphoric, inviting death. Somehow the koaki works on the brain, slowing things down. You get that good glow feeling and yet you function normally."

"Now, Mel, let's say my client just robbed a bank. I'm defending him."

Leventhal closed his eyes, tilting his head back. A smile flickered across his face. He knew his fee was going to be augmented.

"Yes."

"I say he didn't rob Wells Fargo. The authorities say he did. Let's say it all boils down to a lie detector test."

Leventhal still had his eyes closed, his fingers together. "I think I'm with you."

"Did your client actually rob the bank?"

"Let's say he did."

"Okay." Leventhal's eyes sprang open. "Your client pops a few Amitofanils prior to the test."

"Yeah, that's about it."

"It's win or lose according to the test?"

"The DA agrees. Pass the test, you walk."

"Your client's really guilty?"

"As guilty as sin, as we Irish say."

"What you're asking me, Dan, is can he beat the test?"

"Exactly. Say black is white—and get away with it."

"I really don't know. Depends on the individual. Willie Sutton, maybe a *no*. But say some cardiovascular surgeon who is very familiar with the sympathetic nervous system and its reactions to the gamut of pharmacopoeia . . ." Leventhal wiggled his hand. "Anyone you have in mind, Dan?"

"Just hypothetical." Sheridan looked at Leventhal. Both knew precisely whom they were talking about.

"Can you give me a few tablets of this stuff?" Sheridan said. "I want to say black is white and see what the polygraph says."

"Here." Leventhal reached for a plastic bottle in back of his plastic kidney display. "Take—I'll say two—five hours before the test. Just don't try to seduce your secretary."

"Unlikely."

Sheridan drove his car into the J. J. Timilty & Sons Funeral Home parking area in West Roxbury. Visiting hours were 7:00 to 9:00 P.M., and at 8:45, the lot, with only a couple of cars, looked eerily vacant.

He signed the register and stood for a moment before entering the room. A small group was seated in an anteroom, murmuring with light gossip. He noticed a bereaved Mrs. Harrington standing with her one son and two daughters. A middle-aged priest stood next to them, nodding condolences. The Harringtons did not appear to be holding up well. A Beacon Hill background was no help now.

"I'm Dan Sheridan." He grasped the cold, elegant hand of Harrington's widow in both of his. "I'm awfully sorry."

"Mr. Sheridan." She peered at him through teary eyes and tried a semblance of a smile. "Thank you for coming. . . . You and Neil had your battles over the years, but . . . uh . . . he respected you.

"This is Neil's cousin, Monsignor Flynn."

"Padre." Sheridan shook his hand and moved on to the children. They were huddled together in misery. Sheridan made no pretense.

"I'm sorry," he said again, then moved on.

A picture of young naval lieutenant Neil Harrington, white military collar, epaulets, chest bedecked with ribbons, sat atop the closed casket. There were flowers on tripods, flowers laid against the casket, above, along the walls. Tributes but little else. The funeral parlor was almost as deserted as the parking lot. The good that Harrington did would be interred with his bones. The evil would live after him. Sheridan thought of Shakespeare, not really recalling the play but succinctly recalling the adage. There would be no official outpouring, no eulogies delivered by the cardinal. The Catholic Layman of the Year and Laetare recipient would be buried in shame and dishonor.

Sheridan knelt and blessed himself, then paused for a few moments.

"Whatever you were, Neil, you were not a murderer," he whispered. "Just maybe not a hell of a lot different from the rest of us." He blessed himself again, nodded toward Mrs. Harrington, and left.

As he descended the front steps, he noticed Mayan d'Ortega alighting from a gray Mustang parked next to his red Le Baron.

He waited for her. She seemed surprised, almost startled to see him.

"Sheridan," she exclaimed, "you're the last person I would expect to be here."

"Well, maybe Mayor Kane, Normie Wright, and the others came earlier. And of course the cardinal will give Neil a plenary indulgence. He'll bypass Purgatory."

"If you'll excuse me, gringo, I'm not in the mood for . . ."

"I'm sorry." Sheridan lowered his head. "That wasn't called for. When a fellow lawyer—a fellow human—goes out like this . . . I really don't feel too good.

"Do you believe in God, Mayan?"

"What?" She threw him a dismissive look.

"No, I'm serious, Mayan. I have my doubts. I think when you go, you go."

She studied him for a few moments. Then she said, "Look, I've got to pay my respects. There's a little Mexican place over in Brighton, Villa de Mazatlán. We'll have a drink, discuss theology, law, whatever."

"Meet you there," he said quietly.

They sat in a corner decorated with cactus plants and a blowup photo of Pancho Villa, brandishing *pistoleros,* his sombrero tilted rakishly back from his forehead.

"I believe that there is a greatness out there. Not holed up in some nirvana"—her eyes looked upward—"but maybe in mankind itself, with all its troubles, all its tragedies, its bravery in everyday living. I think *we* are God—you, me, Neil Harrington, even your Dr. Dillard."

They had been talking in this sober vein for half an hour.

She sipped her tequila and he toyed with a straight bourbon. He signaled the waiter for the bill, then looked at her carefully.

"Do you think Harrington killed the Williams woman?"

"No." She studied her fingers, avoiding his gaze. "Not in his character. He was too ambitious, driven. And too proud. Then, bang! He's caught in a scandal. The driver, the egoist, doesn't reason or react logically. Maybe he took the only way out he thought was open. I can't be judgmental."

She met his gaze head-on.

"Your client beat the indictment because of McCafferty. He walked scot-free because of the Harrington debacle, with a little help from the media. Gretchen Wilder will broom the case. I probably would, too—but of course I'm not the DA."

"What does the former star prosecutor, now a sister Portia, think?" Sheridan looked into his glass, then drained it.

"With no determinative cause of death, a favorable polygraph, the government's star witness collapsing . . ." Her hand slashed the air.

"What does Mayan d'Ortega, human being, sister goddess, think?"

"It's late, amigo." She glanced at her wristwatch. "Let's lay all this to rest."

"I like you, Sheridan. In other circumstances, we might have been comrades." She reached over and touched his cheek. "*Vaya con Dios.*" She picked up her purse and left the restaurant.

Sheridan fumbled with his wallet, then paid the bill.

He walked across the lot toward his Le Baron. He felt stupid for not escorting d'Ortega to her car.

"Dan," Raimondi got him on the car phone, "a Sean Canavan wants to meet with you tomorrow. Gave Judy his aunt's-estate pitch. He'll be in at eleven, but I can stall him for another day. I think you know who it is."

"Manny, what do you say we broom the whole Dillard thing?"

"Sure, Dan, I can. Can you?"

41

"MEL, I'VE been boning up on toxicology at the Harvard Medical Library." Sheridan had dropped by for another consultation.

"Seems the South American Indians had more than a leg up on acute poisons. Curare, the old dart poison, paralyzes nerve endings and leaves a person helpless."

Dr. Mel Leventhal steepled his fingers together and closed his eyes for several seconds—a characteristic pose.

"Many toxins can be lethal within a short period of time," he said. "In fact, beestings caused three times more fatalities in the United States last year than bites from snakes, spiders, and scorpions combined. A susceptible victim goes into instant anaphylactic shock and it's curtains."

"Can these toxins be detected at autopsy?"

"Not easily. Curare comes from the *Strychnos* plant. Can kill within seconds, and there's no known antidote. And the pathologist has to be alert. He's got to be looking for just that—venoms, poisons. When you get a fatality after a history of snakebite, hornet sting, or beesting, then the pathologist's forensic suspicion is heightened."

"Are there some toxins that can kill without a trace, even if the pathologist is especially tuned and he suspects acute poisoning?"

"Sure, I'm not a pharmacological biochemist, mind you, or a forensic toxicologist, but I know a person can lick a postage stamp laced with potassium cyanide and—zap!" Leventhal snapped his fingers. "Nine times out of ten, even the most experienced forensic pathologists wouldn't be able to pick it up.

"Certain poisons cause cardiac arrhythmia. The heart beats so fast, it fails to express the proper flow of blood to the brain stem, where crucial life-sustaining centers are housed. Again it's fatal, and the diagnosis is usually the catchall category for sudden death, cardiac failure. The real lethal agent goes undetected."

"This koaki frog." Sheridan removed a plastic bottle from his suit pocket. "Professor Erica Fujii, chief of Pharmacology at Johns

Hopkins, describes it as the little angelic monster: You eat its liver, you're in seventh heaven. The liver extract provides the grist for mood elevators." Sheridan shook the bottle.

"But according to Fujii, the skin of the koaki frog, when compressed and ingested, is more deadly than strychnine. There's no known antidote, and it kills without a trace."

"I'm familiar with Dr. Fujii; also read her recent paper in the *New England Journal of Medicine.*

"I'm an internist, Dan. I prescribe drugs, not poisons." Leventhal again went through his ritual, fingers steepled, eyes closed. "But I have to know the chemical breakdown of certain poisons, the antidotes available. Of the twenty-six hundred breeds of snake in the world, only two hundred are venomous. But even in New England, we had eight fatalities last year from rattlesnake bites. So if a medical practitioner screws around with some kid who claims he was bitten by a rattler while hiking in the Blue Hills, three miles from Boston, if you don't institute immediate remedial action, you sure'n hell better have your malpractice insurance paid up.

"So, there are many toxins—no, not many, but more than a few—that can kill, and the best pathologist in the world can't pick it up.

"When do you take your lie detector test?" Leventhal wanted to wrap up this discussion.

"Tonight at seven-thirty."

Leventhal glanced at his watch. "Six hours from now. Pop a couple of Amis right now. Jesus, Dan, these little marvels not only are the ultimate pepper-upper; they're the ultimate pecker-upper. You might screw yourself to death and it would take the embalmer three days to get the smile off your face."

"Hey, Mel, I could do that without any help from the little greenies." Sheridan grinned, shook the bottle, and placed it in his pocket.

"And thanks for the consult." He removed an envelope from his pocket. "Here's an extra retainer."

The exchange was quick, deft. Dr. Leventhal smiled a bright professional smile. They shook hands. Sheridan departed.

Dr. Leventhal sneaked a peek at the check. Another three thousand. Not bad. But somehow he suspected he would earn it.

* * *

Buckley drove Sheridan over to MIT. "We had a pretty good week, Dan, settling the Doyle case and walking Dillard, and the checks have cleared. And best of all, we didn't have to grease anyone's palm."

"You're right." Sheridan had a whimsical smile as Buckley crossed over the Larz Anderson Bridge to the Cambridge side of the Charles River. "And right now, I have a pretty relaxed attitude.

"Do you recognize anything out of the ordinary about me?" Sheridan pulled down the sun visor and took a peek in the vanity mirror.

Buckley gave a quick glance in his boss's direction. "You got a smile on your face for a change."

"How about the eyes?" Sheridan looked over at Buckley.

Another quick glance. "What about the eyes?"

"My pupils. Did you ever see such dilated pupils?"

"Say, you're right. What have you been smoking?"

"I ingested some psychotropic medication this afternoon. That's why we're going over to see Dr. Steinmetz again."

"Christ, Dan, you could have cut me in. The goddamn Dillard case is over!"

A horn blared and Buckley swerved to avoid colliding with a late-model convertible. The young woman driver gave Buckley the finger as she sped off.

Sheridan laughed at the near collision, especially at the driver's reaction.

"Do you remember Dillard's appearance during his test?"

Buckley sighed. "I recall that he was more composed than either of us, even more so than Steinmetz."

"And did you notice Dillard's eyes that evening?"

"Not particularly."

"Well, I didn't, either. But as I look back at it, I think his pupils were dilated, just like mine. I say I think. I don't know for sure. When you're not looking for something in particular, it's not important to you.

"You know that final argument I used in the Clancy case?"

"I remember."

"My witness was tripped up by the DA, a minor discrepancy. Said

he was fifteen feet from the scene of the accident. The DA proved
he was thirty feet away.

"I asked the jury, 'How many light fixtures are there over your
heads—and please don't look up.' "

"How could I forget that argument?" Buckley turned into the
MIT concourse.

" 'Madam forelady,' I said, 'you might say six. You, sir'—I
pointed to the guy next to her—'might say three. Actually, there
are none. Now you've been here for three days, coming and going.
The entire room was in plain view, but the light fixtures weren't
important to you. Just because you didn't guess correctly doesn't
mean you weren't here!' "

"I get it; the jury got it. Just because Clancy was off by one hundred percent didn't mean he wasn't at the scene. Footage wasn't
important; the accident was."

Buckley turned into a parking space in front of Steinmetz's building. "Dan, you think with the help of those trankies you can ace
the exam?"

"Not ace it. I think I can scam it."

"Suppose you flunk?"

"Well, if I flunk it, the Dillard case is history—I promise."

Steinmetz greeted Sheridan and Buckley with unusual exuberance.
His cynical moodiness of the earlier visit seemed to have evaporated.
He stroked his ginger beard and his little blackberry eyes glittered.

"Okay, Doc." Buckley spoke for Sheridan. "Let's go through the
test."

Steinmetz sensed a psychological reluctance in Buckley that almost amounted to fear. "Look, gentlemen, I'll administer the examination. This procedure is a valid indication of what a person
believes to be the truth. If he believes it, although he could be dead
wrong, the polygraph will register that he did not deceive."

Sheridan spoke up. "So if the examinee says he shot Lincoln and
he believes he did, then the polygraph will indicate that he shot
Lincoln?"

"Not exactly. It will demonstrate that he didn't deceive."

"Dr. Steinmetz," Sheridan said, "are you familiar with any
pharmaceuticals that can tranquilize a patient to such an extent

that he can say anything and be believed by that little machine of yours?"

"There are a few drugs that can alter personality, but I haven't had much experience with them."

Sheridan smiled again and rolled up his sleeve.

The test was short. Ten questions. "Is your name Napoleon Bonaparte?"

"Yes."

"False." Steinmetz's lips flattened in satisfaction. "Is your name Mickey Owens?"

"Yes."

"True."

Steinnmetz furrowed his brow and looked at Sheridan and Buckley. Although he was conducting the interrogation, the questions came from a list supplied by Sheridan.

"Mickey Owens. Who in hell is Mickey Owens?"

"Catcher—Booklyn Dodgers, 1936. One of the great ones. Made one miscue. Dropped a third strike. The Yanks went on to win the World Series."

"You're trying to impugn the test," Steinmetz snapped.

"No, Doc. Six hours ago, I took a drug called Amitofanil. It has certain sedative and hypnotic qualities. In fact, your voice sounds very distant, like I'm at the other end of a wind tunnel without the wind.

"Even with the drug, I flunked the Napoleon stuff because I couldn't identify with Napoleon. But Mickey Owens . . . My dad was a catcher for the old Quincy Presidents. I was a catcher. Still am." Sheridan stole a glance at Buckley to see if he picked up on that bit of information. But Buckley's mind seemed to be elsewhere.

"I could identify with Owens. My father idealized him so much that he became sort of a hero to me as a kid."

Steinmetz looked baffled. "The only way I can explain it is that at the moment of your response, it's your belief that counted. Somehow you believed you were Mr. Owens, and the test showed you did not deceive."

The test continued. "Did you ever steal anything in your life?"

"No."

According to Steinmetz's interpretation, that was not a deception.

"Again I fooled the machine." It was Sheridan's turn to shake his head. "I stole plenty as a kid. I stole the final poly sci exam in college in my junior year. Dated the dean's secretary to get it. I don't feel good about it even to this day."

Steinmetz didn't look too pleased himself.

"Well," he grumbled, "all of these questions were inane to begin with, not subject to reality, posed no threat to your personal safety."

"I agree," Sheridan replied. "There was no stress at all. But I did scam the test."

"Maybe we should rerun the exam in a week or so . . . same questions without you being on those super pills of yours," Steinmetz said as he proceeded to shut down the machine and remove the graph paper. He looked more bemused than angry.

"Dr. Steinmetz, I hope I have your confidentiality." Sheridan pulled out an envelope. "Here's a check for fifteen thousand dollars."

"I am a professional." Steinmetz took the envelope. "Confidentiality is the hallmark of our discipline."

Sheridan shook Steinmetz's hand vigorously. "There are few of us left, Doctor." To Buckley, even to Sheridan, the compliment sounded wooden.

"I consider it as sacred as the client-attorney or patient-doctor privilege." Steinmetz opened a desk drawer and swept the graph paper into it, together with Sheridan's check.

"Your Dr. Dillard," Steinmetz said. "I understand he was exonerated by the grand jury."

"Uh . . ." Sheridan checked himself. "Yes, that's the word. Yes, exonerated." The three men shook hands and Buckley and Sheridan left.

"You know, Dan, we're passing out money like it's penny candy." Buckley glanced over at his boss as they drove back to Boston.

"Lucky we have it to pass around," Sheridan said, taking out the small bottle of pills from an inside pocket and peering at the contents as if they contained a secret.

*   *   *

Sheridan sat with Sonny Callahan in the deserted choir loft of St. Denis as the late-morning sun filtered through the stained-glass window.

"Your man Raimondi said I'd find you here," Callahan said. "I think I have some information you should know."

They talked in whispers, even though only a sole parishioner sitting in a pew below and murmuring prayers disturbed the sepulchral silence.

" 'Tis a nice church." Callahan delayed the opening of business. "I like to sit by meself in the quiet. That red light down there means Christ is present on the altar."

Sheridan looked over at Callahan.

"Yes, it's just you and me, that little old lady down there saying her prayers, and the Good Lord." Sheridan's voice had a caustic overtone. "And I don't think the Almighty would want us to be bullshitting each other, especially in church.

"Why this meeting, Sonny? And please don't pat me on my knee like I'm one of your nephews, and don't give me that stuff about what a great Irish Catholic lawyer I am."

Sonny's cheeks bunched. He smiled, but his eyes were devoid of coyness.

"I'm no saint," he began.

"Hey, the confessional is down there next to the altar." Sheridan looked straight ahead, but tilted his head toward Callahan. "And to keep the record straight, I'm not your attorney, I don't intend to become your attorney, and whatever you tell me isn't covered by the attorney-client privilege. Got that, Sonny?"

Callahan paused for several seconds.

"Jaysus, Dan, don't get so uptight. Settle down. To be truthful, I wish you were me attorney. Mouthpieces—I buy and sell them. They're a necessary evil."

"Look." Sheridan glanced at his watch. "I'm due in court at one. Let's not dance."

Again, Callahan paused. He watched the elderly parishioner bless herself, genuflect, and head toward the back door.

"Dan," he said, "you warned me about the FBI. They would have nailed me on all sorts of crazy charges, just like they nailed Liam Hennessey in Brooklyn a few years back."

"Sonny, come to the point. I'm running late."

Callahan looked directly at Sheridan. Their eyes met, held.

"Do you know anything about the SAS?"

"I've heard of them. Kind of a British commando unit. Hit men with Oxford accents."

"You got it." Callahan nodded. "The Williams woman was a British agent, a plant in our operation. She gave our cause a lot of grief."

"Listen, Sonny," Sheridan said, "I'm a lawyer, not a politician. I'll leave the SAS and the IRA to themselves, like the Germans fighting the Russians at Stalingrad."

But Sheridan's mind quickly assessed what Callahan was trying to relate. Dillard or someone under his direction had killed Williams.

Sheridan eyed him coolly. "Sonny, I defended the doctor. I walked him. That was my job. No more, no less. The case is closed. Maybe Harrington took out Williams; ever think of that?"

Callahan shook his head.

"Harrington wasn't in the movement. In fact, he turned against us. I tried to intercede—"

"Intercede?"

"Dan, I never condoned the killing, nor did the doctor. He did what he had to do."

"Why are you telling me all this, Sonny? Trying to brush me with some sort of guilt?"

"Dan, I love you, if you can believe it. Love you, because you're the kind of person I'd want to be if I had it to do over. Sure, they call me a fixer, a manipulator, whatever. But, Dan, I . . ."

Sonny started to choke; tears welled in his eyes. He shook his head, then blessed himself.

"Be careful, Dan." He patted Dan's knee. Sheridan watched him bless himself again and get up to leave.

"Sonny," Dan said as Callahan was about to descend the stairs from the choir loft.

"Yes?" Callahan paused.

"On the way out, put a C note in the poor box. I'll match it."

42

SHERIDAN nursed a bourbon at the Ritz bar, occasionally swiveling his chair to catch the early arrivals alighting from cabs and stretch limos as they headed for Dillard's gathering. He checked them off: Mayor Jimmy Kane with his wife, Kattie. The mayor, attired in a cashmere coat and white silk scarf over black tie and tux, nodded and tipped graciously. Kattie, rotund, summoned up a glassy smile, and looked uncomfortable in her new spangled evening dress from Saks, sable jacket about her shoulders. No rolled-up sleeves or parochial school image on this occasion.

Sheridan chuckled inwardly as he reviewed the power structure; Senator Crimmins, Representative Margaret Devaney, state politicians, city councillors, television personalities, Pat Nolan from the *Herald,* Fletcher Porter from the *Globe,* doctors—the Who's Who of the medical profession. Dillard hadn't missed a trick; all bases were covered.

Sheridan downed his bourbon and ordered another.

Somewhere in the recesses of his mind, the sensors kindled by Sonny Callahan began to smoke. Be careful.

Here's Dillard, he thought, escapes indictment by the craziest of circumstances. He should have taken his family on a long vacation to the Grand Canyon, get out of Dodge, let things abate. No, he holds a victory party at the Ritz, like some Mafia don who had just beaten the rap. Things didn't add up. Dillard never lacked balls. Soul maybe, but he had chutzpah; he might be able to pull it off.

Sheridan shook his head. Why should he care? And why the hell was he even here, mulling over whether to check into the party?

Not everyone was in black tie. He had on a blue business suit, nondescript maroon tie. He could meld in. He hadn't told his office that he might attend, not even young Buckley. And there was a game the next day in New Haven, a good three-hour drive. He stifled a sigh with a swallow of bourbon.

Maybe he was getting too old for baseball. Catcher wasn't exactly first base. And lately, he'd taken some pretty good shots. And maybe, he thought, I'm getting a little too old for the law. Twenty-hour days, making split-second decisions, crunching deadlines, massaging clients, keeping everyone afloat, getting scorched by domineering judges and every practitioner, from assistant DAs to defense attorneys, claims managers, adjusters; even the bar overseers were trying to knock his jock off. A trial lawyer had to run the adversarial gauntlet, day in, day out. It was guerrilla warfare, no game for chivalrous gentlemen. If you were dehorsed, you got stomped. But he knew he loved it—the combat, the intrigue, the vagaries, the elusive quarry—the occasional defeat, the sweet scent of victory. And he knew he'd never be satisfied playing first base, or being relegated to conveyancing for a bank. Being a trial lawyer was in his blood—the maneuvering, the battle, the carnage, saving some poor bastard from the slammer, helping a family in the projects stave off the sheriff.

Perhaps he was too Irish ever to give it up or ever to relinquish his position behind the plate. Nothing like waiting for some Young Turk to come barreling home. Ties didn't count in either game.

He was snapped out of his reverie by the arrival of Sonny Callahan with his wife, Moira.

Well, well. Sheridan smiled to himself. The party's complete—except for Neil Harrington.

Sonny, in black tux and sporting a kelly green bow tie, looked as out of place as the mayor's wife. A few flashbulbs popped. Sonny glared, then grinned as Moira poked him with her gloved elbow.

Be careful. Sheridan recalled Sonny's words of admonition. And Sheridan knew and Callahan knew that it wasn't Harrington who had taken the Williams woman out. Williams was just another war casualty as far as Callahan was concerned. But if she was SAS, they had all been playing with a fierce and deadly adversary. He had heard about the SAS, how they had gunned down four unarmed Irish tourists at Gibraltar on the tip that they were going to bomb a military band. There were no rights, no list of charges, no indictment, no Geneva convention, no counsel. Bam! That was it. Even the Mafia had ground rules, a bizarre code—but a code nonetheless.

There were several late arrivals, urbane types with white boutonnieres, whom Sheridan couldn't place.

He dismissed it. No, those chaps are too smart for a hit on the fifty-yard line at homecoming. Weren't they?

He finished his bourbon, smiled at a leggy airline stewardess hunched over a manhattan, paid his tab, and checked his watch: 7:45 P.M. Time to see whether his invitation was still valid.

The Roof Garden of the Ritz was alive with spring flowers, an arboretum of white and crimson azaleas, potted geraniums, fiery red Japanese crab, and pink dogwood. The black-tuxedoed men with their elegant bronzed women chatted easily, smiled, exchanged a few fraternal slaps on the back. Everyone was upbeat, goodwilled.

The attractive receptionist checked his invitation and proceeded to pin a celluloid name tag on his lapel: DANIEL SHERIDAN, ESQ. Judy hadn't sent regrets, after all.

A trio—blond harpist, longhaired violinist, crew-cut pianist—played Mozart, Brahms, Bach, an occasional tango. No "Wearin' o' the Green" stuff at the Ritz.

Sheridan sipped another bourbon and dipped into the Brie and oyster-shrimp canapes, then wandered, enhanced by his fourth bourbon. He nodded, smiled. Somehow people knew who he was. He was a celebrity—of sorts.

Dillard was talking with a coterie of medical specialists when he recognized Sheridan and motioned him to join the circle. Sheridan hoisted his glass and reluctantly edged his way forward.

"Kim, darling," Dillard addressed his wife, "this is my lawyer, Dan Sheridan." He turned slightly to his associates. "A very capable counselor, believe me." He saluted with his martini.

Kim Dillard had the aristocratic good looks that go with summers in Provence, winters in Santa Barbara—honey blond hair, a fifty-going-on-thirty kind of good looks. Her voice carried in it reminders of fine schools, posh country clubs, autumn leaves smoking on the grounds of some Vermont hideaway. Pleasant, soothingly rustic.

"I've heard a lot about you." She extended her hand to Sheridan, who fumbled between a kiss and a handshake. "The doctor and I are honored you could attend."

What in hell am I doing here? Sheridan chided himself as he gave Kim Dillard a peck on the cheek.

"Yes," Sheridan stammered, "just wanted to give my best to both of you. But I'm running a little late. I think I must be going."

"Nonsense," Dillard said. "We expect the cardinal in a few minutes."

"You've got to be kidding!" Sheridan looked at the doctor. "Can I see you a moment?" He jerked his thumb toward a corner.

"If you'll excuse me." Dillard placed his empty martini glass on the tray of a red-waistcoated attendant who was drifting by.

"Dillard." Sheridan's voice was bereft of sympathy, understanding. The bourbon had done its work. They stood a few feet back of the orchestra's podium. The group had taken a break from Mendelssohn.

"What in hell are you doing? All this crap!" Sheridan's hand swept outward. "Crimmins, Devaney, Kane, the cardinal . . ."

"Hey, Dan, relax. It's a cabaret, party time. Loosen up!"

"Maybe I should have shot a few Amitofanils." Sheridan zeroed in on Dillard, his eyes steely blue.

Dillard intercepted a waiter and took a martini from his tray.

"Another bourbon, sir?" The waiter swiveled his tray toward Sheridan.

"No. No thank you. I think I've had enough."

The waiter gave a courteous nod and continued on his way. Something clicked in Sheridan's mind. The waiter. Tall, carefully groomed dark hair flecked with gray. Too well groomed for an ordinary waiter. Sheridan watched him move off.

"So you know." Dillard gave a slight toast and tasted the martini.

"I suspected it all along," Sheridan said as he watched the waiter depart toward the kitchen entrance. He had seen that guy before. Where?

"You're my counsel, Mr. Sheridan. . . . For a pretty good fee, I might add. Everything told to you or which you learned during your investigation is deemed confidential. Like the seal of the confessional."

"Let's see if I'm reading you." Sheridan placed his half-full bourbon glass on the piano top.

"You obviously know about the koaki frog."

"You've been studying, Counselor." Dillard took another sip of his martini.

"Let's say I injected Angela with koaki serum on the night of April second. As a sedative, mind you."

"Okay," Sheridan interrupted. "She lapses into a coma. You render first aid. She doesn't respond. You don't call nine-one-one or an ambulance service or the police. You drive up Ninety-five, carry her almost the length of a football field into the woods, and dump her. Thick underbrush—her remains probably wouldn't have been found in this century. An unexplained disappearance; you'd be in the clear."

"Well, again let's just say for the point of argument that your assumed chronology is true—which of course I deny." Dillard finished his martini. "Would you have represented me?"

Sheridan was about to answer when Dillard's face suddenly contorted, his eyes widened, and he pitched forward onto the floor, the martini glass shattering on the marble tiles.

Only Sheridan and a few bystanders saw what had happened.

"Quick, call security!" Sheridan barked. He bent down and turned Dillard over, faceup, cradling his head in his arm. The guests began to gather.

"For Christsakes!" Sheridan yelled. "Get the manager! We need an ambulance!"

Sheridan felt for a pulse. There was none. Dillard's eyes were glazed. He was gone.

The inquest was held in one of the older rooms of Suffolk Superior Court. Dr. Vincent Shields, chief of Pathology at Boston General Hospital, testified that Dillard died of a coronary thrombosis, a clotting of the anterior descending coronary artery of the heart, leading to a gross myocardial infarction.

"In layman's terms," he told the panel, "the doctor had a major heart attack. He couldn't have survived. Too much damage to the myocardium was involved; too much heart tissue died. Such an attack, especially in men over fifty, can come at any time. It's due to atherosclerosis, the buildup of sludge that gathers in our coronary arteries at an early age; the progression is inexorable.

"Dr. Dillard had a typical coronary profile—hardworking, driven, successful. And he had been through a lot of psychologic trauma. These factors precipitated the thrombosis."

In Dr. Shields's opinion, the pathologic diagnosis was open and shut: death by natural causes.

Mayan d'Ortega, being the transitional district attorney pending Gretchen Wilder's official appointment, conducted the investigation. She interrogated the caterer, the hotel manager, the head maître d', Sonny Callahan, finally Dan Sheridan.

Sheridan had been the last person to talk with Dillard, immediately preceding his collapse.

"What was the subject of your discussion?" d'Ortega inquired.

"I felt that Dr. Dillard was fortunate to have had the indictment thrown out, and I questioned the propriety of the social affair that was in progress."

"Anything more?"

"Any further conversation is privileged under the client-attorney relationship, which privilege I'm invoking at this time."

"You're refusing to disclose the conversation?"

"That's right."

"The man is dead. The attorney-client privilege doesn't apply to a dead person. You could be subject to a contempt citation. I could seek a court order."

"Do what you have to do," Sheridan replied. "Court order or no court order, you're not getting the conversation."

D'Ortega let it drop. A week from today, she'd shed her prosecutorial garb and enter the world of private practice. She gave Sheridan a dismissive nod. Like enemy fighter pilots, both knew the duel was ended.

As Sheridan sat in Dr. Leventhal's outer office, he was still trying to jog his memory on the identity of the waiter. Why were there only two drinks on his tray? Why one martini and why one bourbon? And the waiter had given a courtly bow when he had declined the drink. Of course, when Dillard collapsed, there was bedlam. If the waiter had reappeared, Sheridan had been too busy to look for him.

"This consultation's on the house, Dan," Dr. Leventhal said as he scanned the pathology report. "You've had your share. . . ."

Sheridan nodded.

"The Williams woman, Harrington, Dillard. I've read the papers."

"Yeah," Sheridan said, "like the last scene from *Hamlet.* I'm not so sure I like the ending." He paused several seconds. "What do you think?"

"I'm no pathologist." Leventhal furrowed his brow. "Only autopsy I ever did was in med school. As you know, I'm an internist with a subspecialty in cardiology."

"This thrombosis or blood clot, could it have been induced by some toxic phenomenon?" Sheridan asked.

"Sure, a lot of medications are capable of triggering heart attacks. The drug ergonovine can cause spasm of the coronary arteries. It's given to patients undergoing coronary arteriography, X rays that show narrowing of the coronary arterial tree. A few milligrams of the drug can cause a fatal spasm. Then there's potassium chloride, and IV thrombin can induce extensive intravascular clotting, which can lead to myocardial infarction."

"How about koaki frog extract?"

"I think you're beating a dead horse, Dan. Shields has impeccable credentials. His finding was death by natural causes and his toxicology studies were all negative."

Sheridan thought for a few minutes. "Dillard died of a heart attack. Right?"

"That's what the pathologist concluded."

"I've witnessed heart attacks before," Sheridan said, "represented several clients with heart claims. Isn't a heart attack, especially a major attack like Dillard's, preceded by shortness of breath, profuse sweating, nausea, chest pains—the victim sometimes gasping for air and clutching his chest?"

"Those are the classic symptoms and signs. But some patients just keel over, same as Dillard. No warning, not a symptom. Dan, accept the path finding and move on."

Sheridan met with Fletcher Porter at two o'clock in the afternoon in a small bar across from the *Globe* building on Morrissey Boulevard. They sat in a booth in the back, next to the men's room. Except for a few transients, at two o'clock in the afternoon the place was deserted.

"Is there a story here?" Fletcher took a deep swallow of his Bud Light, then passed the photos to Sheridan.

"I don't know, Fletch. If there is, you'll be the first to be clued in."

Sheridan studied the six glossy prints. Fletcher Porter studied Sheridan.

"These didn't make the editions," Porter said. "They were taken in the hallway by our photographer during the grand jury deliberations."

Sheridan sipped his bourbon and shuffled through the prints. Sure enough, photo five depicted a tall, immaculately dressed man being led by the bailiffs toward the grand jury room. He quickly noted the date and caption in the lower corner of the photo: *Sebastian Simeone of New York, brother of Williams entering the grand jury room.*

He recognized him alright. He was the waiter at the Ritz.

Sheridan displayed no emotion, lingering a few seconds longer at photo six in an attempt to defuse Porter's curiosity.

"See anything?" Fletcher still scented a story.

"Afraid not, Fletch. If there are any ghosts out there, as I said before, I'll cut you in."

It wasn't difficult to get Sebastian Simeone's New York number. He didn't have to waste a call on Claire Doherty. The yellow pages of the Manhattan telephone directory ran a quarter-page ad: "Simeone Imports, Objets d'Art, Antiques." It listed a lower Second Avenue address. Sheridan jotted down the telephone number.

He worked at the office until ten, then sat at his desk for several minutes mulling over the events of the past few weeks. The bizarre deaths of Williams, Harrington, Dillard, even Father Duffy. He hadn't given Dr. Leventhal all the facts, and the pathologist who autopsied Dillard didn't know what he knew or suspected. Sebastian Simeone was probably SAS like Williams, or maybe just a brother avenging a sister's death.

Was the martini spiked with koaki toxin? Maybe he was getting paranoid. Dillard died from a heart attack; the diagnosis was clear and precise.

He wanted to confront Simeone head-to-head. But why? Maybe, like Leventhal said, it was over, time to move on. If Simeone wanted to have him hit, it would be easy enough. He wasn't going to alter his lifestyle by peeking over his shoulder or listening for footsteps. And maybe it was really over—the IRA and the SAS were even, a king traded for a queen. He removed the slip of paper with Simeone's telephone number from his wallet, crumpled it, and tossed it into the wastebasket.

He reached his apartment shortly after eleven, exhausted but still keyed up. He switched on the television for the late news. The Dillard inquest had already been edged off center stage.

Tomorrow was Thursday. They had a game out in Pittsfield, another three-hour drive. He checked his watch: 12:15. Time to turn in. He yawned and clicked off the set. But he knew he wouldn't be able to sleep. He needed to hash over the events of recent weeks. And pride prevented him from calling the one person who would understand all of the complexities and permutations. But where the hell had pride gotten him lately? He picked up the phone and punched out a number. Sheila answered on the second ring.

"Agent O'Brien, I have a problem and I need to talk to someone, someone I can trust."

There was a small pause, a short intake of breath, before Sheila replied.

"*Agent* no more," she said. Another pause. "I heard what happened to Dillard, the inquest, and, Dan . . ."

"Yeah?"

"Thank God you called." She choked up. "I wanted to say goodbye. I leave for Chicago tomorrow morning." Unsteadiness crept into her voice.

"You okay, Sheila?"

"Yes, I . . . I'm fine, really. . . ."

He said nothing for a long moment. "Sheila, can you get packed in, say, twenty minutes?"

"Packed?"

"My aunt's place down in Chatham. The roof shingles won't last till the fall. I need someone to hold the ladder."

"I'll be ready in ten," she said.

ACKNOWLEDGMENTS

My deepest thanks to:

Peter Matson, my agent and longtime friend,
for his professionalism and helpful suggestions.

Carolyn Blakemore, who corrected many revisions with
a fine editorial eye.

Betty A. Prashker, my editor, for her insight,
invaluable assistance, and especially for her
perseverance, as I stretched a deadline or two.

Catherine McDonald and Elaine Adamson, my superb
secretaries, who crafted the literary journey from
outline to final manuscript.

John Feegel, M.D., of Tampa, Florida, a lawyer and
also a fine writer, for his advice on medical esoteria.